MY DARK EVER AFTER

OTHER TITLES BY GIANA DARLING

The Fallen Men Series

The Fallen Men is a series of interconnected, stand-alone, erotic MC romances that each feature age-gap love stories between dirty-talking alpha males and the strong, sassy women who win their hearts.

Lessons in Corruption

Welcome to the Dark Side

Good Gone Bad

"Fallen Son" (a short story)

After the Fall

Inked in Lies

"Fallen King" (a short story)

Dead Man Walking

Caution to the Wind

Asking for Trouble

King of Iron Hearts (a Fallen Men companion book of poetry)

The Evolution of Sin Trilogy

Giselle Moore is running away from her past in France for a new life in America, but before she moves to New York City, she takes a holiday on the beaches of Mexico and meets a sinful, enigmatic French businessman, Sinclair, who awakens submissive desires and changes her life forever.

The Frenchman (The Evolution of Sin Book 1)

Praise for Giana Darling

"Taboo, breathtaking, and scorching hot! I freaking loved *Welcome to the Dark Side.*"

—Skye Warren, *New York Times* bestselling author

"This book stole my soul and gave my heart a beatdown! This book was hot, suspenseful, and emotional. A perfect read! You get me?"

—K Webster, *USA Today* bestselling author

"Giana Darling weaves a sexy and addictive story that's unlike anything I've ever read before."

—Ava Harrison, *USA Today* bestselling author

"Dark, decadent, and provocative, *Dangerous Temptation* is one of my absolute favorite reads in 2021. Tiernan and Bianca set my Kindle on fire! Giana has weaved an exquisite story. I can't wait for the next. READ THIS!"

—RuNyx, bestselling author of *Gothikana*

"Giana Darling at her absolute best. A raw, gritty, emotional read that draws you in, page by page, until you're utterly consumed with Priest and Bea. Beautiful characters, emotional storyline, and steamy scenes to fulfill all your dark romance needs. Five peachy stars!"

—Dani René, bestselling author

"This book is decadent and delicious, and I devoured it. I love everything Giana Darling writes, but this takes the top spot in my favorites of hers. The romance is outrageous, unapologetically blood pounding. The action is gorgeously choreographed. One click, and then prepare to get lost in the pages of this five-star BANGER! I can't recommend it enough."

—Dylan Allen, *USA Today* bestselling author

"GIANA DARLING HAS MY WHOLE DAMN HEART."

—Kandi Steiner, #1 Amazon bestselling author

The Siren (The Evolution of Sin Book 2)
The Sinners (The Evolution of Sin Book 3)

The Enslaved Duet

The Enslaved Duet is a dark romance duology about an eighteen-year-old Italian fashion model, Cosima Lombardi, who is sold by her indebted father to a British earl whose nefarious plans for her include more than just sexual slavery . . . Their epic tale spans Italy, England, Scotland, and the United States across a five-year period that sees them endure murder, separation, and a web of infinite lies.

Enthralled (The Enslaved Duet Book 1)
Enamoured (The Enslaved Duet Book 2)

Anti-Heroes in Love Duet

Elena Lombardi is an ice-cold, brokenhearted criminal lawyer with a distaste for anything untoward, but when her sister begs her to represent New York City's most infamous mafioso in a murder trial, she can't refuse, and soon she finds herself unable to resist the dangerous charms of Dante Salvatore.

When Heroes Fall (Anti-Heroes in Love Duet Book 1)
When Villains Rise (Anti-Heroes in Love Duet Book 2)

The Dark Dream Duet

The Dark Dream duology is a guardian/ward, enemies-to-lovers romance about the dangerous, scarred black sheep of the Morelli family, Tiernan, and the innocent Bianca Belcante. After Bianca's mother dies, Tiernan becomes the guardian to both her and her little brother. But Tiernan doesn't do anything out of the goodness of his heart, and soon Bianca is thrust into the wealthy elite of Bishop's Landing and the dark secrets that lurk beneath its glittering surface.

Bad Dream: A Dark Dream Prologue (free)

Dangerous Temptation (Dark Dream Book 1)

Beautiful Nightmare (Dark Dream Book 2)

The Elite Seven Series

Sloth

The Impossible Universe Trilogy

Sebastian Lombardi has moved to London to pursue his dreams of being an actor while also providing for his family back in Italy by driving for a luxury car company. It's there he meets Savannah Meyers and her husband, Adam Meyers, who propose a scandalous deal—live with them as their lover and they'll make his wildest dreams come true.

The Moon & His Tides (Impossible Universe Trilogy Book 1)

The Sun & Her Burn (Impossible Universe Trilogy Book 2)

The Stars & Their Sky (Impossible Universe Trilogy Book 3)

Coming Soon

Fallen Men Book 9

My Dark Mafia Romance

My Dark Fairy Tale

MY DARK EVER AFTER

GIANA DARLING

Montlake

Published by Montlake, Seattle

www.apub.com

EU Product Safety contact:
Amazon Publishing, Amazon Media EU S.à r.l.
38, avenue John F. Kennedy, L-1855 Luxembourg
amazonpublishing-gpsr@amazon.com

ISBN-13: 9781662527593 (paperback)
ISBN-13: 9781662527586 (digital)

Cover design by Hang Le
Cover image: © FTAPE LIMITED; © NatalyFox / Shutterstock;
© Tim Mossholder / Unsplash

Printed in the United States of America

To every person who sees life in shades of gray instead of just black and white.

What is done out of love always takes place beyond good and evil.

—Friedrich Nietzsche, *Beyond Good and Evil*

CHAPTER ONE

Guinevere

Wind whistled across the icy peaks of the Huron River and cut through the streets of Ann Arbor, buffeting me like a secondary gravitational force as I fought through the early snowfall across the University of Michigan campus. Bundled in layers of cashmere, swaddled in a thick scarf pulled up over my nose, with a beanie protecting my ears and forehead, I had only a thin swatch of skin exposed to the stinging bite of the brutally cold October day, but I was still frozen.

If I was being honest, I had been since I got off the plane from Italy two months ago.

It was as if all the warmth in my blood had been left behind in that godforsaken country. My warmth, my happiness, and half my heart.

My boots crunched through the freshly fallen snow as I walked from my yoga class back to work in the State Street District fifteen minutes away. Only locals and the slightly insane voluntarily walked outside in weather like this, but I was desperate for anything to distract me from my current state of affairs.

I was back home in Michigan, working for a father who'd barely spoken to me since I'd broken his trust by going to Italy despite the vow I'd made never to set foot in his mother country. My mother, as always, had taken his side, so although I had to work with him and saw her at our mandatory Sunday family dinners, I'd never felt so distant from my family. To make matters worse, the few friends I'd made at college seemed so far away from me after my summer abroad. I found myself uncharacteristically furious at them for their petty complaints.

My sister dropped dead at twenty-six, I wanted to scream at them.

The man I fell in love with is a stone-cold killer, I wanted to divulge.

How can you think this is the be-all and end-all in safe, quaint Ann Arbor? I wanted to demand.

Instead, I stayed quiet while they talked about their lives, retreating deep inside myself to a place I wasn't sure I liked. A place filled with seething shadows that clutched at me, hooking beneath the flesh like talons and threatening to drag me even deeper into my own darkness.

I was sick of the mundane. Routine and schedule and predictability. It made me feel like I was losing my sanity. When I'd returned home, my father had given me the job he'd threatened to take away for staying in Italy against his wishes, saying that it would ground me, and all it had done was drop the bottom out from beneath my feet so I felt like I was in a free fall.

I'd tasted freedom and passion, the sucking black hole of despair, and the shivering bite of terror, alongside the heady mead of lust and a veritable bacchanalia of sin.

How could I go back to water, having become drunk on wine?

Before Raffa, I'd always felt that pull, a low-grade weight in my belly that hungered for sin, for the rough edge of sex, for the bright pain of anger followed by the blood-warming satisfaction of revenge. I'd read books like *The Count of Monte Cristo*, watched action movies filled with violence, and read erotica on a private web browser in the dark of night, alone in bed with my hand between my legs.

It had been enough.

Or at least, I hadn't known then what a shallow form of satisfaction it was.

And now I did.

All the things I had accused Raffa of being—a cold, merciless killer, a skilled liar, a vengeful villain—they were the very things I'd gravitated toward in literature and film and fantasy my entire life.

The hypocrisy kept me up at night, even though I told myself fiction and reality were two totally different mediums.

Killing a man for trying to hurt me was *not* romantic.

Raffa had taken Galasso's life without a qualm. And even though Galasso was a predator, he was still something to someone.

He should have been turned over to the proper authorities, right?

But the authorities never would have found the man who'd threatened me and, most likely, countless other women in his past.

I growled under my breath as I reached the revolving doors of the Beaumont Building, which housed my father's firm, stomping my feet free of snow before pushing into the warmth of the marble foyer.

I was distracted from my thoughts by the sight of a man sitting in the waiting area before the security turnstiles. There was nothing remarkable about him, and normally I might not have noticed him at all. But discovering your lover is a mafioso after weeks of thinking he's Prince Charming opens up an awareness in a person that is hard to quell.

Something almost like paranoia.

And I knew I'd seen that man before, not just earlier that day, loitering outside the coffee shop beside our offices, but also the day before, jogging through the park on a parallel route to my own.

I knew he was the same man because he had dark hair buzzed nearly to the scalp, with an oval patch of silver just above his right ear. It wasn't exactly distinctive, but again, I'd taken pains to be more observant since the summer, and I knew this was my third time in two days crossing paths with him.

In a small city like Ann Arbor, it wasn't unusual to run into people you knew—it happened almost daily—but something about this suited man with his stern countenance tripped an inner alarm.

He looked, almost, like Carmine, Raffa's associate back in Florence. Suave, suited, and inexplicably dangerous despite the veneer of civility.

Without thinking it through, I veered toward him.

He glanced up with a surprised blink when I stopped just before the seat where he was scrolling through his phone. A quick peek showed he was looking at food reels on social media, and I wondered if I was being unduly suspicious.

"Hello, I think I saw you here this morning. Is there something I can help you with?" I asked sweetly, but one hand was curled inside the mouth of my purse, around the can of pepper spray I'd started carrying.

He blinked again, his face utterly expressionless in a way that made me shiver. And then, suddenly, he smiled. A bright, wide grin that could have been handsome if I'd found anyone attractive since I'd met Raffaele Romano.

"Are you Ms. Stone?" he asked, standing and swiftly buttoning up his blazer in a move that was utterly seamless and reminded me, as most things seemed to, of Raffa. He offered a square-fingered hand. "Your father mentioned you this morning, actually."

"My father did," I echoed, taking his hand reluctantly. Noting the calloused ridges not typical of a wealthy man.

"In our introductory client meeting," he elaborated in a flat American accent. "My name is Tom Kirkpatrick. I just moved here from Washington, and your firm comes highly recommended."

My spine softened slightly at the information.

A prospective client.

It would explain why he was around the building. And really, it wasn't unusual for people to run through the many parks in the city. It was one of the appealing aspects of living here.

I let out a long sigh and smiled back at him. "Well, why don't we go up together and get to know each other a bit. If you decide to do business with us, we will be working together closely."

"I hope so," he said a little too baldly, then ducked his head with a wince as if he was embarrassed by his enthusiasm.

Last year, I might have blushed and tried to flirt with the handsome older man. It would have flattered me to know he was interested, that he thought I was pretty.

Now, his attention moved through me like a cold draft, emphasizing the emptiness within me.

It lingered as we stepped into the elevator, his voice a dull drone in my ears.

◆ ◆ ◆

It was late, and the glass walls of our twentieth-floor office were black reflective mirrors highlighting the fact that I was seemingly alone. Everyone had long since gone home for dinner, to their families or friends.

I didn't really have either at the moment, so I stayed.

Burying myself in work because even when everything else went to hell in a handbasket, I was good at my job.

The best, second only to my dad.

He'd trained me for this since I was a girl. While most girls doodled in coloring books and played with dolls, John Stone gave me puzzles and taught me to play chess. When I was older, we spent weekend mornings racing to finish the *New York Times* sudoku puzzles and playing math games over pizza at the dinner table.

Gemma and Mom had left us to it happily, focusing on their shared love of food, wine, and fashion. It wasn't that Gemma wasn't smart enough to participate, but her skills lay in languages and sensory disciplines.

If sometimes I watched Mom and Gemma cooking and laughing in the kitchen and wanted to join them, I never acted on the impulse.

I gritted my teeth as the pencil in my hand broke, a splinter of wood lodging in my forefinger. A bead of blood pooled, and I brought it to my mouth to suck it clean.

"What are you still doing here?"

I snapped my head up to see Dad standing in the doorway to the conference room. Even though it was long after hours, his suit was still totally immaculate, cuffs buttoned, tie perfectly flat against his chest and knotted close to his throat. You never would have known he had old, faded tattoos beneath the silky fabric, only a handful of symbols and Latin words along the backs of his shoulders and the base of his throat. Even at home, he never went shirtless, always covering the marks as if they were scars instead of art.

John Stone gave *buttoned up* new meaning.

But God, I loved him.

He'd been my hero when I was growing up.

Some of my friends didn't understand my often blind love for and loyalty to him, but they didn't know what it was like to be so sick as a child you might die. To go to bed every night wondering if this was the time you wouldn't wake. To have that fear be such an elemental part of your life and then to trust the man who told you each and every one of those nights that he would see you in the morning. That he would be there no matter what, and then he *was*.

Even though he was an important man with a booming financial firm, he never missed a doctor's appointment. Every time I woke up from surgery, he was there beside my bed, smiling at me. Every time I was sick and aching, he was there to hold me, to distract me. My human embodiment of hope.

I knew how lucky I was to have a father like him, and until recently I'd never thought to take it for granted. If he'd asked me to crawl over glass, I might have. That was how much I trusted him. That was how infrequently he'd let me down.

The only thing we had ever disagreed on was Italy.

His homeland and the seat of his hatred.

My ancestral country and the setting of my lifelong dreams.

Gemma had always encouraged me to visit.

Fuck him, she'd say in that flippant, slightly cruel way she had of putting down any and all authority figures. *If he loves you, he won't stop you from doing what you've always dreamed of doing.*

But it was easy for her to say.

As the sick sister, I'd been given more attention through necessity, but they made it up to Gemma by giving her whatever she asked for. Trips around the world, designer bags, a Porsche when she turned sixteen.

We could have been raised by different parents, that was how disparate our upbringings had been.

Her words lingered, though.

Long after she moved to Albania for her year abroad.

And then she sent me that last email before she died.

Listen to me, Jinx, I know what I'm talking about. You don't owe Dad and Mom anything. It's your life, and you've fought to stay on this earth to live it. You owe it to yourself to go to Italy. I hope you find answers there like I have here. I never could have known what I would find when I started looking into who I truly am. Don't let Dad's lies keep you from your truth. I won't let him keep me from mine anymore. Be brave and bold, little sister. I hope when we see each other again, we are both very different people.

It seemed too much like the hand of fate to receive a message like that from Gemma just a handful of days before she died of a heart attack.

So I'd taken it to heart despite the god-awful feeling of lying to my parents and disobeying the strictest order they'd ever set for me.

Do not set foot in Italy.

Even now, after everything that had happened, the lies and heartbreak, I couldn't say I regretted it. My summer in Tuscany had changed me for the better.

Raffa had called me his fawn, his *cerbiatta*, but I felt like a stag now. Something with wariness and horns, something that wasn't afraid to gouge if threatened.

I knew now what I hadn't before.

There were real monsters in the world, and the most dangerous of them all had a face like an angel's.

"No rest for the weary," I responded finally, with a little shrug as I reached into the open bag on the seat beside me for another pencil.

He studied me for a moment, something like fond amusement warring with frustration in those brown eyes that were so similar to my own. "You always preferred to do things longhand. Unusual for kids today."

"I wouldn't say I'm a kid anymore," I said mildly, my attention on the numbers set out before me instead of on my father.

The sight of him hurt me. Knowing he was *there* but not *here*, not present for me the way he always had been before.

It might have hurt less if I'd still had Raffa, but losing the only two men I'd ever loved in one fell swoop had carved me up from the inside out and left me hollow.

"No," he mused with a weary sigh, moving into the conference room to brace his hands on the back of one of the empty seats. The light hit his face full on, highlighting the tired brackets beside his eyes and mouth. He'd always been a handsome man, but right then, he seemed like a faded photograph of someone from a long time ago. "But you won't tell me what happened this summer to take the bloom off the rose."

I snorted softly, dropping the pretense of work to level him with an assessing look. "I've told you. When you are ready to tell me about why you left Italy, I'll tell you what happened in Firenze."

He flinched slightly at the name of the city, a tic he couldn't curb. Curiosity burned in me so brightly I couldn't believe I'd ever been able to contain it. I'd always wondered about what bridges he must have burned in leaving his family and nation behind and moving to America, but I'd respected him too much to press.

No, maybe that wasn't quite it.

I hadn't known enough about the world to question if that past was anything more than uncomfortable. If it was dark and full of secrets that could, years later, affect me.

Now that I did, I refused to settle for silence.

And the only trump card I had to play was my own Italian history.

Dad glowered at me.

Once, it would have worked, but I'd fallen in love with a man whose glares could skin the hide off a rhino, so I only blinked in response.

"Damn it, Guinevere," he growled, slipping the chair out so he could sink into it, hands going to his hair and mussing it for the first time all day. "I thought when we left your teenage years behind that we'd remained unscathed by this kind of rebellion from you. We had enough of it from Gemma."

"Blind obedience isn't something you should be proud of," I countered, wincing at my own past naivete. "You *knew* how much I wanted to go to Italy. How much it meant to me. How I dreamed of it during those long stays at the hospital." Despite myself, tears clogged my throat, turning my voice to ash. "You *knew*, and you never gave me any reason or backstory. You just forbade me like an antiquated king with a princess in a fairy tale."

"You should have respected me enough to take my word for it," he said gruffly, hands white knuckled where they were clasped over the table.

"You should have respected me enough to tell me the truth," I retorted, scalding tears racing down my cheeks.

This was the crux of the issue with both the men in my life.

How could they respect me—love me—if they didn't trust me with the truth?

Vera, Raffa had called me. *Truth* in Italian.

Yet he had offered me none of his own honesty.

He might have been gone from my life forever, but my father was not. There was still hope there. I just needed him to explain himself so I could explain myself to him and we could *finally* reach some kind of understanding.

"Have you ever considered not telling you the truth was to keep you safe?" Dad demanded, slamming a palm flat to the table as he leaned across it. "Did you ever consider I would cut out my own heart before putting you in harm's way and that keeping you from that blood-soaked country was the least I could do to keep you safe? I left for a reason, Guinevere."

"And I went for my own reasons," I replied, suddenly exhausted by the fruitlessness of this conversation. An imitation of the one we'd had every week since I came home in August. "Until we can be honest with each other, we can't fix this rift between us. Are you happy with the way things are?"

The question was bloody, a raw hunk of flesh I carved out of myself to offer to him.

Do you see the way I bleed because of this? I tried to convey. *Do you see the way I ache to make things right?*

But Dad only stared at me, a vein throbbing in his forehead.

"I love you, Dad," I said after a long moment of silence. "But if I learned anything this summer, it's that I have to love myself more than anyone else if I want to be healthy and happy. And I refuse to pretend I'm okay with you keeping secrets from me that affect my own life."

"We can fix this," he said with fervor, opening his hand to me even though I was too far away to take it. "Just put my past to rest, where it has lain buried for years, and look to the future with me. I-I can't say I will forgive you easily for going to that *place* behind my back, but you're home now, and if you promise not to go back again, we can recover."

A bitter laugh coughed up my throat.

Because I could promise that, really.

It wasn't like there was anything for me left in Italy but broken promises and shattered dreams.

So why was it impossible to make that oath?

The idea of never returning was too final, ripping out the last roots of the love that had seeded, grown, and flourished in Tuscany.

It would eliminate the faint whisper of "what if" that haunted me in the darkest hours of the night, when I couldn't sleep for the memories.

Despite everything, I could not make that oath.

The idea of never seeing Raffa again stabbed through me like a cold blade, even though I knew it was one of my own making. I had decided to leave him.

But, a small voice in my head murmured, *he didn't come after you. He hasn't contacted you at all since you've been gone.*

Despite that, I couldn't bring myself to utter the words to repair my relationship with my father and risk permanently deleting all hope of Raffa from my heart.

"I won't do that," I said finally. "That shouldn't be what this hinges on. If I go again—which I do not intend to do at all right now—then I'll give you the courtesy and respect of telling you. But I won't make that promise. It's my life, and I have to be able to do as I please. Maybe you can't understand that, but after being sick and sheltered for so long, I need this independence. Even though what happened in Tuscany changed me, it wasn't for the worse. I'm stronger now. And part of being strong means assuming responsibility for myself instead of hiding behind my parents. Even when I love them."

Dad stared at me, throat working as he swallowed convulsively. When he spoke, he stared at his open palms as if they held the secrets to the universe. "I should have realized before this."

"Realized what?"

His gaze snapped to mine, dark eyes the same shape as my own and filled with fire. "That you are too much like me to understand how to put aside your pride and make the right decision."

Without waiting for a reply, he pushed out of the chair and stalked out of the conference room. I watched with tears drying tight on my skin as he went to his corner office and then reemerged a moment later in his coat and scarf, with his briefcase.

He did not spare me a look as he left the offices.

The only thing that remained in his wake was the cold, dark office and the pile of numbers I had been trying to drown myself in. Left with nothing else to do, I dove right back in and hoped the clarity of mathematics would clear my tumultuous soul.

CHAPTER TWO

Guinevere

When working failed to distract me, I scrubbed a hand over my face and collected my files, phone, and computer to pack away in my messenger bag. It was almost midnight, and even though I knew sleep would elude me, as it had for weeks, it was clear my mind was too distracted to get any work done. I could go home to the little apartment I'd rented above an antique shop near the U and binge-watch a few episodes of *Slow Horses* until my body gave in to sleep.

The building was so silent it almost hummed, a sentient emptiness that felt like a haunting. It spooked me even though I told myself I was being silly. There was a night guard in the lobby downstairs, and you needed a pass to get to any of the levels. The only ghosts between these walls were my own.

But when the elevator stopped on the fourteenth floor instead of going straight to the basement parking garage, I was surprised. Even though we shared space with a number of high-profile businesses, it wasn't usual for people to stay that late working.

Unless, like mine, their lives were imploding.

When the doors parted to reveal a relatively young man in a sharp suit, with a surprised, warm smile, I shouldn't have felt cornered like an animal in the dark. It wasn't even anything he did—nicely dressed, briefcase under one arm, that big, white-toothed smile to put me at ease.

It was something in me that rankled, something that Raffa had ignited.

Paranoia, maybe.

Or a heightened sense of self-preservation.

"Good evening," the gentleman acknowledged as he stepped into the elevator.

Without really processing why, I shuffled closer to the doors, and then, just as they were closing, I slipped out. When I turned back to the doors, I caught a glimpse of the man inside frowning at me before the metal closed.

"You're being ridiculous," I muttered to myself, and I took a deep breath before pushing the button to call another elevator to the floor.

It only took another moment, but when it opened, there was another man inside.

The same man I had seen jogging in the park, loitering by the offices, inside the lobby this morning. Mr. Kirkpatrick.

"Hello, Guinevere," he greeted me casually.

But there was nothing usual about a client being in the building at that hour.

I wasn't sure how he'd gotten in or if he'd never left, hiding somewhere in the multistory tower until he knew I was alone.

"I'll catch the next one," I said, stepping back a little with a tremulous smile, trying to keep a level head even as my heart thumped rabbit-quick against my rib cage.

"I think you'll take this one," someone suggested behind me.

I whirled to find the man from the first elevator standing there, slightly out of breath, no doubt from running up the stairs to get back to my level. In one steady, raised hand, he held a matte black gun.

Fuck.

I threw myself low to the left, catching my balance on the wall before taking off into a sprint down the other corridor. There were two curses in Italian behind me, but I was too busy running for my life to translate what they yelled at each other as one or both of them came after me.

Our offices were laid out in an oval connected by a continuous hall. At one end were the elevators and the reception desk and at the other, a flight of staircases under an emergency exit. It was there that I ran, kicking off my heels so I could pound down the carpeted floor with better traction.

"I will shoot," the man behind me panted.

Because of the curve of the hallway, I didn't think he had a good shot at me, especially when I hugged the wall as I thrust forward. As if to test my theory, a shot blasted through the air, loud enough to ring my bell. The bullet embedded in the wall to my left, too wide.

He couldn't get the shot off unless he got closer.

The red light of the emergency exit had never looked so welcoming. I crashed through the door and stared down the stairs, hoping to get at least a level between us before he entered the stairwell too.

I thanked God that I had started to take my physical fitness more seriously since returning home. Only the hours I'd spent at the gym and the dojo propelled my slight frame forward faster than the tall, athletic man on my heels.

I could hear the metallic bang of the door hitting the concrete wall as he blasted through it, steps clapping against the stairs as he raced after me.

But I didn't look back.

Fear wasn't a noose around my throat but the wind at my back, forcing me forward with a clarity of purpose that eradicated my panic.

I had to get away.

There was no other option.

I hadn't fought so hard to get to twenty-three years old only to die because of some goon with a gun who was coming after me for God knew what.

If I could just get to the lobby and the night security guard, I had a chance of getting away.

Another shot rang out, a thunderous boom in the echo chamber of the stairwell and a click as the bullet ricocheted off the banister.

I pushed hard, the taste of metal on the back of my tongue like my lungs were working so hard they were bleeding.

Eleventh floor.

Tenth.

Ninth.

I was gaining distance on him.

He was in a suit and slick-soled shoes, trying to maneuver his big body around the tight turns of the staircase.

I was barefoot in wide-legged wool trousers, with a slight enough frame to let gravity do half the work in throwing me down the stairs, even with the heavy bag banging against my hip.

Seventh.

Sixth.

Fifth.

My breath was a harsh expletive. My pulse roared in my ears.

Another shot rang out.

Pain like the bite of a horsefly stung against the side of my head.

I blinked away the smarting tears of pain, but a few steps later I slipped in something and looked down to see splatters and smears of blood from where I'd stepped in it.

The blood was mine.

Fatigue started to eat away at the adrenaline, leaving room for fear to bloom in its wake.

I wasn't going to make it.

Behind me, my pursuer was starting to close the gap, and I still had four floors to go.

I thought of my parents finding out in the morning that I'd been killed in the office. Of the last words my dad and I had spoken to each other. Of them grieving the loss of their last living child.

Of the fact that if I died, I would never see Raffa again even if I wanted to.

Thinking quickly, I slammed open the door to the fourth floor and threw my bag into the hall. Then, on light feet, going much more slowly than I wanted to but without making any sound, I slunk down the stairs, keeping to the wall so that I wasn't visible from above.

My heart beat in my throat as I crept down, waiting for my chaser to hit the fourth floor and, hopefully, take the bait.

His loud footsteps stuttered at the fourth floor, and then there was a bang as he wrenched open the door.

I pushed my tired body off the wall and sprinted down the last three flights of stairs without worrying about noise.

He'd taken the false lead.

When I practically fell out the door into the marble lobby, I was already yelling for help through gasping breaths.

No one responded.

I pinched at the cramp in my side and walked forward to peer around one of the thick pillars obscuring my view of the security desk.

The only sight that greeted me was a pool of lacquered blood seeping out from behind the desk and across the polished marble floor.

I sucked in a breath of shock a moment before the cold kiss of metal pressed into the base of my skull.

"Did you kill him?" I asked, surprised by the firmness of my voice.

The man behind me, presumably Kirkpatrick, though that was obviously a fake name, shifted his weight as if caught off guard by my reaction to being held at gunpoint.

"Who?"

"The night guard," I said. "His name is Pedro. He has two daughters."

He made a noise of scorn in the back of his throat and gripped my shoulder so hard it ached before marching me toward the elevators.

While we waited for one to arrive, he turned me to face him, readjusting the gun to press into the soft meat on the underside of my jaw. His expression shuttered when he saw the wound to my temple.

I hissed when he touched it gently, his fingers coming away red. Now that the adrenaline was receding, I could feel the hot throb of pain at the side of my head and the sticky wetness like drying paint along my cheek, jaw, and neck.

"You should not have run," he repeated with a cluck of his tongue, the way a mother might reprimand a child. "They will not be happy with this."

"Who?" I demanded, stepping closer despite the weapon at my throat.

Kirkpatrick scowled at me, but the elevator doors opened before he could respond, and the second man stepped out. He was sweat slicked and disheveled, still breathing hard as he shot me a furious look.

"They said you were sick," he snapped in heavily accented Italian.

"Who?" I asked again, but they were wedging me between them and pushing me into the elevator.

Even though I tried to resist, I was a five-foot-three, 110-pound girl against two six-foot-plus muscle-bound gangsters. There was no way, now that they'd caught me, that I could break free.

Still, the moment the elevator doors closed, I gathered the last of my strength and went absolutely berserk. Leveraging my weight against their hands locked on my arms, I kicked up my legs against the metal doors and gave a mighty push, shoving both men into the back wall. My nails, honed to pretty, sharp points and painted Raffa's favorite red, dug into the skin of the hands holding me, puncturing the flesh and raking up to the wrists.

"*Porco Dio,*" Kirkpatrick cursed, releasing me with one hand only to lash out with the other and slap me hard across the side of my face.

Stars popped and fizzed in my vision as I sagged into the other man, momentarily losing control of my legs. When his arms wrapped around me, I dug an elbow into his gut and had the pleasure of feeling the air rush out of his lungs.

He didn't let me go completely, but I was able to drop out of his loosened hold to the floor. Twisting, I wrapped both hands around the gun he held and wrenched, using all my weight as a counterbalance to try to wrest it from his grip.

When that didn't work, I leaned forward and sank my teeth into his hand, clenching when he rained a fist down on my shoulder to pry me free.

"*Basta!*" Kirkpatrick bellowed, the one word vibrating the steel cage taking us to the underground parking garage. "Enough, Guinevere, or I'll shoot you even though they want you alive."

The man above me, whose hand was clamped between my teeth, reached down to dig a thumb into the bullet wound on the side of my temple. I spat out his palm without hesitation, wincing at the bright edge of hurt that cut through my brain.

"Up," Kirkpatrick demanded with a gesture from the gun trained on me.

My legs shook slightly, with exhaustion or fear I wasn't certain, as I slowly stood. With a muttered curse, they placed me between them again.

"Any more funny business and I'll knock you out," he warned me.

Blood dripped down the side of my head onto my cheek, itching.

I didn't respond, staring straight ahead as I tried to figure out some escape route between the elevator and the car they no doubt had ready in the garage. I remembered reading somewhere that once your abductors had you in a car, your chances of surviving were reduced by more than half.

"The plane won't wait forever," the unnamed man murmured in Italian, probably unaware of my proficiency in the language. "This took too long."

"They'll wait," Kirkpatrick said grimly, adjusting his grip on me. "They want her enough to wait forever."

The elevator dinged as we reached the parking level, their hands tightening on me as the doors slid open to reveal a black limousine waiting ten yards away, idling with the back door open.

Who the hell kidnapped someone in a limo?

As we started toward it, another suited man emerged from the front seat holding a gun.

"What took you so long?" he demanded in Italian.

The only Italians I knew who would do something like this were mafiosi. But why in the world would they want me?

And why now?

Even if this was somehow associated with Raffa, it had been two long months of radio silence between us.

They shoved me toward the car, and no matter how hard I struggled, I couldn't get free. My heart was in my throat, beating so hard I thought I would vomit. Their hands were iron shackles around my arms, bruising and twisting until agony burned through them.

I kicked at the door to the limo, bracing so they couldn't push me inside, but when the third man got involved, they shoved me into the car without issue.

The moment I fell to the floor, I knew with painful clarity that this was it.

I wouldn't see Mom and Dad again.

I wouldn't have this life back in Michigan I'd been hating, and how stupid was I for being so ungrateful while I was living it? At least I was alive! How had I forgotten how precious and inconstant that could be?

Doors slammed around me as the men got back into the car. They didn't bother to pick me up off the floor as the wheels screamed from the velocity of the car gunning forward.

"Where are you taking me?" I asked, my voice hoarse from screaming. The car was moving up the ramp, waiting for the automatic door to lift so they could drive into the deserted street. "Why are you doing this, and who for?"

Kirkpatrick smiled that big, toothy smile at me. "We are taking you home," he said.

Seconds later, as the car pulled out of the building into the driveway, my body flew sideways, slamming into the door as another car barreled into us. I was aware of Italian shouts and the metallic click of guns cocking before blackness swarmed my vision and I passed out.

When I came to, only seconds had passed, my head drumming with misery from the dual impact of the gunshot and the contact with the door. A bullet pierced the window above me, sending glass raining over my body. I curled into a tight ball in the corner, protecting my head with my arms as Kirkpatrick shot from behind the protection of the other back door.

I peered at him as he fired back at whoever had hit us, so I watched as a bullet caught him in the cheek and exploded out the back of his head.

"Oh my God," I murmured, pressing my lips to my knee as I swallowed the bile in my throat.

What the fuck was happening?

A moment later, quiet descended, and I realized that there was utter stillness in the limo around me. Kirkpatrick lay half inside the car, his brains splattered on the upholstery. The other man who had chased me was visible on the pavement beyond him, blood spreading around his body like a red halo. When I found the courage to unravel and peek into the front seat through the transparent partition, two bodies sat in the seats unmoving.

The crunch of shoes over glass alerted me to someone moving my way.

Without hesitation, I fell forward toward Kirkpatrick, groping over his body to grab the gun caught loosely in one hand. The metal was still warm from his grip as I fumbled it between my fingers. After scooting to the other side of the car on my butt, I adjusted the gun, then rested my wrist on my knee so it would stop shaking.

I waited.

It only took seconds for the man to appear in the doorway, just his suited torso beneath an open overcoat. A gun hung loosely in one hand as he kicked at Kirkpatrick and then dragged him out of the way with one fierce tug, depositing him on the pavement like a pile of rubbish.

Done with that, he turned his attention to the inside of the car.

I sucked in a deep breath, my finger fluttering against the trigger, ready to pull at the slightest provocation. When the man stepped into the doorframe and slowly lowered himself to fit through the gap, I pulled the trigger.

The bullet lodged in the frame, a handspan from the stranger's shoulder.

"I'm armed," I announced, my voice thin but loud. "Tell me who the hell you are, or next time I'll put one between your eyes."

Too many films, I scolded myself almost hysterically. I wasn't even sure I could aim to hit the man *at all* with the way my hands trembled.

"You know who I am," the man said before ducking his head into the car and fixing me with that familiar pale-bronze stare.

"Raffa." The word fell from my mouth in an exhale of shock and relief.

"Vera," he said, his voice so soft it reached between us like a silken feather to caress my bloodstained cheek. "What have they done to you, *cerbiatta mia*?"

Without a single second of hesitation, I dropped the gun to the floor with a dull, concussive thud, and I crawled across the distance between us to throw myself into Raffa's arms.

He caught me instantly, cradling me in his arms with one hand palming the entire back of my skull as I fit my face into his neck and burst into tears.

"Hush, hush," he murmured as he slowly worked us both out of the car and stood easily with me in his embrace. "I have got you now. And I will not let you go again."

CHAPTER THREE

Guinevere

The car was silent but for the *shush shush* of snow under the wheels and the faint strain of classical music someone had playing in the front seat of the massive black SUV Raffa had bundled me into immediately after catching me up in his arms.

I was still there, in his arms, even though I knew I would have to leave the false serenity of that embrace before long.

There were too many questions to ask and issues to be solved for me to pretend that all was well between us.

But for now, I was desperate for some peace, however short lived. So I'd been silent and pliable as he'd handed me water to swirl the taste of blood out of my mouth, then as he'd carefully inspected the bullet graze on my temple and declared it had stopped bleeding.

The scent of Raffa—oak and moss and burning firewood—suffused my senses as I curled into his strong chest, one hand wrapped in the fine silk weave of his suit jacket, smearing it with blood. He was warm and solid, a living shield I knew, even after our acrimonious split, would shelter me from anything.

Though that just reminded me that he might have been the reason I was in danger in the first place.

"Why did they come after me?" I asked, my voice cutting up my sore throat so badly that I winced. "Was it because of you?"

It was Raffa's turn to wince. It was so faint I only noticed the gesture because I was in his arms. "I am not sure, though I would have to suppose that yes, they came for you to get to me. Things have . . . escalated back home."

"Because they were undermining you?" I surmised, staring out the window at the icy landscape, unseasonably early in the year, and feeling the echo of that cold deep in my bones.

"Because they attempted to hurt you," he growled, the words rumbling through his chest and into me. Reflexively, his hands tightened around me almost to the point of pain. When I whimpered softly, he relaxed, smoothing a big palm down my spine. It was unconsciously done, and there was something beautiful about his instinct to soothe me.

Something I wanted to lean into even though everything was so fucked up.

"So more violence and death as an answer to violence and death," I concluded, pulling away slightly to look into his face.

God, it was a good face.

The nicest one I'd ever laid eyes on.

If it was possible, he'd grown more handsome in the last two months. The dark stubble that usually only appeared at the end of a long day was thicker now, almost long enough to be called a beard. It emphasized the steep cut of his cheekbones and the hollows beneath and highlighted the unique pale maple of his irises. His mouth looked soft amid the bristles, a smooth and pale pink I wanted to deepen into red with lascivious kisses.

I dreamed of kissing him every single night. Literally. My sleeping hours were filled with erotic dreams I couldn't escape from. I woke up every morning hot and bothered and angry with myself for being so turned on by the memory of a man who had deceived me.

Now that mouth and the man attached to it were so close we were breathing the same breath. I could count the striations in those cool metallic eyes and the lashes fanning out thick and dark around them. I could press a kiss to the scar on the edge of his chin and ignore the fact that it was probably from some Mafia misdeed.

In this moment, so close to me, he was just a man, and I was just a woman. Nothing else existed if I focused on the beat of his heart beneath my palm and the murmur of mine rushing in my ears.

I realized then that love didn't die. You could shoot it in the face the way Raffa had shot the man in the closet, but it didn't drop dead. No, love bled out like a nonfatal wound, sluggish and painful, over time, even when you wanted it to stop stone cold.

Two months wasn't enough to bleed out the love I had for this man.

Two years, two decades—I wondered if any length of time would drain his existence from mine.

He was staring at me as intently as I was him, and he seemed to find something in my gaze that had that full mouth curling.

"You are not as opposed to violence as you wish to be, I think," he noted. "When I broke that man's finger for insulting you, I saw the flush in your cheeks. The way your pupils blew to black. You looked . . . hungry, Guinevere. Not disgusted."

My heart knocked against my breastbone as if desperate to allow Raffa inside.

"No," I said, but it lacked conviction.

I had lain awake too many nights struggling with that truth to discount his words now.

"*Si,*" he argued, tipping his head so that he could ghost his mouth along my cheekbone. "I think there is some bloodlust in you. I think I would not feel this way about you if there was not."

"Which way?" I dared to ask, holding still so I wouldn't give in to the urge to bare my throat to him.

"You fought back against those men. Oh, you think I did not notice the scratches and teeth marks? You may be a little fawn, but perhaps under the right conditions you can be feral."

"I was fighting for my life," I countered.

"*Si*, and you would fight for others this way too. I know you, Vera."

His words popped the bubble around us like a knifepoint. I wrenched myself out of his arms with a wince and took my own seat next to him, turning my face to the window.

"Well, I don't know you," I rebutted softly.

He had nothing to say to that.

Or maybe he did, but I was shaking slightly as the shock wore off, and my head was aching as if the bullet that had grazed me was lodged deep inside my brain, and I knew he wouldn't press if I was unwell.

I touched my hot forehead to the cold glass. "Did you know these men?"

"I did not recognize them, no. I took their phones, though, and if they are not burners, we should be able to get something from them."

"But they're probably burners."

A small hesitation. "Yes."

I sighed, my breath fogging the glass. "I'm not safe, even an ocean away from you."

"It would seem that way," he admitted. "I am sorry, Guinevere. Even though it is not a good enough excuse, this is the reason I did not tell you the truth about who I am. This is why, though I could no longer imagine my life without you, I did not ask you to stay. Your safety is more important than my happiness."

"Yeah, well, honesty is more important to me than my happiness or my safety," I said, and found it was true. "I am a grown woman, capable of making my own *informed* choices."

"*Capisco*," he said. I understand. "But you have to understand what it does to a man to know that his own actions could put someone he loves at risk."

I thought about my father and wondered if he had done something horrible in Italy, something that had echoed across years and continents to place Mom or me in danger. It was the only reason he would keep something from me like this.

If it was a matter of my safety.

If he felt guilty because he was the one who had put a bull's-eye on my back if I ever went back to his motherland.

"My father has been keeping secrets from me his whole life about why he left Italy and never wanted me to visit. Then, I take a chance on something for myself, to find out who I truly am in a new setting entirely of my own choosing, and I find this man. He's kind and thoughtful and gorgeous, and most of all, he makes me feel seen. Like everything I am and everything I'm still discovering about myself is precious and wonderful."

I glanced up at him, and our gazes clicked like magnets aligning. Neither of us could have looked away if we'd tried.

"And then I discover that everything I thought I knew about him is a lie. It's not just about the love I had for him. It's the way that deceit taints the love I'd started to feel for myself and this new version I'd been working on that whole time I was falling in love with him."

"The man you fell in love with is not the lie," he insisted, the words a sibilant hiss. "How can you not see that it is everything else that is the lie? The man I am with you is the truest me in every sense. The man I wish I could be if circumstances were different. The man I am inside the heart I gave to you."

"I gave it back," I reminded him coldly, because every atom of me was yearning to hold him and kiss him and love him even though he was more monster than man, more stranger than lover, really.

There was so much I didn't know and couldn't understand.

"I don't want to talk about us. I want to know why they came after me when we broke up months ago and I live in a different country."

Raffa sighed, a furious rush of air that ruffled my blood-stiff hair. "I am sorry they were able to get to you at all."

"Wait," I said, fighting through the myriad of emotions and the probable concussion making my thoughts blurry to realize something important. "How are you here? How could you have possibly known I was in trouble?"

Something shifted in those light-brown eyes like bodies stirring in a shallow grave beneath the earth.

"You had me watched?" I asked, more breath than voice.

A tic of muscle in his square jaw was my only answer.

"Jesus, Raffa. Are you serious?"

"Be happy that I am, or else you would have ended up dead or worse at the hands of those *bastardi*."

"Be happy? That you were essentially stalking me?" I asked incredulously.

But deep inside that locked box at the center of my being where light couldn't reach, something thrilled at the thought.

"*Si*," he said curtly. "I had you watched. You think it is because I did not respect your decision to leave me? *Cazzate*. I had you followed because there was no other way to keep myself away from you. How could I live without knowing if you were all right? How could I breathe?"

The silence between us bloomed like a bruise, painful right through to the bone.

"Did you know something like this might happen?" I asked, the starch gone out of my tone because how could I yell at a man who said things like "How could I breathe" about not knowing if I was safe?

"No, truly. If I had thought they would come for you, Renzo or Carmine would have been here to oversee things himself. One of my top *soldati*."

"If it wasn't one of your men, who was it?"

"I had the capo of the New York Camorra send someone," he admitted. "He is a good man and did not hesitate. In fact, he and his wife offered to shelter you in New York if anything should happen."

"How did you know to come?" I pressed, because Raffa was good at providing information adjacent to what I really wanted to hear.

"His man noticed someone tailing you two days ago. He tried to track them down but lost them somewhere on campus."

"And so you came?" I said, a little stupidly, staring over his shoulder into the dark and neon blur of the passing nightscape. "Just like that."

"Guinevere," he said, all exasperation and heat, his fingers gently pinching my chin so I was forced to meet his gaze. "I would have been on the next plane out if you so much as broke your little toe."

"Feeling guilty, eh?"

A subvocal growl purred at the base of his throat, and his eyes looked so dark then, devoid of light as we passed under a bridge. "I would have taken any excuse to see you. It was the hardest thing I have ever had to do, keeping myself in Italy and away from you. Do you not understand that?"

"No, I guess I don't," I murmured, prying my face away from him.

It was so easy to say the words, those sweet Italianate phrases of love and affection that seemed to roll off his tongue with uncharacteristic ease. It was much harder to illustrate love and trust in action, and Raffa had proven he didn't trust me, and therefore, I honestly felt, he could not love me.

At least not like I had loved him—*did* love him.

A sharp exhalation ruffled the side of my hair. He took my limp hand in his, rubbing a thumb along my bloodstained skin as if it didn't bother him.

"If you do not want to believe that I love you, then at least believe this: I would do anything to keep you safe. And yes, that means I would happily take a red-eye to America. Yes, I would rip a man apart with my bare hands for so much as leering at you. Yes, I would raze this whole city to the ground if it turned against you. No one is safe from me but you," he vowed darkly, eyes deep enough to swallow the world. "If you believe anything of me, believe that."

Looking at him in the dim interior of the car, shadows cutting his handsome face into something stark and terrifying like a death mask, I could believe it. He had shown how violently he felt about me before—the rude driver, Galasso, the intruder. It was a ferocity that I inspired in him that was never aimed my way. As if I was his dark muse.

I shivered, but it wasn't from the cold.

It was from the feeling it gave me—like a key fitting into the lock of the darkness at the heart of me and slowly clicking open.

I opened my mouth to say something—*Thank you*, maybe, or *I hate you for making me feel this way, like violence is a love letter*—but the partition in front of us whirred as it lowered, distracting me.

"The plane is ready for takeoff, boss," a man said from the front seat. "We should be there in twenty."

"Plane?" I asked, blinking owlishly. It suddenly occurred to me to question, "Where are you taking me, Raffa?"

His hand tightened around mine, his calluses catching on the curves of my hand, fingers metal bands around my own. When I looked up into his eyes, they were the color of the inside of a flame, a pale yellow so bright they burned.

"Home," he declared. "I am taking you home."

CHAPTER FOUR

Guinevere

"Absolutely not," I declared, yanking my hand out from between Raffa's. "I'm not just going back to Italy with you."

"You are not safe here," he reminded me, his entire body taut and poised like that of a predator about to pounce. "How can I keep you safe when you live across the world from me?"

"We broke up!" I shouted. "Exactly so I would not have to be involved in this kind of mess. I'm not going back to Tuscany with you to become ensnared in it further. I think it's fair to say you can't keep me safe even when I'm in your bed, given an intruder almost blew my head off on my last night spent in your home."

Oh, he flinched. Like I'd slapped him full across the face. No, like I'd punched him, closed fist, all my weight behind it. The skin of his cheeks flushed, surprisingly visible in the dark interior of the car, as if I really had hit him.

I watched as his throat worked around a hard swallow and his eyes clenched closed for a single second before he fixed them on me again.

When he spoke, it was in the voice of a capo, a made man of the Italian Camorra.

"You will come home with me until I put down the dogs who stalk us both, Guinevere. In this, I do not care about your opinion. You can rage. You can call me the devil. You can think this means every awful thing you have imagined about me since you learned I am in *la mafia* is true. I do not care. Your safety comes before anything."

"Even if it means I despise you?" I seethed.

"Even then," he agreed with a solemn head tilt.

"Be reasonable," I tried to suggest calmly, though I couldn't believe his audacity. "I have a life here. A job. A family. And both of those are entangled. I can't just disappear without people worrying about me."

He shrugged one shoulder. "So call them. Make something up."

"It's not that simple, Raffaele," I snapped. "My father still won't talk to me properly after I defied him and went to Italy the first time. You're asking me to irrevocably damage my relationship with my father."

One slow blink of those annoyingly beautiful lashes. "Better a damaged relationship than mourning his second daughter, no?"

"I'm not going to Italy with you," I repeated firmly. "Please, take me back to my apartment so I can get cleaned up."

"And then what?" he demanded, shifting closer, teeth glinting in the orange light spilling in from outside. "You can protect yourself from all the things that go bump in the night? You are a fawn, not a huntress. They will eat you alive."

"You think I came home after almost being shot in the head and thought, meh, I'm fine being defenseless?" I scoffed, but my belly tossed and churned. I felt sick with fear and anger and the impossibility of going to Italy and remaining in Michigan. "I've been taking MMA classes twice a week."

Something like a smile seized Raffa's mouth before he bit it off. "You think two months of MMA is going to stack your five foot nothing, a hundred ten pounds soaking wet against a trained mafioso?"

A noise of frustration bubbled up my throat. "I think I could take you by surprise."

"Oh?" The word was a curl of smoke through the space between us, heady enough to drug me. "I would like to see you try."

Lust pulsed between us in time with our heartbeats, tangible enough to feel, to touch.

I sat on my fingertips to keep myself from reaching out.

With a suddenness that made me gasp, Raffa lashed out with one hand, palming my entire throat, fingers folding around my pulse point with just enough pressure to make me feel the drag of breath through my airway. There was a knife in his other hand, sparking in the passing streetlights like stop-motion film as he lifted it from somewhere hidden to press it featherlight against my cheek.

"You think because I am a made man that I have no rules or morals, but you are wrong. I am Rex Infernus, and in the world that I rule, I am the one who makes the rules as I see fit. No one acts against me, little fawn, not without serious consequences." The knifepoint skimmed the ridge of my cheekbone and moved down to the corner of my mouth, where he pushed the flat of the blade into the center of my lower lip as if testing its plushness. "You have unmasked me, so there is no point in pretending any longer that I am not the kind of man who would make any man suffer magnificently for any second of pain they gave you. I would skin them with this knife. Butcher their organs into mash. And keep them alive until the very last moment so they could feel every second of agony."

I was breathing too hard. The sound of air rushing through my lungs was like that of the ocean churning violently through rock. It should have been fear coursing through me, or anger.

But it wasn't.

Arousal moved hot and slow through my veins, volcanic. If he'd pressed his tongue to my lips beside the skin-warmed edge of that blade, I honestly might have erupted.

"I am who I am to keep those I care about safe." He was whispering now, a husky drawl that steamed up the knife between us. "You are one of those people, whether you like it or not. And I will keep you safe, even if it is from yourself."

"I'm not going with you," I said, but the words were threadbare, my conviction buried under drifts of lava at my molten core.

The edge of his mouth curled into a cruel little smile as he dropped the hand from my throat and moved the hand holding the knife into my hair. He kept the blade away from the strands as he threaded them between his fingers to tug my head back so he could duck down to nose at the thrumming pulse point in my neck.

"I would rather have you alive and hating me than dead. So hate me if you will, Guinevere, but you are going back to Italy with me, and there is nothing you can do about it."

◆ ◆ ◆

I yelled at him.

Which was strange because I don't think I'd ever yelled at anyone before in my life.

But when you realize that you've fallen in love with a man who seems like an angel only to discover he is the absolute devil, it's only fair to lose your mind a little.

The anger, though, didn't get through to him.

It was only when I exhausted myself, the last of the adrenaline drained from my shocky, weak limbs so that sorrow and helplessness could seep through me in their wake, that Raffa seemed to care.

Men can never withstand a woman's tears, my sister Gemma had told me one night after she returned home tearstained but euphoric from a date. Her college boyfriend at the time hadn't wanted to take her to her silly high school prom, but the moment she'd started to cry, he'd capitulated.

It was shocking to see Raffa's steely resolve waver as he watched me dash a hot tear from my cheek as I twisted toward the window to look at anything other than him.

"I have to take you," he said quietly. "How could I live with myself if you died because of me?"

It was a fair question, but it did nothing to mitigate the fact that abandoning my life in Ann Arbor was reckless and foolish and potentially life ruining. What would I have to return to when all was said and done? An estranged family and no career.

I mentioned that to Raffa, but he merely gave me one of those minuscule shrugs and said, "You are very smart, with two degrees and work experience. You might not work for your father again, but you will be able to find other employment. If not, I will help you."

I shuddered to think what Raffa's offer of "help" might entail.

"So once again I'll be in Italy without any of my things," I muttered, thinking of the dishes I'd left in the sink that morning, the half-read copy of Virgil's *The Aeneid* on my bedside table, my medications.

At last, this seemed to give him pause. "Will that be a problem? We were able to get your medication just fine in Firenze last time."

"I'm on a new protocol," I admitted, my lids scraping over my dry eyes as I blinked. "It's an injection to lower the oxalate in my blood."

Out of the corner of my eye, I saw Raffa pull out his phone. His fingers flew as he researched, asking me for the name of the drug.

A sigh hissed though his clenched teeth before he leaned forward to press a button and say, "Tony, change of plans. Take us to 1211 Burns Avenue."

"How do you know my address?" I asked and then realized, around the same time that Raffa slanted me a look, that the answer was obvious.

Raffa was rich and powerful enough to know anything he wanted about me.

"We can grab some of your things," he allowed, "but we must be quick."

I sucked my bottom lip between my teeth to keep from thanking him and nodded tersely.

Happily, it only took us ten minutes to get to my apartment building, but I had to wait as Raffa and his two goons secured the perimeter of the building before he let me out of the car. He tried to help me through the snow because I'd lost my shoes in the chase at the

Beaumont, but I'd literally rather have walked through ice than accept his hand right now.

Still, he walked close behind me, and I caught the way he had his hand raised just in case I slipped.

The apartment building was dark and quiet at this time of night, so no one interrupted us as we took the stairs to the sixth floor. There was an elevator, but I decided after one quick glance at it that I was not ready to get inside one of those again.

Raffa let me unlock the door to my apartment before pressing me gently by the belly to the wall so he could enter alone, gun raised as he checked out the space. When he came back into sight, there was a crooked grin on his face and a photo pinched in one hand.

I knew without having to study it closer that it was a selfie of us at Piazzale Michelangelo after we had jogged to the top to catch the sunset over Florence. The sky was a brilliant smear of tangerine and fuchsia, the light turning the red roofs of the city into shimmering fire. But that wasn't why I'd kept the photograph, printing it at a local shop so I could tuck it into the vanity in my bedroom.

It was the look on the face of the man I'd thought I'd known.

His dark, overlong hair was pushed back from his sweaty forehead, the ends curling like swirls of ink at his neck. One deeply tanned arm was wrapped around my side, hauling me up into his torso so that I was his height, my mouth pressed to the five-o'clock shadow along his strong jaw. My eyes were squeezed shut as I kissed him, but there was something like a smile in the expression anyway, an exuberance in the way my arms were thrown around his neck.

But it was his smile that took my breath away.

Relaxed and wide, a full-lipped, eye-crinkling expression of pure joy.

He looked young in it, much younger than his thirty-four years, and more carefree than I'd ever seen him. Just a man without a care in the world, embracing his woman like he'd never tire of it for as long as they both lived.

"Do not forget to pack this," Raffa said, delight and happiness ruffling the edges of his serious tone.

I blinked at him, unamused, as I brushed past him on the way to the bedroom at the back of the apartment. "I just liked the way Florence looks caught on fire behind us."

"Mmm," he hummed, following me into the bedroom to lean against the doorjamb. He crossed his arms, one hand holding his gun, the other the photograph.

What a fitting contrast.

"I think it is the way we look on fire with happiness, but you can lie to yourself if it will make you feel better," he allowed with faux magnanimity.

I ignored him in favor of dragging my suitcase out of the closet.

"It is still warm in Toscana," he told me as he unnervingly watched me pack. "But it will grow colder by the end of the month."

I nodded, pulling out the bin of summer clothes tucked away at the back. It was hard to think about how long I might be stuck in another country. Even harder to admit an elemental part of me was absolutely euphoric about the idea of going back.

"You don't need to supervise me," I said after another disquieting moment of his scrutiny. "I'm capable of packing."

He made a noise in his throat that was halfway between laughter and a grunt of acknowledgment before he pushed off the wall to explore the rest of my space. I pretended I didn't hate that even more than him watching me.

In his absence, I quickly shucked my bloody, torn clothes and stuffed them in the garbage bin because there was no way I would wear them again. I took an oversized, faded U of M tee and a soft pair of leggings from my drawer. My feet were cold, cut up and bruised from running for my life, so I swaddled them in thick socks and then stuffed them into my Uggs. The outfit was decidedly different from the silks and designer garments Raffa had bought for me, but I felt safe and comfortable in the familiar garb.

When he returned a few minutes later, I was almost done. He paused a moment in the doorway, obviously staring at me, his gaze a heated press against my skin. I startled when he passed me a secured plastic bag filled with my medicine from the fridge.

"You will teach me to help you with this," he told me, crouching beside me in his spotless designer suit, strong thighs splayed distractingly. "It must be uncomfortable to dose yourself."

It was, but it also wasn't the end of the world, and I absolutely did not want Raffa's man-killing hands gently tending to me. It wasn't something my heart could survive.

I knew because I had started to fall in love with him the first time he'd taken care of me when I arrived at his palazzo in Florence.

"You should pack this," he said, his gaze having snagged on the red fabric I'd left in the summer bin.

I watched as he pulled it from the tangle of clothes and carefully folded it, stroking down the silky fabric. When he looked up at me, his pale eyes were warm with memories.

"I never got to see you in a field of poppies, wearing this dress," he murmured. "Pack it."

"Poppy season is over," I reminded him, taking the dress he'd bought me from Maria Lucia's store and stuffing it back into the bin.

I stood to go to the bathroom to grab my toiletries, and when I returned, Raffa was sitting on my bed, looking at the framed photo of my family I kept on my nightstand. It had been taken at one of my father's work events, so we were all done up in finery, though nothing so fine as what Raffa was used to. I was seventeen in the photo, a fresh high school graduate wearing an almost childishly demure white dress that covered me from throat to wrists to ankles, while Gemma was in a scandalously low-cut orange dress that brought out her curves and summer tan. My dad had his arm around me, a proud smile on his face, and my mom was holding Gemma around the waist, laughing at something she'd said.

It was a good photo, one of the last ones we had as a family because Gemma had always been traveling and then moved away when I was twenty.

"You look different here," Raffa said, his thumb sweeping over my image. "Young and soft, even more a *cerbiatta* than the girl I found on the road in Tuscany."

"I was," I agreed. "Young and foolish. I guess I still am."

He flinched just slightly at the comment. "Your father looks very Italian, but your mother is fair."

"Her parents were Albanian," I told him as I bent to zip up my suitcase. "Are you ready?"

He was frowning down at the photo, but nodded, standing with it still in his hand. "Yes, go to the door and give your case to Tony. He will take it down for you. Then come back."

I wanted to question him, but exhaustion was settling deep into my bones, weighing every step, so I just did as I was told.

When I returned, the bathroom light was on, and Raffa was inside, my little first aid kit open on the closed lid of the toilet.

"*Vieni*," he ordered, tapping the sink.

I stepped closer automatically, and by the time I hesitated, Raffa had me by the hips, carefully lifting me to sit on the basin.

"I'm fine," I said, even though my head was throbbing and every inch of my body ached.

"*Stai zitta*," he told me.

I hated hearing him speak Italian because it was so damn lovely, even when he was telling me to shut up.

Still, I quieted, sitting calmly as he tilted my head to inspect the bullet graze. The tap ran for a moment, and then a warm cloth was pressed to the wound. I winced, but he shushed me softly as he cleaned up the injury.

"This will hurt," he warned before dabbing antiseptic onto the long cut, and I sucked in a sharp breath, nearly choking at the pain.

"Good girl," he praised me. "Almost done."

I shivered, clenching my teeth against the invasion of pleasure those words made me feel.

"It is not so bad," he declared after collecting the garbage and throwing it into the little bin beside the toilet. "It will hurt and then itch as it heals, but your hair should cover any scar."

I nodded because my voice was somewhere near my toes, and I didn't know what to say anyway. My body had a mind of its own when it was being tended to by him, and all it wanted to do was curl close and feel safe after this horrible night. He used a new warm, damp cloth to wash the dried blood from my face, and I had to close my eyes to shield myself from the tenderness in his expression.

The cloth landed with a wet splat in the sink behind me, so I peered through my lids to see him bend slightly at the knee until we were eye level with each other. Only then did he cup my clean face in his big, rough palms. I noticed how exhausted he looked up close, the lines of strain beside his mouth, the sooty circles beneath his eyes that spoke of a long time without proper sleep.

"I am sorry, Guinevere," he murmured, thumbs sweeping over my cheekbones. "Sorrier than I have words in English or Italian to say."

The ache that opened up in my chest like a crater threatened to eat every last inch of my resolve. If I just leaned into his touch, I knew he would wrap me up in his arms and make everything okay.

At least for a moment.

I'd learned better than to think it could last.

"Let me say goodbye," I whispered through the vise around my throat. "I promised my dad that if I was ever going to leave again I would say goodbye."

His mouth flatlined, and his hands fell from my face. "No. You do understand that they could be hurt because of this? The less contact you have with them, the better."

Fear pierced my breastbone, setting fire to my lungs. "I can't just leave them here, then! What if they send more . . . goons after them because they can't find me?"

"I will keep someone here to monitor them." Raffa waved my question out of the air with the back of his hand as if it was of no consequence. "They will be safe. But only if you are not here to put them in danger."

My head thunked against the mirror behind me, making me wince. I closed my eyes to breathe deeply through the chaos of tangled emotions in my chest. It felt like drowning. Like I would die if I didn't take Raffa's offer, even though it felt safe to trust the hand he gave me.

"The last thing on earth I want to do is go back to that place with you," I admitted, my mind racing as I thought of another alternative. "I could leave," I said. "But I could go to London or Paris. Somewhere no one would think to look for me. My French is pretty bad, but they speak English in the city. I have a friend who lives there whom I could stay with."

"No, Vera, you will not disappear from me, and you will not disappear from there. This is *la mafia*. There is no escaping to any part of the globe."

"I could try," I insisted, but I still didn't open my eyes, unwilling to see Raffa in front of me, his resolute expression or, even worse, one of pity.

"No, you will be where you belong," he said intractably, with the authority of an ancient Roman emperor no one would dare to defy. "With me."

The pressure around one of my wrists as it lay in my lap was cold enough to shock me out of the shivering stasis.

"What the . . . ?" I gasped as I looked down to see the handcuff locked to one of my arms. "Raffa! What the hell is this?"

The grin on his face was pure wolf, sharp canines and red lips. He lifted his own hand between us, rattling the metal linking his cuffed hand to mine. "My insurance policy."

"You are insane," I shouted, wrenching my hand back even though there was no way I could break out of the cuffs. "My whole world is being turned upside down because of you. I-I hate you, Raffaele. I freaking hate you."

"Fine," he said flippantly. "Hate me in Tuscany."

"This doesn't mean anything for us," I declared, everything in me shutting down like a house before a Category 5 hurricane. Shutters closing, doors locking, battening down every last hatch so that nothing more of him could get in. "We're still done, Raffaele."

The silence between us was flat and disquieting, the dense air before the storm hits when the animals are silent and the hairs on the back of your arm rise in alarm.

"I know," he acknowledged finally, voice rough and deep as if the words cost him. "There is no happily ever after for a man like me. I have always known this. It is my fault that for a moment I considered . . . Well. It is done now."

"Good," I said softly as I closed my eyes and turned back to the window, pressing myself to the cold mirror like I secretly yearned to press myself to the untrustworthy stranger I used to know beside me. "I'm glad," I lied.

CHAPTER FIVE

Raffa

Seven weeks. Five days. Twenty hours.

The excruciating length of time I had lived through without seeing Guinevere.

As much as I had wanted to refuse to let her go back to America, and then as much as I had wanted to fly to her side to convince her to return every day after she had gone, I had managed to restrain myself.

At first, it was a simple matter of respecting her decision when I was made to acknowledge I had not respected her enough before to divulge my truths. If she did not want me, the rejected and aching part of my mind declared feebly, then I would not force myself upon her.

Especially when doing so could be dangerous.

And there came the rub.

A man had entered my home, somehow slipping past security, in order to come after not just me but also my woman.

That was unacceptable.

It did not matter that the would-be assassin's brains had been blown out all over my walk-in closet. The threat had not passed.

Even if I wanted to bring Guinevere back—bring her *home*—how could I do so knowing I would be putting her life in danger again?

Therefore, there was only one course of action to be had.

Find the people who were after me and mine and end them in no uncertain terms.

Not just their leaders but also their foot soldiers and informants, their women and their fucking children. I wanted to eviscerate them all for daring to go after the one woman who had ever touched my soul.

For her, I would burn down all of Firenze.

I set the Sala brothers and Ludo on the matter exclusively, because if anyone could root out the enemy, it was Renzo, Carmine, and the best hacker this side of the Mediterranean Sea. We interrogated everyone in our own clan with access to and knowledge of the palazzo who could have passed information along or helped the intruder inside.

Our search yielded nothing.

My men and women were loyal because I did not take them on without extensive trials and experience. I had not doubted them, not really, but it did not explain how someone could have entered the palazzo so effortlessly.

Unless we had another mole like that fucker Bruno who had tried to assassinate me in Rome, just days before I'd met Guinevere on that lonely stretch of Tuscan roadway.

The only thing we knew was that this San Marco character seemed to be puppeteering everything. The assassin had been wearing a traditional Venetian mask, Bruno had admitted he had been introduced to the Pietras by this man, and when we looked into the dead assassin's identity, the man was revealed as Iacopone Basti, a supposed glassblower out of Venice.

It didn't make sense.

Neither I nor my father had history with Venetians, especially because he had overseen the Mafia outfit out of the Venetian port for decades. Our local capos there, under the supervision of Donatella Verdi, had been happy with the status quo when Carmine and Renzo went to do the rounds. In fact, Donatella was unwaveringly loyal to us because we had backed her play for capo over her idiot brother years ago when her father passed. The idiot brother was not the problem either. Donatella had ended his life with his own gun.

It had to be someone closer to home, but who I could not say, no matter how I searched.

The Grecos had taken over the Albanian operations in Livorno, and they had clearly expressed interest in expanding their power base, but our successful sting operation using the Direzione Investigativa Antimafia (DIA) and its overzealous deputy director, Sansone Pucci, had razed their operation to ash. While Pucci was too morally high-minded to be corrupted, the arrests had earned him national acclaim and a pay raise, and we both knew I had been the one to help him. With his attentions fixed on hamstringing Clan Greco and the rival family facing prison and a systematic dismantling, I did not think they had the power to continue to come for me.

Which left the Pietras and their hatred of our leadership. They had killed my father, so I had personally killed Gaetano Pietra's two oldest sons. He was an old man now, in his mid-eighties, without an heir to his underworld throne, and he was grasping at power and revenge by colluding with this San Marco to come after me.

I did not view him or his people as a serious threat.

I knew where each one of them lived, worked, and bedded their mistresses.

I knew how to kill each of them without drawing the attention of the DIA. Poison, a staged car accident, a fall down the slippery stairs, or a drunken accident off one of Genoa's many docks.

But there was no point in killing the messengers before I could get to the man using them to send the message.

Despite the acute frustration of hitting dead end after dead end, I could breathe easy knowing that Guinevere was safe from harm in quaint little Ann Arbor, Michigan, and I knew that because I had made a deal with Dante Salvatore to watch over her.

"I will not ask why you need this favor," he had said over the phone in that strange accent that was accounted for by his upbringing in England and time spent in Italy. "Because I am a man very much in love too. And like yours, my heart was taken by a fierce woman who made me work for her."

My laughter was a bitter cough. "This woman is almost impossible to win back."

"Ah," he'd said, and the sound of children's laughter could be heard in the background. "What is it they say? The night is always darkest before the dawn. I will keep your woman safe, Romano, no questions asked."

And then, weeks later, to wake up in the middle of the night to my phone ringing, with Dante Salvatore's name flashing on my screen . . . my blood had run cold.

There was no hesitation in leaving.

Not even with a potential mole in my ranks, not even with my mother and sisters in Tuscany, well guarded as they were, not even with the proverbial wolves at my door.

Nothing mattered as much as getting to Guinevere before any harm could come to her.

And I had failed.

By the time I landed, Dante was on the phone with me again, announcing that his man had been taken out after checking in to say they were watching her office building.

Abject terror had pierced me like a blade, slicing from head to toe until I radiated with restless agony. I had nearly pulled a gun on Tony for stopping at red lights in our race to reach her.

My fawn had been alone and unwittingly trapped in a cage with predators who would know exactly how to ensnare and, perhaps, murder her to get to me.

For as long as I lived, I would never forget arriving at the Beaumont Building to see an unmarked limo careening out of the garage, knowing that my girl was probably inside on her way to be raped, tortured, or killed.

I had held the gun to Tony's head and demanded he ram into that car so they could not get away.

The ensuing firefight was over before I broke a sweat. The men were trained, but not well, not compared with me and the four of Dante's men who had met me at the airport.

In the vibrating silence that followed, I had no idea what I would find.

Was she hurt? Scarred or crippled? Tied up and gagged, violated?

Bile surged up my throat as I walked to the broken car and tugged the dead body out from the entryway to the back seat.

And then, there she was.

La cerbiatta mia.

Pressed to the opposite door of the car, bracing a gun on her knees, eyes squinted as they stared through her own blood down the barrel at me. Ready to end whoever might come for her.

If I had not loved her before, I would have loved her forevermore after witnessing the tableau she made in that dark interior.

My innocent Guinevere covered in blood and trembling, but facing off fearlessly against her probable death.

Dio mio, she was brave.

Gorgeous and sublime.

Too good for me even to look at, let alone touch.

It rocked me further to see the way relief broke through her fierce expression like sunlight through a storm cloud, completely transforming her entire countenance as she dropped the gun and threw herself into my arms.

Like I was her hero.

It was bizarre to admit that it was one of the best moments of my life, knowing that even after everything that had happened, the ways I had let her down and betrayed her love, she still trusted me to save her.

I tried to hold that feeling close to me as I sat on the plane to Firenze, on the opposite side of the cabin from where Guinevere had settled herself as soon as I had uncuffed her.

She had curled up in one of the big cream leather chairs and promptly fallen asleep as if I did not exist.

Maybe she wished I did not.

I watched as she slept fitfully, lids jumping, limbs twitching, the odd whimper getting stuck in her throat. It was almost impossible to stay away from her, so eventually I gave in and moved to the seat across from her. When I reached out to cup her foot as it kicked out, she froze and then softened back into a more comfortable sleep.

In sleep, it seemed, her body recognized mine as friend instead of foe.

It was when she woke that she would distance herself from me again.

Rightfully so, maybe, but it still felt like a dozen knives stuck through every one of my ribs like a pincushion.

It did not matter that she hated me, I told myself. What mattered was that she was under my purview again so I could actually keep her safe.

And there was no safer place than Villa Romano. The seat of my house, my family, and my power in the north. The sprawling estate was nestled in the hilly region of Chianti between Firenze and Siena. It comprised a main villa that housed my mother and youngest sister, Delfina, while Stacci and Carlotta each had their own homes on the property with their husbands and children. To the left of the acreage lay Tenuta Romano, our world-renowned vineyard, with the winery and visitor center down the road at a separate estate, and to the right our olive groves. The barracks for my on-site *soldati* were in a converted barn near the groves, close enough to the house for a one-minute response time. There were guards twenty-four seven in the tower at the gates and still more patrolling the acreage.

Leo was currently living in the main house with Philippe, a childhood friend and trusted soldier who had once killed three men using only a toaster.

Throw in a state-of-the-art security system, and Villa Romano was one of the most heavily guarded fortresses in the country.

No one would harm Guinevere there.

Which meant it was the only option, even though I knew taking her there would open an entirely new world of problems. My nosy mother and siblings prying into our history, Leo's strange animosity toward Guinevere, and my own reluctance to fall even more deeply in love with her after seeing her interact with the other few people I loved in this world.

I sighed, exhausted from being awake for well over forty hours, but unable to sleep until I had called and emailed everyone on the ground to ready for our arrival.

The only person who dared to make the situation harder than it already was, of course, was Martina.

"Raffa, this is a bad idea," she said softly, or as softly as a woman like her could manage. "You'll torture yourself having her around but being unable to really have her."

"You think I do not know that, Tina?" I rubbed a hand over my eyes, trying to rid them of the sandy grit of fatigue. "There is nothing for it. Do you think my comfort is more important than her safety? I am the one who brought those thugs upon her head."

She made a vague noise of distress. "You don't know that for sure."

My laugh was a quiet, bitter bark. "*Sei seria?* Do not be foolish. You think Guinevere has her own enemies in Italy?"

It was such a preposterous idea that I laughed again. But it reminded me of the photos I had taken from Guinevere's apartment. I pulled them from the inner pocket of my suit and arranged the one I wanted on the table beside me to take a photo of it that I could send off to Ludo and Martina.

"I just sent through a photo of Guinevere and her family. She says that her father left Italy abruptly and has never agreed to tell her the reason why. Find him for me."

"For you? Or as a present for the girl you wish to win back?" she quipped.

I was silent for long enough to make my point.

She sighed. "It is not wrong to want someone good for yourself, Raffa. None of us had ever seen you so happy as when she was living in the palazzo with you. None of us had ever dreamed of seeing you so at peace."

"Peace is always temporary. It is chaos you can count on."

Another sigh. "Unfortunately, you're right. But maybe this time, you can see if Guinevere is capable of surviving the chaos. Of surviving and loving the true Raffaele. I may be biased, but he is as good a man as they come."

It was rare to receive a compliment from Martina, so even though I was sunk knee deep in self-recrimination, I let her words soothe me.

"Good for the circumstances of our lives, perhaps," I allowed quietly, working the words past the knot in my throat. "I try to be."

"I know, *fratello*," she said, lowering her voice too. "It does not go unnoticed. Have you . . . have you considered telling her why they call you the reluctant mafioso?"

Across from me, Guinevere stirred in her sleep, calling out weakly. I stood to grab the cashmere afghan from the couch, balancing the phone between my ear and shoulder so I could carefully lay her beneath its folds, tucking the ends up under her feet so they would not get cold.

"No," I finally answered, hesitating over Guinevere, caught by the magnificence of her beauty even in slumber. Her full red-pink mouth was the only spot of color in her pale face, framed by all that long, dark hair still tangled and bloodstained in places. She looked like a fairy-tale princess, someone meant to be kept safe and hidden away for her own safety in a tower until a good and kind prince could prove himself worthy of her affection.

The reality was that I was no Prince Charming, and I never would be. The only tower available to her was the guard tower at the gates of my fortified mansion, a necessity because I was a criminal with more enemies than sense. Instead of proving myself, I had betrayed her and then dragged her kicking and screaming into the dangerous waters of my world once again.

"No," I repeated. "I will not tell her why I became *capo dei capi*. The point is, I am who I am, and there is no turning back."

Truthfully, despite what my naive teenage self had hoped, there never had been.

There was no getting out of the Mafia alive.

And now Guinevere was a part of that world.

So I had to find some impossible way to free her, even though it meant leaving myself behind forever.

CHAPTER SIX

Raffa

To my surprise, Guinevere slept through the transfer from plane to car. She curled herself into my chest as I carried her down the stairs to the waiting vehicle on the tarmac at the private airport outside of Firenze, and when I tried to move her onto her own seat inside the SUV, she whimpered.

It was a good excuse not to let her go.

Carmine shot me a look in the rearview mirror as he drove us through the countryside to Villa Romano, but he did not say a word, turning the volume up on classical music instead. Affection pulsed in my chest like a second heartbeat. It was good of him to give me that moment without teasing—uncharacteristic too.

Clearly, I was not the only one who had missed the American girl.

The sun was setting when we finally pulled up to the wrought iron gates of the Romano estate. Rose-gold light spilled over the vines on the left side of the road and turned the grass to luminous metal sheaves on the right.

"Guinevere," I said, gently rousing her because I knew she would love the view, and some part of me was eager—proud—to show her the beauty of my home. "Wake up. We have arrived."

She stirred in my arms, mauve eyelids fluttering before they peeled back to squint up at me. The long rest had done wonders, adding some color to her cheeks. I held still as she groaned and stretched in my arms, a sleepy smile tugging that full mouth into a pink crescent I wanted to kiss open and plunder.

"Raffa," she murmured, still asleep enough to forget herself. "I always dream about you."

It was as if her small hand had reached into the cage of my ribs and wrenched out my heart.

"This is not a dream, *cerbiatta mia*," I told her softly, taking advantage of the situation by running a calloused finger down the suede-soft edge of her jaw. "You are awake, you are safe, and I have finally brought you home to Villa Romano."

Even though I knew it was coming, watching her warm, open expression ice over made my stomach clench.

I let her scrabble out of my lap onto the seat beside me, smoothing down her threadbare, oversized college tee as if she was insecure or somehow immodest.

"Look," I encouraged her, pointing out the window. "I woke you to watch the sun settle."

Her mouth dropped open, her eyes tight with anger before she instinctively shot a glance out the glass over her shoulder. She arrested, one hand lifting to gently touch the pane the way she had done those early days back in Firenze, when she was discovering its beauty for the first time.

"Wow," she breathed, turning completely to face the window and the glimmering, deeply orange sun kissing the tops of the endless stretch of vines leading up and away from the top of the hill we were cresting. "It's like something from a dream."

I swallowed the urge to tell her this was *my* dream. Her in my home, meeting my family, seeing the sweet and sour memories that haunted this place for me.

"How many vines do you have?" she asked, forgetting her acrimony in the face of her undying curiosity.

"One hundred twenty-five acres of vineyard," I told her. "Tenuta Romano is one of the oldest wineries in the country. My ancestors have lived here for over one thousand years. The tower by the gate is an Etruscan ruin, actually, and the main house on the hill is hundreds of years old."

"So cool," she whispered.

The tangerine light kissed her face as she turned it fully into the fading rays, limning her in a neon glow I wanted to trace with my fingertips.

"I thought you would like it here," I confessed.

It was the wrong thing to say.

She slid me a sidelong look, shoulders tensed. "Yet you didn't bring me here."

"It would have been . . ." *Unbearable.* "Hard to introduce you to my family knowing you were leaving shortly."

"And now? I'll still leave, Raffa. After you take out whoever it is who is coming for you and, by proxy, me."

I tilted my head at the tone of her voice, trying to decide if I was reading into it too much. Because there was something there. A reticence or a lack of conviction. Something that said she was attempting to convince herself as well as me.

Outside the window a dog swooped into view from between the vines, a *segugio maremmano* purebred my sister Stacci had named Aio. He ran beside the car as we ascended the circular road climbing up the hill, his dappled body glowing gold.

"What a beautiful baby," Guinevere breathed, her hand clenched against the window.

There was yearning there, and awe.

"You like dogs?"

Her laugh was wistful. "Always. We didn't have time to take care of one because I was always in and out of the hospital, and my parents felt it wasn't fair to leave a dog alone so much. Gemma had a hamster for about two weeks before it escaped the cage and got stuck in a drawer. My dad decapitated it accidently when we were searching for it." She winced. "Needless to say, we never got another one."

I laughed, shocked that even when she was angry with me, she could still be sweet and funny.

"We have had dogs all my life. Stacci breeds *segugio maremmano*, a type of Italian scent hound. Her husband, Emiliano, is a hunter, and Aio there is good enough to take on a boar if he needs to."

"Wow," she said again, then laughed at herself, pushing a lock of hair out of her face as she turned to face me. "I'm sorry, I forgot, I guess."

"Forgot?"

She shrugged, chewing on her lower lip for a moment before admitting, "How magical everything is here. How much it feels like a fairy tale."

When she looked up, our eyes caught, and even though she jerked her chin as if to wrench her gaze away, it did not work. We stared at each other across mere inches, and yet it felt as if the entire Atlantic Ocean still separated us.

"A Grimms' fairy tale," she corrected. "The bloody kind."

I inclined my head in agreement. "Let us hope this one ends happily."

At least for one of us.

She pursed her lips, but the sound of screaming children drew her attention out the window again.

Maximo, Vitale, Zacheo, and Mattia all waited at the crest of the driveway, the latter two jumping up and down and waving their arms.

"*Zio Raffa*," they cried, out of sync with each other.

Aio barked in agreement, racing up to them and dancing between their wriggling bodies.

I laughed despite the tense atmosphere in the car and lowered my window so I could call out in Italian, "*Ciao, ragazzi! Sei stato buono con le tue madri?*"

Hello, children! Have you been good for your mothers?

"No!" they all cried before dissolving into giggles, running alongside the car as it started to pass them.

I chuckled, grabbing at Maximo's hand when he pushed it through the window, leaning forward to clutch him under the arms and pull him swiftly into the slow-moving car.

His laugh was a high-pitched squeal as I buried my face in his neck to blow a raspberry after he settled in my lap.

"And how is my favorite nephew today?" I asked in Italian.

He screwed up his face in irritation. "You call *all* of us your favorites, Uncle!"

"Why, yes, I do. But let me tell you something, I missed you very much."

Truthfully, Stacci's and Carlotta's sons were one of the only reasons I came back to Villa Romano at all. Without them, it was too easy to live in the past. To see my sisters silent and subjugated when my father was present. To see my mother valiantly trying to raise her children when her husband was out sleeping with whomever he pleased, carousing and acting like a bigwig in Firenze.

The boys brought new life to the villa, swept away the ghosts with their laughter and silly games.

Before I had gone to Michigan to save Guinevere, I had only been home once in the two months following her departure. My mother and sisters had noticed my melancholy even though I had done my best to hide it, and I did not want to answer any more questions about "that American girl."

So it was good to be home.

It was even better, in a bittersweet way, to have Guinevere there at my side.

When I looked over Maximo's curly head at her, she was staring at me with wide eyes, holding her body so still she seemed almost afraid of me. When she noticed my gaze, she gave a shake of her head as if to rid herself of a bad memory, and then shot me a tight smile before turning toward the window and the house as it loomed ahead of us.

The pale-gold stone structure may have been old, but my family had always been wealthy, so it was in incredibly good repair. Cypress trees lined the last stretch of gravel driveway, and a stone fountain with a female statue pouring water from a basin had been erected centrally in the circular courtyard before the front door.

Angela, my mother, stood outside with Stacci—who was holding her youngest, Nico—and Carlotta, Delfina, Ludo, and Leo.

"They pull out the welcome committee," Carmine murmured from the front seat.

"Carm!" Guinevere exclaimed, leaning forward to place a hand on his shoulder and grin at him in the rearview mirror. "I didn't know you were driving. I'm sorry I was ignoring you."

"You've had a rough day," he allowed, eyes sparkling as he raised a hand to place it over hers before pulling to a stop in front of the house. "It is about to be more exhausting after you meet the Romano women. I was happy to let you rest."

"Well, I am happy to see you," she admitted, though a shadow crossed her expression, and she dropped her hand from his shoulder. "Even if we are more strangers than friends."

Before he could respond, Guinevere was opening her door and slipping outside.

I looked at Carmine, who winced and shrugged. "It's going to take time, boss."

Fortunately, time was one thing I seemed to have, given we had no leads on who was provoking the Pietra and Greco clans into turning against us.

"What do you say, Maximo—should we enter the fray?" I asked my five-year-old nephew.

"No," he declared imperiously. "I think Carmine, you, and me should go have a boys' night. You can take me for gelato in the piazza."

I laughed, swinging him into my arms as I got out of the car. "I promise we will have a boys' night soon, but I think your mother and aunties would be very angry with me if I left without even saying hello."

He pouted, but also shook his head. "They're kind of demanding like that."

I was still laughing when I stopped beside Guinevere where she was frozen at the side of the car, hugging herself as if it was cold. Without thinking, I placed an arm around her shoulders, balancing Maxi on my other hip as I led us toward my waiting family.

"Ciao, mamma." I greeted my mother first, stepping away from Guinevere to kiss her on both cheeks and then doing the same down the line of sisters waiting for me. When I hit Leo and Ludo, I exchanged back-slapping hugs. "You saw fit to create a welcome committee, I see."

"We were eager to meet your American friend," Carlotta said with a sly smile. "I've been very jealous that Delfina got to meet her and we didn't."

"I told you, it was a coincidence," Delfina said with a roll of her eyes before stepping up to Guinevere. She grabbed her by the shoulders and pressed a kiss to each cheek. "Hello again, friend. It is nice to see you."

Whatever frostiness Guinevere had dredged up for me, she could not do the same for my sister. My fawn was a naturally warm, open woman with a big heart who had spent most of her life feeling lonely and shuttered away. It was no wonder she yearned for connection, and something in my chest ached at seeing the way she flushed and smiled shyly under Delfina's attention.

"*Ciao di nuovo*," she said in Italian.

My sister's grin almost split her face in two. I knelt to deal with my swarm of nephews and an enthusiastically barking Aio, keeping an eye on them as she led Guinevere up to meet the family. Even though part of me yearned to do the introductions myself, I knew it would only make things more awkward. I had called ahead to tell my family I was bringing a female guest to visit, and Stacci, who had been the one to answer, had crowed with delight when I confirmed it was "my American girl." There was no doubt they would treat her kindly, with the kind of overenthusiastic warmth characteristic of the female Romanos.

"*Che bella*," my mother exclaimed, opening her arms wide for a hug. "*Vieni.*"

Guinevere hesitantly stepped into the circle of her embrace and then laughed breathlessly when Mamma squeezed her tight.

"Welcome to Villa Romano," Mamma pronounced, punctuating the words with a kiss to each cheek. "We are very happy to have you."

◆ ◆ ◆

Dinner at the villa was always a production. Guinevere seemed almost in a daze as my mother and sisters press-ganged her into helping in the kitchen, placing her before a crate of melons and prosciutto to make the antipasti and then shuffling her to the other end of the kitchen to cut the homemade bread Mamma made each day.

A happy daze, though.

I watched through the archway in the dining room as Leo, Ludo, and Carmine updated me on developments in the last two days.

"The Grecos and Pietras aren't really working together," Carmine was telling me. "Apparently, they both have issues, but Alfonso Greco and Gaetano Pietra hate each other."

"Who told you that?" Leo asked, updating his notes on his tablet.

Carmine glowered at Leo. A level of professional competitiveness would always exist between them. Leo was my oldest friend, and his father had been my father's consigliere, but Carmine and Renzo had been with me in London. They knew the man I was now in ways Leo did not.

"Does it matter? It is from a reputable source."

"It does not matter," I agreed. "What does is finding out who sent the funeral chrysanthemums and the assassin. Tell me we have a lead on that."

"I got something," Ludo grunted, raising his hand like we were in a classroom. It was a gesture that would have endeared him to Guinevere even more. She had once told me that she found Ludo—the best hacker in the Italian Mafia—adorable. "You remember Angela Greco was married to a Tancredi? Well, Iacopone Basti, the assassin? He's listed as going to school every year until graduation with Mario Tancredi."

Tombola!

That was the connection we were looking for.

"So it was the Grecos who sent a man into my house," I said darkly, fury moving hot and slow like lava beneath my skin. It was hard to harness that power until the right moment, until the right people were in my vicinity, so I could unleash all that volcanic rage to the ultimate consequence.

Leo frowned. "Are we really going to base our conclusions on something so tenuous? I want to eviscerate the people who threatened us just as much as you do, but going to school with someone is not exactly telling. *Cazzo*, Raffa, you and I went to school with two judges and one of the heads of the DIA. Doesn't mean they are corrupt."

One of them was. The money I had funneled to him had bought him a charming mansion in Mallorca last year.

But Leo had a point, as he usually did.

"Besides, we both know the Pietra family has a much better reason to want you dead than the Grecos do," he added.

"Look into it further," I told Ludo. "In the meantime, Carmine, set up a meeting with the Albanians. I want to talk to someone in the Shqiptarë inner circle about their dealings with the Grecos. See what they know."

"On it," he agreed. "Renzo and Martina are waiting for you at the palazzo. They have some more things to go over. Martina heard a rumor about the Pietras, but she said she wouldn't tell anyone but you."

"I'll leave after dinner," I said, then caught sight of Leo's face. "What is it?"

"You just got here, *fratello*. Your family misses you. At least stay the night. If you need someone to go to Firenze tonight, let it be me. You are tired and much missed."

A wan smile claimed my mouth as I stepped forward to a clap a hand to Leo's shoulder. "You are a good man, Leo di Conte."

"And you," he told me. "Stay and see your woman settled and your family happy. I'll go see Martina."

I nodded my thanks, squeezing his shoulder. "Could you also be eager to leave to see that woman you are sleeping with?"

Leo blinked. "How the hell did you know?"

A shrug. "I recognize the look of a man in love, maybe. Tell me, what is her name? When do we meet her?"

His mouth twisted, but he rubbed his hand over it after to massage out the kink. "Not yet. Soon, though. We are still . . . figuring things out."

"Tell me about it," I said dryly, my own smile just as mangled.

From the kitchen, an explosion of laughter. Even amid the tangle of sound, I could parse out Guinevere's lovely laugh.

It made me ache to hold her. To eat that happiness off her tongue.

I had missed the taste of it.

"*Ragazzi*," Mamma called. "Dinner is served!"

◆ ◆ ◆

If Guinevere was overwhelmed by the chaos of a Romano dinner, especially after running for her life yesterday, you could not tell. She laughed with Lando, Carlotta's husband, about the first time she tried a tripe sandwich with me at the Mercato Centrale and asked Emiliano questions about how to hunt boar, given that we were eating a pasta sauce made from one of his successes. She fielded questions from my eager sisters as if she was used to holding court, evading the more invasive inquiries by offering an interesting story or asking her own questions. Luckily, the heavy sweep of her dark hair hid the bullet graze over her temple, or else I was sure we would have faced a furious barrage of questions about how I could have let Guinevere get hurt.

I already felt enough guilt and grief as it stood.

The candles lit amid the various platters of food on the table cast her in sepia tones that made her seem otherworldly, transcendent. My fingers itched to test her skin, feel if it was flushed and real against my own. I wanted to brush out that long, dark hair until it shone and braid it back away from her face before folding her into fresh sheets and tasting every inch of her to see if it was as ambrosial as I remembered.

I would have settled, though, for a single glance from those long-lashed doe eyes.

Instead, she spent the entire three-hour repast smiling and engaging with everyone who was not me.

She had cast a spell over the table, even Leo, who regarded her with solemn eyes, that odd quirk in his mouth that said he was reluctantly enchanted.

"She's lovely," Mamma told me when some of us started to clear away the dessert plates and empty glasses.

Leo was popping the cork on a dessert wine that he insisted Guinevere sample, and Zacheo was asleep in Carlotta's lap, drooling on her dress. It was a tableau I had been a part of countless times, but never with Guinevere at its heart, shining brighter than any of the candles on the table or stars winking above us in the clear night sky.

"Yes," I agreed as I carried the plates inside to the kitchen, where Stacci and Ludo were washing up.

"I can understand why Carmine says you were instantly infatuated. *Un colpo di fulmine.*"

A lightning bolt.

The Italian phrase for love at first sight.

"It was not that simple, Mamma," I replied.

Guinevere had been hit with something the moment we met, but that something was my car.

At the sink, Ludo snorted.

"Perhaps that is when it started," I admitted with a glare at my *soldato*. "But does a lightning strike alter your DNA? Does it carve out space for something so big in your chest that you cannot breathe around it?"

"*Si*," Mamma said, reaching up to cup my cheek. "It does, *ragazzo*."

I was not so certain. Surely an actual lightning strike would not hurt so much as the pain of Guinevere's rejection.

"I'm heading up." Guinevere's voice came from over my shoulder. When I turned, she was in the archway, swaying slightly with obvious fatigue. "Leo insisted when I almost broke my jaw yawning," she added bashfully. "It must be jet lag."

Or running through a skyscraper trying to avoid two Italian thugs trying to murder you, I thought, but I did not distress my mother and sister by saying that aloud.

"Yes, bed for you," Mamma declared. "Raffaele will show you to your room. Emiliano already put your suitcase there."

I sighed, because my mother was incapable of not playing matchmaker, but I still went to Guinevere's side.

"Do you need me to carry you?" I asked quietly, noting the drawn, pale cast of her face.

I wanted to carry her to my room and tuck her into my body so I could shield her from the world and bury myself in her scent.

"No," she said simply, carefully moving away to avoid touching me.

I let her lead the way up the stairs even though she did not know where to go. When she hesitated at the second landing, I eased by her to walk down the left hall all the way to the last room on the right.

"Every room in this house has a name," I told her, my hand on the knob, the shadows thick around us, only a shimmer of moonlight pooling in from the large window at the end of the hall. "I thought it was appropriate you have this one."

I stepped aside so she could read the little ceramic plaque on the wooden door.

Papavero.

Poppy.

She made a thin noise like air escaping a puncture wound, but followed me without objection into the dark, cool room.

I flipped a switch on the lamp beside the bed, illuminating the large space for her to study. There was a large bed with a carved wooden headboard and matching nightstands, a floor-to-ceiling gilt mirror propped against the wall between two windows, and an ornate chest of drawers and matching bureau. Everything was done in soft creams and reds—passionate, romantic colors that suited my *cerbiatta*.

"It's beautiful," she admitted, stepping into the room timidly as if she was afraid to be alone with me.

I could not blame myself later, when I lay awake and unblinking in my own room, for what I did next. It was the wine, maybe, or the late hour and the fact that I officially had not slept in over two days.

Mostly, though, it was the sight of her in that old college tee with all that thick, dark hair spilling around her shoulders, the pale oval of her face exhausted but utterly, devastatingly beautiful. All of it amplified by having this woman, my wish on a shooting star, here in my house after a long, wonderful dinner with my family, who seemed to like her almost as much as I did.

Whatever magic it was that moved me beyond rational thought, I found myself stalking across the room toward her.

"R-Raffa," she stuttered, stepping back against the partially open door so that it swung shut with a shudder.

Seconds later, I was on her, shoving her into the door with the full press of my body, my hands diving deep into those tousled locks to hold her head back for the kiss I bent to seal over her mouth.

She tasted divine.

Like something holy. Something that could absolve me of my sins and baptize me anew.

I understood suddenly what it must have been like for Dante's fallen angels to have known heaven and to have been cast from its light forever.

Something like a sob lodged in my throat as I thought about never holding her like this again.

Only the fact that she kissed me back for one euphoric moment allowed me to swallow it down, chased by the heavenly taste of her mouth against mine.

"Raffa, no," she said against my lips, even though it was her thigh hitched over mine and her fist caught up in the collar of my shirt.

"What do I have to do to earn your forgiveness?" I rasped against her neck as I pressed kisses like question marks into her skin. "Tell me, *mia stella cadente*, what I must do, and I will do it."

The fist in my shirt flattened to push me away farther.

Only the heaviness of our breath punctuated the room. I could not take my eyes from her swollen mouth, slick from my kisses, sweet from that single taste of dessert wine.

"Space," she said finally with a shiver as she pushed me away again. She waited until I reluctantly stepped back before saying, "Give me space, Raffa. Being back in Italy with you . . . it's enough to make me lose my head, and I'm not willing to be your blind *bambolina* anymore."

"You are not blind. You are here in my inner sanctum. In my *home*, with the people I care for the most, because I count you among them now."

Do you not see? I wanted to shout. *Do you not see how my love for you eclipses all else?*

But I could not and would not say it.

She did not want to hear it, for one thing.

And for another, what did I expect? That she would forgive me and love me enough to make a life with me here in Italy as the Proserpina to my Pluto? That she could accept and love the dark in me just as she had been drawn into the light?

Even if she did, could I keep her safe from all the enemies forever at the gate, seeking to take the power and glory of my empire from me and mine?

Could I condemn her to the kind of lifestyle where she could be hurt or killed because of me?

Could I even bear to live with that responsibility and the shame of bringing danger to her door?

It was as hopeless a situation as I had found myself in nearly five years ago, when my father died.

Sometimes in life, you are shown the things you most desire just as a reminder that you do not deserve to have them.

"Space," Guinevere repeated, canting her chin into the air, the dimple in her left cheek flaring as she pursed her lips. "And time."

"*Bene*," I said, rubbing a hand over my mouth as if I could erase the taste of her enough to willingly leave the room. "I will give you space and time, Guinevere."

I stepped to the side so she could move deeper into the room and I could turn to leave. The knob was in my hand, my body already in the hall, when I hesitated, peering through the shadows into the golden-lit room.

The words were out of my mouth before I could rein them in with rationality.

"You may need time and space. You did not ask what I need, but I will tell you anyway because hope has been a hand around my throat, strangling me, every day we have been apart. Love is not something that recognizes just the good in someone. It sees the bad and ugly. It acknowledges the dark because it accepts every part of who a person is. I am not all good. I am not even divided wholly in half. But whatever good I am I would give to you. Whatever bad I have I would use to shield you from harm. All I ask for in return is that you love me for who I am. Not Prince Charming, but *tuus Rex Infernus*."

CHAPTER SEVEN

Guinevere

Raffa was gone when I woke up the next morning.

I knew before I even left the gorgeous room he'd placed me in. It was something in the air, or maybe I was back to being too fanciful.

My body was still sore from the escapades in the Beaumont Building, but it felt good to stretch it out in the big, soft bed. The bullet graze to my temple was already scabbing over, a superficial injury that had bled so much because it was a head wound. The room smelled faintly of lavender, and as I unpacked my suitcase, I realized it was because each drawer was filled with little sachets of the dried flower. Even though the house was hundreds of years old, they had spared no expense on the upgrades. The en suite bathroom housed an enormous tiled walk-in shower with such amazing water pressure I moaned the entire time I stood under the spray.

It felt incredible to get clean. I brushed out my hair, moisturized my body with the olive oil–based products on the sink basin labeled with "Romano Toscana," and did a full skin-care routine. Even the pinch of the needle when I injected myself with my medicine didn't ache as much as it usually did. The self-care routine made me feel human again, so when I reentered the bedroom, I finally noticed the box on the side table beside the door.

It was a new smartphone with fancy card stock attached to the box with a piece of tape.

To call home.

You have your space and your time, Vera.

I will return in a week.

—Rex Infernus

Even when I hated him, he looked after me.

I huffed out a frustrated breath and took the box with me to the bed, where I flopped back with a groan as my muscles twanged.

In the absence of my Raffa dilemma, I was faced with another.

Calling my parents.

The phone was already programmed when I opened the box, my wallpaper set as a photo Martina had taken of Raffa and me on the day we took the boat out in Livorno. We were both wet, hair slicked back, droplets like diamonds where they caught the sun on our cheeks and lashes. Raffa was smiling that closed-lipped, private expression of deep joy, and my teeth were bared in the widest grin I'd ever seen on my own face.

We were so happy together.

It felt both good and bad to see evidence of it, like pressure on a knotted muscle.

The only contacts he had inputted were Ludo, Carmine, Renzo, Martina, Leo, and himself.

My thumb hovered over his contact information and then pressed down to open a new text thread.

Guinevere: Thank you for the phone.

Guinevere: And the space.

He didn't respond, but then I didn't expect him to. He was probably busy doing whatever it was mafiosi did all day.

Besides, I was just delaying the inevitable.

The phone ringing sounded like a death knell.

"Hello?"

"Hi, Mom," I said.

"Oh my God," she whispered, then louder but angled away from the speaker, "John! John, it's Guinevere."

There was a cacophony on the other end of the line, and then both of my parents started to speak over each other.

"Guinevere, where the fuck—"

"Honey, are you okay?"

"I'm fine," I said loudly, cutting them both off. "I mean, well, I'm okay now."

"There was a break-in at the offices," Dad said, voice gruff but discernibly relieved. "The night guard was killed, and there was blood in the staircase. They found two men dead outside the parking garage who seem to be the culprits, but when you didn't answer your phone . . ."

His exhale was shaky, so much pain in a single breath I could feel it through the phone.

"I'm fine, Dad," I said softly, cradling the cell to my ear like it was his hand. "I was still there when they broke in, and they tried to hurt me, but a . . . a friend ended up saving me."

"A friend?" he said flatly.

Silence echoed between us like the aftermath of a nuclear bomb, poisonous and impossible to breathe through without wanting to gag.

"A friend," I repeated, quiet but intractable.

"Where are you now, honey?" Mom asked, and I knew she had her arm on Dad as if she could physically restrain him.

I paused, wincing as the words came out of my mouth. "I'm back in Italy." Then, over Dad's blustering, I added, "I had to come back. I know you won't understand, but when I left Tuscany, I left a piece of me behind."

I figured it wasn't truly a lie. I had left half my soul in Italy, not just behind Raffa's breastbone but in the streets of Florence, in the fabric of Tuscany. It was easier to sell my parents on an epic love story than it was to tell them the truth.

The man I loved was an Italian capo, and the dangerous men who wanted to kill him had set their sights on me, so this was the only way to keep me safe.

"And your job?" Dad demanded. "I taught you better than to just walk out on your career, Guinevere. You're leaving your clients and colleagues in the lurch with this stunt."

And me, he was no doubt thinking but didn't say.

That wasn't why he was mad, really, but I addressed it all the same. "I'm more than willing to work remotely while I see out my two weeks' notice. I know it was irresponsible of me, but I was scared. I almost died two days ago. Not because of any illness but because of violence. And my . . ." What did I call Raffa? *My boyfriend* sounded too juvenile, *my partner* too platonic. "My man makes me feel safe. When he offered to fly me out on the next plane, I was still in shock, and it seemed like the only place I would be okay."

"Jinx," Mom breathed, devastated. "You're safe here with us."

"It hasn't felt that way lately," I admitted. "And part of that is my own fault for lying to you about coming to Italy in the first place. Whether or not you respect my choices, this is where I am meant to be for now. Gemma always followed her heart, and you never had a problem with it. I'm asking now for you to let me follow mine."

"Gemma ended up dead at twenty-six," Dad snapped harshly.

The silence that bloomed was acrid, like smoke from a dying fire.

"John," Mom scolded quietly.

"At least she lived before she died," I countered. "She traveled, she fell in love, she made mistakes. She was the most alive person I've ever known, and she made me realize how pathetic I was to let the fact that

I'd survived being sick be enough for me. Surviving isn't good enough. I want to thrive."

"You can thrive here, baby," Mom coaxed. "Come home. You can move in with us again if you're scared. We haven't touched your bedroom."

"Come back," Dad said, his voice as raw as a bleeding wound. "Please, Guinevere. I know you think you're safe there, but I promise you aren't."

"I'm staying," I said firmly. "But the offer still stands, Dad. You tell me yours, I'll tell you mine."

Another long pause, this one stale.

"At least tell us who you are with," Mom asked. "I ought to know the name of the boy my daughter is in love with."

I winced a little at the word *boy*, given that Raffa was eleven years my senior.

"Raffa Romano."

"What does he do?"

"H-he runs a multimillion-dollar business," I admitted, which was true. It just wasn't entirely legal.

"Oh," Mom said over the sound of her clapping her hands together. "A wealthy, handsome Italian? I should have known nothing less would entice my romantic girl."

"Mom! You don't even know what he looks like."

"Is he handsome?"

My pause made her laugh.

Dad was conspicuously silent.

"How long will you be there, though? Is this a vacation or . . . You aren't planning to stay there forever, are you?" she asked.

And I didn't have an answer.

How long would it take Raffa and his *soldati* to hunt down the enemy? How long could I be forced into his proximity and survive with my willpower intact?

"I don't know, Mom."

"Well, okay." Her voice was velvet soft with sadness. "I expect you to check in every day, okay? Or else your father will worry."

"Okay, I will."

"Give us a minute, Elizabeth?" Dad asked, then waited until the door clicked shut to sigh heavily into the speaker. "Does Raffa Romano have any affiliation with Clan Romano? One of the biggest Mafia families in Italy?"

I blinked in surprise at the ceiling and then sat up as my heart kicked into a trot. "Um, *no*. Why would you even assume something like that?"

He grunted. "I read up on him some when I saw you pictured in the paper with him. There was an article about his father being associated with the Camorra. That's dangerous stuff, Guinevere."

"No kidding," I said, shocked by how easy it was to funnel my past self's woeful obliviousness. "You know I wouldn't be with someone like that."

He was quiet for a moment. "Lately, I'm not sure I know you as well as I thought I did."

As he'd intended, the words hit the mark, puncturing something in my chest so I had to suck in a sharp breath or drown in my own blood. All my life I'd wanted to make my parents, especially my dad, happy. It seemed incredibly unfair that pursuing my own happiness directly countered his.

"That was your choice as much as my own," I reminded him. "I've got to go, or I'll miss breakfast."

"Be safe." The words were sudden, edged with desperation. "I wish I'd taught you more about protecting yourself . . . but please, Jinx, stay out of trouble."

"I always try," I told him.

"And yet it always finds you," he murmured before hanging up without another word.

◆ ◆ ◆

It should have surprised me to find all the clothes I had left behind at Raffa's Florentine palazzo in the walk-in closet of my new bedroom at Villa Romano, but it didn't. It was just utterly like him to go overboard for me. I could admit that seeing the familiar designer clothes we'd bought together my first week in Florence warmed my heart, and I knew that had been his game plan.

After switching my pajamas for a long dress and cardigan, I walked downstairs to the cacophony of voices, startled into almost falling over when a toddler ran headlong into my legs.

"Oh," I said with a little laugh as I caught the dark-haired boy around the shoulders. *"Stai attento, piccolo."*

Watch out, little one.

He dropped his head back between his shoulders and smiled a gap-toothed smile at me. "I speak English good!" he practically shouted.

Carlotta swept into the room looking harried but gorgeous. All Raffa's family was beautiful, which wasn't surprising given how stunning he was, but still. It seemed vaguely unfair that they should have genes this good.

Carlotta dashed a stray lock of golden-brown hair escaping her ponytail behind one ear and shot me an exasperated look. "Zacheo, Maxi, and Nico are all too young for school. I am afraid you will have to put up with them all day every day, just like the rest of us."

I chuckled, tentatively stroking a hand down the boy's messy locks. "I don't mind at all. I babysat all through my teens, and I . . ." I cleared my throat. "I lost my sister over a year ago, so it's nice to be around family."

"You will regret saying that," Carmine said as he came into the hall from the kitchen, chomping into an apple. "Now they'll have you as the live-in nanny."

Carlotta shoved him into the wall as he passed. "Ignore him. There is so much gel in his hair it makes him stupid."

I laughed at their camaraderie, feeling, for the first time in two months, like I wasn't alone.

"Come on, Zacheo," Carlotta urged. "Let Guinevere go have some breakfast."

"Do you like Nutella?" he asked me, still clinging to my legs. He had his mother's wide-set dark-brown eyes.

"Everyone likes Nutella," I replied.

If possible, his grin widened. "Me too," he shrieked, twisting to grab my hand and tug me down the hallway out the open French doors to the flagstone patio off the kitchen.

The same enormous wood table we had eaten at the night before was laid for breakfast with ceramic pitchers of juice, a platter of whole fruit and another of fruit salad, and others piled with breakfast pastries. From its place on top of a hill, you could see over the entire valley from the villa in a 360-degree view that included vineyards, olive groves, and weaving roads lined with cypress trees. It was so perfect it didn't seem real, even as I paused to absorb the view.

Carmine and Ludo sat at one end of the table, the former reading the *Corriere della Sera* newspaper and the latter doing something on his tablet. The only other people at the table were Stacci and her baby, Nico, in her lap being fed yogurt.

"*Buongiorno*, Guinevere," the adults called almost simultaneously as Zacheo dragged me to the table and pushed me down onto the bench.

I laughed when he immediately crawled up beside me and then half into my lap, already reaching for the enormous jar of chocolate-hazelnut spread.

"Zach, you have already had enough Nutella this morning," Carlotta reminded him as she came out to grab some of the discarded plates to take inside.

The little boy stared at her with huge eyes, blinking innocently. "It's for her!" he corrected, swinging the mini spatula from the jar in a wide arc so chocolate lashed out across the table. "She *loves* it, Mamma."

Carlotta bit back the edge of her smile, but the rest of the adults laughed. "All right, if Guinevere says it's okay, then you can help make her some Nutella toast."

On my lap, Zacheo wriggled with delight, reaching for a *cornetto*.

"You'll have to get used to lack of personal boundaries, I'm afraid," Stacci explained with a soft expression on her face as she watched Zacheo rip open the pastry and spread an obscene amount of Nutella on it. "With five boys under nine years old in the house, it's pretty chaotic."

"I don't mind," I said, which was the truth.

How could I take umbrage at such a warm reception? The way the family instantly enveloped me into their ranks. Emiliano had offered to teach me how to shoot so that he could take me hunting, and in the meantime he and Stacci had told me they would take me out hunting for truffles with their pig, Tonio, who was apparently named after Leo's father. Carlotta and Angela had offered to teach me to cook some regional dishes, and Lando had proposed to take me on a tour of local churches through Tuscany and Umbria some weekend when he was off work. Two of Raffa's *soldati* who lived on the property had also introduced themselves as Michele and Philippe, brothers who ran security for the villa under Leo. When I'd mentioned taking a jog around the property, they'd both nearly fallen over themselves to illustrate the best routes on a map for me.

I didn't know what Raffa had told them about me, but it was obvious I had not arrived a perfect stranger.

Only, their lovely reception brought with it an ache, that bitter edge of knowing they seemed utterly genuine and almost perfect on the surface, but that they were, in fact, a family of criminals. Or if not criminals themselves, then complicit in the activities of their patriarch.

Did sweet Carlotta with the messy hair and soft smile know that her brother didn't flinch when he shot someone in the head?

Had he ever killed someone for Stacci, who was beautiful enough to draw all kinds of attention?

Had he ever kidnapped Delfina "for her own good"?

It was hard to accept kindness now. I was always looking for the catch, and in this instance, it was an obvious one.

They were Raffa's family.

And if I fell in love with them, how hard would it be to keep my distance from the mafioso who had unfairly stolen my heart?

But as Zacheo offered me a Nutella-laden piece of *cornetto*, insisting on shoving it into my mouth himself, I already knew it was a losing battle.

"So these are our last days of freedom before the harvest starts," Stacci said, wiping Nico's messy mouth. "What do you say we go into town and grab something you might have left behind? Have you been to Greve? It is touristic but still cute."

"That sounds wonderful, thanks. What are you harvesting? The olives?"

"No, it is too early for those. Because we are Northern, Lando will not begin the harvest until later in November, even early December. We begin *la vendemmia* on Sunday. You won't see Delfina much for the next couple of weeks because she runs operations at Tenuta Romano. The whole family goes out for the first few days to help. It's a kind of a . . . community ritual."

"Everyone nearby comes out too," Carmine added, looking at me over the top of his newspaper with a wry grin. "You can meet the locals and get a sense for the flavor of true Toscana. The countryside is very different from Firenze."

"Less cold," Stacci agreed.

"Less civilized," Carmine countered.

It was worth noting that even sitting in a villa, eating breakfast in the country, Carmine was wearing a bespoke three-piece suit. Before I'd grown to know him, I might have thought him haughty for doing so, but I knew it was part of his identity—his mask.

I realized now that Raffa and his *soldati* all had them in various ways.

Raffa most of all.

The expensive suits, the carefully tamed waves pushed away from his handsome face, the pose he commanded all the time, arms crossed, feet braced like those of a general at attention. There was not one cultivated ounce of him that did not command respect.

Only a select few got to see him as he had been last night at dinner, sitting back casually in his chair with his thighs spread, a nephew on one knee, tucked to his chest as he dozed off against his uncle. His hair had fallen over his forehead, his stubble overgrown and a direct contrast to the ruddy softness of his mouth. He'd laughed once or twice, that rich belly laugh that made my skin break out in goose bumps.

Only a select few, and I was one of them.

Love is not something that recognizes just the good in someone. It sees the bad and ugly. It acknowledges the dark because it accepts every part of who a person is. I am not all good. I am not even divided wholly in half. But whatever good I am I would give to you. All I ask for in return is that you love me for who I am.

His words from last night echoed in my head like a song stuck on repeat.

Because he was right.

I had finished reading Dante's *Divine Comedy* when I returned to Michigan, as if Dante's words could keep me connected to Italy, a last lifeline I wasn't willing to relinquish. There were dozens of quotes I'd annotated with red pen, but one stood out more than most.

"The day that man allows true love to appear, those things which are well made will fall into confusion and will overturn everything we believe to be right and true."

The truth of those words was a mirror held before my face, impossible to ignore. Loving Raffa had turned my world upside down not once but twice. Here I was back in his country, in his stronghold, held against my will in order to ensure my safety in a contradiction that embodied the nature of our entire relationship.

He wanted to keep me safe, but he was the danger.

He wanted to love me, but he did not trust me.

My soul called out for the beauty of his even as my mind turned away from the horrible things I knew he'd done.

My body was a battlefield between rationality and passion, and Raffa was right—eventually there had to be a winner. Not just for my sake, but also for his.

I just wasn't sure which side would win out.

Even if I loved him enough to accept his darkness, I didn't know if I was brave enough to harness mine.

Zacheo finished eating the rest of my chocolate-covered *cornetto* and then smacked a sticky hand on my cheek, smiling so bright he took my breath away. For one brutally vivid moment, sharp and bright as a diamond, I imagined that my children with Raffa might look something like Zacheo.

"Che buono!" he exclaimed.

"*Delizioso*," I agreed, giving in to the urge to rub my nose against his.

He giggled, squirming to get away from me even as he kept his hand on my cheek.

"Will you go to the festival with Mamma and me this weekend?" he asked, moving his dirty fingers to the gold chain around my throat and flicking the *cornicello* lucky charm back and forth. "There's dancing."

"It is the Grape Festival in Impruneta," Carlotta told me as she came back outside and sat with a sigh of exhaustion on the bench beside me. "We take the little ones every year."

"We can all go together," Ludo grunted, then shrugged at me when I shot him a surprised look. "They give out free wine."

"You can walk on the grapes with your toes," Zacheo shouted into my face, smacking my cheek to emphasize his excitement.

"Lower your voice," Stacci and Carlotta reprimanded at the same time.

"You can walk on the grapes with your toes," Zacheo repeated quietly. "Want to come?"

"Definitely," I agreed, ready to let this family distract me from reality, at least until Raffa returned.

CHAPTER EIGHT

Guinevere

The grape festival in Impruneta was incredible.

I was used to parades. We had them for Easter and Christmas, but this was something else entirely. There were floats shaped like wine bottles and stands for local wineries, dancers in wonderful costumes that were later judged for the prize of a terra-cotta wine cup. It was the last day of a monthlong celebration, the crowd large but jovial, kids running around while parents sipped wine and chatted in clusters.

Zacheo held my hand while we watched the parade and then demanded to be put on my shoulders. I wasn't very tall, but I perched him there anyway, grateful when Emiliano asked the man in front of us to move to the side so his son could see the proceedings.

Carlotta's mouth was stained red from wine, and Stacci was lured into dancing the traditional steps of a local jig with some friends of hers, who had us all clapping and laughing along with them.

It was idyllic.

So perfect I felt inexplicably like crying.

The last five days at Villa Romano had been their own kind of exquisite agony. The entire family was wonderful, if a little chaotic.

Angela Romano was clearly the matriarch, but she was made of sugar without an ounce of bitterness or vinegar to offset her sweetness.

She happily enlisted me to cook before mealtimes in the kitchen, patiently teaching me how to hand roll *orecchiette* and cured *lardo di Collonata*, when to take a braised lamb out of the oven and how to bake *schiacciata alla Fiorentina*, the traditional dessert of Florence. She did not speak English as well as her children, but it gave me the opportunity to flex my Italian, and she delighted in teaching me obscure expressions and dialect from her youth in Naples, where she was born.

Stacci and Carlotta stopped apologizing for their sons on my second day in the house, when they caught us playing *nascondino* (hide-and-seek) swiftly followed by a rousing round of *palla prigioniera* (basically dodgeball) out by the small field beside the pool. Zacheo had become my little shadow, but the rest of the boys delighted in having an active adult to play in their games. I didn't have much to do before the US market opened and I started my remote work, so I spent most of that time playing games.

It was hard to be confused and sad when I was surrounded by sweet, rambunctious children.

Delfina was busy preparing for the harvest, but when she rolled in at the end of dinner and grabbed a plate to eat standing up in the kitchen while the rest of us cleaned, she always made it a point to talk to me. I liked her perhaps even more than sassy Stacci and sweet Carlotta. Delfina was blunt in a way that reminded me of her brother, and she had a fascination with film that I could relate to. She had ducked into my room the last two nights after dinner to sit on my bed and watch Sebastian Lombardi movies with me. He was from Naples, but he was still Italian, and Delfina told me she'd had a crush on him since she was ten and he was the sole reason she was still single.

She made me laugh.

Emiliano and Lando were both kind, the former more gregarious than the latter, but they both worked long hours, so the only men I really spent time with were Carmine and Ludo.

I could not complain.

Even though I wasn't allowed to leave the estate without an escort, Ludo took me for a jog every day down the hill, around the looping road, and back up. It was still warm enough that we were dripping with sweat by the time we returned, but my stamina was getting so much better. He also helped me with sparring, something he excelled at. Unlike my teacher at the dojo, Ludo had real-world fighting experience, and he taught me what a true fight for my life might look like. The first time I landed a punch, he gave me a fist bump that felt like a trophy.

When I had to work, Carmine shared his temporary office space with me. I tried not to eavesdrop, but it was impossible not to be drawn in by his phone calls and conversations with Ludo. The Romano business had interests in everything from green energy to agriculture to imports and exports. I learned that they owned a few genuine luxury brands and a number of factories that reproduced fake designer products, which seemed counterproductive, but Carmine only smirked at my expression and explained that they could corner both markets.

It was fascinating.

So much so, I found myself gravitating to Carmine's desk when I was done with my own work. He didn't say a word, only shifted a portfolio across the tabletop toward me; it contained a financial pitch from a wind turbine company near Turin.

"What do you expect me to do with this?" I asked, even though there was a pen between my fingers already, my eyes on a pad of paper beside Carmine's elbow.

He handed it to me without looking away from his screen. "What do you think?"

What a powerful question for a curious mind.

An hour later, I'd written a summary of why I thought the company itself was a bad bet but that the idea had merit.

Another hour after that, Carmine casually pushed a folder across the desk at me; it contained five companies that could do the same work the original one had proposed. I found the right candidate in the time it took me to eat the panini Carlotta brought me for lunch.

I didn't ask if the business they intended to conduct with the company was wholly legal because I already knew the answer and found I didn't want to acknowledge it. Even watching Carmine work, overhearing conversations that were not always kind in tone, I tried to ignore what was right in front of my face.

It was considerably harder than it had been my first six weeks in Tuscany.

Five productive, fulfilling days in Italy, five days I never would have assumed I'd enjoy, given that I was technically there against my will.

And all five of them spent away from Raffa.

You shouldn't miss him, I thought as I leaned against the stone wall of the bell tower in Impruneta with Ludo while the others socialized around us. I was tired, both from lingering jet lag and from chasing the kids through the square. The sun was dipping behind the red-roofed buildings, but there was no sign of the festivities halting anytime soon. It wasn't very smart of me, but I'd had my share of wine with the sisters, sampling the local offerings and toasting to this, that, and the other. I wasn't used to drinking, and my head was spinning like a top about to stop, wobbly and slow.

"I'm going to grab a coffee," I told Ludo in Italian, and when he moved to join me, I shook my head and pointed to the café four yards across the crowded street from us. "I will be right back. Stay and have fun."

His lips twisted in an eloquent way that said clearly, *Yeah right.*

I laughed as I walked away from him, swerving through the bodies to get to the busy coffee shop and the collection of people standing in the open doorway, drinking wine and espresso. The interior was just as busy, but I wedged myself into a small gap at the bar and fluently ordered myself an espresso when the server noticed me.

It felt good to taste Italian on my tongue again. To stretch the muscles I'd honed for weeks in Florence and know that I hadn't lost any skill over the past two months.

I leaned against the counter, taking deep breaths to settle my spinning head, and hoped the coffee would cut through some of the haziness.

"Guinevere," someone said in surprise over my shoulder.

It was Leo with an older man who looked vaguely like him, though his expression was blank where Leo's was charming. I assumed this gentleman was Tonio, an uncle Stacci's and Carlotta's kids had named their pig after, and Leo's father.

"I didn't expect to see you." Leo stepped around someone to put a hand on my shoulder and kiss me on both cheeks. "What are you doing here?"

"I'm with the family. The boys wanted to see the parade. I could say the same for you, though. I thought you were in Florence with Raffa."

"Ah, of course. I returned just this afternoon, and I decided to have dinner with my father." He indicated the man behind him. "Have you two met yet?"

Tonio stepped forward with a warm smile and clasped both my hands in one of his before he kissed the air beside both of my cheeks. "I am happy to meet the woman who has made Raffaele smile."

I beamed back at him. "Thank you. I am happy to meet Leo's dad and Raffa's uncle."

"I am not truly either," Tonio explained. "Leo is my adopted nephew, and Raffa's father was my best friend, so the title is merely an honorific."

I didn't know quite what to say to that, so I replied, "You have the same kind eyes."

Tonio laughed, squeezing my hands sharply before dropping them to wipe at his eyes. *"Grazie."*

Leo's smile was thin. "Where are Ludo and Carmine? You shouldn't be alone."

"Relax. Ludo is just outside," I explained, though it felt good to know Leo was concerned for my safety. He hadn't taken to me like Raffa's other friends had, and I still wasn't entirely sure why.

"*Bene, bene*," he said, staring somewhere over my shoulder like he was considering something before he nodded sharply, expression clearing. "Are you enjoying the festival?"

"Yes, it's incredible. Then again, I'm very easily enchanted," I said with a self-deprecatory laugh.

It used to be one of my better qualities, I thought. That innocent wonder and curiosity. Now I wondered if it wasn't why I'd earned the nickname Jinx from my family. I never seemed to know when it was better not to follow trouble.

"A side effect, maybe, of being very enchanting yourself." He was smiling at me, pale eyes bright, but there was an artifice to it that made me think he was trying too hard. He was the last of Raffa's friends I had to connect with, and I had the feeling he was making a sincere effort to be kind to me. "If you want to see something truly worthy of wonder, you should climb the bell tower to watch the last of the sunset. Raffa mentioned you enjoyed watching the sunsets from Piazzale Michelangelo in Firenze, but watching one over the hills of Chianti is a true spectacle."

"It's open to the public?" I had noticed the old stone tower as soon as we'd walked into the piazza that afternoon. It was no doubt the best viewpoint in town.

"Yes, yes," he assured me, distracted by his father leaning close to whisper something in his ear. "Let me show you the entrance before I leave."

I agreed, pleasantly surprised by his overture of friendship. "*Grazie*, Leo."

"I will leave you two youths to enjoy the festival," Tonio suggested. "It's time for this old man to go home to bed."

We both said our goodbyes, and then Leo offered me his arm with a little bow as his father took off for the exit without us. I smiled as I slid my hand over Leo's forearm and let him lead me through the crowded entry, around the milling bodies in the street, and toward the bell tower.

A band had started to play in the square, the music amplified by the crowded buildings surrounding the open bowl of the piazza.

"I am sorry about before," Leo said over his shoulder. "I was rude when we first met. It didn't have anything to do with you. Not really."

I waited for him to continue as we finally reached a closed wooden door that swung open easily under Leo's big hand. He was a handsome man, dark-gold hair and pale eyes contrasting nicely with olive-toned skin. He had to be Northern Italian with coloring like that. Gemma had ended up with similar looks, our Italian father's skin and our Albanian mother's flaxen locks.

The door closed behind me with a loud clanging, which startled me into yelping, hand flying up to cover my lurching heart.

Leo only peered at me through the dark. "I fell in love with a foreigner once too. She was charming and beautiful, and I thought at the time that I would give up anything for her." He paused, one hand clenching tight at his side. "It didn't end well. I didn't want to see a man I consider my brother go through the same thing."

I stepped closer to place a careful hand on his closed fist. "I'm sorry, Leo. Losing someone is never easy."

"That's the thing, though, isn't it?" he asked. Among the shadows, his face was hard, almost cruel. His teeth were flat and square, not like Raffa's pointed canines—they looked brutal enough to chew through bone. I was seeing monsters in every man now that Raffa had pulled back the veil on his underworld, even kind and good-looking ones like Leo. "You haven't lost your love. Not really. You're making the choice to let him go. You wanted the truth, yet when he gave you honesty, you couldn't handle it."

Before I could think of what to say, Leo's phone started ringing, and he pulled it out of his pocket, frowning down at the screen.

"I'm sorry, Guinevere. This is important. Will you be okay to find your way to the top without me?"

"Is everything okay?" I asked, because there was real distress on his face as the phone continued to ring in his hand.

"It will be," he stated firmly, like his belief alone could make it so. "Enjoy the view. I'll make sure Ludo knows where you are."

I nodded, turning away from him to the shadowy mouth of the stairwell.

"Follow the light to the top," he instructed before closing the door and leaving me alone in the dark.

I listened to my own harsh breaths for a moment, willing my heart to slow and my equilibrium to balance. When I felt steady, I sucked in a deep breath and started up the narrow, winding stairs.

Leo's words had touched on the questions that lay at the foundation of my tension with Raffa.

Was I brave enough to love him for who he was and courageous enough to stand beside him in the criminal underworld he reigned in?

And did I really know the whole truth?

Both Raffa and Leo had implied that I did, but knowing that Raffa was a mafioso was the tip of the iceberg. Had he killed many men? Any women or children? Did he have morals or rules of conduct when he was free to write them as he pleased? What was the ethical tapestry of a made man? What was the structure of that kind of business and organization?

There were considerably more questions than answers. If I wanted to know Raffa, the real man and not the one I'd idealized, I would have to let my natural curiosity lead me into trouble once more. Only this time my eyes would be wide open, fixed on the treacherous nature of the steps I took forward.

The first questions I had to ask were of myself.

I wasn't a stupid woman.

College educated, bright enough to graduate top of my class, I had always been complimented for my intelligence and puzzle solving.

So had I really been so blind to the hints that Raffa was something darker than Prince Charming? Or had those very clues drawn me in even closer, a glittering lure leading me through murky waters?

I might have been the good sister and daughter, the A+ student and sheltered sick girl, but I was also the woman who fantasized about spankings and bondage. The one who thought a necklace of love bites was just as pretty as one of jewels. The one who watched violent movies because the action excited her, and the one who got aroused, sometimes, when she learned MMA and took an opponent to the mat. There was something hungry in the heart of me, and Raffa had been the first person to see it. To feed it full.

So maybe I hadn't acknowledged his darkness, but had I secretly known or willfully turned a blind eye to continue living out the fantasy of my Italian hero?

Maybe.

Pink light splashed across the stones at my feet, warming my ankles like tropical water as I reached the top of the stairwell and stepped out onto the small platform under the peaked tower roof. The bell was almost as big as the space, a great big iron bulb. Archways opened the enclosure at regular intervals, revealing a stunning view of the piazza filled with colorful, costumed revelers and the band playing away in one corner. Beyond that, down the slope of the hills leading away from town, were countless rows of vines marking this as a part of the famous Chianti region. Everything was covered in honeyed light dripping from a multihued sky that seemed to melt into itself, vivid pink to orange to softening yellow and blue.

It was breathtaking.

I followed my impulse to lean through an archway, elbows braced on the warm stone and chin propped on my hands so I could enjoy the rest of the sunset by myself, way above the teeming mass of Italians.

I don't know what it was exactly that alerted me to the presence of someone in the stairwell, because they didn't make a sound. It was just a vague sense, honed over months of paranoia and recent trauma, that tickled the back of my neck like a cool breath.

I was no longer alone.

Adjusting my stance casually, I moved so the entrance of the stairwell was in my peripheral vision and the blurred movement in the shadows of the lowering dusk light solidified into a human form.

I had nothing on my person except the cell phone in my cardigan. Carefully, so my arm hardly twitched, I dipped my fingers into my pocket and pulled out the phone. I thumbed the screen open and hit Raffa's name in my Favorites.

Just as the faint whisper of a ring began, the person stalking me decided to pounce.

They lunged out of the darkness onto the small platform, intending to tackle me, maybe, or force me into the corner.

But I was already moving, twisting with the half wall at my back so I was no longer in the corner. The man couldn't stop himself mid-motion, so I could use his own momentum against him and shove him harder into the half wall. His head cracked against the stone with a sickening sound, but he recovered quickly.

When he turned to face me, forehead split and bleeding heavily above one eye, his hands were lifted as if in surrender.

"I am not here to harm you," he said in slow, careful Italian. "I am a friend."

I could hear Raffa's voice calling out from the phone in my pocket.

"I don't know you, and usually when someone sneaks up and lunges at you, they don't have friendly intentions," I countered, shifting so I was closer to the stairs.

To my surprise, he grinned, and there was something genuinely warm in his expression that gave me pause. "True. I'm sorry for scaring you. I had hoped to take you quickly and quietly."

"Where? And why?"

"The Venetian wants you," he admitted. "That's all I can say at the moment. But please, you must come with me."

"No." I had nothing to defend myself with, but I bent my knees and rolled slightly to my toes, grateful I had decided to wear practical flat sandals because of the Romano children. "I'm not going anywhere."

"I have something," he said as I eyed the distance to the stairs. He kept one hand in the air as the other reached for his pocket, which was coincidently next to his holstered gun. "I was told to show you this."

My breath arrested when he pulled a shiny gold chain from his pocket, unraveling it until the pendant swung into sight. It was a gold cross, something that adorned the necks of countless men and women in this country.

Only I knew who had worn that necklace.

The cross was the size of my palm, large but thin and made of delicately twisted filaments of metal, with a diamond the size of my pinky finger pressed into the apex.

"That was my sister's," I breathed, stepping forward as if by magnetic force.

"It was," he agreed.

Before he could say more, the sound of footsteps echoed through the stairwell. We shared a look, just for a split second, but it conveyed his distress that we had been found and my own that this stranger couldn't finish telling me why the hell he had Gemma's necklace.

The next second, he was dropping the necklace back into his pocket and gripping his gun, training it at the mouth of the stairs. A shape appeared, rounding the curve, and he shot at it.

The sound of Ludo cursing in Italian reached my ears, and I knew if I did nothing, this stranger was going to hurt him. There was no way Ludo wouldn't find a way to get me. I might not have trusted Raffa's goodness, but I knew he wouldn't let me be taken and that those orders meant something to the men in his inner sanctum. Not just because they were orders from their capo, but because I truly believed I meant something to them too.

Just as they meant something to me.

Raffa wasn't the only person I'd missed in Italy.

There was no way for Ludo to get to me except by storming up the stairs onto the small landing, exposing himself to the gunman's bullets.

But he seemed to have forgotten about me for the moment.

My mind worked so fast it ran into the idea headlong, making me wince.

Ludo fired a round of shots that didn't connect and then was forced to duck around the curve as the man returned fire.

I sucked in a deep breath as I tried to gather every ounce of courage I possessed and transform it into kinetic energy.

When the man ceased firing to move slowly toward the staircase with his gun raised, I took my opportunity.

The landing was small enough that it only took me a single leaping bound to ram myself into the unknown gunman with the full weight of my charging 110 pounds. The force made him stagger sideways, his head hitting the bulbous iron bell with a dull knell that vibrated faintly through the tower. I almost winced in sympathy at the contact, but he was already reaching for me, probably trying to use me as a human shield against Ludo, who was charging up the stairs.

I evaded his reaching arm, but he raised his gun with the other and fired off a shot. It was poorly aimed, but that didn't matter with Ludo racing up to the stairs toward us, caught between the narrow walls. The sound of Ludo's pained grunt drew my attention momentarily away from our assailant, and I watched my friend fall to one knee at the top of the stairs, hand pressed to his side.

Before I'd come to Italy for the first time, I had never known violence. It had been as abstract as a staged fight scene on the television screen or a chapter in a spy thriller, something intangible enough that I had never had to think about how it would apply to me.

Did I have the capacity to be violent?

I would have laughed and said, unequivocally, even righteously, absolutely not.

I'd never even killed a spider.

Yet there I was, standing at the top of an ancient bell tower with shots ringing out around me, a wounded friend at my back and a strange shooter before me, and the only thing I could think about was protecting Ludo, protecting myself, at all costs.

So as the gunman righted himself against the wall and took a step forward with his weapon trained on Ludo, the small American girl completely forgotten, I rushed him again.

Throwing all my weight low into the side of his exposed torso, I pushed the stranger up against the half wall in the open archway, and then, when he tried to swing the gun my way, I planted both hands on his chest and shoved with all my might.

Our eyes locked for one unnaturally elongated moment, the previously pleasant mask he'd worn to convince me to go with him quietly eradicated by fury and disbelief.

I felt his weight give way under my hands, the rush of air as his body tipped over the ledge, legs kicking up to try to regain some semblance of balance. A foot kicked me hard in the shoulder, a parting blow before he was suddenly gone.

I lunged over the stone wall to watch, morbidly fixated and horrified by my own actions, as he went tumbling through the air to land with a sickening thud in the piazza. The wine revelers nearby screamed and scrambled away while one or two noble people ran to the fallen man's side to see if they could help.

There was no help for him.

He was dead, and I had been the one to kill him.

When a hand clamped over my shoulder, I screamed before I remembered that Ludo was up here with me. I turned to find his face pale and sheened with sweat, one hand pressed to his side, blood bubbling between his fingers.

"*Grazie*," he murmured, reeling me in for a hug against his uninjured side. "*Grazie, amica mia*. I am sorry I could not stop him before you had to."

I curled into Ludo's body, oxen-strong and steady even with a serious wound. He smelled like cypress trees and gun oil. It shouldn't have been comforting, but it was because it reminded me of Raffa.

"I killed him," I whispered into his chest. "I killed someone, Ludo."

"*Si*, Guinevere," he agreed in as soothing a voice as I had ever heard from him. He led me toward the stairs with one arm around my shoulders, as if I was the injured one. Even though my shoulder ached and I felt close to vomiting, I wrapped my arm around Ludo's waist in an effort to support him too as we started down the spiral stairs.

"I'm a killer," I breathed as the dead man's face flashed in my mind like a strobe light at a disco, something epilepsy inducing that jerked through my entire system.

"No, *sei colei che mi ha difeso*," Ludo grunted over the chaos of the door at the base of the tower slamming open against the opposite wall and multiple footsteps thundering up the steps toward us.

"It doesn't matter why I killed him," I murmured, knowing that taking a life had shifted something fundamental, tectonic, inside me, revealing dangerous cracks in the foundation of my soul for something hot and hazardous to seep through. "Only that I did."

CHAPTER NINE

Raffa

I was meeting with six of my most trusted capos in a restaurant in Siena when my phone vibrated in my pocket.

Usually, I would not have answered during such a meeting, but I had set a special tone for Guinevere that thrummed like a heartbeat against my thigh. There was very little that could have made me ignore a call from her, and it certainly wasn't half a dozen of the most powerful men (and one woman) in Italy.

"*Scusate*," I murmured to them as I stood, buttoned my blazer, and stalked out of the closed restaurant dining room into the back hall to take the call. "Guinevere?"

The sound of a scuffle came through the phone line, punctuated by a vicious, almost metallic thud.

"Guinevere!" I snapped as my heart tripped inside my chest and broke into a sprint. "Vera!"

When she did not answer, I stormed back into the room, where Renzo waited by the front door.

"Call Ludo and Carmine. Find out where Vera is," I ordered, the phone still at my ear so I could hear what was going on. Then I turned to my capos and said, "Thank you for your time, friends. Something has come up. I trust you will do as we discussed. There is a healthy bonus for whoever unveils San Marco."

"Do you need help with this emergency?" Pamina Riva, the only female capo in the northwest, known infamously as La Vampira for her bloodthirsty ways, offered with a sharp grin.

"No, *grazie*, Pamina," I replied just before a voice came through the phone.

"*I am not here to harm you*," a male voice said distantly. *"I am a friend."*

A growl worked itself up my throat like something rancid and bilious.

"The car is out front," Renzo told me, his own phone in his hand, fingers flying.

I made for the door without further comment until I heard Pasquale, the son of capo Ernesto Ricci, mutter, "Never thought I'd see the day Il Gentiluomo was under the thumb of a woman."

Without pausing in my stride, I called out, "And I never think you can get any stupider than you already are, yet you constantly find ways to prove me wrong. You will double your dues to the family for three months for your son's insult, Ernesto."

A sound of outrage exploded from his mouth, but Renzo was already opening the door for me.

I turned just enough to let the light hit the side of my face, highlighting the vicious grin curling one side of my mouth. "Next time you think to speak about my woman, I will take out your kneecaps, understood?"

Ernesto reached over to clamp his meaty hand around his son's forearm and answered over his squawk. "*Capisco, capo*. I apologize for my son. Let me know if I may be of assistance."

I jerked my chin before the door swung shut behind me and listened to the phone as I raced to the curb and got into the town car Martina had idling out front.

"They're in Impruneta for the wine festival," Renzo told Martina as he got into the passenger seat, and we took off with a squeal of tires into the twilight streets.

"Go," I barked, even as I heard the unknown man say to Guinevere, "*The Venetian wants you.*"

Porca Madonna, that fucking Venetian.

"It will take us fifty minutes to get there, boss," Martina told me.

"Break every speed limit."

"That *is* with breaking every limit," she countered.

Gunfire exploded on the other end of the phone line. My hand gripped the phone so tightly the metal edges cut into my flesh, spilling blood across my palm.

"Where the fuck are Ludo and Carmine?" I demanded of Renzo.

"Ludo isn't answering his phone, but Carmine is on the way. He was watching your sisters across the piazza. He said ETA is three minutes. He left Michele and Philippe to protect your sisters."

Three minutes with Guinevere alone somewhere with an unidentified shooter.

Fear turned my blood to battery acid, bitter enough on the back of my tongue to make me gag, burning in my veins until I thought I would catch fire from the inside out.

"Why the fuck did they even leave the estate?" I asked.

Renzo winced. "They were with Ludo, Carmine, and a handful of men who kept to the shadows. It seemed extremely unlikely they would find trouble."

My family calls me Jinx because I'm so unlucky, Guinevere's sweet voice came back to me as she explained her idiosyncratic ability to find trouble wherever she went.

"*Cazzo*, I never should have left her," I snarled, as more gunfire sounded and a female cry exploded over the airways.

I'd never believed in God, even though I was born and raised a good Catholic Italian. It did not make any logical sense to me to appeal to an entity we had no science to back, no actual data on.

But I sat there in the car as the countryside blurred around us, and I begged whatever God might prevail that he would keep Guinevere safe from harm.

And then when that did not seem like enough, both because I doubted his existence and because I doubted even more that I deserved to be heard by him, I appealed to the devil, offering him my cold soul in eternal damnation in exchange for Guinevere escaping this alive.

My heart stopped when the gunfire ceased abruptly and silence followed.

"Guinevere!" I bellowed, hoping she would hear me—could still hear me and wasn't dead.

If she lived through this, I would not spend a moment more battling guilt and the inane idea that being away from her was ever a good idea. I would sew myself to her side if I could, pocket her against my chest in the inside of my suit jacket so that I might always feel her against my heart. Insane, overpossessive—I no longer gave a fuck.

Even if she could not accept me as her lover once more, she would live with me as her shadow whether she liked it or not.

No harm would ever come to Guinevere Stone again.

The words rang truer in my thoughts than prayers to God or deals with the devil.

I was the only authority that mattered.

Over the line, a gasping, choking sob that was soon muffled. A minute later, a cacophony of clatter and raised voices.

"Someone answer this goddamn phone!" I shouted.

Finally, someone did.

"Raffa?" Carmine asked, panting heavily.

"What the fuck is going on over there?" Even though I had never been a creative person, my mind was imagining all the dire ways Guinevere had been maimed or killed. "Is Guinevere okay?"

"She's okay," he said immediately, but there was an edge to his voice like he didn't want to confess what came next. "I mean, she is healthy but for some bruising. It's Ludo who took a bullet to his side. He's on his way to the hospital now."

"Put Guinevere on the phone." I needed to hear her voice before my insides could unclench.

"Um, I don't think that is the best idea right now, boss," he admitted. "She's hysterical."

Hysterical?

I flashed back to the look of abject terror on her face, bits of bone and brain matter flecking her nightgown and skin in the aftermath of the assassin's death.

"Do not let her run," I ordered through gritted teeth, adrenaline like acid in my veins as I sat caged in the car with nothing to *do*. "Carmine, do you hear me? Whatever happens, do not let her run again."

"It's not you or us she wants to run from," he explained. "If she could, I think she'd be running from herself."

"What the fuck happened? Stop being cryptic with me. I need to know how to help her," I bit out.

"He's dead." His words were heavy enough to land like blows against my ear. "The man who shot Ludo and tried to take Guinevere? She killed him."

◆ ◆ ◆

The family had been put to bed by the time I reached the villa, but warm light greeted me as I stormed inside and found Leo sitting with his head in his hands at the kitchen table. A sweating glass of amber liquor—his preferred whiskey, probably—sat untouched by his right elbow. He looked up at me as if I was the Grim Reaper come to deliver his death.

I was not far off from doing exactly that.

Ludo had already briefed me that Leo was the one to suggest Guinevere take in the sight of Impruneta and the surrounding valleys of grapes from the bell tower, and though he had gone straight to Ludo to tell him where Guinevere was, those few minutes when she was on her own had been enough to endanger her life.

Such carelessness with the woman I loved and breathed for made my very bones quake with suppressed fury.

"I am so sorry, Raffa." Leo's heavy voice punctured my thoughts and drew my attention back to his hangdog expression. "Honestly, I was trying to bond with her, not endanger her, when I offered up the suggestion. I feel . . . I feel absolutely sick that I was the one to put her in harm's way."

"You should." My voice was a death knell, hollow and dark.

Behind me Martina hovered, perhaps waiting to see if this conversation would end in bloodshed.

"I already apologized to Guinevere," he continued, eyes glassy as he looked out the dark window and then back to me. A thin smile flickered at the end of his mouth. "She told me what she saw of the view was lovely."

Warmth cut through the cold anger burning up my gut.

"She is the most resilient woman I have ever known," I agreed.

Leo's mouth pressed into a firm line as he looked down at his palms. "A woman must be if she wants to live this life with us."

It was true, of course. A reality I had been wrestling like a giant beast for almost the full length of time I had known Guinevere. Now that my worst fears had come true, both in Michigan and now closer to home in Impruneta, it settled something in me to know that my *cerbiatta* could hold her own until help arrived.

This did not mean I was willing to forgive Leo, not when he had been rude to her since the beginning. Perhaps if it had been Carmine, Renzo, or Ludo who had put Guinevere in that position, I would have forgiven one of them more easily.

"I have not been fair to her," Leo said, reading my thoughts as only a lifelong friend could. "It wasn't about her so much as the woman I loved and lost. She . . . she reminds me of her. The courage in the face of new horizons. Even her laugh . . ." He lost himself to memories, and a part of me that had loved Leo my whole life ached for the loss of this woman I had never known.

Their brief affair had only lasted a handful of months a year or two ago, but it had left an indelible mark on him, a measured, melancholy kind of maturity he had not possessed before.

"I am sorry for your loss. You know I am. But I will not tolerate anyone treating Guinevere with hostility. I will not even tolerate her being treated as anything less than the most precious creature in this house," I admitted, crossing my arms to level him with a declarative glare.

Leo blinked. "I guess I hadn't realized how much you cared for her. To say that . . . when your mother and sisters and nephews live here? Well, I'm shocked."

"You shouldn't be," Martina finally chimed in, stepping up beside me to press her shoulder into mine in a show of solidarity that soothed some of my agitation. "When have you known Raffa to take risks? When have you known him to allow himself to be vulnerable? If I did not love Guinevere myself for the woman she is, I would love her for his sake alone."

"I was just trying to protect you back at Fattoria Casa Luna," Leo argued. "Can you blame me when I have been trying to do that my whole life?"

"Sometimes you should worry more about being a good friend than a good soldier," Martina snapped.

And it surprised me that she was right.

Renzo, Carmine, Martina, and even Ludo, who was almost as unfeeling as they came, had all made it a point to get to know Guinevere on a personal level because I clearly cared for her, and only Leo had not.

But Leo was also the only one of my inner circle who had not witnessed the man I was allowed to be in England at university and in my financial career before coming home. He did not know I was even capable of falling in love like an ordinary man.

Though there was nothing ordinary in the way I loved my Vera.

"I am sorry for that too," Leo added, his expression broken open with earnestness. "I will make it up to you both, I promise."

"Okay," I said simply. "You can try, and I want you to succeed. But you have to know, Leo, that if it came down to it, I would end your life before I ever let you endanger hers again."

Leo studied me for a long moment, awe and regret and sorrow playing over his features before they settled into something like resolve.

"I understand." He spoke quietly. "You have found the kind of love worth ruining the world for."

"I have," I agreed, even though I had never been less sure that love would come to mean Guinevere and I would be together in the end. "So you will excuse me while I go to her."

"Please." He waved his hand at the stairs. "She wouldn't even let Carmine or Angela inside to tend to her. I think the only one she wants is you."

Hope burned a hole in my chest like a bullet wound to the heart.

With a curt nod, I moved swiftly up the stairs toward Guinevere's bedroom. The light was on under her door, but when I tried to open the door, I found I could not.

"Guinevere?" I called softly so as not to wake the house.

How my sisters had managed to get their children down after such a night, I had no clue, but it was only one of the many reasons I admired them. To think our father had thought women a "lesser species."

"Guinevere," I called again, only to be met with silence.

The door locked from the inside, but no one ever bothered to lock their doors unless they were being intimate, and I did not have a clue where the ancient key might be kept.

"I could look for the key?" Martina asked softly from the mouth of the hall, where she had lingered after following me up. "You don't think . . . you don't think she's harming herself or anything, do you?"

I had not before she uttered the words. Even though I knew Guinevere was not the kind of woman to self-harm, not when she was so grateful for her health, alarm trilled through me.

Bracing my shoulder against the door, I heaved my weight into it while twisting the painted ceramic knob. The wood shuddered but did not give until I stepped back and threw myself into the panel again.

The door popped open with a sharp crack, the lock having punched through the jamb on the inside of the room.

"Wait here," I told Martina, who walked toward me and then slid down the wall beside the door to sit on the floor as sentry. *"Grazie, amica mia."*

If she was startled by my uncharacteristic heartfelt thanks, she did not show it.

I pushed into the room and closed the door behind me before looking to the perfectly made bed.

It was empty, as was the rest of the room.

I walked toward the closed bathroom door and heard the telltale rush of the shower running. When I tried the knob, it opened easily, steam wafting out in a thick stream. It obscured the bathroom as if the space had been stuffed with wet cotton, but I followed the damp wall until I reached the glass enclosure and then opened the door, stepping inside fully dressed in my bespoke Brioni suit.

Only that close could I see through the steam to Guinevere.

She sat curled in on herself at the base of the rushing water, her skin pomegranate pink from the scalding spray, hair a wet slick of black down her back. Her arms were banded around her legs, face pressed to her knees, and even though she had to be ridiculously overheated—burned, even—she was shivering.

"*Mia stella cadente*," I murmured, squatting before her so I could reach out to tip her chin up. "What are you doing to yourself?"

She did not want to lift her chin, but my grip was inexorable. I was greeted by an expression that rent my chest in two like the swift slice of a katana through the rib cage. Her huge, luminous brown eyes were bloodshot and filled with so much self-loathing I could not bear it. I recognized the emotion because I had found it too often staring back at me in the mirror.

"I was dirty," she whispered, tipping her head back and closing her eyes so that the hot water splashed across her face. "I'm trying to get clean."

I realized on closer inspection that her hands were still bloody, clasped under her calves where the water wouldn't hit them. It must have been Ludo's blood, because she was uninjured, and the *stronzo* who had tried to kidnap her had been tossed from the bell tower rampart.

"Will you let me help you?" I asked softly, because there was no doubt she was a fawn right now, hurt and cornered with nowhere to run.

I wanted to be the refuge she did not realize she could find if only she accepted the hand I extended to her.

She stared at it for a long time. Minutes dissolving into each other as my suit grew heavy and wet, my shoes pooling with water. I did not move. I barely breathed.

Trust me, I willed her.

It had once been so effortless for her to do so, to curl into my chest as early as those first few days of knowing each other, when she was too sick to let societal norms curb her impulse to find solace in me.

Now, even shaking with trauma, she was unsure.

Of all the things in my life I had not wanted to do and regretted, lying to her and letting her run home to Michigan without fighting for her was the worst of them. Worse than all of them combined.

Eventually, though, she unwound her arms from her legs and reached a shivery hand up to clasp my own. It felt so small and frail within my grip that for a moment I thought I would break her bones tugging her to her feet. She rose gracefully, with that lithe elegance she seemed to embody no matter the circumstances, so I was surprised when she suddenly collapsed again. I caught her, lifting her against my torso and securing her there with one arm banded around her back. The too-hot water burned even through my suit jacket, so I used the other hand to turn the temperature down and then returned my attention to the woman in my arms.

She had frozen, ramrod straight and stiff like a wooden plank, but after a second, she loosed a long sigh and sagged inch by inch against me. The last point of contact was her cheek resting against my chest, nose turned into the drenched lapel and wet lashes spiky against her pale cheeks.

"I'm dirty," she repeated quietly. "But I'm so tired."

"I will clean you, *cerbiatta mia*," I told her solemnly, and even though it was difficult to do with one hand, I kept her pinned to my chest while I reached for the almond oil soap on the shelf.

She was content to rest heavily against me as I started with her right hand and then moved on to her left, lathering the soap thickly between her fingers, rubbing with the natural sponge in little circles to banish the blood clinging to the ridges of each fingerprint. Then her arms, slim and pale from the Michigan autumn. She would always be slight because of her illness, but I found beauty in every inch of her. It was not a sexual kind of appreciation, tending to the small swells of her breasts and the tender apexes under her arms, between her legs. It was something sacred that sluiced through my insides like the warm water around us, cleansing me of the impurities I had felt since she had last been in my presence.

Loving Guinevere was my absolution. Worshipping her the only kind of freedom I had felt in the last five years. Because there was nothing responsible about our pairing, nothing acceptable or free from obstacles, yet it was the only thing I had ever wanted viciously enough to fight for without capitulation.

No one would take her from me unless she walked away herself.

Even then, I knew, in a way that settled the panic I'd felt for months, that there would never be a time I did not watch her from afar and care for her however I could get away with. Guinevere's unluckiness had come to an unnatural end the day she met me. Any lottery she entered, she would win. Any dream she aspired to, I would help her attain. Any future monsters who might come for her would find me there to scare them away.

I was, quite clearly, born to love her.

So after weeks of being unable to express it, I let all the love I harbored for her in my black heart spill over into the simple act of bathing her.

I went to my knees, placed her foot on my shoulder, and used both hands to sweep over her lightly muscled thighs straight down to her calves and the oddly lovely bones in her feet. She shivered still, but this time not from the shakiness of adrenaline giving way to horror.

Gradually, the flush of heat from the too-hot water was replaced with a different kind of warmth beneath her skin.

When her hands slowly sank into my hair, tangling in the strands and tugging gently, I looked up at her through wet lashes to see her pupils blown wide with desire.

"Do you want me to clean you up with my tongue?" I murmured against her skin before licking a droplet of water from the crook of her groin.

She nodded immediately, swaying a little into my mouth.

I hid my smile against her skin and then trailed my lips to the top of her mound, pressing a chaste kiss to the bare skin above her clit before I started to enjoy her in earnest. Even with the water still beating down on us, I could taste the sweet sluice of her arousal against my tongue when I delved between her lips to play at her entrance with my tongue.

She gasped, legs quaking with a mixture of lust and exhaustion. I moved my hands to her pert ass and lifted her against me, moaning in approval against her pussy when she wrapped her legs over my shoulders and clung even tighter to my hair for balance. I shifted slightly so she could lean back against the travertine tiles if she needed to and then devoted myself wholly to the task of feasting on her gorgeous cunt.

I ate like a man starved, and I was. For two months I had assumed I would never get to touch her like this, taste her like this, love her like this again. The idea of sex without her felt bleak, sepia toned where I had once had vibrant technicolor, and my previously voracious sex drive had diminished astonishingly unless I was thinking of Guinevere. The way she moaned in these breathy little gasps like she did now, writhing on my tongue as I fucked it inside her clutching heat. The way she fisted my hair too tight and dragged her nails down my shoulder, marking me in the most primal way as hers.

I was so hard beneath my wet, painfully constricting trousers that I throbbed fiercely, but I made no move to adjust myself.

This was about her.

Sucking the toxin of self-hatred out and replacing it with soothing caresses full of all the love I had for her.

When she came, it was with a sigh that spun out like a ball of yarn, long and loose, her muscles tightening around me before going completely lax so that just my hands on her ass and her back against the wall kept her from falling over. I lapped at the delicious spill of cum until her swollen folds tasted only of water, and then I pressed another kiss to the top of her mound.

Carefully, I adjusted her legs so they slid from my shoulders, down my arms, and to either side of my hips before I gently rose to my feet and carried her out of the shower into the slightly less steamy room. I perched her on the closed toilet so I could remove my sopping-wet suit jacket and grab a towel. Almost asleep where she sat, limbs warm and malleable, Guinevere let me dry her.

Once she was dry, I frowned at her mass of wet hair and searched the cupboards for her hairbrush. When I came back to her with it and a hair tie, her eyes widened for a moment, lips parting. I wished I knew if she remembered the first time I had done this for her, braiding her hair when she was too ill to care for herself.

She was not sick now, not physically, but the mental strain of realizing that you have ended another life is something even more insidious.

I secured a towel around my waist and settled behind her on the back of the toilet to start combing through her wet hair. She only moved to lean forward so I could get to the long ends. I worked in silence, only our shared breath and the rhythmic tap of water droplets against the shower floor filling the space.

"I killed someone today," she said finally in a wooden whisper. "Did they tell you?"

I hummed, working a tangle out of her dark hair. "They told me you saved Ludo's life and yours by acting quickly and bravely."

She was quiet for so long, shoulders slumped and head drooping, that I wondered if she'd fallen asleep with my soothing fingers and the brush in her hair.

"*Sono un'assassina*," she said, her voice more resolute, shoulders snapping straight like those of a soldier called to attention. "I am a killer."

"There is a difference between killing for pleasure and killing to protect yourself and others," I told her. "You are not a killer, because your heart is good and your motivations were honest. *Non sei un'assassina; sei una cacciatrice.*"

You are not a killer; you are a huntress.

"A hunter kills only to provide for the family or to protect their village," I lectured as I pulled her hair into three parts and began to braid the damp strands. "They do not teach you this in school, Vera, but there is a price for saving a life, and that is often paid in the taking of another."

"It's too easy to believe you," she admitted, leaning back slightly so I had to pull the tail of her braid up in order to finish it off with the elastic. "It's always been too easy to believe you."

"You have slept beside me for many nights," I reminded her. "Do I have trouble sleeping? Now you know I am a killer too. Does that surprise you? Does that make me a callous man in your eyes?"

There was bitterness in her voice when she asked, "Are you saying every life you took was to save another?"

"Yes," I responded instantly. "Unequivocally yes. If I did not kill the men who came for me, they would kill my brothers-in-arms and eventually my family. Stacci, Carlotta, Delfina, Mamma, Zacheo, Nico, Mattia—"

"*Basta,*" she snapped.

Enough.

"I understand," she continued, hunched into herself, pulling her feet up to rest on the closed lid beneath her so she could hug her knees once again. "But it is too general an excuse to use so often when you could just . . . stop putting people in a position where their lives are at risk."

"Life is so simple in your eyes," I said, even though I knew she would recoil, bunching tighter like a wood bug, ready to close off completely and roll away from me. I fought the urge to pull her close. "Sometimes you are not born into a position where freedom is a viable option."

"You don't like being a mafioso." It wasn't a question. "I've thought back on our conversations, and you always seem so . . . reluctant to play your part. So why do this? Why kill and steal and lie? It . . . it doesn't suit you."

Just as killing doesn't suit me, she didn't say, but I could hear the thought clearly enough.

I could have told her that I had cut ties with my father and banished myself to London. I could have explained that when he was killed, I had no choice but to take up his mantle because the wily bastard had not named another heir, and Camorra tradition dictated that a new *capo dei capi* outside the family should kill the previous family members to eradicate any contestation about their reign.

I could have explained all that to my sweet Guinevere, and she might have felt empathy for me, might have even let herself love me again, a little.

But what was the point in that when the truth remained?

I was who I was, a stone-cold killer running an underworld empire. No matter how I had arrived here, it was who I was and, more importantly, what I was good at.

My sigh shuddered out of my lungs like steam from a failing engine. I climbed down from my perch and rounded Guinevere so I could crouch on her level to look into her eyes.

"But it does suit me," I explained patiently. "I am good at hiding money from the authorities and slipping beneath their notice. I am clever enough to play games with the power-hungry capos just waiting for me to fail and ruthless enough to put them down when they act against me. Like the moon, I have a dark side of my heart too. I just so happen to love you with all of it, the shadowed soul and the light."

"You're saying that you'd love me enough to kill for me," she countered, a cruel edge to her tone, a sneer on her pretty mouth. "And that makes it okay?"

"I am saying I *have* killed for you, *cacciatrice mia*," I corrected, cupping the entire side of her face in one big palm. "I would kill for you again until the streets of Florence ran red with the blood of your enemies. And when it was all over, I would pull you into our bed at night, slake my lingering bloodlust with your body, and fall asleep as easy as a babe with you in my arms."

"That's psychopathic," she told me primly, but her eyes were dark and hungry, enormous black pools I could fall into for the rest of eternity.

"That is the reality of my life," I argued. "To me, that is the highest form of love."

She scoffed, biting her lip as she wrenched her gaze away from me.

"Tell me this," I said with a soft hiss, hoping the words would slip through the crack in her armor against me. "If it had been you alone on the tower, would you have resorted to sacrificing yourself and going with that *bastardo* to keep the family safe from him?" I paused to let the words register, to watch the way her shoulders tensed with wariness, sensing a trap. "It was only when Ludo had been shot, when it was no longer only yourself in danger, that you killed him. You did it because you love Ludo and you could not stand to see him die."

Her silence was answer enough.

"Love." I punctuated my point quietly but clearly. "In this life, violent delights often beget violent ends. To love so much is to do anything to keep your people safe." I hesitated and then added, "You can say it is because I am a mafioso. That I was raised habituated to brutality, trained in the language of blood and death, that you are an American girl from Michigan with no such background, and you can deny it all you want, but I *see* you, Guinevere. I see you, and I know you love just as savagely."

She raised a shaking hand to scrub it over her face as if she could wake herself up from a nightmare. When her hand dropped, her expression had been rubbed raw, mouth sagging open like a puncture wound, eyes weary and ancient.

"I judged you for being a murderer," she said softly. "Only to become one myself. It's a horrible kind of karma, I guess."

"You are twenty-three years old," I allowed with a thin smile. "You have a lot of time left to learn about the kind of person you are. You just have to be brave enough—like you were tonight—to ask yourself the truly hard questions."

"Like what?" Her lids were fluttering, too heavy to keep open. She was slumped back against the toilet now, a bruise blooming along one shoulder from her scuffle with the dead man, her face pale and clean and so young looking it made me ache inside.

"There are three types of people," I said, sidestepping her question momentarily. "Those who run from danger, those who would give up their lives to save others from it, and those who would stand and fight against it." Her gaze found mine, eyes filled with questions and yearning. "Most people never have to answer the question of which type they are except for in the abstract, in a philosophy or ethics course, maybe. In the life I lead, the one I led you into, you have to answer the question in a very real way. Even though I believe I know which woman you are, it is up to you to decide. When you are ready, you will tell me."

"What if I don't give you the answer you want?" The words were so quiet they were more breath than sound.

I could feel the awkward pull of the wry smile on my mouth. "Do you not understand yet, *stella cadente*? Whatever wish you make, I will see done."

"Even if it's not what you want for yourself?" There was desperation there, but I could not tell how she wanted me to respond, so I gave her only the truth.

"There will never be a day that I will stop loving you," I confessed with a blasé shrug, as if that love did not dictate every beat of my heart. "So yes, even then. There is nothing I would not give you. Nothing I would not do for you."

"Even murder," she whispered, eyes drifting closed for a slow blink I was not sure she would wake from.

"Especially murder," I agreed easily before standing to collect her into my arms.

As soon as her body pressed into mine, she curled into my chest, cheek over my heart, and promptly fell into a deep doze.

The sensation of pride her trust and comfortableness instilled in me was cataclysmic, a shifting of tectonic plates in the very foundation of my life.

"I love you," I couldn't help but tell her as I carried her into the cool bedroom and tenderly deposited her beneath the sheets. "Even if you are not brave enough to be Regina Inferna."

CHAPTER TEN

Guinevere

I woke up the next morning with the echo of Raffa's mouth between my thighs and the phantom sensation of hot, wet blood on my hands.

It was an alarming contrast, but oddly fitting for my current situation.

My shoulder ached from where the dead man's boot had connected with it, but I rolled away the stiffness as I got ready for the day. My face was a pale oval in the mirror, bleached of color and hollow beneath the cheeks and eyes. I looked skeletal and vaguely frightening.

With a sigh, I opened my makeup bag and got to work making myself presentable, even though I felt like squirreling the whole day away locked in my room. There was no doubt in my mind that Raffa, or one of his well-meaning but interfering sisters, would have dragged me out of bed at some point.

Besides, it was the first day of the grape harvest, which meant that I had already slept too long and most of the family would be out in the field of vines extending all down the left slope and valley beside the house. I had been eager to participate in such a cultural phenomenon, questioning Delfina about the harvesting process and Angela, Stacci, and Carlotta about the community feast they hosted among the vines that first night to celebrate.

It was going to be glorious.

I could wallow in self-pity and flagellation another day, I decided, as I donned the most casual outfit in my closet, a white linen dress with straps that buttoned close on my chest, and slipped my feet into sturdy leather sandals. My hair was wavy from Raffa's braid, and even though it was impractical, I left it down because I liked the way it made me feel to know his fingers had been in it, caring for it and for me in one of my lowest moments.

Not thinking about the fact that I had killed someone—and watched him splatter open across the cobblestones beneath me like a much too macabre Humpty Dumpty—was utterly exhausting, and I'd only been awake for half an hour.

When I left the room, I noticed the splintered doorframe, thumbing a sliver of wood as I passed by. It hurt to think of Raffa's panic when he'd listened to the entire bell tower encounter through the phone, knowing he couldn't reach me. He must have been driven crazy with helplessness and rage, but when he'd handled me in the shower, he had only been tender and so patient it set my throat to aching.

Every touch of his hands seemed to reanimate me, breathing life into my two-dimensional spirit. The ghost I had become after turning that random Italian assailant into one himself was banished by the immensity of Raffa's worship. For a man like that to cherish me? It felt nothing short of holy, some ancient pagan ritual involving sacrifice and blood as offerings to a god that was just as merciful as it was full of spite.

I could not deny that it made me feel powerful, especially after I'd felt so helpless on the bell tower, to know that this behemoth of a man knelt only for me. Knowing, as I did now, that he was truly dangerous had been an extra thrill, the spark that tipped the edge of my pleasure into a cleansing, vibrant climax.

I could be honest with myself about that, at least.

Ask myself the first of the hard questions Raffa had alluded to the night before.

Did Raffa's criminality affect how I felt about him physically?

Quite the opposite.

All those dark fantasies I'd harbored about being tied up, fucked hard, left wanting for hours, and then being made to come until it hurt only raged hotter now that I knew he could be cruel and shocking. I wondered just how far down he could take me, just how thoroughly he could take every inch of me apart with his teeth and cock and bare, man-killing hands.

"*Cazzo*," I murmured as I left my bedroom behind. "Who are you, Guinevere?"

The answer to that question was much more difficult to answer.

I hurried downstairs, eager for the distraction of the harvest and, if I was being honest, eager to see Raffa again.

Even though he was the cause of all this chaos, he was also the only one who made me feel slightly sane, even remotely safe. Not just from external forces but also from myself. This new version that was emerging from the darkest depths of my soul and swallowing whole parts of my previous identity whole.

That he could still look at me like he saw every inch of who I was, even the new bits I wanted to hide away from, made it impossibly harder not to love him.

"*Buongiorno*, Vera."

I closed my eyes for a moment to savor the richness of that voice because Raffa was turned away from me, pouring coffee from a hand-painted Dolce & Gabbana Moka pot into a matching cup.

He was wearing casual khakis that hugged his thickly muscled thighs and sculpted ass and an oversized white linen shirt. When he turned with the coffee cup in one hand, I noticed his shirt was open indecently low to reveal most of his carved, tanned chest and the crisp black hair that made my mouth water.

Merda, why did he have to be so gorgeous?

"Did you sleep well?" he asked, concern so obvious in his usually stoic expression that I hesitated mid-step, thrown off by the tenderness there. "I kept the door open to my room, but I did not hear you cry out in the night."

He'd been listening for nightmares.

My traitorous heart skipped a beat.

I accepted the coffee he extended to me, breathing in the delicious aroma to take a moment to compose myself. "I don't remember any dreams. I was out like a log."

"*Bene*," he said with a firm nod, turning away to the oven, from which he pulled out a full plate of food. "The family left two hours ago to begin work, but Mamma made you a plate."

I never thought I would see a powerful, arrogant man like Raffaele Romano *fuss* over someone, but there he was, making me coffee, grabbing utensils and a full plate of food to give to me, even laying my napkin in my lap.

I gaped at him, and when he noticed, he laughed. It was that full-bodied chuckle that he only ever used with his close loved ones. My eyes fell closed for too long a beat while I absorbed the beauty of it.

"I'm fine, Raffa," I reminded him. "It wasn't me who was . . . hurt."

"We will agree to disagree, hmm?" he decided, nodding at my hand where it was loosely clasped around a fork, hovering over a mound of eggs. "Eat your food."

"Are you being so sweet out of guilt?" I asked, even as I obeyed and dug into the perfectly seasoned scrambled eggs and vibrant slices of prosciutto.

"I am being sweet because I am a sweet man," he qualified, and then shot me a wicked grin over his shoulder as he poured himself a fresh cup of coffee. "When I want to be."

I didn't respond, because, of course, I knew this. Raffa was the man who had taken an unlucky American girl into his home for safe harbor when she had no money or clothes to her name, who had provided for her and indulged her whims.

Of course, we had shared a basic attraction from the start, and I was sure if I'd been another kind of woman, he would have seen me off with a wad of cash to the nearest hotel, but that wasn't how it had gone.

I wondered if I wasn't so unlucky as I had always believed.

Raffa's words from my last week in Florence in August echoed in my head: *sfortunato al gioco, fortunato in amore.*

Unlucky at cards, lucky in love.

And then his words from the night before . . .

There is nothing I would not give you. Nothing I would not do for you.

I knew in my bones they were spoken from the heart. He would do whatever it took to make me happy, even if it made him unhappy.

And the truth was, I did not want Raffa to be unhappy.

He had so obviously been unhappy for a long time when we met, and I thought it would be a crime if he stopped laughing that throaty chuckle and smiling that almost boyish, mischievous grin.

But could I be the kind of woman who fought—and killed—for what I wanted and those I loved? Even though I technically *had* the night before, I couldn't say actually ending that man's life had been my intention. It was more an accidental by-product of my desire to stop him from shooting Ludo.

Could I ever go into a situation with premeditated murder in my mind? Because if I stayed here with Raffa as anything other than his reluctant hostage, I knew there might come a day when I would need to.

"How many people have you killed?" I asked suddenly, shocked by my own frankness.

Raffa only blinked as he settled across from me with the *Corriere della Sera*. It was flipped open already to an article with a bold enough headline that I could read it upside down.

Suicidio! L'uomo salta dal campanile di Impruneta.

So that was how they'd spun it. That the man had committed suicide after drinking too much wine at the local festival. I had to admit, it seemed plausible. It cowed and scared me slightly to wonder at the reaches of Raffa's Camorra. That they could rewrite history so clearly when there had been an entire piazza of citizens who must have heard the gunfire even over the live band.

"I do not count," Raffa said before snapping open the newspaper crisply and perusing a different headline. "To do so would be . . . *inopportuno*."

I had to cede that to him. "Okay then, have you ever killed women? Children?"

Raffa dipped the newspaper so he could narrow his eyes at me, that pale-maple brown almost bronze in the bright autumnal morning light.

"Why are you asking me this?"

"Why aren't you answering?" I countered, dropping my fork to the plate. "You told me to ask the hard questions."

A surprisingly proud grin curled the edge of his mouth, and I noticed that he hadn't shaved that morning, his stubble an inky spill across his firm jaw and square chin. I wanted to drag my teeth along that bristly edge.

"So I did," he agreed. "No, I have not killed children. Just because I kill when I must does not mean I do not have a code."

"You didn't say you haven't killed women," I noted.

He shrugged. "I am what some would call a progressive capo and what others would call *un'idioto*. I have female capos in my organization who are more frightening than most of the men in the outfit."

"Are you going to make this about equality?" I asked, a little burst of shocked laughter stuttering up my throat. "Really?"

He arched a brow. "I am not making it about anything. I am merely saying that, as you have observed yourself, gender does not matter to *la mafia*. If you are involved, you have equal opportunity to die."

"So you have killed women?" I persisted.

Raffa rolled his eyes. "Guinevere, I have three sisters and a mother. I have not killed a woman before, but that does not mean that someone somewhere in my organization has not. As *capo dei capi*, I am responsible for them all."

I thought about it for a moment and nodded curtly. "Okay, I suppose that's fair."

He inclined his head magnanimously, and I couldn't help but laugh as he meant me to. It was crazy, really and truly, that he could make me laugh the morning after I'd ended a life, but there we were.

"You feel better this morning," he noted, gaze trailing over my skin like hot fingers.

"I do. You . . . you helped last night. Thank you for taking care of me." Even though I didn't necessarily mean the orgasm he'd given me, I couldn't fight the blush that bloomed beneath my skin.

The edge of his mouth pressed into a firm line to fight his knowing smile. "It was my pleasure, Guinevere. As I told you, whatever you need, I will see done."

"Tell me . . ." I hesitated, swallowing thickly. "What was his name? The man I killed."

Raffa sighed. "He was Federico Mancini. A cook from Venice. He has a brother we are trying to secure in order to question him about why Federico might have been all the way over here in Tuscany to abduct you, but he is proving hard to find." He paused before admitting, "His girlfriend filed a missing person report on him a few weeks ago."

"You think he is involved too?" I asked, even though I knew the answer. "That he might come after me as well?"

"I will not let him," Raffa said with an arrogant shrug. "You are safe so long as you remain here in my home, under guard."

I didn't relish the idea of being trapped at the villa, beautiful as it was, but I nodded because I knew Raffa would not budge on that point. He was an overprotective mafioso; there was only so much room for negotiation.

So I tried my hand at an easy ask. "I want to join the harvest."

"Eat the rest of your breakfast first. It is serious work," he ordered, watching me until I lifted my fork and resumed eating. "Now, before we join the others, can you tell me any details about last night? I know it might be difficult to speak of it, but I need to know."

My fork dropped with a clatter. "Oh! God, I can't believe I almost forgot. He had my sister's cross." At Raffa's furrowed brow, I quickly explained, "When he came up the tower stairs, he lunged for me, but when I evaded him, he told me that he was only there as a friend. He said that 'the Venetian' wanted to see me, and he'd been told to show me something. It was Gemma's cross, the one my father gave her when she turned sixteen."

"Are you sure it was the same?"

I was already nodding. "It's very specific. Twisted, delicate gold filaments and a two-carat diamond at the center of the cross. I would know it anywhere. I was always a little jealous that she was the one to get it. It's the only family heirloom we have."

"It wasn't returned to you when Gemma died?" Raffa said as he folded the paper up and exchanged it for the phone lying on the table, typing away quickly.

"No, my dad was upset about it, but the authorities said it wasn't on her person when they found her, and it wasn't among her possessions in the flat she was renting. That's all we got back of her. A box of trinkets and clothes, along with this ugly black urn she would have hated. The local authorities had her cremated before they could find and contact us."

Raffa paused in whatever he was typing to look up at me with bright eyes. "Did she die in the States?"

I shook my head. "No, I think I might have mentioned she was living abroad in Albania. It's where my mother's people are from originally."

He hesitated a moment and then put the phone down to lean over the table, gathering one of my hands to hold tight in his own. "Where exactly?"

"Durrës," I said. "She was there to study at one of the top wineries on the coast."

"The port of Durrës also happens to be the main point of drug exportation for the Albanian Mafia," Raffa told me slowly. "Did your sister . . . did she take drugs recreationally?"

I blinked at him as my stomach clenched into a hard knot. Memories seeped through the locked box I kept shoved to the back of my mind. Gemma returning home from a party in eleventh grade with a nosebleed, giggling too loudly and practically bouncing off the walls.

"What did you do, Gem?" I'd asked her when she came crashing into my room, happy that our parents were still out on a date night.

"I had *fun*, Jinx," she'd told me as blood dripped onto her sparkly shirt. "You should try it sometime."

The day Mom had found a bag of marijuana stuffed in the back of Gemma's underwear drawer and a bag of white powder stuffed into a bundle of socks, she had argued that she was only hiding it for a friend. It became clear who that "friend" was on our next family trip to Gun Lake, when Gemma and her boyfriend, Sam, had gotten so high they crashed the speedboat into the dock and had to be taken to the hospital.

After the colossal fallout of her actions, Gemma had seemed to quit her partying and focus on her dream to become a winemaker and study at the famous Dukeshës Winery.

"Yes," I whispered through the clogged emotions in my throat. "She had a bit of a habit for a while, but it was more that she partied too much and didn't know when to stop. She went to rehab before moving to Albania."

Raffa's lips rolled under his teeth as he considered something and then retrieved his phone again to dash off another few messages.

"Do you really think she went to Albania to study wine?" he asked me.

"It was her passion," I argued. "She was always closest to my mom, and they shared a love of wine and the old country. I think she went with honorable intentions, but I can't say what might have happened if she met the wrong person. She tended to choose the wrong kind of guy."

"The irony," he murmured, clearly indicating the situation I found myself in now with him.

I cracked a smile even though my mind was reeling. "You think Gemma had something to do with the Albanian Mafia, and that's why she died?"

"It's a possibility. The Albanians did business with us until last year, when I decided to pull back from the drug-trafficking game because it was too hot and we have countless other options for investment. When I asked you for help with the shipping manifests, it was to uncover who had taken over their operations in Italy, because we knew whichever clan was involved was likely the same coming after my life and my seat of power. The Greco family also had ties to Venice." My eyes widened at the link. "Yes, one of the capo's daughters married into the Tancredi family that rules that city. The Venetian has been terrorizing my organization, and you, for months. When your flat was broken into, they left a winged lion figurine with a wolf in its mouth."

"The symbol of Venice and the symbol of Rome," I murmured as the wheels turned. "I don't suppose the Romano family originated in Rome?"

"*Tombola*," he said. Bingo.

"Wow," I breathed, both fascinated and chilled by the fact that threats and mind games such as these were Raffa's reality. "So this isn't just about power, then."

Raffa tilted his head, a lock of wavy hair falling like a comma across his forehead. My fingers itched to push it off his golden skin. "What makes you say that?"

"Using metaphors, sending threats, going after your girlfriend?" I ticked the items off on my fingers. "It seems pretty obvious to me. They want revenge against you for something."

The smile that earned me was wide and bright, those sharp teeth glinting. For a moment, I thought he might actually slow clap for me.

"*Bel lavoro*, Vera," he praised warmly. "*Sì*, I believe they are after Clan Romano and not me specifically. My father, he was not a good man even by Camorra standards, *capisci*? *Era cattivo*. Rotten. He cheated on my mother, ignored my sisters because they were women, hit me or blackmailed me when I did not obey him. I have no doubt he killed women and children if it could not be helped. It is because of Aldo Romano that there are enemies at the door."

"What happened to him?" I asked.

Raffa had never spoken about his father before, and it was obvious from the twisted knot in his brow and the bitterness in his tone that he harbored a deep hatred for the man.

"He was killed," Raffa told me, utterly emotionless. "The Pietra family killed him over four years ago now."

"So you became capo," I murmured, trying to reconcile the man who could treat me and his family so kindly with the one who had killed so many men he did not bother to keep track.

Raffa's mouth flatlined. *"Si può fare tutto, ma la famiglia non si può lasciare."*

It took me a moment to translate it because he spoke so quietly, and by the time I did, he was shoving out of his chair to take my plate to the kitchen sink.

You can do anything except leave your family.

I thought about Gemma leaving us for Albania and never returning home. I thought of my dad and mom back in Michigan, separated from me not just by the Atlantic Ocean but also by the sea of lies and secrets stacked up between us.

The phrase seemed entirely suitable for what I knew of Italian families and their makeup, but I wasn't sure it applied to my own, however much I might have wanted it to.

"For better or worse?" I quipped to lighten the heavy expression crinkling Raffa's handsome face.

His laugh was a short, bitter bark. "*Nel bene e nel male*," he agreed. "Speaking of family, *andiamo*. Let us enjoy the fine weather and allow me to teach you a little something about wine."

"I certainly enjoyed the first lesson you gave to me on the subject," I said, smiling at him as I stood to join him at the front door.

Raffa's pale eyes burned with intensity at my words, the air between us crackling palpably. I swallowed thickly, wondering why I'd flirted so boldly when I was still so unsure about where we stood.

He'd given me an orgasm with his mouth the night before, and there I was *flirting* with him like there was nothing wrong between us.

And maybe that was the problem.

There was nothing wrong between Raffaele and Guinevere. It was everything around us, wedged between us, that seemed so insurmountably problematic.

"Those shoes are pretty, Vera, but they will not work today." Raffa interrupted my reverie to grin down at my sandals before he opened a heavy wood bureau and emerged with a pair of dark-green gum boots. "There will be debris on the ground that you could hurt your feet on, and these offer protection from *vipere*." When I made a horrified face, he grinned. "*La vendemmia* is not for the faint of heart. You will sweat and toil like the rest of us, and at *un lauto pranzone*, when you are so tired your hands will not make a fist and your back aches, we will all come together to eat the feast Mamma and her friends will spend most of the day creating for us."

"Who is looking after the kids if everyone is out working?" I asked as I undid my sandals and took the socks and boots Raffa handed to me.

"They are with some teenage cousins, playing their own games in the areas we have already harvested," he explained. "Sometimes they want to help, but really they only like to play in the vines and feel like they are taking part with the rest of their family. Delfina always sets aside a few of the grapes she will use for the family's table wine so that the young ones can stomp them with their feet. It was a tradition we did as children, too, with our uncle Tonio's wife."

"That sounds like fun, if a little unsanitary," I admitted, and watched Raffa's ruddy mouth bloom into a bright smile.

"In order to have fun, we must get a little dirty," he teased me before offering his hand. "Come, Guinevere, let me watch you fall even more in love with my country. It reminds me there is more to love than hate here, especially with you to share it all with."

"Raffa," I breathed, staring at his hand as if it was a *vipera* peeking its triangular head through the vines. "Don't say things like that to me."

"No," he said, voice strong and even, the cold flat of a blade at my throat. "I will tell you every day exactly what you bring to life in the previously barren fields of my heart, so you know how excruciating it was to be without you for two months. How excruciating it will be for me if you choose to run away scared from the truth of me and this life. I will survive, of course, because only in Dante's works do the heroes have the luxury of wallowing in their tragedies, but I will not thrive. I did not a single day before you came, and I will not a single day after you leave."

"Are you trying to guilt-trip me?" I demanded, clinging to the negative by the ends of my fingertips so I did not plummet headlong into the blinding brightness of unconditional love I had occupied before I knew better. "Because that's not fair."

"*L'amore domina senza regole*," he said, stepping closer so that suddenly he was looming over me, so much taller and wider, a mountain of a man who would not be moved. "Love rules without rules, and so do I. There is no room for *fair* when I am trying to convince you to stay here with me forever and be *la cacciatrice mia*."

"Not your little fawn?" I asked before I could stop myself, transfixed by the way he was staring at me as if nothing existed for him but me.

This time, his small smile was wry with self-deprecation. He reached up to pinch my chin gently, a quick caress I hadn't realized was one of his idiosyncrasies with me, one I missed.

"No, Guinevere," he said. "If you stay here with me, you will have to be more than a *cerbiatta* caught alone and innocent in the middle of the road. You will have to be a huntress. So that the next time some man comes for you, you will not hesitate to put him in the ground where he belongs. So that, after, you will not lock yourself in the bathroom unless it is to drag me in there with you to fuck you hard and long in celebration of your own sexy-as-hell gumption."

My mouth was dry, but heat pooled between my thighs at the thought. Raffa pinning me against the travertine tiles, pressing my face to the cool stone with one hand while a foot kicked apart my feet roughly to make room for his narrow hips and hard cock. His teeth at my neck almost painful, biting a claim into my flesh that would linger for days.

"I can see what it does to you." His whisper curled like smoke around me, insidious, inside my lungs before I could think to stop breathing. "The thought of being powerful, of taking charge. You came to Italy to find yourself and your independence. I know you were not looking for the darkness you found, but I think, perhaps, it found you for a reason, and I am starting to believe you could be glorious, my Vera, as Regina Inferna at my side."

His mouth was so close to mine, and I wasn't sure when that had happened. The scent of him, like the forest floor shrouded in fresh dew, consumed me, and his mouth, framed in inky black stubble, the color of the inside of a seashell, was all I could see.

There was nothing in me but the urge to kiss him. I rolled to my tiptoes in the rain boots so that I hovered closer, swaying into that beckoning mouth. His smile was a slow, long curl, like a ribbon under scissor blades.

"Next time you kiss me," he murmured, "you will be sure of what you want. So sure, you will be the one to fuck *me*, to push me against the nearest surface and take your pleasure from me however you want. You will use me to get off and cry my name to the sky because you know there is no God for us but each other and no heaven but the kingdom down under we could reign over together."

He dipped just slightly to tongue at the center of my bottom lip. My tongue chased after him, but he pulled away from me between one blink and the next, cold air suddenly rushing in against my chest. When I blinked again, he was gone through the open door, whistling with his hands in his pockets as he started to walk down the hill into the vines.

CHAPTER ELEVEN

Raffa

La vendemmia was a sacred time for winemakers in Italy, and an even more sacred one for the Romano family. Though my father had been a hard man, the weeks of the harvest had brought with them a different side of him. He spent every night at home with the family, flirting with his wife, joking with Uncle Tonio, Leo, and me, and throwing crumbs of affection to his daughters. It was the best version of him, one that lasted a few fleeting weeks. So it was no surprise that we all loved *la vendemmia* more than Christmas at Villa Romano.

It was a time of celebration and peace.

I stayed those few weeks at the villa, along with my most trusted friends and *soldati*, bonding over the rigor of picking grapes and carting plastic crates stuffed with purple bunches into the backs of trucks to transport up the hills to the main production facility a few acres away from the family home.

Though in all those years, I had never brought a woman with me to the grape harvest. I had never thought to.

It was time spent with family, something intimate and holy someone had to earn the right to be initiated into.

Of course, Guinevere had earned that right.

The links in the chains binding the Camorra together were forged in blood, and she had let enough of hers to be considered a made woman for life.

Despite the fact that she did not want to be here, both here in Italy and here with my family, in the Camorra, or in my vicinity, I could clearly see that a part of her belonged on this Latin soil. It was evident when I watched her at work with our community in the endless sea of green vines, dark head bent intently on her task as her mobile mouth moved around sound and smiles as she chatted happily in shockingly good Italian to the men and women around her.

Even Uncle Tonio, quiet and reserved, smiled at her through the gaps in vine leaves as she raced Carmine to collect the most bunches on a single trunk.

She had soil smeared on her forehead from pushing her heavy hair out of her face with her work gloves, and sweat glistened on her small nose, but she looked like some kind of model from a *Vogue* spread on the idyllic beauty of Tuscany. Stacci had lent her a drab brown apron to cover the bottom of her dress, but even that suited her, emphasizing the richness of her wavy hair and laughing dark eyes.

If I had not already been in over my head in love with her, seeing her work and laugh among the vines with my people would have done it.

"You are drooling," Carlotta informed me, jostling me from my study of Guinevere with a shoulder bumping into mine. "Close your mouth, Raffuccio."

"Do not call me that," I said automatically, because I had been doing so since I was eight years old and none of my sisters had ever stopped.

"I see why you catch flies when you look at her," Stacci murmured from my other side, looking at Guinevere through two rows of sloping vines as she petted Aio, whose tail was thwapping hard into her side. "There is something about her that is . . . *incandescente*."

"Like a shooting star," I murmured before I could curb the impulse. "Streaking across my life for only a brief time."

"It is good to know you have not outgrown your dramatics," Stacci huffed, sharing an eye roll with Carlotta.

I snorted as I clipped another bunch of Chianti classic grapes and dropped them carefully into the bucket so the delicate skins would not burst. "If I am dramatic, I learned it from my sisters."

"Why are you so convinced she will not stay?" Carlotta asked. "She looks right at home to me."

I followed her gaze back through the leaves to Guinevere to find she was pelting Carmine and Martina with debris, laughing so hard there were tears leaking from her eyes. She had stayed close to my *soldati* for most of the day, but had taken pains to introduce herself to the townsfolk too. At one point, I had caught three older men—all brothers, and all widowed or divorced—crowding around her in a blatant attempt to flirt. She had laughed—that vibrant, bells-ringing, celebratory sound—and indulged them, though Ludo, confined to a comfortable chair because of his gunshot wound, had scowled at them all.

Santa Madonna, she was glorious.

"You both do not understand what it is like to fall in love with a person outside the life. She thought she had fallen in love with someone else entirely until circumstances meant the real me was unmasked."

"The real you?" Stacci scoffed. "Raffa, you are not so subtle as to be able to affect multiple personalities. Even as a boy, you were always exactly who you wanted to be, take it or leave it. If she loved you, Guinevere loved who you really are."

"You are only saying that because you do not understand what it must have been like for her," I argued in a sharp, sibilant hiss like the *vipera* everyone watched out for with wary eyes. "She did not know her lover was a killer."

"She did not know she would become one either," Carlotta pointed out with a raised brow as she carted a heavy plastic container of grapes in her arms, barely breaking a sweat at the load she carried under the warm

October sun. "The best kind of people change and adapt. Especially if they are rewarded for it."

"I am hardly enough reward for having blood on her hands," I derided, grasping a bundle of grapes too firmly so they burst apart in my gloved hand, the vibrant skins staining the white canvas purple red.

"Does she at least know *why* you became *capo dei capi*?" Stacci asked. "Knowing you, she doesn't."

"It hardly matters why when the end result is the same."

"It does matter, and you know it," she pressed, poking me with a hard finger to the chest. "Does she know you did it to save us? Does she know the first threat came with the news that *papà* was dead? Does she know Leo had to stop a gunman from storming Carlotta's delivery room? No one knowing these things could hold what you do against you."

"She is a twenty-three-year-old girl from America," I growled, thinking of Guinevere going to college classes, sunning herself with her family at Gun Lake. "What does she know about *la mafia*? What right do I have to want her to stay in this life with me where a gunman could storm her delivery room, eh?"

"Women in the life do not have to do much but stay silent and obey," Delfina said, suddenly over my shoulder.

I scowled at her, but only because I was so mired in my own turmoil that I had not been alert to her arrival.

"Not my women," I said firmly, raising a brow at my wayward, headstrong sister, who had insisted on going to college when our father disapproved, who had dated a woman last year even though it was tittered about behind lifted hands at church and in the piazzas. "My women do as they want because they know I will protect them. If worse comes to worst, they know how to protect themselves because I have made sure of it. Above all, they *know* what they want because they are smart enough to go after it."

"And you want Guinevere to go after you," Martina said, popping through the leaves with a childish grin, happy to have the opportunity to eavesdrop and meddle. "You want her to do more than just stay."

"*Si*," I answered, lifting my chin as if I expected to be punched and was bracing for the hit. It was what my father would have done if he had known I wanted to bring an *estraneo* into the family. "I want her to stand at my side, without secrets and without shame. My partner in all things."

"You don't think she is too innocent for that?" Carlotta asked, watching as Zacheo raced down the row of vines away from his older cousin to throw himself into Guinevere's side.

She laughed and swung him up into her arms, blowing a raspberry into his cheek.

"She pushed a man off a roof to save Ludo," I said without taking my eyes off her. "She would do worse to save me, to save any of you now that she knows you and has shared a meal with you. The biggest heart is the most ruthless of all because it knows no bounds when it has to protect those in need."

"That may be true, but you are *capo dei capi*. Let us not pretend what you do is entirely altruistic. I know you came home and took vows to save us, but you lie, murder, and steal almost every day, and you cannot tell us there isn't a part of you that loves it," Martina rejoined.

"There is. A large part," I admitted with a blasé shrug, like my own bloodlust and savagery did not alarm me sometimes. "But I have told her that, and she has seen it for herself more than once. I know her in ways you do not. She has darkness in her, seething and hungry. I just have to be patient and find a way to set it free."

"*Buona fortuna, fratello mio*," Carlotta said, squeezing my arm as she moved away with her crate of grapes to load them onto the waiting truck. "I have a feeling you will need it."

Stacci and Delfina laughed, bumping shoulders as they took their own wares to the truck behind their elder sister.

But Martina lingered, her gaze a warm weight on my cheek like a cupped hand.

"I do not think you need luck," she whispered to me in Italian. "Guinevere is too curious about the world, too hungry for experience, to be satisfied with the norm. Look at her. She fell in love with a mafioso eleven years her senior who never made light of his dark side, even if she did not know the extent of your underworld career. She sees you and she wants you, Raffa."

"Then why the face?"

She pursed her lips. "You told us earlier this morning that Guinevere's sister was involved with the Albanians. She mentioned when she was last here that her father forbade her from ever setting foot in Italia. Why do you think that is? Maybe she has secrets just as dangerous as your own."

It was not an unfair comment, though the idea of Guinevere keeping secrets from me did not sit right. She was honest, my Vera, straight through to the bone, even when she was deluding herself into thinking she was not aroused by the very thing she claimed to be repulsed by.

"Ludo is checking out her parents," I confessed in a hushed voice as I turned my attention back to the vines. "John Stone was originally from Italy, but all we know is that his given first name was Mariano Giovanni. Though Ludo has already discovered her mother, Elizabeth, was born in Albania."

Martina sucked a breath in through her teeth, thoughts turning like gears behind her dark eyes. "Does Leo know? He warned you that she could be a plant, and I know we thought he was being ridiculously paranoid, but Raffa . . . Italian and Albanian parents? When both are involved in our troubles?"

"It does not look good," I admitted, my head jerking up at the sound of Guinevere's shriek as Maximo, Vitale, and Mattia joined Zacheo in pulling her to the ground for a tickle war. "But you have spent time with her—do you really think she is capable of such duplicity? To seduce me to destroy me and mine?" The idea was so absurd I almost could not speak it without laughing, and there was nothing much to laugh at. "You think she was waiting in the grass at the side of a random Tuscan country road to throw herself into the path of my Ferrari so that we could meet?"

Martina's jaw flexed. "Well, no. You are not the only one who fell in love with her in the summer. But this is too strange for coincidence, no?"

"No," I agreed. "There is something there. A connection between Gemma, at least, and the Albanians and maybe the Grecos. Otherwise, why would they have her cross? The man in the tower told her that he was a friend. I do not like the idea of someone trying to get to Guinevere because of Gemma."

"You think she could have owed the Albanians drug money," Martina surmised. "Not a bad possibility. It's hard to imagine a sister of Guinevere's doing something so foolish."

I arched a brow. "She is more reckless than she would like anyone to think. I just have to prove it to her."

Martina watched me watch Guinevere for a moment and then clucked her tongue. "You have thirty minutes until dinner, and the sun is already dipping. No one will notice if you go off together. We can discuss business tonight when we have finished here."

"I told her the next time we touched it would have to be because she begged me," I explained. "I will not go to her."

"No," Martina mused, her eyes pinned over my shoulder. "But I think she is coming to you."

I turned my head again to track Guinevere as she made her way up the row of vines two over from where I stood, walking north, farther up the hill. Just as I was about to respond to Martina, Guinevere turned, her gaze locking unerringly with mine across the dozens of yards between us.

"*Vieni*," she mouthed clearly before turning on her heel and moving deeper into the vines.

My mouth went dry when she untied her apron and dropped it to the ground behind her, and my heart almost stopped as she reached the top of the incline and flipped one of her buttoned straps open and over her shoulder so that material gaped between her shoulders and—no doubt—at the front.

She disappeared over the crest without looking back.

But I was already stalking after her, thinking that my little fawn was smart enough to lure a predator into any trap.

The air was heavy with the sweetness of ripe fruit and the sharp tang of the sunbaked limestone protecting the bases of the vines. I cut through the field on quick strides, eating up the space impatiently, eager to get my hands on Guinevere once again. The thought of her seducing me with my family and friends only a field away was making me half hard already, but when I conquered the hill and started down the slope, I did not find her waiting for me.

Instead, she had paused a handful of yards down the row, on her tiptoes, the hem of her skirt rucked up in her hands to expose her slim, pale legs. Her dress gaped open on one side, revealing the edge of a pale breast topped with a hard nipple the same shade as the red wine grape stains saturating my hands. As soon as I caught sight of her, a wicked grin curved her mouth, and she took off, sprinting through the vines away from me.

Without hesitation, I followed.

Leaves whapped against my shoulders as I raced down the narrow gap between trunks. My heart was sprinting even faster than my body, churning blood so hard through my veins it burned. Or maybe it was the violent edge of desire that heated me through to the bone as I chased after my *cerbiatta*. There was something primal and unbelievably erotic about having to hunt her down and earn her capitulation. Sweat broke out on my brow, and my erection pressed uncomfortably against my trousers as I ate up the space between us.

Finally, blood roaring in my ears, I was close enough to swipe at her.

My fingers passed through the ends of her silken hair, and she laughed.

Bright and crystalline like a nymph leading a god on a merry chase, intoxicated by the unusual power shift.

A growl sneaked up my throat and rent the air a second before I reached for her again, lunging to wrap both arms around her small waist, encompassing it entirely. Our joint momentum carried us forward to the ground, but I twisted to take the brunt of the fall, landing on my shoulder and back with Guinevere plastered to my front. Her breath whooshed out of her in a rush of exhilarated laughter. The thick, dark length of her hair curtained our faces, blocking out what remained of the sun at the base of the vines. In the shadows, her smile glowed.

"Well, I have hunted you down," I rumbled, arching up to nip at her chin. "Now do I get to enjoy the spoils?"

"I think you'll find it was me who hunted *you*," she corrected haughtily, gathering my hands away from her hips to pin them above my head in the grass. "I was the one who set the trap. You were just the *uomo sciocco* who ran headlong into it."

Pride and warmth crowded inside my chest, making it momentarily hard to breathe. It did something to me to hear her call me silly again and to know she was comfortable enough with me to play coy once more. "What are you insinuating?"

"I watched you play with your nephews all day, chat with your sisters, and help some of the elderly townsfolk with their work. A man with money and power like you would never have to do an honest day's work in his life if he didn't want to, and yet I saw you tend to each bundle of grapes you clipped as if it was a religious experience." She paused to dip closer to me, an elbow in the ground on either side of my head, her nose near enough to bump mine. When she spoke, it was through a smile that made her dimples flash. "I recognized you today. As the man I used to know, the one I . . . liked very much."

Her fingers tightened on my wrists, pressing my hands deeper into the earth as her expression shuttered.

"It helped to see that side of you, that sweetness you like to pretend isn't there. It . . . it reminded me that I have the same tendency, but reversed. I was raised to be a good person, but the truth is, everyone has a little darkness, and I do more than most. I-I killed a man yesterday, Raffa." She sucked in a quivering breath, and I drew the tip of my nose down the line of hers to give her comfort. "And I think I would do it again. To save Ludo or Martina or Zacheo or . . . or you."

Then, so quiet I almost did not catch it even though she was practically speaking the words into my mouth, she added, "Especially you.

"I can't say I'll stay," she whispered against my lips. "I can't say I'm suddenly okay with any of this. But I also can't deny that being with you is *il mio posto felice*. My happy place. That while your life and you are clearly dangerous, I never feel safer than when I am near you. And I'm so tired, Raffa. I've been tired since I left you in August, and now I feel it straight through to my bones. I don't know enough about the life of a camorrista to commit to the *capo dei capi*, but I am willing to let my Raffa convince me to stay, if he can. So please"—she paused, but only to suck in a deep breath and adjust her tone to be as firm as iron—"make me beg for you."

Before I could reply, her mouth was sealed over mine, tongue pressing firmly between my teeth to rub sinuously against my own. I let her take the lead for a second, stunned and aroused, with the knife's edge of hope pressed to my throat so that I could barely breathe.

Convince me.

Make me beg.

Oh, I could do that. If keeping Guinevere with me was only contingent on fucking her brains out, I had no doubt of my victory.

It was the other unavoidable issues that whispered insidiously into my ear like the devil on one shoulder. *Can you keep her safe? Can she really love the monster beneath your mask? Can she withstand the cruelties of your dark world?*

I banished the voice and let my instincts, roused by the chase, overcome me.

With a snarl against her plush lips, I thrust my tongue over hers and canted my hips, throwing my bigger body so Guinevere slid off my hips and I could roll over on top of her seamlessly. She groaned at the display of strength and tried to sink her hands into my hair.

"No." My voice rasped harshly between us as I reared up to pin her hands as she'd done mine. "You wanted me to make you beg, *cacciatrice*, and you will get what you wish for."

I adjusted us slightly so that we lay diagonally across the narrow expanse of grass with our hands resting at the edge of a trunk. Without speaking, I raised her hands to curl around the wood.

"Do not move them," I instructed her, watching as her eyes blew straight to black, mouth parting on a soft pant. "If you do, I will have to spank you again . . . though for a greedy girl like you, I am not sure that is a punishment."

"No," she agreed, tongue dipping out to touch her lower lip in a little tease. "It's not."

I pressed a hand to her mouth. "Do not speak unless it is to beg me for more, *cacciatrice*."

She nodded before I moved my hand away to unbutton the other strap of her dress and peel the fabric down to her hips. Exposed, her nipples beaded in the cooling air as the sun kissed the edge of the green Tuscan hills. I ducked to take one into my mouth, sucking hard and testing the furled flesh with my teeth until she squirmed.

"*Stai ferma*," I ordered against her wet breast. Be still.

She released a breathy moan of protest but instantly relaxed for me. The alpha animal inside me practically roared at her supplication and immediately took advantage. I lowered myself between her thighs, lifting the heavy linen skirt until it rested above her hips before pushing her legs as wide as they would go. Only a thin pair of white silk ruffled panties obscured her beautiful *figa* from view.

With a light snarl, I rent them off with my teeth.

Guinevere gasped, hips canting up toward my mouth as if the idea of my teeth so close to her sensitive flesh aroused her. I tested the theory by biting softly into the tender meat on the inside of her thighs, leaving impressions like stamps of possession in her pale skin.

I leaned back, braced on my forearms between her thighs to draw my thumb down the center of her cunt, revealing its wet, pink center. Moisture pooled at her entrance, and I slicked it up to her clit with the pad of my finger, rubbing light, tight circles over the nub until I could feel the tremor of her barely restrained vibrations under my hand.

"*Scopami, per favore*," Guinevere gasped, arching up into my touch.

Fuck me, please.

In the deepening shadows, she seemed like a beautiful illusion, something flickering between here and some otherworldly there, half in my realm and half without.

I gripped her hips a little too hard, flexing my fingers into the muscles of her pert ass.

"*Non ancora*," I said with that cold edge of cruelty I knew made her toes curl. "Not yet. You have not nearly begun to beg for it."

With that, I dipped my head and dragged my tongue from her leaking entrance to the top of her pussy, sucking at the hot, swollen crest of her until she cried out senselessly. The vine leaves rustled in the breeze, cooling as the sun disappeared degree by degree over the edge of the hilly valley, but Guinevere's skin was hot, almost burning to the touch.

I had set a fire inside her that I intended to nurture into an inferno and see through until she was nothing but ash in my hands, ready to be reborn into something new.

"Raffa," she cried weakly as I fucked into her heat with my tongue, curling it inside her in a way that made her hips leap like a struck live wire. "Raffa, *dio mio*, *per favore*, please!"

"Tell me, *cerbiatta*, do you want to break apart on my tongue?" I asked her, my voice a deep, broken rasp as arousal threatened to strangle me. "I will lick you clean and share the sweet taste of your *figa* with you when I work myself inside this tight cunt."

I did not wait for her answer. Instead, I twisted two thick fingers inside her, pressing them along her front wall as I used my mouth like a weapon against her clit, sucking while lashing my tongue over the bundle of nerves.

I held her body down with one forearm, and she almost choked on a sharp breath, body bowing, fingernails digging audibly into the bark of the Chianti tree, and then shuddered apart on a broken wail of completion.

"Raffa, Raffa, Raffa," she sang like some ancient invocation, a spell that wove itself through the very fabric of my being and eradicated whatever was left of the civilized man inside me.

I reared back to undo my belt and trousers with one hand while the other still pumped inside her convulsing pussy, driving her orgasm on and on until she was a writhing, serpentine creature locked at the base of the vines. A *vipera*, dangerously beautiful, utterly toxic to a mere mortal.

She was still coming when I replaced my fingers with the head of my weeping cock and drove relentlessly inside her.

"Fuck," she cried out, her hips flinching away from me even as her head crashed back into the ground on a fierce moan of pleasure. "Oh my God, Raffa."

"There are no gods for us but each other," I reminded her through clenched teeth as I started to fuck her brutally, hauling her legs up over my thighs so they were splayed wide around my torso, held open for me to watch as I wedged my thick cock inside her mouthwateringly pretty little pussy. "When you pray for help, it is me who will come. When you ask for your deepest wishes, it is me who will fulfill them. When you want to come, Guinevere, it is me who will drive you out of your mind with pleasure. *Capisci*?"

"*Si, si, quello che vuoi*," she said in a slurring rush, driving her hips down onto mine, small breasts swaying with each thrust. "*Meus Rex Infernus*. *Raffa mio*. Please, just fuck me harder."

There she was. My insatiable girl. A wanton, vibrant temptress only ever for me.

Possessive pride surged through my veins, tightening my balls and the base of my spine. I wanted to come inside her and watch my seed leak out that reddened, lightly gaping hole. I wanted to come on her belly, her breasts, rub it in so that we would both know she wore me beneath her dress when we went back to dinner. I wanted to brand her inside and out so that she would know the truth I was enslaved to . . .

She was mine as much as I was hers, and there was no reality—hers on the side of good, mine on the side of bad, or any other—where the two of us were not meant to be together.

This was just the first of many ways I would show her.

I lifted one of her slim legs higher, propping it onto my shoulder so I could fuck into her more deeply. Her eyes screwed shut, lavender lids fluttering, mouth open in a soft O as she trembled and clutched tighter to the tree for more leverage to grind back onto me with every thrust.

The force of our coupling made the vines sway and overripe grapes drop from overhead. I bent to retrieve one that rolled between her breasts, breaking the thick, slightly bitter skin between my teeth and then rubbing the purple-red skin into her nipple until it was stained the same color.

Guinevere shivered violently as I did the same to the other side and then drew it into my mouth with a hard suck. The sound of my balls meeting her drenched pussy was loud in the twilight quiet, underscored by the rustling leaves and the harsh rasp of our breath.

When I looked up into her eyes as I ground deep and felt the tremor of her oncoming orgasm, she had a ripe wine grape between her teeth, an offering she made by canting her head up toward me.

I bit into her lower lip first just to feel the clutch of her pussy around me and then ate the fruit out of her mouth, the two of us sharing the sharp, tannin-rich juice between our lips. The kiss was almost sloppy, panting breaths and punctuating moans.

"I love this," she confessed onto my tongue, like a wafer placed there during a religious ceremony. "I missed this so much."

"*Anche io, mia stella cadente*," I told her. "*La mia vita è tornata nell'oscurità quando te ne sei andata.*"

I missed you too, my shooting star. My life returned to darkness when you left.

"*E guardati adesso*," I continued as I collared her throat in one hand and then used my thumb to smear the grape juice across her bottom lip. "*Non sei mai stata più bella di quando sei mia.*"

And look at you now, never more beautiful than when you are mine.

A groan rattled through her throat as her tongue chased my thumb across her lips. I bent my head to nip at her ear as I shifted my free hand to the place we were joined, splitting my fingers across the broad stretch of me inside her, grinding the heel of my palm into her clit.

"Come for me now," I demanded, pausing to drag my teeth down the line of her neck. "Take your pleasure from me, and then I will fill you up with so much cum you will be leaking for hours. Squirming at the dinner table as it drips down your thighs. Only you and I knowing you are my good, sweet little slut."

Guinevere choked on her scream as my teeth fixed to her throat, sucking hard enough to bruise, and she came as if she had been struck by a lightning bolt, juddering in my arms, robbed of breath and filled with electricity.

"*Brava*," I praised as she came, finally giving myself over to my own pleasure as it seared like an electrical current from her flesh into mine. The ecstasy was so keen, it ripped through me almost painfully, and my vision fizzed out, white blurs and black stars behind my lids.

This was it.

Raw, primal connection between two souls.

She could say she did not trust me, but enticing me to hunt her down and fuck her into the grass was not an act between two strangers. She could say she did not love me, but as she released the wood trunk and sank her trembling hands into my hair to hold my cheek pressed tight to her breast, over her beating heart, I thought that too must be a lie.

I could hear it in that very pulse, an echo of something like my name in its rhythm.

"Raffa," she said, as if she could hear it too.

There were tears in her voice, roughened by pleasure, waterlogged with confusion and remembered sorrow.

"Guinevere," I murmured back before pressing a kiss to her breastbone, running my thumb over the faint scar from her kidney transplant curving over her lower abdomen. *"Cacciatrice mia."*

"Not yet," she whispered so low, I thought she was speaking to herself. "But maybe one day."

CHAPTER TWELVE

Guinevere

We returned in time for dinner, but there was no way to get back to the house to tidy up without being seen, so we did our best to make each other presentable. It must not have worked well, because there were a few low whistles and Italian catcalls when we emerged from the shadowy vines into the lights of the terrace, where five long tables had been placed end to end and filled with most of the community members who had helped out that day.

Raffa quelled the calls with one superior look, and placed a comforting hand on my low back to lead me to one end of the table, where the head chair remained empty, along with one to its left. Martina winked at me as I took the seat beside her, and Renzo gave me an assessing stare from where he sat across from me on Raffa's right. Carmine, next to him, waggled his brows.

"You have a grape stain," Ludo said in his monotone, face utterly expressionless as he motioned to his own chest. "Just there."

I peered down at my white dress and noticed the vague mottled pink handprint over my dress. As we were getting dressed, Raffa had collected a handful of grapes and crushed them in his palm, then made me laugh as he lifted his fist to let me drink the juice dripping down.

After, he had tugged me into a searing kiss that had left me with even fewer working brain cells than I had after two spectacular orgasms.

So I hadn't really noted the way he'd used that grape-stained hand to fondle me through the fabric.

I cut a look toward the head of the Romano clan, who only smiled mildly at me as he reached for the glass of wine already set out for him and lifted it into the air.

"Attenzione, amici miei." Raffa's voice carried easily over the cacophony of diners dispersed over the extra-long table, and people immediately quieted. "Thank you for being here with us today on the first day of the harvest. My family has worked this land and produced Tuscan wine for generations. Even in our darkest days, the vines have brought us solace." His gaze dropped to mine, a slight tip to the edge of his firm mouth the only nod to what had just happened between us among those very vines. "There is nothing more important to me in this life than protecting and nurturing my family. Every single one of you is a part of the fabric of this family, and this family is the reason I am here today. Thank you for everything.

"*Salute*," he called out, raising a chorus of the same as everyone lifted their wineglasses at the toast and then sipped from their Tenuta Romano wine.

Only, when I lifted the glass to my lips, it was sparkling grape juice instead of wine.

Something in my chest overinflated, making it ache.

Of course Raffa would remember I couldn't really drink. Of course he would have taken the time to make Angela and the other organizers aware so that I wouldn't have to sit awkwardly without a drink or stick to water when there was cause for celebration.

Raffa had told me from the beginning that he wasn't the kind of man to play the hero, but his actions were almost always contrary to his words. He'd taken care of me since the beginning, and even when I'd run from him, he'd seen a way to take care of me all the way in Michigan.

Coaxing him away from the group this evening hadn't been a well-thought-out plan. I hadn't even consciously decided to lure him away to seduce him. When I'd watched him chatting with his sisters, interacting with his community, and laughing with his mother, something seismic had occurred in my chest. A tectonic shifting of morals and values I had clung to for years.

It wasn't that I suddenly understood why Raffa lived life the way he did as the head of a criminal syndicate or that I was instantly okay with the myriads of decisions he'd made to get there and stay there. It still disturbed me to think of the bodies that lay littered throughout his past, the blood that had seeped beneath the skin of his hands to stain even his bones red.

It was that I realized something fundamental about myself in relation to him.

I was willing to bury my morals alive in a deep grave for just one more kiss.

Eager to cut out the tongue of my conscience to hear him call me his *cerbiatta* or *stella cadente* just one more time.

Happy to blind myself to his flaws and failings completely if it meant feeling those calloused, wide-palmed hands on me just once more before I died.

This was my ugly truth. The one I'd been trying to hide from since the realization of who Raffa was the night after the San Lorenzo party.

I was willing to lower myself to the dark depths of his underworld if it meant I could keep the flame of this brilliant love alive inside my chest.

It was chilling, really, to acknowledge that about myself after a lifetime of being told to follow the rules, be a good girl, watch what I said and how I acted so no one would judge.

But it was also frighteningly freeing.

And empowering.

Walking through the vines and feeling the predatory eyes of Raffa stalking my every step had encouraged me to embrace the sizzle of wicked fantasy burning the edges of my brain. I'd started running without thinking it through, my blood rushing loudly in my ears but not loud enough to cancel out the thud of his footsteps gaining ground behind me.

Being hunted like that was strangely erotic. Knowing he wanted to catch me because I was a cherished prize, that when he did he would undress me, devour me, give me what the French called the "little death."

It felt like a death, coming under those grape-stained hands knowing they'd frequently been tainted by real blood, knowing as they parted my thighs gently that they had taken lives violently, knowing as he praised me for taking him inside me that he had threatened men more than twice my size into submission . . .

It was something out of my most depraved fantasies. Thoughts I only ever allowed myself at night without a stitch of light to lend them any kind of reality.

And there I was, hunted and fucked open beneath a clear sky, just a hillside away from a group of sixty people toiling away in the vines.

When I cried out, a small, wanton part of me hoped they would hear it.

"Did you have fun on your walk in the vineyard?" Martina's voice pulled me from my revelry. I blushed at the look on her face, dark eyes sparkling, brows raised as she took a sip of wine.

"It was stimulating," I responded in the blandest voice I could summon.

We stared at each other for a moment before we both burst into laughter.

"You are not so much the *ingenua* anymore, are you, Vera?"

"No," I agreed. "Though I'm not sure exactly what I am anymore, to be honest."

"You have time to find out," she said, but the smile fell from her lips, and her eyes were matte black, the color of a gun. "You should take it. All the time you need. Because once you make a decision about this kind of thing, there is no going back. Trust me."

"I know. The problem is, I feel like I made the decision before I knew exactly what I was agreeing to," I admitted, sneaking a glance at Raffa, who had his head bent to Renzo, nodding at something intently.

Martina hummed, studying the quality of the wine by hovering it above a candle flame. It shone darkly, like stale blood.

"I was married before. Did you know this?"

"No, I had no idea." It was hard to picture the strong, no-bullshit Martina with anyone but Renzo, even though I knew they weren't really together.

"I fell in love when I was very young, just sixteen. Umberto hung around with some of the local crew, and he was beautiful, with hair that curled over his head." Her voice had a distant quality, a voice-over playing over an old memory. "I used to put my finger inside the curls and pull. We got married when I was eighteen, and I moved from my parents' home into one he bought for us. We both joined the *forze armate italiane*, him for the prestige he sought and me because I had always been drawn to combat.

"I realized quickly that I didn't know Umberto like I thought. Seeing him after school for a few hours a handful of days in the week and on weekends was not a large snapshot into what he was really like. I had not seen him stressed or in pain or slept with him after a particularly bad day."

She paused to take a long draft from her glass and then carefully set it down to show me her left ring finger. The shape of it was wrong, crooked like the gnarled trunk of a tree.

"It wasn't until Raffa left for England that he started to get physical with me. We had moved away from town to a military base in the south, and there was no one, now that Raffaele was gone, to check in on us. Renzo and Carmine had gone with him. The first time he hurt me, it was because the butcher I went to every week called out hello to me when I went for dinner with my husband. Umberto was livid. He thought I was having an affair. He broke my finger so that the ring would never come off."

I hissed at the horror of the story, reaching out to run my own finger down hers. There was no ring at the base anymore, not even a tan line.

"The emotional and physical abuse started to get worse when I was promoted over him in the ranks. Umberto was mean and impatient, and you can be mean in the military, but impatience never goes over well. The second time I was promoted over him, he beat me so badly, I passed out and woke up in the bathtub with a broken arm, clavicle, and eye socket."

"Martina," I murmured, clasping her hand in both of mine.

It was almost impossible to comprehend someone as strong as Martina being abused, but I knew it happened to many women across the globe. I made myself stay still and silent for the rest of her story even though feminine rage surged like bile up my throat.

"I called Raffa that day," she continued, staring down at our hands and then offering me a thin smile. "He knew the moment I said hello that something was wrong, mostly because I had been avoiding his calls until then. Somehow, I didn't cry when I told him what Umberto had done."

"He must have been furious," I murmured. "What did he do?"

"He told me to check into a hotel, where a doctor he trusted would meet me to do an exam. He said not to waste time on packing anything, to get out of the house as fast as I could. When the doctor came, he was holding a plane ticket and my passport. I caught a night flight out of Naples to London, and Renzo and Carmine were waiting for me at the airport."

At my frown, she huffed out a breathy laugh. "Raffa wasn't there because he was already on a flight to Naples. By the time he came home two days later, I had been honorably discharged from the armed forces, and Umberto was dead."

Her stare burned into mine, holding my gaze without flinching. She had her chin tipped, eyes narrowed, shoulders squared as if she was daring me to come for her or Raffa.

"Depending on your perspective, Raffa could be seen as the hero or the villain of that story," she said in a low hiss that undercut the cacophony of chatter at the table. "The truth is, he's often both, or one in order to be the other. Life is so much more complicated than slotting people into boxes, don't you think?"

I swallowed, my dry throat clicking. "Yes."

"Don't give him hope if you don't mean it," she said, kinder this time even though she took her hand from mine. "He deserves someone who is willing to be both the hero and the villain for him as well."

I nodded a little woodenly as Martina turned away to accept a platter of *papa al pomodoro*. She ignored me completely as she filled her plate, and I mutely did the same, layering the ceramic with fragrant Tuscan delicacies that made my mouth water even as my stomach was tied in knots.

"Stai bene, cerbiatta mia?" Raffa asked, sliding a palm over my thigh under the table.

I nodded, summoning a thin facsimile of a smile to my face. "Yes, tired. But happy to be a part of this."

Raffa's answering grin was small but genuine, a closed-mouth curling of that firm pink mouth. Without thinking, I reached out to press my thumb to his lips.

When he arched his brow, I answered the unspoken question. "I like the shape of your smile."

"*Bene*," he responded against my finger. "Because this smile is only ever for you."

My heart throbbed like a wound in my chest at his words. His eyes crinkled as the smile deepened before he bit the tip of my thumb and then leaned back to raise his wineglass.

Even when he turned to talk to Renzo again, he kept one hand on my thigh, eating his dinner with only the right.

After everyone had finished, a group stood from the table to set up a makeshift stage for their band. I watched in awe as five men set up and started to play using an interesting mix of guitar, bass, flute, drum, and violin. To my surprise and joy, Angela Romano stood up to take the microphone, launching into a smoky version of "O sole mio."

"May I interest you in a dance?"

I blinked before looking over my shoulder at Leo, who stood with his hand extended and a slightly sheepish smile on his face. Raffa squeezed my thigh, drawing my attention, and inclined his head as if to encourage me to dance with his friend if I wanted to.

I didn't, not really, but I figured it would be rude to refuse, so I slipped my hand into Leo's and stood up.

He grinned as he led me to the section of the stone terrace where a few other people had started to dance, including Stacci and Emiliano. With sinuous grace, Leo pulled me into his arms and moved us into a simple box step.

He smelled good, like expensive cologne, and even among the candle flames and twinkling strands of lights poorly illuminating the space, his blond hair glittered like gold. I was sure most people thought Leo was handsome and charming, but I was still wary around him. Though I knew he was making an effort for Raffa's sake, I still wondered if he didn't like me very much. He had been kind to me during the grape picking earlier that day, trying to joke with me about Italian traditions and American slang, but the rapport was not as natural as it was between me and the rest of Raffa's crew.

Maybe we had too much baggage to ever truly be friends for our own sake instead of Raffa's.

It was strange that Raffa, dark and intense looking, with a permanent scowl and guarded personality, could have made me feel so much more comfortable even from the beginning.

"Raffa told me he calls you his fawn," he said with a wan smile. "But that recently, he is trying to convince you to become a huntress."

"Yes. He wants me to stay, and the only way that is possible is if I embrace the darkness in myself as well as him. In order to survive all this," I said with an inelegant wave of my hand to encompass everything and everyone around us.

His small smile was twisted. "He's right. I called the woman I love my little dove. But doves are too easily caught in cages and kept as pets. You want to be something strong enough to break free."

I could imagine Leo calling his lover something so romantic. Despite our chilly beginnings, it was clear to see he was handsome and personable enough to have nearly any woman he wanted.

"I wanted to apologize again for the night in Impruneta," he said quietly, real distress marring his brow. "I truly thought you would find something lovely on top of the bell tower, and instead you found only danger and death."

I shivered at the memory of killing that man, the lack of resistance as my shove forced him back over the half wall into open air.

"You are very brave," he continued solemnly. "Brave enough to stand with Raffa against whatever comes, I think. He deserves that."

I swallowed thickly, because he was right about Raffa's merit, but I was not so sure I was strong enough to take whatever chaos would come, even though I wanted to be. The face of the man on the bell tower haunted my dreams.

"Ludo told me your family is originally from Tuscany."

I was surprised by the non sequitur but nodded. "My father's family, though I don't know exactly from where. My mother's people were Albanian."

"Is that what brought you to Italy? A desire to know where you come from?" His voice was innocent, but his body was stiff as we danced.

He was a big guy, leaner than Raffa but just as tall, and it hurt my neck to look up at him, so I settled for looking straight ahead instead. His shirt was unbuttoned to the top of his chest, and the corner of a tattoo scrawled in black ink peeked out beneath the blue fabric.

"Mostly," I agreed.

He waited for me to go on, but I didn't.

Leo hadn't liked me from the start, so there was no way I was opening up to him.

"Ludo was having trouble searching for information," he continued conversationally. "He said you only knew your father's birth name was Mariano Giovanni. I suggested he might have translated his Italian last name to the English equivalent."

"Oh, that's actually a good idea," I said, brightening. "Sasso isn't that common a last name either."

"No," he agreed. "It isn't. But there are many ways to say 'stone' in Italian. *Sasso, roccia, masso*—"

"May I cut in?"

Raffa's uncle and Leo's adoptive father, Tonio, stood beside us with a pleasant smile on his creased face. The only resemblance he had to Leo was the same pale-blue eyes; otherwise, he was a blandly handsome man, with a tanned complexion and a thin mouth that became lovely when he smiled. He might once have shared Leo's golden hair, but his pate was bald and shiny now, speckled with age spots.

We hadn't spoken properly at all, so I was surprised by his request, but Leo seemed overly irritated by it. He tried to move me into dancing again as he shook his head at his dad.

"No, we were just in the middle of enjoying Angela."

As if on cue, Raffa's mother finished the song and bowed at the influx of applause before handing the microphone over to another woman.

"She's finished, and I would love a dance with the woman who has stolen my nephew's heart," he insisted, stepping closer so that Leo had to let me go in order to move out of the way.

I let Tonio take my hand and touch my hip, keeping a respectable distance between us as a new song started, and he swept me deftly away from his son, who stood staring at us from the dance floor with his jaw ticking.

"You speak Italian, don't you, *cara*?" he asked, and then shifted into the other language when I nodded. "Well, it is good to finally have a moment to get to know the woman who has taken Raffa by storm."

I arched a brow in an imitation of Raffa's haughty disbelief. "Hardly by storm. He helped me when I was down on my luck, and we became . . . friends."

"Friends do not look at one another the way he looks at you," Tonio said with a sly smile and touch to the side of his nose.

When I opened my mouth to argue, he spun me purposefully so that I could see Raffa standing by the side of the dance floor with his arms crossed, ostensibly talking to a few young men from the village as his eyes tracked me darkly across the terrace.

He looked voracious, like a man who had not eaten in weeks, despite the fact that we'd just finished a Tuscan feast.

Even though he'd just filled me with cum an hour earlier, the remnants of which were still damp on the insides of my thighs beneath my dress.

"You are the first woman who has ever stood a chance of taking him away from it all," Tonio continued, as if we were having a two-sided conversation.

I frowned, stumbling a bit so that I stepped on his foot. "I'm sorry."

"Do not worry, dear," he said with a big smile. "It can't be surprising to hear what you must know. Raffa would give it all up for you, I'm sure."

Honestly, the idea of Raffa renouncing the Camorra had never even occurred to me. It didn't seem likely the *capo dei capi* would up and leave his organization for some pretty, young American *or* that the camorristi would let him just walk away. He knew too much. In books and movies, people like Raffa who tried to leave the life were always killed before they could touch their toes to the white sand beach of their happily ever after.

"I'll have to disagree with you on that," I said finally, happy that my voice gave nothing of my inner turmoil away.

Because now that he'd planted the seed, I couldn't help but think of a different reality where Raffa moved to the States with me. Maybe he took over Dad's firm with me eventually, the two of us expanding it and making it into something of our own. Maybe we started fresh somewhere away from my parents, in California or North Carolina, somewhere warm enough to appeal to my Italian boyfriend.

Boyfriend.

That thought alone burst the fragile bubble of fantasy.

Raffa was not my boyfriend. He could be no one's boyfriend. He was a thirty-four-year-old mafioso. To think he could be something so . . . *trite* and juvenile as my boyfriend was ridiculous. To think that he could just uproot his life from Tuscany, with his family, friends, and entire underworld empire, was absolutely idiotic.

And despite what Tonio obviously thought of me, I was not an *idiota*.

"Raffa would no sooner leave his family behind than he would cut off his own hand," I replied dryly, shooting Tonio an unimpressed look. "Clearly, you do not know him well if you think he would give all that up for someone he met a few months ago."

He stared down at me with those narrow, watery blue eyes, and I wondered how old he was, because he seemed ancient and omnipotent in that moment, something peering out at me from the dark with knowledge I'd never have.

"Clearly, you do not know his heart as well as you should, given it is in your possession," he countered softly, a disappointed twist to his mouth as he dropped my hands abruptly and stepped away from me. "If you asked, he would give up everything for you. Raffa never wanted this life, and now that he has a tangible reason to leave it, you are too cowardly to give it to him."

He walked away from me without another word.

I decided then and there I did not like the di Conte family very much.

"What did you say to upset Uncle Tonio?" Raffa asked, appearing between swirling bodies at my side.

Before I could respond, he was taking me into his arms, flattening me against his torso with a hand pressed firmly at the base of my spine while the other took my hand and started to swirl me around the terrace.

I laughed breathlessly as he pushed me out under his arm in a twirl and then hauled me back into his side.

"He seems to think you're in love with me," I said, rolling my eyes. "Your whole family seems to have an opinion on our relationship."

"They are Italian," he said with a shrug. "It is our way to be nosy about each other's love lives. We invented the soap opera, you know." He smiled slightly as I laughed. "Besides, Uncle Tonio has a soft heart. He adopted Leo legally, but he also fostered half a dozen of our *soldati* when they were boys, Michele and Philippe among them. He was also the one who encouraged me to go to school in England, even though Aldo forbade it." He paused, dipping closer to run his nose along my hairline. "And Guinevere, you must know, because I have said so in both English and Italian, I do love you."

The words dropped through the center of my chest like a stone in a pond, sending ripples throughout my body to the ends of my fingers and my toes.

"It is you who does not love me," he murmured quietly, ducking his head to nip at my ear. "Because you fear only a monster could love another monster."

"True monsters aren't capable of love at all," I retorted before I could think of how he might take my words.

His flinch was imperceptible, but I felt it against my body and ached for him.

"No," I said, the word harsh between us. "I meant you cannot be a monster when I so clearly see how much you love your friends and family."

And me, I thought but didn't have the courage to say.

"Your uncle was implying that if I asked you to give it all up for me, you would," I confessed, because I didn't want to have a secret with the older man and because I wanted to see how he might react to the possibility.

Raffa's brows lifted, a lock of dark hair curving over his forehead as he stared down at me. "Mmm, I had not thought about that."

I was startled into laughing. "You know, I thought the same thing. It doesn't seem like a practical solution."

"Practical? No. Not at all. But something I would have to seriously think about if you asked it of me," he mused as if I'd asked him something casual, whether he wanted sugar in his coffee.

"Are you kidding?"

He blinked slowly as he puzzled through something and then shook his head as he looked into my eyes again. "No, I do not *kid.* Are you asking me?"

Adrenaline sluiced through me like acid, chewing up my bones and muscles until I felt like I might dissolve into nothing.

"No," I said, more breath than voice. "I'm not asking."

"And I am not saying it would be possible," he returned easily. "But when I told you that whatever wish you made I would see done, I meant it."

"This is real life, and you are not a genie," I rebutted, an edge to my voice even I didn't understand. "You couldn't just . . . leave easy as you please from this life."

"You are right. It would take violence and planning. You would have to live with knowing I would kill many people who would try to come for us. Whatever happily ever after you might have imagined for yourself will never happen with me, Guinevere. Even in America, even living another life, I will always have a dark heart, and therefore we will always have a dark ever after. We will never be truly safe—no matter which life you think is best for yourself—as long as you are with me."

Suddenly exhausted, I stopped dancing and tugged my hand from Raffa's.

"Why is violence always the first answer with you?" I asked before turning on my heel and heading into the house.

There were people in the kitchen cleaning up and laughing, a couple in the room by the stairs making out heavily on the sofa, but I ignored them all to climb the stairs to my bedroom.

Behind me the clack of dress shoes followed.

I entered my room and tossed the door shut behind me only to have Raffa catch it in his hand and throw it closed once he entered after me.

"Why do you insist on being naive?" he demanded, his expression as fierce as that of a gladiator facing down three adversaries and a lion in the Colosseum. "You think your father escaped whatever hell he was running from in Italy without bloodshed? You do not think he was running away from his own sins?"

He stalked toward me. Automatically, I backed up until my knees hit the end of the bed and my momentum forced me to sit down. He kept a foot of space between us, but it felt superheated, the earth between us about to split apart.

"Do you think I dreamt as a boy of being some gangster with a gun and chains? Do you think this was what I aspired to when I went to Oxford? Sometimes life is cruel and we must be cruel in order to survive it, Guinevere. How can you, a survivor of your own kind of hell, condemn me for that?"

"I am not condemning you, Raffa," I said, surging to my feet so that we were pressed torso to torso and I had to drop my head back between my shoulders to snarl up at him. "I am just saying, if you wanted to, you could stop it. The killing, the lies, the criminality. You could come clean."

His laugh was harsh, like something put through a meat grinder.

"I have told you, I will never be clean. Even if I left it all behind and went with you to America, I would still have lived the life I did as a mafioso. The hands that touched you at night would never be unsoiled, and the soul you'd claim to love would never be without the darkness it needed to do what had to be done to protect my loved ones."

"You like it, then," I pressed, already knowing the truth but needing to hear it again anyway. My hand slapped over his heart. "The killing. The lies. Going against the law."

"I love it," he seethed, leering down at me with a snarl on his mouth that should have been terrifying but was instead bizarrely beautiful. "I love watching those who would hurt me and mine be snuffed out like a light. I go to bed easily each night knowing they won't come for any one of us ever again. I love being cleverer than the police and the government, sneering in their faces when they sniff around looking for tells they'll never find."

He lifted me in his arms so abruptly, I let out a cry. Suddenly, we were at eye level, his arm banded under my ass to keep me high enough to look into that seething, cold gaze, straight to the ninth circle of Dante's hell, where Satan himself reigned from his throne.

"I did not want this life, but there was a part of me born to thrive in it, and I am not capable of turning it off. I might be tempted to give up everything for you, *stella cadente*, but not when I am not sure if you love the real me. Dante spent his entire life worshipping a woman he did not really know, projecting onto her all the things he desired most in a partner because it was safe to do so. I will not be just an ideal to you."

He took my lower lip between his teeth in a savage bite that rent the skin and made blood pool between us. With his eyes open and locked to mine, he licked up the metallic tang and then slicked his tongue over mine to share the taste.

"I do not want a meek lover or a girl who is happy to turn a blind eye. I want someone brave and bold enough to take my hand even when it is blood soaked, even when what I do is wrong. If you cannot do that, Guinevere, I will go to the palazzo in Florence and stay away until I can be sure you are safe, and then I will send you home."

"I told you," I said with an edge of desperation, hands sinking into his hair when he tried to pull away. "I do not think you are a monster. I see the tenderness in you."

"But what if I am? A beautiful monster. And Guinevere," he whispered against my mouth. "What if you are too?"

His kiss tasted of blood and ash, something dark dredged up from the deep. I felt like Proserpina kissing Pluto, tasting life and death, riches and devastation, all in one set of beautifully formed lips.

Just as I was losing myself to the embrace, he tore his mouth from mine, sat me on the mattress, and planted one hand on my chest to push me down onto the bed.

By the time I landed, the door was closing firmly behind him, and I was left alone with the taste of blood and Raffa on my lips.

CHAPTER THIRTEEN

Raffa

When I went downstairs the next morning after a sleepless night, I was surprised to see Guinevere already awake and sparring with Ludo outside the kitchen window as I made an espresso. The gunshot wound had been a through and through without hitting any major organs, but he still had his side wrapped, and he was moving carefully to protect his left torso. It was not his first bullet, and it would not be his last. It was impossible to expect Ludo or any of my *soldati* to take any kind of bed rest unless they were unconscious or unable to walk.

"They do that every day," Carmine said as he trailed into the kitchen in an immaculate three-piece suit. Even I did not dress so formally at the villa, instead wearing trousers and a thin cashmere sweater the same color as the Chianti wine we had drunk last night.

I watched as Guinevere ducked under one of Ludo's meaty fists and planted a jab to his kidney. Even though I could not hear them, I could see Ludo laugh and give her a fist bump at the move. Beginning a new sequence, he seemed to be teaching her to climb a bigger opponent by bracing a foot on his thigh to get enough height to land a hit to his face.

"She mentioned she had taken some MMA classes in Michigan, but she seems proficient," I admitted as heat kindled in my gut.

She was fierce as hell in black spandex, taking on my *soldato* like she had been born to do it. Even though she was slight, she was quick, easily evading the bigger man's slower movements.

"Saw you have a tiff on the dance floor last night. Everything okay?"

I sighed, scrubbing a hand over my face before shooting him a look. "Why is it never easy with women?"

Carmine guffawed. "You find the answer to that question, you'd save a lot of men a lot of issues. Guinevere, though, well, you did it to yourself, boss. Should've been honest the moment you started to fall for her."

"It took me by surprise. I was in love before I could guard against it." I downed my espresso and turned away from the window. "Did you set up the meeting with Drita?"

"This afternoon at five," he confirmed. "You wanna head out now? Leo asked me to tell you he went into Rome for a meeting for the Romano Group today, so he's out."

"Where are Renzo and Martina?"

Carmine pulled a face that made me chuckle.

"Go knock on their door," I told him.

"I don't want to be within sixty feet of my brother in bed naked with Martina," he grumbled as he moved out of the kitchen to do as I asked.

I was still grinning when the front door crashed open and Guinevere darted inside, Ludo hot on her heels. She cried out in an approximation of a warrior as she spun sharply, leg raised to deliver a kick to Ludo's uninjured side. Only, he was ready for it, and because of her short stature, it was all too easy for him to clasp her foot and hold it hostage in the air.

My chuckle made them both pause, gazes snapping to mine.

"*Buongiorno, ragazzi*," I greeted them, crossing my arms as I leaned back against the counter.

"Oh," Guinevere said before blowing an errant lock of hair out of her face from where it had escaped her ponytail. "Good morning, Raffa."

"Boss," Ludo grunted, still holding Guinevere's foot.

"Let Vera go, Ludo. Ren, Martina, and I are heading out in twenty minutes, so you'll need to be working from here today."

He dropped her foot without a care, sliding out of her vicinity when she reached for him to balance herself. His faint snigger trailed after him as he climbed the stairs.

"Where are you going?" Guinevere asked, walking on her toes into the kitchen to pull a pitcher of water with lemon out of the fridge and pour herself a glass.

I watched, a little distracted, as she tipped her head back to gulp down the entire contents, her throat working the way it did when she swallowed around my cock.

"Firenze," I said, clearing my throat with a rasp. "I have work in the city."

She tilted her head, dashing the back of her hand over her wet mouth.

Cazzo, why was even that attractive?

"What kind of work?" she asked innocently enough, but there was calculation in those *occhi di cerbiatta*.

"The kind you do not want to hear about."

She had made that clear enough last night.

Her small white teeth clamped into her plush bottom lip. "Will you come back?"

"No," I said simply, because she knew why.

There was no way I could be in her orbit and not be drawn by the gravitational force of our shared attraction into kissing her, fucking her, loving her even more than I already did.

And I loved her enough that I felt it in my lungs with every breath I took.

"I'm coming with you," she announced, throwing her shoulders back pugnaciously. "To Florence. I haven't been back yet, and I would like to visit."

I arched a brow. "I have work in the city. I will not be able to join you. With someone after me, and by extension you, I do not relish the idea of sending you off into the city alone."

"I'll wait while you do your business," she offered hastily, and I had to wonder at her angle here.

Did she want to go into the city that badly, or was she reluctant to see me go?

"We leave in twenty minutes," I said, against my better judgment. "Will you be ready?"

In answer, she ran to me, raised to her toes to press a kiss to the hinge of my jaw, and whispered, "Thank you," before she darted up the stairs.

I pressed my fingers to the place her lips had touched and shook my head.

◆ ◆ ◆

It was almost impossible to keep my hands off Guinevere on the train to Florence. She was dressed in uncharacteristic black, a tight pair of trousers that tucked into black Ferragamo riding boots she'd borrowed from Delfina and a silk shirt that closed in a series of red ribbons from between her breasts to the bottom of her belly. I wanted to rip those bows open with one flick of my fingers, lay her out on the table in the first-class train car, and feast on her again until this rapacious hunger in my gut slackened.

We were only taking the train because of Guinevere, who had told Renzo and Carmine train travel was one of her favorite things.

Peaceful, she'd said wistfully while we waited for Ludo to bring the car around for us.

A quick change of plans, and Ludo was dropping us off at the local train station.

The look of delight on Guinevere's face was more than enough to warrant the irritation of traveling by train. Which did not help the aforementioned problem of keeping my hands off her, even though our relationship seemed to have hit an impasse.

Fortunately, we were surrounded by people, including Martina, Carmine, and Renzo. Carm was trying to help Guinevere improve on tresette, a complicated Italian card game, with the other two while I took calls and responded to the dozens of emails I had not seen to yesterday because of the harvest celebrations.

One of the calls was to the deputy director of the DIA, Sansone Pucci.

"Signor Romano," he answered. "What can I do for you? Ready to come in and confess all your sins?"

"Are you a priest now, Pucci? I have to say, you might be better suited for it. After all, I heard the Greco clan was given to you on a shiny platter and not thanks to your own sterling police work."

The pause was ripe with fury.

"What do you want?" he repeated.

"Merely a favor," I corrected mildly. "No, it is not illegal. I just want you to look into someone for me."

It was annoying that our search had come to this, but I had to use every resource at my disposal.

"Have you heard of a mafioso who calls himself the Venetian?"

Sansone scoffed. "You gangsters and your monikers. No, I have not."

"Keep an ear to the ground," I suggested. "He has been ruffling feathers for some of my father's old associates."

There was a note of interest when he replied, "I will. Does this have anything to do with the Greco case?"

"It could," I said, unwilling to spoon-feed him the intel. "Look into it and let me know if you find anything of note."

I hung up without saying another word, but I knew I would hear from him after he conducted his own investigation. Now that Sansone could confirm I was a potential tap for inside information, he would not be able to resist getting my input.

"It seems dangerous to use the police," Guinevere murmured as the train pulled to a stop at the Santa Maria Novella station in Firenze. "Why bother?"

"Raffa likes to live on the edge," Carmine quipped as we stood to get off the train.

"Do you really want to hear about this?" I asked Guinevere. "Perhaps it is simpler if you stay removed, given where our . . . friendship stands."

She sucked her bottom lip between her teeth and looked almost shyly up at me as she said, "I would like to know more about your . . . business, if you trust me enough to tell me."

"There is a reason to every aspect of my madness," I told her after a deliberative pause.

There could be no harm in her knowing more about the outfit. She may not have wanted to be my Regina Inferna, but there was no path in Guinevere's future where she would ever betray me or mine. This I was willing to bank my life on.

I let Renzo and Martina step in front of her, Carmine and me at her back.

"Most people believe I never recovered from my very public falling-out with my father. They believe I came back to Italy to set up shop after he died just to be close to my sisters and mother. Tonio and Leo run the Romano Group, and I do not even sit on the board of directors for the company. By all rights, I am completely removed from Aldo Romano's ties to the Camorra."

"Did people know he was a capo?" she asked softly.

"Not really, but those who did suspect something did not suspect the same of me." I shrugged. "Hush now. Such conversations can wait until we are in the car."

As soon as we were safely ensconced in the vehicle, Guinevere continued her questioning. "If you have nothing to do with the Romano Group, does that mean your investment firm is totally clean? If so, how can you conduct any of your . . . shady business?"

The laughter that flowed out of me felt immeasurably good. I had missed Guinevere's insatiable curiosity and quick mind almost more than I had missed the feel of her in my arms.

"My primary business, Lupo Nero Investments, is totally aboveboard. The only way it benefits my other business interests is that I manage the wealth of some of Firenze and, indeed, most of Northern Italy's most prominent movers and shakers. The party I took you to at the Pitti Palace? Do you remember some of the people we spoke with? The mayor and his wife, an Italian prince from the house of Savoy, the head of a famous fashion house? All clients. It helps to have a reputation built in high society—they tend to protect their own. And *certo*, they are very connected and often extremely loose with their morals should I need something from them or they need something more than financial advice from me."

There was a flush in Guinevere's cheeks that spoke of her excitement. There was no doubt she was sapiosexual, aroused by intelligence just as much as she was by my good looks or edge of menace.

"My 'shady business' is conducted by a number of different companies. It was foolish of my father to have so many interests under one umbrella. The companies that remain under that corporation are now mostly legal enterprises because I do not need the headache of an audit or investigation leading like one toppled domino into more."

"Smart," she said, leaning forward in her seat like an eager student.

I rolled my grinning lips between my teeth so that she would not think I was making fun of her eagerness. Though this was exactly what I had hoped for, that her big, beautiful brain might latch on to the complexities of running a multimillion-euro business and find endless interest there.

I knew I did.

"What is it, Martina?" I asked my right-hand woman. "About three hundred twenty different companies?"

"About," she agreed, fingers flying over her phone as she worked in the seat across from us while Renzo drove us through town.

"How can you possibly manage so many?" Guinevere asked. "My father and I run one of the biggest investment firms in the Midwest, and we have just under two hundred high-grossing households, with eight staff working more than full time. That's just to manage the *money*, not the companies that gross it."

"Well, to put it into perspective, I have approximately six hundred staff between Lupo Nero Investments and my other, more clandestine companies. Most I have no contact with, as they are not even aware for whom they work. Laborers in our textile factories, engineers involved in our green tech projects, and the like. Renzo takes care of the larger grossing companies, and Martina has oversight of the rest. I have managers, usually one for two or three companies because they are not all always in play or very labor intensive. For example, Imelda, whom you met at Fattoria Casa Luna, manages her business and two other small vineyards in the region. I have three other managers of top-grossing wineries in the country, and they all report to Delfina, who also runs Tenuta Romano, as you know. Though our family winery is completely legal."

Guinevere's eyes were wide and bright, those *occhi di cerbiatta* that had first drawn me to her. "Delfina works for you too."

"You mean she knowingly commits fraud for me?" I teased. "Yes. My father would roll over in his grave to know one of his daughters was in the life, but Delfina insisted that being born the wrong gender did not mean she should be cut out of the family business." I shrugged. "I agreed. The capos at the head of each clan or family in the north report to me as well and run their own businesses. They give us a cut of the profits, while we often provide infrastructure and protection for them."

"Like a tithe to the church?"

"An ill-begotten tithe to a church filled with sinners, but yes, that is a good comparison."

"Wow," she breathed. "So what do you do most days, then?"

"What doesn't he do?" Martina muttered. "Sticks his hand in everything."

"I do," I said, baring my teeth at my friend and colleague. This was an old argument. "Not because I do not trust my team, but because in this life, if you do not keep tabs on everything, one little problem can slip by unnoticed, and next thing you know, you are incarcerated or dead."

"So you're a workaholic," Guinevere sighed. "I mean, I knew that. My dad is too. I was when I went back home, and even as a student I worked long hours."

"*Cerbiatta mia*, you sound jealous," I declared, watching a warm blush spill from her cheeks to her clavicles. It hurt to flirt with her, so I was not sure why I continued to do it. Sobering my voice, I added, "I am the King Below, so I make my own rules and my own hours. I have been known to take time off."

"What do you do when you aren't working?" she asked, and I heard the unspoken *or when you're with me* as clearly as if she had said the words.

"I collect cars, as you know, and travel to watch Formula 1 races. One of my very good friends is Leandro Volta," I said, flippantly mentioning the race-driving legend. "And I own many, *many* properties that I like to visit now and again."

"How many?"

"Twelve. In Lago di Como, Capri, Roma, and Venezia, and outside of Italia, in Mallorca, Seville, Geneva, Nice, Sarandë, Tahiti, and London."

"You should really consider starting a charitable organization," she said in that prim voice she used to reprimand me, which should not have made my dick twitch but did. "I think you have more money than is sensible."

I laughed, bright and bursting. *"Dio mio, sei una bella persona."*

My God, you are a beautiful human.

She turned toward the window to hide her smile, but I caught sight of it before she did.

I did not know what her play was in asking such questions and asking to spend the day in the city, but even though I was slowly, painfully coming to terms with the fact that she would never truly be my woman, I would also take whatever time with her I had left.

The Albanians were like vampires and did not like to meet during the day. When they did, it was always in basements or sewers, places that rarely saw the light. It was an idiosyncrasy of working with the Mafia Shqiptarë that I was used to. The earliest they ever agreed to meet was five o'clock, and after an hour's journey in the car, we had most of the afternoon to kill.

I should have headed to the office per my original plan, but watching Guinevere as she gazed out the window at the passing streets of Firenze like a warrior returned home after a long period abroad made something in my chest flip and catch.

"Drop us at La Chiesa," I told Renzo.

Martina raised a brow at me from where she sat across from me. "Do you want me to handle the meetings you have booked?"

"Reschedule to teleconferences," I said. "The ones that want to meet in person can come to the office next week."

She nodded, already pulling out her cell phone to make the changes for me.

"You don't have to change your plans for me," Guinevere said softly, her pinky finger nudging mine on the leather seat between us. "I know you're busy. I was just going to walk around and take in the sights I missed so much. Maybe treat myself to a gelato."

Her cheeks burned at the mention of gelato, no doubt thinking, as I was, of the time I had licked the sweet, cold cream from her chest in a back alley.

"I wanted to take you to this place before," I admitted, looking away from her gorgeous face to stare out the window. "But we ran out of time."

Or really, she ran away before I could.

She was silent after that until we pulled up to the mouth of a narrow, pedestrian-only street and I ushered her out of the car.

"Five o'clock," I said by way of goodbye to my *soldati*.

"Philippe is in the car behind us," Martina said. "He'll follow behind you and then drive you to the meeting when it is time. Carmine is already on his way to Drita to sweep the space and discuss preliminaries."

"He is there to fuck her," I responded. "But I am sure he will find time do those too."

Martina grinned at me, then softened to say quietly, "*Stai attento, fratello.*"

"I always am," I replied, knocking on the roof of the car once before I shut the door and watched them take off.

When I turned to face Guinevere, her long, rippling sheets of dark hair were stirring in the cool autumn breeze, her mouth pinker and eyes darker from the all-black ensemble with the bright slash of red ribbons she wore. She looked just as fey as she always did, but dire, like something that only came out at night to play with unsuspecting victims.

I swallowed thickly as my heart rate quickened with desire.

"*Vieni*. You will like this."

She fell in next to me without hesitation, our steps syncing up instantly. It should not have made my pulse hitch, but the little act of synchronicity only seemed to underscore what I honestly believed to be true.

Guinevere and I belonged together.

I could only hope that fate would not conspire to keep us apart as it had so many other great Italian love stories: Dante and Beatrice, Romeo and Juliet, Petrarch and Laura.

This was my last-ditch attempt to show her how deeply I knew and admired her.

"Oh," Guinevere said, stopping in her tracks as she saw the plaque by the inconspicuous stone building we were walking toward.

Chiesa di Santa Margherita de' Cerchi.

Otherwise known as La Chiesa di Dante.

"Dante and Beatrice's church," she breathed, turning to look at me with eyes filled with starlight. "You know, I kicked myself when I went home for not making the time to visit."

"Well, we are here now," I said through a dry throat. "It is not much, really, but I think the historian in you will love it nonetheless."

She followed mutely as I held the heavy wooden door open for her to slip inside. It was midafternoon on a Wednesday in the offseason, so the small, humble church was not busy. Only three other people gathered at the back of the last pew, an elderly woman in mourning black with two preteen boys.

I shifted a hand to Guinevere's low back as we walked down the aisle to the front of the church. It was very minimal, as many small Italian churches were: whitewashed walls, small wooden pews, scant decor with only a stone tomb and tall wood cross to mark the altar. It meant the eye was drawn immediately to the painting done by a British artist of a scene from Dante's *Inferno* that hung on the back wall.

The true item of note, though, was the large wicker basket beside the stone tomb that read **PIETRA TOMBALE DI BEATRICE PORTINARI**.

The tomb of Dante's beloved Beatrice.

The basket was filled with handwritten letters locals and tourists alike had been leaving for centuries.

"You know, apparently she isn't even buried here," Guinevere whispered as she took in everything like it was dripping with gold and jewels. I knew to her the history and lore were what made it priceless.

"She is most likely entombed in Santa Croce," I agreed. "With her husband's family. But it is more romantic to think that the same church Dante was married to another woman in might also be the resting place of his eternal love."

Guinevere hummed her agreement, drifting over to the wicker basket.

"It's so . . . full," she mused, looking up at me. "People really still leave her letters."

"They say if you write your deepest wish, Beatrice will grant it. Can you blame people for seeking out their dearest desires in any way they can?" I asked.

Her lids shuttered as she turned away, letting a sheaf of dark hair curtain her expression as she peered down at the basket again.

I left her to it in order to cross to the pulpit, where a stack of papers and envelopes waited alongside a donation box. After depositing a fifty-euro bill into the box, I took what I needed and returned to Guinevere, who was seated in the pew in front of the tomb.

She frowned as I extended the stationery and a pen to her.

"Your life has been complicated of late. I thought this place might bring you enough peace to parse out what your deepest desires are now. Beyond the chaos of myself, your issues with your father and his control, what is it that Guinevere Stone truly wants?"

Her eyes glimmered in the low light, reflective black pools under a waning moon. I could not read anything in them even though I tried.

Silently, she took the parchment from me and crossed her legs to write on her thigh.

I took my own piece of paper and pen back to the pulpit and stood behind it like a macabre farce of a priest, bent to write a different kind of sermon.

It did not take long to make my wish to Beatrice.

Desidero solo l'amore di Guinevere e la sua sicurezza.
I wish only for Guinevere's love and safety.

It felt important to manifest that in sight of the fact she might be gone from me for good before too long. I did not have to wish for the love and safety of my family because I would always have a way to influence that.

If Guinevere decided to go home to America, all I would have remaining in my power would be wishes and prayers to protect her.

And perhaps a few well-placed *soldati* to keep an eye on her for the rest of her life.

I waited for her to be finished with her longer letter, then watched as she licked the envelope closed and carefully placed it at the top of the basket. I followed suit, dropping my own beside hers.

"Do you believe in this?" she asked as we turned in tandem to leave. "That Beatrice or the universe might actually grant you what you want just because you wrote it down here and now?"

"No," I mused as I held the door open for her again, checking over my shoulder to see that Philippe was doing as I'd asked and collecting Guinevere's note from the basket. "I told you, I believe in no god but myself. Still, it is good practice to put what you want out into the ether. You never know what might come of it."

"I agree," she said as we stepped into the narrow road and I led us toward one of my favorite sandwich shops, l'Girone de' Ghiotti.

"Dante himself wrote, 'Do not be afraid; our fate cannot be taken from us. It is a gift.'"

"So you believe in fate?" she asked, her hand brushing mine as she swayed a little closer to me.

I reached out with my pinky to brush hers purposefully. "It is the reason I am what I am today. Who my father was and what he did meant that even when he died, he had placed my family in a treacherous situation. Do you know what the new *capo dei capi* does to the family of the previous leader of the Camorra in Italy, *mia dolce cerbiatta*? They murder his family so there will be no one to contest his reign."

Her head snapped to face me, mouth agape in shock. "That's barbaric."

"We are barbarians in suits." I shrugged. "This has been our way for centuries. It was stupid of me to think it would ever be different just because I willed it to be."

"That's why you returned from London."

"*Certo*. I had never wanted anything to do with the Camorra, but how could I leave my mother and sister to the wolves?" I had not wanted to share this with her, but the stakes were so low now. She had already rejected the man I was—it could do no harm to explain the true terrors of my world.

"What about an amicable transfer of leadership?" she asked. "What if someone like Leo or Renzo had taken over?"

My laughter was hollow and hard, spent shell casings at our feet. "That is not how things are done. You take power either through blood right or by blood. Even if we had wanted to do things peacefully, it would have upended the hornet's nest. Men would have felt shunned or angry that they were not chosen, and angry mafiosi argue with their fists and guns and knives. My family still would have been forfeit in the ensuing power struggle."

"Barbaric," she murmured again, obviously horrified by the practice. "So you always knew you would go back. England was just a brief reprieve."

"Yes and no. I had suggested to my father that he adopt Leo," I confessed, rubbing a hand over my mouth wearily. "Leo was raised by his mother's brother after her death, and Tonio happened to be my father's consigliere, his right-hand man. He took to the life like a duck to water. By the time I had made my first kill, Leo had made a dozen. My father loved him like a son, admired him more than his real son." My smile was flat and warped on my face, like hammered metal. "It would have made sense."

"But?"

I sighed as we turned the corner to the sandwich shop. "But nothing is so simple. My father was a man of tradition, and most Italians do not like change. Why should he adopt Leo when he had a son who could do the job, as was my birthright?"

"But you didn't want it."

I wondered if she noticed the parallels, though my stakes were so much higher, between her relationship with her father and my own.

Both had wanted us to follow paths we did not truly want to walk, and we had both succumbed to the pressure. Guinevere had a chance to rebel, but it seemed she would not take it. I was the last person who should be able to judge her for that.

"That did not matter to my father," I said with a bitter twist of a smile before I turned slightly to face her just outside the shop. "I am who I am because of the way the world made me. You might see blood on my hands, but I wish you could see that they have never held anyone as tenderly as they have held you."

"Raffa," she murmured. "It's just not that simple."

"No, nothing worth fighting for ever is."

"I want you to know," she said, taking one of my hands between both of hers, clutching it tight as if she did not want to let me go. "I do not think you are a monster, no matter what you say or how much you try to scare me away. I may have fallen in love with only some part of you, but I realize now that was the best you had to offer me. Knowing what I do now, I can say you let me fall in love with your soul, and it's as beautiful as anything I've ever seen."

"Even bloodstained as it is?" I asked, because it hurt to hear her say the words but not follow them up with any apologies or promises to stay, to love me still.

"Red is your favorite color," she retorted with a wry grin. "And it's definitely growing on me too."

CHAPTER FOURTEEN

Guinevere

Raffa did not let me join him for his meeting with the Albanian Mafia.

"If you were my partner," he said with an easy shrug, "it would be different. I would introduce you to the Albanians so they knew who reigned with me. As it is, it is better for you to remain unseen. We do not need more criminals with a memory of your name and face than are necessary."

It irritated me, but the only person I could be annoyed with was myself.

I wanted to be there beside him, both because I wanted to support Raffa and because I was rabidly curious about the inner workings of his business. With every subject I learned about, there were that many more questions to ask. I turned the idea of the Camorra business structure over and over in my brain like a Rubik's Cube, studying its bizarre and wonderful complexities.

I thought that, if given the chance, I might have a lot to offer such an outfit.

I wondered if Raffa knew what he was doing in keeping me away, stoking the fires of curiosity and hidden desire until they burned under my skin.

"What the fuck are you doing?" I whispered to myself as I banged my head back against the seat.

"*Mi dica, signorina?*" Philippe asked from the front seat.

"I need to go for a walk," I said, suddenly desperate to get out of the car. "Can we?"

My bodyguard/driver peered at me in the rearview mirror, obviously weighing my desires against whether or not his boss would crucify him for taking me away somewhere.

"I can text him to let him know where I've gone," I suggested. "He might not see it right away, but it will mean he won't worry. Please, Philippe, I don't know when I'll be back in Florence."

He sighed, rubbing a hand over his buzzed head. "I see why the boss likes you," he muttered. "Americans are persuasive."

I huffed a shocked breath of laughter. If I was more persuasive, I would be at the meeting with Raffa, Renzo, Carmine, and Martina.

We were close enough to the Duomo that I headed there automatically. Even in mid-October, the city was thriving, packed with tourists looking through their telephoto lenses and locals swerving deftly through the masses. I loved the hodgepodge of Italian, English, and other languages, the sound of a street performer singing one of Raffa's favorite songs by Pavarotti.

Philippe followed soundlessly behind me, but his presence didn't feel oppressive. After what had happened in Impruneta, I was grateful for a bodyguard.

When we reached the Piazza del Duomo, I ducked into the cathedral, which was free to the public, and wandered the illustrious interior. It gave me goose bumps to think about the first stone being erected in the 1200s, to know that so many lives had touched this place and been touched by its existence in return.

It didn't surprise me that my feet took me to Domenico di Michelino's painting of Dante and scenes from *The Divine Comedy*.

It was ironic that Raffa had read to me from the volume and that we both liked to quote the famous Italian poet when the story had specifically been crafted as a warning to people not to sin and forfeit their immortal souls. Each of the nine circles of hell had its horrors, and none of them were sugarcoated.

Did I want my liver pecked at by a bird of prey every day for the rest of time?

Did I want to be as Sisyphus was, eternally rolling a boulder up an endless hill?

Raffa liked to say he was the only god in his life and he made his own rules, and something of that philosophy must have rubbed off on me.

Because I truly believed there was no deeper level of hell than a life without Raffa Romano at my side.

Even if, in the end, when I closed my eyes to greet death, I faced eternal damnation. Better to have lived free and well than not at all.

I had to think even Dante, with all his moral wisdom and posturing, would have sinned with his beloved Beatrice if he had been given the chance. It was easy for him to write that he "never allowed Love to govern" him when he had never once met the object of his affection. Knowing her, being intimate with her, could he still have allowed reason to rule?

I was a reasonable person, a numbers-based, fact-oriented thinker.

Yet the love I had for Raffa and the feelings he had unearthed inside me about life and myself defied all my previous expectations and experiences.

Knowing him and loving him made it easier to know and love myself.

And the truth was, we were not so different as I thought we should be.

He was a good man born to the dark, and I was a girl born in the light who had always yearned for something peeking out at me from the shadows.

Eravamo come due gocce d'acqua.

Two drops of water. Made of the same substance.

Anime gemelle.

Identical hearts or twin souls.

"*Scusi*," a female voice said from over my shoulder.

I turned, startled out of my reverie to see an elderly woman staring at me with wide eyes. She was dressed entirely in black, her silver-streaked dark hair a vivid contrast, her eyes a brown so deep they seemed almost black.

"*Io ti conosco*," she murmured, reaching out with a shaking hand to clutch at my forearm. Her knuckles were like the gnarled roots of a tree, big diamonds winking from a ring on every finger, even her thumb.

I know you, she'd said in a thin, wavering voice.

"I'm sorry," I said in Italian, placing my hand over hers. "You don't. I am just visiting from America."

"No," she insisted, and suddenly her frailty fell away like a shroud, her grasp on my arm painfully tight, her thin lips twisted into a snarl. "I know you. Why do you lie?"

"I'm not lying," I argued, gently but firmly trying to pry her hand off my arm.

Philippe moved forward from where he had taken a seat to wait for me in a pew just a handful of yards away, but I shook my head. She was just a confused old woman. I didn't want to frighten her with big, stern-faced Philippe.

"Why do you lie?" she repeated, her voice getting louder so that we were starting to draw attention. "Why did you leave without saying goodbye?"

"Nonna." A preteen boy who was all limbs and knobby bones appeared at her side, taking her arm and shooting me a helpless smile that was half grimace. "I am so sorry. My grandmother is not very well."

"It's okay," I said as he helped remove her hand from me. "Just a misunderstanding."

"My baby's baby," she whimpered, clutching at her grandson even as she kept her eyes pinned on me.

"Signora Pietra." An older man wearing clerical robes hustled out a side door and offered his arm to the elderly woman. "Please, why don't you come sit in my office for a moment and calm down."

Something in the back of my mind lit up, an internal alarm I wasn't even aware I had set up.

"Pietra?" I asked, stepping forward as they started to move away.

The preteen boy shot me a wary glance and helped hustle the group faster toward the door, then closed it behind them with a resounding thud without answering my question.

There was something working at the back of my brain, chewing over a problem I half remembered.

It had started germinating when I'd seen Beatrice's supposed tomb.

"Pietra di Beatrice" had been inscribed on the side.

Pietra. Another word for "stone."

Sasso, masso, roccia, Leo had said before he was cut off.

He might have finished by adding *pietra*.

My heart tripped into a sprint, knocking so hard against my rib cage it ached. I scurried over to Philippe, who was standing just on the other side of the pew, having watched the entire interlude with the elderly woman.

"Philippe, can you take me to the Uffizi?" I asked in Italian. "Raffa said they would be a while, and there is something I would like to see."

He frowned at me. "They will be done soon, Guinevere. I think it best if we go back to the car and wait as Signor Romano wanted."

"Please?" I asked, utilizing the doe eyes that Raffa liked to refer to so much. "It won't take long."

He sighed wearily but nodded, walking toward the exit with his hand on my arm to keep me by his side through the swarms of warm bodies.

I bit my lip to keep giddy laughter from escaping, my knee jiggling with restlessness the entire drive to the Uffizi's Historical Archive and Research Department. Usually, you needed an appointment and a supervisor to visit the archives, but a quick search on my phone helped me figure out a plan to get through the protocols. As soon as we parked, I leaped from the car even though I was aware that Philippe was shadowing me.

"*Buongiorno*," I greeted the woman at the front desk. "I know you typically need an appointment to visit, but I was hoping to visit my aunt Simonetta. I'm visiting from Pistoia as a surprise."

"Oh." The receptionist, who wore a name tag that read **Paola** and looked almost as ancient as some of the records she guarded, beamed at me. "That is so sweet of you, dear. Margharita, isn't it?"

"Frederica," I corrected, just in case she was testing me instead of showcasing some memory loss in her older age. "But my sister's name is Morena—maybe that's who you are thinking of."

"Ah," she said, even brighter than before, sinking slightly into her chair as she relaxed. "Of course—Morena is off at school in the south. Well, Simonetta should be in her office. I assume you know the way?"

I nodded. "Of course."

"Well then, just sign in and I'll let you through."

She pushed the attendance sheet toward me and watched as I carefully wrote "Frederica Abate."

"Thank you, Paola," I said with a warm smile as I started to move toward the turnstiles, holding my breath for a moment before they gave way and let me through into the archives.

I turned to see Philippe frowning after me before he reluctantly took a seat in the reception area to guard me from there.

I was grateful for the space, because I had no idea what I would find if my hunch was right, and I wanted to be able to process it in peace.

It wasn't my first time in the archives. I'd visited once with Ludo in the summer, so I knew where to go to find the documents from the early seventies, when my father was born somewhere in the region. There were no other people in the stacks with me, but I couldn't help feeling on edge, as if someone might come across me at any second and arrest me for my curiosity.

At worst, they would make me leave.

So why did it feel like I was on the edge of a cliff, staring down at the churning sea below, my toes hanging over the rock?

My fingers trembled as I came across the year 1973 and then caught on the section of surnames starting with *P*. I took the entire file out of the metal drawer and carried it to a table in the back behind stacks of utilitarian shelves.

Piazza, Piccola . . . Pietra.

There were only four births in the region that year with the last name Pietra.

And one of them was Mariano Giovanni Gaetano Pietra.

Born March 3, 1973, outside Pistoia, Tuscany.

My pulse boomed in my ears like thunder after the lightning strike of new information left me paralyzed.

"Oh my God," I whispered as my fingers shook the paper too hard for me to read it.

I didn't need to read the information again to know.

This man was my father.

Setting the papers carefully aside, I pulled out my phone to do some digging. I was no hacker like Ludo, but I had been trained to investigate companies we wanted to invest in thoroughly enough to bank on their return, so I had more than enough skills to find what I needed.

Especially because I remembered the name Pietra from discussions Raffa had with his *soldati*.

A family in the Camorra that ostensibly worked under the umbrella of Raffa as *capo dei capi*, but that had, lately, been rebelling against him. They had bad blood, he'd said, because they had killed his father.

Bile rose in my throat at the implications and settled, bitter enough to make me gag on the back of my tongue.

"Please, no, please, no," I whispered as I searched deeper and deeper through the internet, checking Italian forums and newspaper archives until I found what I had hoped so deeply not to find.

> Gaetano Pietra welcomed his third son on March 3 with his wife, Giulia; named Mariano Giovanni after his paternal and maternal grandfathers. He will be baptized next Saturday at the Cathedral of Saint Zeno.

My head thunked against the table as my spine suddenly lost its rigidity.

Someone who was very thorough had gone through and scrubbed most mentions of the mafioso's third son from digital existence, but this article in a small local paper remained, with the announcement of his birth.

I killed his two eldest sons in retribution, Raffa's words echoed back to me.

My lover had killed my uncles.

My father's family had killed Raffa's father.

What were the odds?

My mathematician brain tried to calculate them and found it wasn't as far fetched as it should have been.

I had come to Florence because I knew Tuscany was where my father had been born. Of course, meeting Raffa had been incredible serendipity, but the odds of meeting someone associated with the Camorra who might have known my father's people didn't seem unlikely. If Raffa had six hundred people working for his outfit, not including the dozens of capos who operated in other regions of the north, there had to be hundreds of cogs in the machine that would lead me back to the Pietra family.

But still.

My vision blurred as I exited the internet app on my phone and dialed a number I knew by heart.

"Hello?"

"Dad." The word fell out of me like an anchor, dragging me down, down, down into panic. "Dad, I need to know . . . are you related to a man named Gaetano Pietra?"

The silence that echoed back at me was colossal. I had the sudden, incredibly surreal feeling of being alone in the Arctic tundra, surrounded by ice and endless quiet.

"Where did you hear that name?" Dad said finally, voice textured with weariness.

"*Cazzo*," I breathed.

"*Modera il linguaggio*," he barked out of habit, only this time the parental admonishment was said in rusty Italian.

"Dad, what the fuck?" I said, ignoring his warning to watch my mouth. "Were you a part of the Italian Mafia?"

It made so much sense I felt ill and dizzy with it. The metal edges of my phone cut into my fingers from how hard I was holding it.

His sigh seemed endless. "I left that behind when I was a much younger man."

"So yes," I surmised. "How . . . ? God, I have so many questions I don't even know where to start."

"Start with how you discovered this at all. Is it because of *that* man, Raffa Romano?" His words lashed at me through the phone.

"You are in absolutely *no* position to be high and mighty about Raffa when you were in the Camorra yourself, Dad," I snapped back.

"So he did follow in his father's footsteps, then." He made a noise at the back of his throat like a dying animal. "Fuck, Guinevere. When I saw that photo of you in the paper with him in August, I did some asking around, and everyone said he was clean."

Despite the circumstances, I grinned, a feral expression to match the wicked pride I felt that Raffa was so good at his job.

"This isn't about Raffa. It's about you having lied to me my entire life. No wonder you didn't want me to come to Italy."

"Yes, no wonder," he shouted. "You do not know how dangerous it is for you to be there, Jinx. With your luck, someone could figure out who you are related to. Raffa Romano could find out! And you do know what he would do to the granddaughter of one of his rivals? Your mother and I would never see you again."

"How could you let me exist in the world not knowing something this big?" I demanded. "Even if I had just been traveling through France and England, how could you have known I wouldn't run into someone who might recognize me?"

"It was incredibly unlikely anyone would recognize you out of context and based on looks alone, even if you did bump into someone who once knew me. The odds were minuscule. I calculated them," he said with a scoff.

Of course he had, just like I had tried to.

"Only, you betrayed my trust by doing the one thing I ever asked you not to, and you spent the summer in Italy. You met a fucking mafioso, for Christ's sake, Guinevere. I thought I raised you better than that."

"I didn't know at the time," I seethed. "Though if I'd had all the information about my family and my background, maybe I would have recognized the signs."

My mind was reeling like I'd gone for a spin on a merry-go-round and couldn't get off, the wheel just spinning faster and faster until all my thoughts swirled into a chaotic muddle.

"If Romano is in the Camorra, you need to leave him. Now," Dad was saying, urgency vibrant in his tone. "I'll buy you the next flight out of Florence. Come home, and we'll figure out how to keep you safe. He obviously found you once before, but—"

"He saved me once before," I corrected. "Raffa wouldn't hurt me, even if it meant saving his own life."

I knew as soon as I spoke the words that they were true. Raffa would move heaven and earth to keep me safe and happy, despite the fact that, recently, I hadn't done anything to deserve that kind of devotion.

God, I thought, I had judged him so harshly when my own father was just like him.

"How can you have raised me on this intense rhetoric about being good and kind in a world that is anything but? When you know its dangers and atrocities better than almost anyone? Instead of arming your daughter, you declawed her and left her vulnerable to predators."

"Predators like Raffa Romano."

"No. Never Raffa." Dark, bad, and dangerous to know he might be, but Raffa would never hurt me, and more than that—more than my dad—he *wanted* me to be both his *cerbiatta* and his *cacciatrice*. His fawn and his huntress. "He is the only one who wants to help me make myself a weapon."

"You don't need to be a weapon, for fuck's sake. You're just a girl. Your life is in America as a financial adviser. You have a serious chronic illness, Guinevere! Come home, and I'll protect you."

"I am more than just my illness, Dad. How many times do I have to say that? I'm not some frail princess you can stuff away in a tower," I argued, fury building inside me, turning the confusion and despair into something actionable. "I should have known the truth so that if anything came for me, I could defend myself. Now, you've left me in an impossible situation, and I'm playing catch-up. If anything happens to me, Dad, it will be *your* fault for not trusting me with the truth."

He made a sound like I'd run him through with a blade.

"I don't know if I can forgive you for keeping this from me," I whispered through the mass of emotion in my throat, which was clogging it like debris in a drain. "This is just . . . too much."

"We can speak about it when you get home. I'll tell you everything you want to know," he promised, and I could feel his desperation through the phone. "Just come home—now."

"No. You can't keep me safe there. They already got to me once before."

"The break-in," he murmured. "The police said it was a disgruntled employee from the Enrich Company, but I should have recognized the shoddy cover-up. It must have been Romano's business catching up to you."

"Maybe, but how can you be sure it wasn't *yours*?" I countered.

"They haven't found me in two decades," he said shortly. "There is no way."

"Well, apparently the Pietra family has reignited the feud with the Romanos, so who knows. Maybe they've been searching for the long-lost heir to the throne for a long time now, and they've finally found you to bring you home."

"I will never set foot on Italian soil again," Dad spat like a curse.

"Good, then I won't have to see you for a while," I said calmly before slowly ending the call and blocking his number.

When Mom called minutes later, I muted hers too.

I sat in the enormous, mostly empty archive room for a long time after that, just staring into space as my brain worked.

CHAPTER FIFTEEN

Raffa

The Albanian Mafia Shqiptarë were unlike any other criminal organization in many ways, but the most obvious was that they were dominating the global cocaine trade without cropping up on any of the international policing organizations' radars. It was the reason I had been eager to work with them when Leo and Carmine had brought me their contact information. I was not interested in the days of old when Italian mafiosi whipped their dicks out for measuring contests in public forums. And in the nearly five years of my reign as *capo dei capi*, not only had arrests within the outfit decreased by over 40 percent, but I also had managed to mostly keep my name out of the mouths of rivals and policemen alike.

Raffa Romano, respected Florentine businessman, was almost an entirely separate entity from Il Gentiluomo.

Which might have explained why it was so easy for me to hide that part of myself from Guinevere.

It certainly made the decision to leave her out of the discussions an easy one.

Drita Hoxha was an ally and had been since we were first introduced five years ago, even through the ups and downs of her tumultuous relationship with Carmine, but she was *not* a friend.

There was no room for true friendships between other crime syndicates. You never knew when your interests might diverge or an insult might be handed down, and suddenly you were at war.

So I liked Drita, and I put up with her and Carm, but I would never trust someone like her with Guinevere's well-being.

Especially when my woman had declined to take her throne beside me. If she had . . . well, I would have decked her out in jewels and finery, told her about Albanian culture so she would not make the mistake of flinching away from Drita's kiss of welcome, and then watched as she made the Shqiptarë eat out of the palm of her hand.

It was easier this way, I told myself, but there was something beneath my breastbone that ached like a bruise.

"This is not good news," Dren, Drita's younger brother, muttered after I explained some of what was going down with the Venetian.

"You have to understand, when you took over again from the Grecos, we were thrilled," Drita explained. She had short, dark hair slicked back from her forehead so that her large, ice-water-blue eyes dominated her face, and a large, mobile mouth that was always painted a dark red reminiscent of blood. "The Romano clan is known for its discretion and efficiency now that you are capo. In the years we've worked with you, we've had no issues. With the Grecos, this was not the case. We are not happy to hear that now you might not be without issues too."

"If you think I am happy about it, then perhaps our language barrier is deeper than I realized," I said dryly in Italian.

Drita and Dren both spoke Italian well, having been raised on it for the express purpose of being the Albanian liaisons on the ground in Italy.

They did not like my insinuation that they were not fluent.

"You motherfuck—" Dren started to curse, leaning over the table to growl at me.

Drita held up one hand. "Do not be a cliché, Dren. How many times do I have to tell you? If you can't keep your temper, take a walk."

For a vibrating moment, Dren bared his teeth at me before he crossed his arms and sat back in his chair.

His sister nodded curtly and folded her hands. "As I was saying, we are not happy to hear about your . . . woes. So we will do what we can to help."

"For a price?" Renzo inserted, because he knew her well.

Drita's smile was almost blinding in that bloody red frame. "If we can be of aid, I think a grateful ten percent off your cut of the deal would be fitting."

Renzo scoffed, but I held her cold eyes and offered my own wolfish grin. "As thanks if you *do* discover something of value, I will set you up with the Montucci family in Ravenna."

It was Dren's turn to scoff. "They hate Albanians. They will not work with us."

"Carlo Montucci is an old friend," I said, without divulging that I had saved him from bankruptcy last spring and he would be in my debt for life. "I am sure we could figure something out. I know you've been eager for more east-coast entry points."

Drita's mouth pursed unhappily, but there was a sparkle in her eye she did not try to hide. "I can agree to those terms. *Besa*," she said, an Albanian oath.

"*Besa*," I mimicked, taking her proffered hand.

"Excellent. Now that we have negotiated terms, I do believe I can help," she offered, snapping her fingers so that a man waiting against the wall behind her stepped forward with a covered tablet he opened and presented to her. After taking it without looking, Drita slid it across the slick wood tabletop to me. "We should start with this."

The screen depicted an image of a blond-haired woman with tanned skin and vibrant blue eyes smiling into the camera with her arms wrapped around a squat older man and woman, a field of vines curving up behind them. Though I had never seen her before, there was something familiar about her features. The large eyes topped by delicately arched eyebrows that made her look young and especially vulnerable.

I knew before Drita said anything whose name would pass her lips.

"Gemma Stone. The sister of the woman you've been sleeping with since the summer."

Her hand was suddenly at the top of the screen, swiping to the next photo in the gallery, one taken of Guinevere and me in Firenze before she'd gone back to Michigan. She was in a short red dress, raised up on the toes of her sandals to meet my kiss, my hand cupping her ass under the fabric, my entire body bent to curve over hers like a shield.

My reaction was so immediate, it could not have had time to filter through my brain. It was just gut instinct. An animal response to the sudden threat of knowing someone had been shadowing us.

I gripped Drita's outreached hand by the wrist and tugged so forcefully she was upended over the table and dragged before me in an instant. Before she could recover, the knife I kept sheathed at my hip was in my hand and pressed to the junction of her jaw and throat, the flat of the blade digging deeply enough to make her breath stutter hard through her throat.

Around me, I was distantly aware of Renzo, Carmine, and Martina standing off against Dren and the other two Albanians.

I curved over Drita's prone body, not like a shield as I had with Guinevere but like a weapon homed in on a target.

The words I spoke were deceptively soft, but as sinister as the wrath barely leashed within me. "You have one chance to tell me why I should not gut you like a fish for following us."

Drita stared up at me, miraculously unperturbed, given her position. She looked almost . . . curious. "So she is not just a bit of fun for you, capo."

A growl ripped up my throat in answer.

She smiled thinly. "I did not take the photo, nor did any of my people. It was delivered to one of my men by a fellow who called himself the Venetian."

My heart hammered so hard it reverberated in my bones. It was hard to hear her over the cacophony of my internal stress.

"Why the fuck would the Venetian give you that photo?"

"Because," she said calmly, "I knew Gemma Stone."

I blinked down at her as the world tilted just slightly. "Excuse me?"

"Perhaps you can lower your weapon and I can take a seat to explain things?"

Reluctantly, I took the blade from her neck, neatly sheathing it even though I did not retake my seat until everyone else had slowly reclaimed theirs.

"Gemma was seeing Dren for a time," Drita explained, gesturing to her grim-faced brother. "They met at a club in Durrës, and he was quite smitten. So much so that he started to bring her around."

There was a grimace on Dren's face that did not speak of a happy ending.

"He even introduced her to members of Clan Greco when they were visiting to renegotiate terms for our smuggling deal. The day after, she broke up with Dren and, presumably, started to see one of the Italians."

"Who?"

It was Dren who grunted, "If I had any clue, he would be dead."

Ah, so he had been very smitten, then.

Merda, well, Guinevere had mentioned her sister had terrible taste in men. And poor decision-making, if she'd gotten involved with an Albanian gangster and then abruptly dropped him for an Italian mafioso. The Stone girls were not big on self-preservation, clearly.

"But you are sure she was with an Italian?" I asked, thinking of the cross necklace Gemma had supposedly given the stranger who'd tried to kidnap Guinevere on the top of the bell tower.

"Very. I followed her the day before she died," Dren admitted, then scowled at my look of suspicion. "Only to try to speak with her. There was no closure."

Beside me, Carmine hid a laugh behind a very fake bout of coughing.

Dren's scowl deepened, and an angry flush burned his pugnacious face. "She ducked into an Italian restaurant by the harbor that is often frequented by the Grecos."

"Did you see her leave?"

"No, she stayed very late, and I decided it was over. The next day, she collapsed in the street dead." There was misery in his voice, as if he missed her despite their end.

The magic of the Stone family, perhaps.

"In what context did you receive the photo of Guinevere and myself?"

"A member of the Greco family who escaped persecution after you set the Italian dogs on them came forward to offer it as a bargaining chip so we would not kill him." Drita's smile was vampiric. "It did not work, of course. But he assured us that the Grecos were still on top and had recruited the Pietra family to work against you and claim the north. They planned to use the girl against you."

"To kill her," I corrected. "They came after her in Florence during the San Lorenzo festival."

"No, Alessio Greco told me they were going to take her. She was worth more alive than dead because they could use her as leverage against you."

"They tried to take her in Michigan, which is why I brought her back to Italia. Another attempt was made to kidnap her in Impruneta just last weekend," I admitted.

Drita frowned. "Impruneta could not have been the Grecos. I killed Alessio myself."

"There are other Grecos," Dren pointed out.

But . . . "No," I said, looking at Rezo, who nodded. "Alessio and his cousin, Ricardo, were the only two higher-ups left in the organization after Sansone Pucci incarcerated the rest without parole. Ricardo was last seen belly-up in Lago di Como."

Where Renzo had left him two weeks ago, after I had killed him myself in the basement of Trattoria Umberto. He was the last of the scuttling bottom-feeders in the clan who had escaped Pucci's police net and whom I had had to put in the ground myself.

"So not the Grecos," Drita allowed. "But still someone under the power of this Venetian and the Pietras. After I killed Alessio, they reached out about meeting face to face."

"Why?"

"To take over operations in Livorno and the rest of the north from you."

Fury burned like banked coals in my belly. "I am still *capo dei capi*."

"Yes, but"—Drita's grin was wicked—"you have to admit, their plan is good. After all, do you know where your woman is at this very moment? They know what you were willing to sacrifice to save your mother and sisters from certain death. It is fair to surmise you might do something drastic like give up your kingdom for a girl. Obviously, they do not know you as well as I do. You wouldn't give up a penny to save some *zuskë*."

The hairs on the back of my neck stood on end as electric panic sparked through my blood. "What do you know, Drita?"

"Nothing," she said with a little shrug, but her gaze slid to Carmine, who was watching her with something like mounting dread. "Maybe next time you think to dip your wick in another woman, Carmine, you will remember today."

"Call Philippe," I said calmly to Martina even though my blood was acidic with rage. When I addressed Drita, it was through a smile like a knife wound cut into my face. "You know, Drita, we have always had an amicable, mutually beneficial relationship. I would hate to see that change over a lover's tiff."

"There's no reason it should," she agreed. "You understand, they might not even have her yet. I gave you a heads-up. Which, I think you'll find, means that I conformed to our agreement."

"Philippe isn't answering," Martina murmured. "Guinevere isn't either."

I raised a brow at the Albanian gangster. "Not enough of one, it seems. A shame. Carmine always complimented you on your legs."

"Wha—"

The gun I held against my thigh under the table recoiled hard into my grip, spitting the bullet directly across from me and into Drita's thigh.

She screamed, hitting her head against the table as she bent down over her ruined leg.

The room erupted into activity, Renzo throwing his huge body over the table to slam Dren against the floor, Dren's gun flying out of his fist to clang against the wall. Martina was on the man who had stepped forward with the tablet, someone twice her size she latched on to like a spider monkey, strong thighs clamping his arms to his sides while she slid a small stiletto blade into his neck. Arterial blood splashed vibrantly across her white dress shirt and face, but she held on until he bled out. It only took seconds. Carmine grappled with the last man, a short, burly, hairy man who had my *soldato* by the throat until Carm elbowed him in the balls and then knocked him out with a sharp elbow to the temple.

Meanwhile, I stood slowly and rounded the table to Drita's side. Through her pain, she had managed to find her own weapon, and she swung it wide to take aim at me. I sidestepped her first clumsy attempt, lunging forward before she could try again and seizing her arm, breaking the bone with a clean snap so the gun clattered to the floor.

She cried out, eyes squeezed shut in pain.

"Listen to me carefully," I told her in my passable Albanian so there would be no misunderstandings. "I will not kill you, because you did not know, perhaps, that this woman is not just any other woman to me. She is *the* woman. The one I breathe for. If I find she has been killed because of your pathetic power play, I will hunt you down and skin you alive before I hang you upside down by the ceiling to bleed to death drop by slow drop. You will beg me to end your agony, and I will not, because you will have instigated mine the second Guinevere died. If she is, by some fucking miracle, alive when I find her, I will consider you in my debt, Drita. I think an increase to a forty percent cut might ease the sting for a while. What do you say?"

She hissed at me as I clasped her broken arm a little too tightly.

"I did not hear you," I said pleasantly.

"Yes," she snapped, eyes blazing like sunlight on ice. "Fuck you, Romano. Yes, fine."

"Where are they taking her?"

She glowered at me, but Renzo had the good grace to drag Dren's knocked-out carcass in front of us, his gun pressed to Dren's temple.

"Well?" I asked.

Her breath shuddered out of her. "They were meant to take her from the train. Someone told them you would be on the eight o'clock."

There were exactly ten people who knew which train we were taking back home.

My mother and my sisters Stacci and Carlotta.

Renzo, Carmine, Martina, Leo, and myself.

Guinevere.

And Philippe.

There was a chance any of them could have told someone else, but it was marginal. The most obvious answers were frequently the correct ones.

Which meant that Philippe was our turncoat.

"Where are they taking her?" I demanded, twisting Drita's arm slightly like the valve release on some of the anger steaming up my throat.

"Fuck!" she screamed. "I do not know. It didn't matter to me."

"Kill them," I said to the brothers.

Carmine locked eyes with Drita as he lifted the heavy gangster onto the table with his head hanging over the edge. Only then did he leverage his weight against the man's head in a savage blow that resulted in a crackling crunch as his neck broke.

Less dramatic than his brother, Renzo immediately drilled a bullet into Dren's head.

Drita shouted through her tears, but I ignored what she was saying to lean in very close, my mouth a whisper against her cheek.

"They call me the Gentleman not because I believe in mercy, Drita," I explained, "but because I always follow through on my word. If you ever keep important information from me again, I will kill you. If you ever even so much as speak Guinevere's name, I will cut out your tongue and asphyxiate you with it. And if you ever think to turn on me, I will hunt down and destroy everyone in your clan, just like I have with the Grecos. Is that understood?"

Her mouth trembled as she pressed it into a tight line and nodded.

"*Molto bene*," I said, dropping her arm to the table so she cried out again. "*Andiamo*. We have to find my huntress."

And I had to hope that was what she would be if they had her.

Not *la mia cerbiatta*, but the *cacciatrice* I had seen peeking through those doe eyes.

CHAPTER SIXTEEN

Guinevere

By the time I left the Uffizi, I knew three things.

The first was that all those late-night, dark-coded cravings I had experienced my whole life had a root cause. I might not have been born into *la mafia* like Dad or Raffa, but clearly it was part of my birthright and part of my destiny.

It was impossible not to believe I'd met my fate when Raffa hit me with his car that night on a lonely, random Tuscan road. That forces beyond our measure had orchestrated our meeting because we were meant to be.

Even when I'd fought it, my heart had been inextricably his from the moment he curled me into his bare chest and read to me from Dante's *Divine Comedy* when I was sick.

I brought out the best in him, I thought, and that did not necessarily mean I brought out the *good* in him. It meant that I made him happy after years of turmoil and loneliness. It meant that I gave him a safe place to play the hero he'd always secretly wanted to be but had never been given the chance to play.

And he brought out the best in me too. Again, not the *good* by its most basic definition. He made me fiercer and more honest. He gave me the freedom and security to be who I truly was and go after what I really wanted.

Raffa had added spice to the banality of my life, the heat I had been longing for since I was that sick girl daydreaming in her hospital bed.

So why had I condemned him for it? How ridiculously hypocritical of me to crave the burn and say I was unable to stand the intensity.

What a stupid lie I'd force-fed myself to maintain the image my parents had drummed into me. How ironic that they were liars too.

My entire world as I'd known it had been eviscerated, and in its wake, I was determined to rebuild myself from the ashes in exactly the image I wanted.

Brave and bold, like Gemma had always encouraged me to be.

A huntress instead of a fawn, like Raffa knew I could be.

Someone who pursued her pleasure, societal judgment be damned.

Which led to the second thing I had decided.

I wasn't going home.

Even if things did not work out with Raffa, my heart and soul had imprinted on Italy. I knew in my bones there was no other place for me in this world. The vibrant people, the food and culture, the history, the very smell of the cypress trees, and the view of endlessly rolling grapevines intermixed with golden fields of hay and thickets of olive trees.

Fate had led me here, and I was not going to spite it again by leaving.

And the third?

I could not live happily in a world where I was not with Raffa.

He was not a Prince Charming, but hadn't I always turned my nose up at those heroes? Two-dimensional, shallow expressions of female fantasy.

Raffa was so much more than that.

He was troubled and dark, but he had a moral code, even if it was skewed. He put his family before everything and stood by his friends no matter what. He'd killed Martina's abusive, piece-of-shit husband because in his mind that was the punishment for putting your hands on a woman he loved. He'd broken a man's finger because he had called me a whore.

I understood now, after killing someone to save Ludo and myself, that sacrifices were called for in the life he'd been born into, and there was no escaping it unless you wanted to roll over and die yourself. With stakes that high, it was no wonder that violence bled into non-life-or-death situations as well. It was a punctuation mark on an order. An oath someone unwittingly wrote in blood not to fuck with you again.

Whenever I'd read about antiheroes or fantasized about deviant, toe-curling seductions, I had been thinking about Raffa. Before I even knew him, a part of my heart had hungered for him. To deny the part of myself that longed for violent delights was to deny myself the love of a man who was not by any definition good but was wholly good for me.

Perfect for me.

The only hard question that remained was this.

Was I good enough for him?

"*Andiamo*," I said to Philippe as I strode through the exit, the Italian stumbling behind me in his haste to catch up.

"Did you find what you wanted?" he asked me as we walked down to the parked car together.

I was surprised because Philippe was not the kind to make idle conversation. Like most of the other *soldati* at the villa, he was there to protect and serve, not to socialize. Only the core four, Leo, Renzo, Carmine, and Martina, seemed to hold a higher standing, doing as they wanted and interacting with the family as if they were key components of it.

"I wouldn't say I wanted to find it, but yes," I said with a little smile as he beeped open the door of the Maserati Levante and held the door for me to get inside.

When he took his place in the driver's seat, he peered at me in the reflection of the rearview mirror. "What did you discover?"

I frowned, but answered smoothly. "I was curious about my ancestry. Apparently, I am distantly related to Petrarch."

Most likely, I wasn't, but Petrarch's real surname was Petracco, which was a derivative of Pietra.

"You look like them," he surprised me by saying.

"Excuse me?"

Philippe smiled, a slightly goofy grin because it was crooked and he had a chip in his front left tooth. "You look like the Pietras."

A shiver ran down my spine like a needle point.

"How do you know the Pietras?" I asked calmly, even though there was no way he should have known I was related to them. He hadn't been with me in the archives, and no one else knew.

"My boss does some work with them," he explained with a shrug.

Which could have been a fair thing to say, but his wording was strange.

His *boss*.

Why not just say Raffa did work with them?

Unless his boss was someone else entirely.

"Where are you taking me?" I asked, because I knew the city well enough to realize we were not heading south, back over the Arno to the building where Raffa was having his meeting with the Albanians, but north.

"The train station. Boss said to meet him and the others there since you took so long. They're already done and waiting for us."

"*Va bene*," I murmured, slipping my phone out of my pocket so I could text Raffa to confirm.

In the right-hand corner, a small symbol denoted I didn't have service.

Impossible.

We weren't in the countryside but in the cosmopolitan hub of Florence.

Unless . . . unless Philippe had done something to the reception in the car?

Porco dio, this was not looking good.

I searched the back of the car for anything I could use to defend myself if I had to and found absolutely nothing. Trying to leash the panic daring to break free and run rampant through my body, I focused on the best course of action.

Act calm, like I was as stupid as he clearly thought I was.

"I can't wait to get back to the villa," I said mildly. "I could sleep for a week. Grape harvesting is hard labor."

Philippe smiled that crooked grin, and I was shocked by the lack of malice in the expression. How could he betray Raffa and take me toward some no-doubt-horrible end and look so . . . amicable?

"Saw you dancing with Leo. I basically grew up with him. He's a good guy. Better than most of the rest of us."

"I could say the same thing about Raffa," I said carefully, just to test his reaction.

It was a swift lowering of his brows. "Yeah, he's a good guy too. He deserves more than his lot, though, you know? He never wanted this."

"He told me. But he is what he is, and I think he's made some kind of peace with it," I offered. It was true—even when Raffa could have told me the circumstances of becoming a reluctant mafioso, he hadn't. Instead, he'd insisted again and again that he enjoyed what he did.

The lying, the stealing, and even, when necessary, the murder.

"There are always other options," Philippe said with a shrug as he pulled into a parking lot. "We're here."

This was my opportunity to run. I just had to time it right, because I was quick, but Philippe's legs were twice the length of mine, and he was built leanly like a runner and not thickly like Ludo, who was slower than me.

My heart panged thinking about Ludo back at the villa. He hadn't wanted me to go into town without him, but he was still recovering from the bullet wound he'd gotten at Impruneta, so Philippe had been assigned to me instead.

He was going to be almost as pissed off as Raffa when they discovered me gone.

When Philippe opened the door for me, he took my arm and wedged it through his own.

"Rush hour," he explained. "It gets busy."

Merda.

I smiled at him. "Right. I'll stay close."

He tugged me into the crush of people heading toward the station, moving quickly without rushing. I kept my eye peeled for a police officer or somewhere I could give him the slip, but the open area around the station was too exposed.

There was no room to operate as Philippe dragged me through the turnstiles and onto the platform, and he held me pressed tightly to his side as we walked toward our train car at the end. Overhead, an announcement claimed there were two minutes to board before departure.

"Hey, stop that," I said suddenly, a little too loud.

A couple waiting for the train across from ours turned to stare.

"Stop touching me," I said again as I struggled away from Philippe, who was scowling at me. "I said *stop*!"

"Hey." An older man with a German accent stepped forward. "Hey, you should not be touching her like that."

"Please, help. He won't let me go," I begged.

The man in the couple to my other side started forward to help, and two women joined him, converging on us.

For the first time since I'd left the Uffizi, Philippe looked alarmed.

"Take your fucking hands off her," one of the women demanded. "I'm going to call the police."

"Do it," someone else agreed. "He's harassing her."

"Let go!" I demanded, leveraging all my weight against Philippe.

He had to use both hands to clamp me close. "Stop this," he hissed.

I tipped my head back to cry, "Help!"

The two men and a few more who had joined our group surged forward to manhandle Philippe off me.

A voice over the PA system announced the train was about to depart, so I pushed off Philippe, leaving him to the crowd of Good Samaritans, and sprinted onto the train just as the doors started to close.

I watched in horror as Philippe broke away from the group by punching one man in the throat and dived into the closest train car.

From my angle, I couldn't tell if he made it or not, but I decided not to wait around to find out.

I moved down the aisle of the train away from where he might have gotten on, making my way to the end car. It was first class only, but luckily I had my ticket, sweat-damp and crinkled in one fist. I took the steps to the lower level and found a place in the nearly empty car at the very back. Slumping low in my seat, I trained my eyes on the door to the car. I wasn't sure what I would do if Philippe showed up other than try to hide, but I didn't want to be taken by surprise.

"Waiting for someone?"

I jerked, my head slamming against the window as I recoiled. A shaky laugh escaped my mouth at the sight of an elegantly dressed woman sitting by the window across the aisle from me. She was handsome, with a strong jaw and thick brows over liquid brown eyes.

"Not really," I said, even though it wasn't much of an answer. "Just relieved to be going home. I thought I was going to miss the train."

She smiled at me, a closed-lip expression that was more considering than it was warm.

"You do not sound as if you should be able to call Italy home."

I had become incredibly fluent in Italian, but I knew my accent continued to give me away. "I'm from the US. Originally," I tacked on, because it felt good to tell a stranger this was where I was going to stay.

"And how do you like my country?" she asked, shifting her body to angle toward me, settling in for a longer conversation.

I was exhausted, so weary my head swam. I hadn't had enough water to drink today, and it was starting to affect me. But politeness was so deeply ingrained in me, I did not even think of ignoring her.

"I like it enough to now call it my home," I confessed with a small smile, eyes flickering back to the entrance to the car. "It's as Robert Browning said: 'Open my heart and you will see Graved inside of it, "Italy."'"

"Poetic," the stranger said. "But I understand the sentiment. The country and its foibles have taken much from me, yet I could never part from it. Not even when others in my family have left it behind for good."

"I tried." I shrugged. "But somehow, here I am again."

"Somehow," she mused before getting up to cross the aisle and take the seat facing mine. "Perhaps you should tell me the story."

I arched a brow at her, unconsciously mimicking one of Raffa's expressions. "Do you often ask people for their life stories?"

She lifted one shoulder and opened her gloved palms. "It is why I deign to take the train."

That startled a laugh out of me.

"Let me guess," she said in that low, smooth voice. "It involves a man."

"Doesn't it always?" I asked dryly.

"Yes," she agreed. "Though not always one's lover."

"It sounds like you have a story too."

"I do." She looked out the window at the smeared Italian countryside rushing by. "Would you like to hear it?"

"Sure," I said, because I would.

It was that insatiable curiosity that had always gotten me into trouble. Happily, I seemed to be out of harm's way for the moment, though my gaze kept vigilant watch on the door for Philippe.

"I was born into a family of men with only a fragile mother to keep me company. She tried to raise me to be a good, sweet girl, but the influence of my four brothers and my father kept me from staying in the kitchen, attached to her apron strings. My younger brother was my best friend because, unlike the other boys, he always invited me to play. We were inseparable until he turned eighteen. Then my father took him from me and turned him into something neither of us liked very much."

Her eyes were glazed by distant memories, her lip firm but caught between her teeth as if she was afraid it might tremble.

"I hardly saw him for the next five years. Only on the night I was planning to run away with my lover to get married did he appear in the doorway of my hotel room in Rome. My boyfriend was beside him, a gun pressed to his head. My brother shoved him into the room on his knees and closed the door behind him. He told me our father had sent him to remind me of my one duty as a girl in the family. Marry for the advantage of the family, not for love."

What kind of family, I thought as my heart picked up speed, *had rules like that?*

The family.

La mafia.

A chill settled over me like an icy cloak.

Behind the woman, the train car doors hissed open mechanically and revealed Philippe. He looked tousled, panting hard with a wildness to his expression as he searched the car until his gaze landed on me.

And then he relaxed visibly, shoulders collapsing, his tread heavy like that of the man at the end of a marathon who sees the end in sight.

I watched him like a fawn caught in a snare as he came closer and the woman kept talking.

"He was going to kill him," she continued. "I thought for sure by the look in his eye that my lover would die and so, maybe, would I for disobeying our father. And then something strange happened." She leaned forward, snatching my hand in a cold, fierce grip. "He knocked Said out, sat in the chair before the vanity, and started to drink my wine. Then, he told me that if he killed the person I loved for being the wrong kind of fit for the family, then he would have to kill the mother of his unborn child. Something he was not willing to do."

Her gaze was so intense on mine that the ink of her irises seemed to spread to encapsulate my entire scope of vision.

Such a dark eye, thick lashed and large like mine.

Like my father's.

My heart was beating so hard now that it ached in my chest. My fingers and toes tingled, and the hair on the back of my arms stood up, my entire body primed like the air before an electrical storm.

"You see," she murmured, "he had fallen in love with the daughter of an Albanian gangster, and our father did not believe in mudding our blood with that of foreigners. It was why he did not like Said. It was why, if he had known about Mariano and Elizabeta, he would have killed them and the baby. So do you know what my brother did?"

I parted my lips when she paused long enough that it was clear she expected an answer, but my tongue was adhered to the roof of my dry mouth. There was an audible noise as I peeled it off my palate and swallowed so hard my throat clicked.

"He ran away with Elizabeta to America," I croaked.

"He ran away with Elizabeta to America," she echoed. "Very good. He left Said alive but had him smuggled out of the country, never to see me again. He sent me back to my father with the promise that I would never breathe a word of his existence again to anyone. As far as my family was concerned, he died taking out Said. And in twenty-eight years, I have never breathed a word of that story to anyone until now."

She paused as Philippe took the seat beside her, his gun held against one thigh. My gaze flicked to it and then back to the woman who was undoubtedly my aunt.

"I think he would understand me telling his daughter, though, don't you?" she asked, releasing my hand to sit back in her chair. The way she did it made her seem like a queen on her throne and not a woman on a swaying train in a blue polyester seat.

"Because you are my aunt," I said and the words dropped like stones between us.

"Because I am your aunt," she agreed. "In fact, you were named after me."

I looked to Philippe, who sat placidly beside her as if he had done so dozens of times before.

"You asked Philippe to bring me to you," I said, thinking through everything aloud. "Is the Mafia so antiquated you didn't think a phone call would do?"

Her mouth ticked up, then fell flat. "I think a reunion warrants more than a phone call."

"This doesn't feel like a reunion," I said honestly. "It feels more like a kidnapping."

"Semantics," she offered with a little shrug. "It is what you make of it."

"And if I wanted to get off this train at the next stop without you?"

"Well." She sighed as Philippe lifted the gun in his lap to train it on me. In the back of the mostly deserted train car, no one could see the threat. "Sometimes family fights."

"I could scream," I pointed out, because there were a few people at the other end of the car who would notice and help a young woman in distress.

Philippe glowered, but my aunt raised a hand and leaned forward again to grab my hand. I tried to snatch it away, but she was too fast, and her grip was shockingly strong for a middle-aged woman. Philippe followed some unspoken cue and reached into her black purse to hand her a needle very much like the kind I used to administer my medicine each day.

"No," I said with a gasp as she held my hand flat to the table and Philippe approached with the syringe. "No!" I shouted.

The needle pierced my hand a moment later, a cool rush of liquid as it was emptied into my bloodstream. Almost immediately, I could feel the effects tingling through me, slowing my pulse, dragging my thoughts sideways off a linear path.

"Excuse my niece," my aunt said as my body lost its structure and I sank back against the window in my seat. "She talks in her sleep."

I wanted to argue that my eyes weren't even closed, but I found they were. And then when I went to open my mouth, I found it was sewn shut, my tongue heavy as lead.

I have to scream, I thought just before I fell back into blackness, where thought no longer existed.

CHAPTER SEVENTEEN

Guinevere

I woke up because someone was jostling me none too gently. Even though my head felt stuffed with cotton and pounded like a pillow beneath the fists of a restless sleeper, memories came back to me instantly.

I lashed out even before I forced my sticky lids open, my fist landing in the throat of the man who carried me.

Philippe let out a crackling grunt, his grip loosening so I slid from his arms onto my own two feet. I landed in a crouch and immediately sprinted away from the people in front of me waiting around the front door of an actual castle.

I didn't get far before someone tackled me hard into the dirt road. My chin hit the packed ground, and the sharp edge of a canine tore through my lip.

Still, I did not stop fighting.

Raffa's voice in my head urged me on.

La cerbiatta diventa la cacciatrice.

The fawn becomes the huntress.

I managed to kick out, happy I'd worn boots that day, landing the heel in the chin of the man who'd caught me by the legs. It gave me space to roll onto my back, even though he kept hold of one ankle.

When he reared over me, I went for his eyes with my thumbs, digging into the inner corners with my nails until I felt the thin membranes pop and warm, wet blood sluiced down my forearms.

The man howled above me, tossing his head back with the yowl of pain. It gave me time to squirm out from under his weight, but by then, like wolves called to the hunt, more men surrounded me.

"*Basta!*" someone ordered in an old, creaky voice that still managed to hold serious authority.

For just a second, I found myself frozen as well.

When I tried to get up again, one of the suited men stepped forward to press the mouth of a gun to my forehead, a cold kiss.

I stilled.

The bodies around me parted to reveal an old man stalking toward us with the use of a gold-tipped cane. Where he had once been tall, he was now stooped over, the joints and bones beneath his silken, loose skin like the gnarled roots of trees. Even in old age, there was something beautiful about him, almost majestic, like one of those paintings you saw in old British manor homes and museums of white men who had ruled the colonial world. He was swarthier than that, with deep-olive-toned skin and eyes like black olives between knitted, scowling brows.

It was obvious that this man was John Stone's father.

Gaetano Pietra.

He did not stop until the tips of his black leather boots were pressed into the side of my belly. With him looming over me, the shadows of night thick on his face with the blazing lights of the house at his back, I thought he might actually kill me then and there.

A man so ready to kill his daughter's lover would not draw the line at his estranged granddaughter.

But then he was offering his hand down to me, each finger glinting dully with the metallic shine of heavy rings.

"This is my granddaughter you tackle into the dirt," he said in that scratchy Italian. "Touch her again like that, and I will let her gouge out your eyes to the root."

I blinked up at him, shocked by his vehemence.

Irritated with my hesitancy, he bent down to grab my hand himself and leveraged me to my feet. Given the cane and his knotted bones, I was not expecting his strength.

He turned me with one hand so that the light from the house spilled over me before taking my chin in his hand to lift it to his.

"You look like him," he said after a long minute of scrutiny. "Pretty, but like him very much."

"A compliment," I said, tipping my chin higher in his grip.

A fleeting smile struck his face, there and gone so fast I almost thought I'd imagined it.

"Inside," he called to everyone in the courtyard, at least ten *soldati* and my aunt lingering on the periphery.

As one, the group moved toward the house.

Even though curiosity ate at me, I knew I would use the first chance I got to escape. These people were strangers even if we shared the same blood, and they had a deep, dark history with the only man who did matter to me.

Raffa.

Somewhere out there going mad knowing I had been taken.

Gaetano's hand was an iron vise around my biceps, and he took me inside what was clearly a small castle. It was grander than Villa Romano, with marble floors and curling staircases to the second level. Old walls had clearly been taken down to make the main floor mostly open, built around the two central staircases. In the back, stone had been taken out to allow for a huge panel of windows to let in natural light. Under other circumstances, I would have fallen in love with it.

The house was filled with people, at least a dozen, all of whom were staring at me.

What the *hell* was going on?

"*Famiglia*," Gaetano said in a voice that boomed and crackled like sound over speakers. Everyone held still to listen, a vibrating anticipation echoing throughout the room. *"Ci è stata restituita."*

My family, he said, she is returned to us.

Um . . .

What?

I blinked as a few women started to cry, and everyone else clapped somberly, as if after a particularly resonant eulogy.

"What is going on here?" I whispered, only because I didn't have the breath in my lungs to speak louder.

Gaetano turned me to him by the shoulders, a grin folding the skin back away from large white teeth. "I am sorry it took us this long to retrieve you."

"Retrieve me from where, exactly?" I asked, completely dumbfounded.

A frown pinched the skin between his thick brows before he looked beside us to my aunt, who winced slightly.

"You were held hostage," he said almost soothingly, rubbing my shoulder. "By those cretins the Romanos."

I blinked once, twice, before slightly hysterical laughter bubbled up my throat. I tried to cup it in my hands at my grandfather's worried expression, but it just kept spilling between my fingers.

"I think we better talk privately before we celebrate," my aunt stepped forward to say, placing a gentle hand on my back to push me toward the hallway to the right of the open-plan area.

Gaetano nodded, speaking rapid-fire Italian to a few men, who instantly converged on him while my aunt led me down the dark hall toward the back of the house.

We stopped at the door to an office, where I was pushed unceremoniously into a high-backed leather chair before a palatial desk. Unlike Raffa's offices in the villa and palazzo, this was chaotic, stuffed with books, files, and loose papers trapped under lamps, empty plates, and oddities like a skull painted with laurel leaves and a trophy of a man fishing. It was dark and seemed cramped because of the mess and the old, chestnut-stained furniture, but there was something comfortable and charming about it that put me more at ease than the modern, open-concept house had done.

I wondered if my father had sat in this chair as a young man, and tried to make sense of the surreal reality unfolding around me.

It took a few minutes for Gaetano to join us, the tap of his cane heralding his progress down the hallway, but no one spoke a word until he filled the doorway and made his way behind the desk.

"I wasn't kidnapped by the Romanos," I said as soon as he sat down, sitting straight in the chair, hands folded as if they'd take me seriously because of my prim bearing. "If anything, Raffa Romano saved me. More times than I can count."

My aunt scoffed. "That *bastardo* would not save a cat from drowning."

"He saved this American girl from a sexual predator," I snapped at her. "You do not know him."

"Nor do you," Gaetano said, folding his hands and propping his elbows on the desk to peer at me over them. He spoke English beautifully, with that same gramophone warble that came from old age but that gave his speaking voice a resonant quality. "You are just a child in a foreign land with foreign ways. You do not know of what you speak."

It was my turn to scoff. "I know that Raffa Romano is the *capo dei capi* of the Northern Italian Camorra. I know that therefore you should not be acting against him, but one of your family killed his father without provocation."

"Shut your mouth," my aunt ordered.

"Ginevra." Gaetano silenced her with a raised hand. "Let her speak."

"Thank you. As I was saying, I know more than I should if I was merely a captive of the Romanos. When Raffa found me, I had no money, no clothes, and no identification. He took me in, and . . ." I faltered for the first time, my damp fingers playing with the hem of my silk shirt. "I fell in love with him because he is a good man."

"Tell me," Gaetano urged, a kind, grandfatherly smile on his creased face. "Did you know he was Il Gentiluomo? *Il mafioso*?"

I frowned at the moniker but nodded. "I did. Eventually."

His smile thinned. "Not because he wanted you to."

"Are you trying to tell me that Raffa Romano somehow found out I was related to your family before I entered the country and then, knowing I would arrive exactly when I did on the side of the road, he hit me with his car so we could meet 'by accident'? I don't think so."

"Stranger things have happened," Ginevra opined.

"Yes, like being kidnapped by my own aunt."

"I saved you," she argued, her expression the very same one I'd seen so often on my father's face when he was being particularly obstinate.

"You took me from the man I love," I declared, staring down my nose at her before leveling the same look at Gaetano. "Why should I believe *you* over the man who has shown me nothing but kindness? When you have tried to kill me more than once?"

Gaetano reeled like I had slapped him. "No matter what you think of Il Gentiluomo, you cannot believe that after losing so much of my family I would order the death of my own granddaughter."

"Maybe you did it before you knew who I was," I suggested, crossing my arms.

If I had been standing, I would have braced my feet apart. Raffa's power stance.

Something flickered in my grandfather's expression, and I knew there was some truth to my accusation.

"We did not know who you were until the Venetian told us you had been kidnapped," he admitted softly. "It was easy enough to confirm. Even one look at you." He shook his head. "You have the Pietra pout."

I tried to flatten my lips, which only made him smile.

"Did you try to have me killed at the Romano palazzo in August on the night of the San Lorenzo festival?" I asked. "Someone sent chrysanthemums and then sneaked into the house at night to try to shoot me in the head."

Beside me, Ginevra bared her teeth and made a noise at the back of her throat like she wanted to rip that man to pieces.

"No," Gaetano emphasized with a weary shake of his silver mane. "You have to understand. The Venetian told us you had been kidnapped in order to keep us in line. We had laid our feud with the Romanos mostly to rest. I lost three sons to this war, two to death and one to abandonment. The Romano clan lost their father. It was enough. Then, the Venetian came to us—"

"You know who he is?" I interjected.

Gaetano glowered as I hit an obvious pain point. "I know he is a tall man, but that is it. I have met with him twice, and both times he wore a cloak with a hood and a Venetian mask. Very theatrical. He came to me to influence me to join his campaign to wrest power from Raffa Romano."

"So you could take over as *capo dei capi*?"

"Guinevere, look at me." He opened his hands to encompass what his advanced years had done to his body. "I am an old man with no male heirs. Ginevra does not want to take over from me, and she has two young sons who would not be appropriate choices for some time. What would happen to my family if I became *capo dei capi* and I died?"

"Whoever came next would kill them," I murmured, because Raffa had told me the very same thing.

It was powerful coercion for the next generation to toe the Mafia line.

"*Esattamente*. This wasn't what the man offered. He wants to be head of the Northern Camorra and promised retribution for our family as payment for our help."

"You didn't want to give it?"

"As I said, I am an old man. I want to enjoy what time I have left with my family. I do not need to begin a war when I am eighty-five, hmm?"

"Fair. So then why did you get involved?"

"When we refused, the Venetian went to the Grecos," he scoffed. "The scum that they are, of course they joined such a farcical rebellion. They thought the reluctant mafioso would be easy to take off his throne."

He clucked his tongue and shook his head. "Just because he did not want to be capo does not mean he is not a good one. It was not until some months had passed that the Venetian returned to us, this time to inform us Raffa had taken the daughter of my estranged son, Mariano Giovanni, hostage. He would not give us more information than some photos and the results of a DNA test he had performed."

A DNA test?

If the Venetian had access to my DNA, then he had access to *me*. The palazzo in Florence, certainly, to gather hair from my brush or something of the sort.

This turncoat was inside Raffa's family or his inner circle.

My stomach turned over at the thought of Renzo, Carmine, or Martina being the mole, and my gut immediately discarded it.

They would not cause Raffa harm under any circumstances.

I could not believe Annella, his housekeeper, or his cook would either.

Which left his sisters, their husbands, Leo, Tonio, and whichever *soldati* had access to Villa Romano and the palazzo. It irritated me that I had not thought to ask more questions about the structure of the Camorra's security. That I hadn't been more involved with helping Raffa end this Judas scheme at once.

"So you tried to kidnap me in Impruneta?" I asked, trying to fit the pieces together.

Gaetano frowned. "No. This was our first attempt. Though we did know the Grecos had sent an assassin to Romano's palazzo, we were assured you would not be hurt."

"And what about Philippe? Has he worked for you this entire time?" I demanded, infuriated on behalf of Raffa.

"He does not work for us," Ginevra spat. "He is a soldier of the Venetian. It was Philippe who came to us with the plan."

A growl rose in my throat, shocking me. I swallowed it back and spoke through bared teeth. "Well, he was not doing it to help you. He was doing it to hinder Raffa. I can assure you I was not kidnapped"—though, technically, Raffa had coerced me to come back to Italy, it was truly for my own safety—"and I would like to return to Raffa immediately. He will be out of his mind with worry."

"*Cara,*" Ginerva said, sliding forward in the chair beside me to grab for my hand as she had on the train. This time I did not let her take it. "You are so young. You don't realize what made men are like. They will do anything to skew things in their favor. Even manipulate innocent girls like yourself."

"Please," I said acidly. "I am a twenty-three-year-old woman with a master's degree. I may have been sheltered most of my life, but in the last few months I have seen men murdered, killed one myself, helped incriminate the Greco family, and fallen in love with a mafioso. I know myself and my relationship much better than you do."

"I am your family," she snapped.

"My father didn't think so," I countered coolly. "Or else he would not have left you for America. You are strangers, and while I can appreciate your motives may have been kind, I am asking you now to return me to Villa Romano and my chosen family."

When I looked to Gaetano, his brows were raised, and I had a vague impression that he was impressed with me. Too quickly, that expression dissolved into sadness.

"I am afraid we cannot. You are too valuable a tool to be used against us. So you shall remain here until we can decide what must be done with you, and with the Venetian, if what you say is true and he has manipulated the situation for his own gain."

"So you are my kidnappers now?" I hissed. "So much better than the Venetians and the Grecos and the Romanos, aren't you?"

This time when Gaetano grinned, it spread like a knife wound across his face, filled with bloody intent. "As you said, you are still a stranger to us, child. And you have not proven any kind of loyalty to those who share your blood, so we shall not either. Eduardo, take her downstairs."

I turned, but hands were already coming down on my shoulders, wrenching me to my feet. Eduardo wasn't large, but his grip was like iron manacles around my wrists as he started to drag me from the room.

"At least let me call Raffaele," I asked. "He'll come for me, and you said you don't want to start another war."

"He won't come for you," Ginevra said, a pity in those eyes that were so like my own. "You'll see."

Raffa's voice echoed in my thoughts.

Il mio posto felice. My happy place.

La mia cerbiatta. La mia stella cadente. La mia cacciatrice.

My little fawn. My shooting star. My huntress.

There is nothing I would not do for you.

Even start a war.

CHAPTER EIGHTEEN

Raffa

We were too late.

The train had already left by the time Renzo pulled up onto the sidewalk outside the train station and we all spilled out of the car into a sprint.

But the beautiful thing about modernity was that you could find records of everything.

Including footage of the platforms.

Two hundred euros greasing the right palms, and we were crammed into the security room with the adviser, watching in black and white as Philippe dragged Guinevere up to the train. Pride blossomed like a night-blooming flower in my chest when I watched my *cacciatrice* call for help and slip out of his grasp, only for an icy draft to obliterate it the moment I saw Philippe escape the crowd and get onto the train himself.

"*Pezzo di merda*," I cursed, hitting the side of the small television so the image spasmed with static. "How the hell did Philippe pass inspection when we went through our ranks?"

"He's known us since we were boys," Carmine said quietly, his gaze still fixed on the screen, shock wide in his eyes. "He was never even on the short list."

"Fuck," I shouted because English curse words hit differently, and anger was roiling through me like a cyclone. "Call Ludo. I want Philippe found *now*."

"And Guinevere?" Martina asked softly.

"Ludo is on Philippe. The rest of us do not sleep until we find where they have taken her," I ordered.

And sleep we did not.

The first night Renzo and Martina tracked down passengers who had been on the same train, using the CCTV footage and Ludo's facial recognition software. A German man claimed he had been one of the few to try to help Guinevere get away from Philippe, and when Philippe had followed her onto the train, the German, Karl, had followed him too, even though it was not going to his destination.

He had followed him through the cars until he reached the end and watched as Philippe sat beside Guinevere and an older woman who looked like her mother.

"She did not even blink when the man sat down with them," Karl had admitted with some confusion. "So I watched for a few minutes, but they chatted calmly, and then the girl settled in to take a nap. I figured I had interrupted a lovers' quarrel and left them. Was I wrong to have done so?"

"Yes," I shouted when Renzo relayed the information.

How could he have left her with a man she had tried to run from? I did not care for his logic, and my gums and fingers ached as if I could sprout fangs and claws and eviscerate him for his poor decision-making.

When it was I who had made the critical mistake.

But I could not understand Philippe.

He had been boyhood friends with Renzo, Leo, Carm, and me. We had played in the vines and pelted each other with olives. We had gone to school together and been pimply-faced teens.

How did someone like that turn on me so viciously?

Abducting the key to my heart right out from under me.

I felt like half a man knowing Guinevere was somewhere out there with the enemy.

"They won't kill her, boss," Carmine said quietly on day two while we watched hours of CCTV footage collected from every stop the train passed through, looking for Guinevere as she left the train with her captors. "They could've done it on the train, and they didn't. They could have done it in the street. They wanted her alive."

"To manipulate me," I growled.

Later that day, the demand came by way of a hand-delivered envelope. The courier, when pressed, explained it had been dropped off at the reception area of his firm, and he had no idea who it was from.

Fatti trovare alle due in Piazza de Miracoli, vieni da solo e sii puntuale, altrimenti la ragazza perde un occhio.

Two o'clock on Saturday in the Square of Miracles. Come alone and on time, or the girl loses an eye.

Fury blinded me, white-hot rage eviscerating my insides. I sat very, very still so that it would not split my skin and explode everywhere. Giving in to wrath would help no one. Calm, cool heads reigned supreme, especially in this world where hot-blooded men abounded.

"The Venetian and the Pietras have at least one man who truly knows me," I said as I sat in my office at the palazzo with Martina, Carmine, and Renzo late the second night. "So I need to do something they would not think me capable of."

"Leave her with them?" Martina asked, then held up her hands at my glower. "I'm just saying they would not expect that."

"That is not an option, obviously."

A cacophony outside the closed door prompted all of us to reach for the weapons we had been wearing since Guinevere was taken. When the door swung open and hit the opposite wall with a bang, it revealed Ludovico, panting hard and wincing, with a hand pressed to his healing side.

"Ludo." I dropped my gun back into its shoulder holster and stalked toward him. "What takes you from Villa Romano? Who is watching the family?"

"Leo," he promised, sucking a breath in through his clenched teeth. "I had to come. This should not be said over the phone."

"What is it?"

He lumbered over to the desk, and Renzo stood so he could take his seat. Once settled, he checked his white shirt to see blood coming through the bandage. Martina got up to fetch the medical kit from the cupboard along the wall behind me.

"You asked me to find out who Mariano Giovanni was," Ludo said finally, pulling his leather satchel from his shoulder gingerly to retrieve his computer. "Well, I finally found him."

Renzo and Martina crowded behind me at the desk to peer over my shoulder at the screen Ludo swiveled my way.

It showed a photo of a young man with thick dark hair and large eyes framed with almost feminine lashes.

I would have recognized those eyes anywhere, in any face.

They were *occhi di cerbiatta*.

Guinevere's doe eyes.

It was a photocopy of an old driver's license from 1989 that read "Mariano Giovanni Pietra."

Pietra.

"*Dio mio,*" Renzo breathed, struck dumb for the first time in his life.

I echoed the feeling.

Could this be possible?

That Guinevere was the granddaughter of Gaetano Pietra, the man who had feuded first with my father and now with me?

It seemed so wildly implausible, so absolutely absurd, that a small part of me felt like laughing.

But then my brain kicked in, puzzling the pieces together that I'd had all along.

Guinevere's father had fled Tuscany before her birth and forbade her from entering the country. Such an extreme aversion for him to have merely disliked what Italy stood for or its governmental policies. No, this was much more personal, obviously diabolical.

It was for her safety, he had said on the phone with her that day in the bathroom with me when he had discovered she was in Florence. She had to leave at once for her safety and never return.

Because if the Pietras discovered who she was, they would never let her go.

The family had been growing weaker for years. Even before they killed my father and I went after their two eldest sons, they had lost a son to a drunken bar fight.

Mariano Giovanni.

Only, he had not died.

He had relocated to the US and changed his identity.

Given birth to Gemma and Guinevere Stone, who'd spent their entire lives not knowing that their bloodline was one of the oldest in Mafia history.

"I am a friend," the man from Impruneta had told her when he tried to take her away.

Somehow the Pietras had found out exactly who was living in my house. Not just a tool to use against me, but one they felt they were owed.

A granddaughter returned home.

"*Cazzo*," I muttered, staring hard at the image of her father. "The woman on the train was Ginevra Pietra. The German said she looked like her mother, and if she looks anything like John Stone, né Mariano Giovanni Pietra, then it had to be her."

"They wouldn't hurt their own blood," Carmine said, but he didn't sound so sure.

Gaetano Pietra was of a school like my father's.

Cold and ruthless as the edge of a blade.

"You don't think she knew . . ." Martina whispered like she could hardly stand to suggest the words.

"*Assolutamente no*," I said, voice rough as I spoke through the weight of this new information. "She was not the kind to keep secrets, especially not after her father and I kept some egregious ones from her."

"She could have been frightened to tell you." Martina continued to speak gently, as if that would soften the blow of her implication.

"No. She did not know, and she did not enter into our lives as some kind of ruse to bring down the Romanos." I shook my head. "I told Guinevere the other day a quote by Dante, 'Do not be afraid; our fate cannot be taken from us. It is a gift.' Maybe this was John Stone's karma, that his daughter would find love in the country he hated because he never saw fit to tell her why he hated it. Maybe it was Guinevere's destiny all along. She came to Italy to find herself, and in so many ways, she has. There was always this side of her that liked the darkness in me, that was called to it."

"We all saw it," Ludo agreed with a grunt. "But now she is with the wrong family, and we have to get her back."

"The Venetian will expect me to show up at Pisa's Piazza dei Miracoli on Saturday because he believes I love her enough to die for her."

"Do you?" Carmine asked, head cocked.

The rest of my *soldati*—my friends—peered at me in much the same way.

"Yes." It was the truest truth I had ever uttered.

Would I die for Guinevere?

A hundred times over.

But I was not willing for either of us to die when we'd had so little of this life together. There were still things I wanted with her, things I had never hoped to dream of until she had appeared in my life like a fairy-tale mirage.

My worst nightmares and hers had come true with this kidnapping, but I would devote every moment of the rest of my life to making it up to her and wooing her to the dark side. Failure in either was not an option.

"I would die for her, but I will not play the sheep led so easily to slaughter. I am the wolf, the head of this family, and *capo dei capi*. If the Venetian wants what is mine, he will have to try much harder to outsmart me, because blunt force trauma will not take me down."

"So what is your plan?" Carm asked.

"First," I said, as something outlandish started to form in my mind. "Nothing we speak of leaves this room. Not even to Leo. Let us hope Philippe was our only mole, but until we know for sure, our circle of trust is the four people in this room. I have an idea, but I have to admit, I am not sure it will work."

"What is it?" Martina asked impatiently.

I sighed even though I knew this was the best course of action to get Guinevere back.

"I am going to call her father."

◆ ◆ ◆

They left me to make the phone call, going into the kitchen to eat and discuss how best to approach the Pietra castle near Pisa.

I sat in my chair, looking at the painting on the wall behind my desk, which I had purchased after Guinevere had left for Michigan. It was John Collier's portrait of King Arthur's Guinevere, crowned queen and resplendent with flowers riding a white horse. It appealed to me for many reasons, not least because the image depicted the scene in a legend where the queen is kidnapped, but her portrayal is of a serene, noble beauty ready to take on the world.

She reminded me of my Guinevere. The peace and stability she brought to my life, her elegance despite her youth, and the sincerity of her curious, insatiable mind.

I had taken to staring at it when I was lost in thought. The two framed photos on the desk I had of Guinevere and me together—one the very same selfie she had kept back at her apartment in Michigan—were too hard to look at for long. Painful reminders, like an urn kept on a mantel.

I dialed the number Ludo had given me and listened to the monotonous ring, which had never sounded more portentous.

"Hello, John Stone speaking."

His voice was stripped of Italy, flat and almost nasal like Midwest accents could be.

"Hello," I said. "My name is Raffaele Romano."

"What's happened to her?" he asked almost before I was finished rolling the second *R*.

I wished I could have proven his assumption incorrect, but there was no getting around the truth.

"It seems your family, the Pietras, have taken her."

The pause that followed did not feel like true quiet. It came down the phone line like a silent scream, something with force that hurt my ears even without sound.

"When?"

"The day before yesterday—"

"And you are only just calling now?" he bellowed.

"I did not know until fifteen minutes ago that Guinevere was related to them. How could I when she did not know herself?"

I found myself holding my breath, because there was a chance I could have been wrong about it all. Her knowing, her role in my life.

Leo's suspicions when he'd first met her echoed back at me.

"Fuck," John Stone cursed viciously. "Fuck! She only found out the same day she was taken. I'm still not sure how."

Ah.

We had tracked the GPS on the Maserati Philippe had been driving, so I had known they went to the Uffizi, but I had assumed it was just to pass the time viewing some of her favorite pieces while I was meeting the Albanians.

But the Uffizi archives were just the place she would visit if she had an inkling about the truth.

Unbidden, my lungs collapsed, punctured by my continued ache and longing for this brilliant slip of a girl who could see rhyme where there was barely any reason.

"Something must have triggered her to finally put it together. She and one of my men had been searching for some time for answers about her ancestry."

John snorted rudely. "There was hardly anything left to find. I scrubbed most of my identifying records when I left that godforsaken place. How did you discover the truth if she didn't tell you?"

"I have a talented sleuth on staff. When this is all said and done, he will help you remove even those trace amounts, but for now, I need your help."

Another pause, this one a vacuum, as if John had reared away from the phone.

Finally, he said, "A Romano asking me for help. I never thought I would see the day."

"Nor did I," I snapped, impatient and at the end of a very short, very frayed rope that tied me to Guinevere. "Now, will you do as I ask to save your daughter from those vultures you call your family?"

Even though Guinevere had always spoken highly of her father, going so far as to *rave* about him, I had not seen a glimmer of anything in my own observations to warrant her praise.

Until, without hesitation, he said, "Anything for her."

Finally, something to bond over.

CHAPTER NINETEEN

Guinevere

They kept me locked in a room in the basement for four days.

Four.

Truthfully, I did not expect to be kept longer than two. That was how much faith I had in Raffa and his crew and their ability to get through any obstacle to reach me. Raffa had literally saved me from being taken by thugs while I was an entire ocean away from him in Michigan. Surely, he could do the same here in his own country, in his own territory.

Even as the morning of the fourth day crept over the horizon and spilled weak pink light onto the ceiling of my stark but comfortable bedroom, I did not worry.

I knew he would come.

And if it was taking a little longer, it was only because he would eviscerate them when he was done.

I had not seen Gaetano again, but Ginevra visited me.

The first day, I refused to speak with her, but she told me stories about her youth with my father. In some ways, she spoke of a stranger, a man named Mariano instead of John, whom I had no memory of. This man was taught to play with guns and knives the way normal children would their toys. She spoke of Gaetano's idea of after-school care, a mini boot camp for his sons to arm and defend themselves and learn about the family business. As a woman, Ginevra herself was not sanctioned to participate, but she had grown sly and clever enough to practice in the shadows and tutor with my father at night before bed in their limited free time. She knew more than enough, she said, to teach me how to take care of myself.

Even though I enjoyed the sentiment, I didn't deign to answer her. When all this was over, and I knew in my bones it would be soon, Raffa and his crew would teach me all I needed to know and more. They could be excessive like that.

The second day, she tried to ask me questions about my life. What did I like to do back home in Michigan? What was my mother like? Did I speak Albanian as well as Italian?

Each time she was met with silence until she gave up and stalked out of the room, punctuating her frustration by slamming the door behind her.

On the third day, she arrived with a tablet, and the only questions she asked were about the Romano family.

How many people lived at Villa Romano? And how many of them were guards?

Where did Raffa spend most of his time, at the villa or the palazzo?

Was I aware of the names of any of the Romano holding companies? Maybe I saw them on his desk sometimes.

When I didn't reply, Ginevra had sighed and said, "Truly, I am your best ally in this entire compound, Guinevere. I told you the story of my brother." Her eyes skittered to a camera fixed in the corner by the door. "I only want what is best for you. So please, hear me when I say that if you do not answer my questions or give me any inkling you might be converted to our side in this, things will go very poorly for you."

I had merely stared at her as I had done for the past two days.

She could say whatever she wanted, but her actions thus far had proven she was under Gaetano's control, and my grandfather definitely did not have my best interests at heart.

It wasn't surprising then, on the third day, when the man named Eduardo opened the door instead of Ginevra, followed closely by Gaetano.

"I hear you are not finding Ginevra a pleasant conversationalist," he said in that faux-jovial way of his as Eduardo started to move some of the furniture to the side of the room.

I watched him wearily, a metallic taste like blood on the back of my tongue. A premonition maybe. I was sitting on the bed with the only book in the room, Italo Calvino's collection of folktales. It seemed fitting I had just been reading about Sfortuna, the unlucky heroine whose fortunes change after a series of unpleasant events when she catches the attention of a prince and earns his love.

My own happily ever after had been within my grasp, and I'd squandered it out of fear. Now, based on the way Eduardo was rolling up his sleeves and then rolling back the carpet, I wondered if that chance was gone for good.

"What is he doing?" I asked quietly.

"Eduardo? Oh, we don't like to get any stains on the carpet," my grandfather explained with a smile as he sat in a chair at the edge of the room. "It's an eighteenth-century Persian carpet."

"Of course," I said dully, my gaze tracking Eduardo as he grabbed a wooden chair from the desk and dragged it into the middle of the room before, surprisingly, he left.

"Now, we are just us two," Gaetano said, opening his palms as if to symbolize he wasn't hiding anything. "Why don't we have a candid discussion about your future, hmm?"

I didn't reply because there was nothing to say. Gaetano had complained that the Venetian was theatrical, but it was clear my grandfather was playing his own game, and he did not really need my participation.

"It is clear that you hold affection for Raffaele Romano, but my daughter has told me it is likely a symptom of Stockholm syndrome and that with enough time you'll come to see the light about him."

I let my scornful doubt shine through my expression, but he ignored me.

"He killed my eldest sons," he continued. "Did you know this? Giorgio and Giuseppe. A car bomb in Genoa took out my firstborn, and poisoned wine my second."

"I thought you had put the idea of revenge to rest?" I asked as fear skittered down my spine and sank sharp teeth into my tailbone.

He cocked his head, tapping his cane against the floor. "Yes, and I thought I had. But now you are here, and I find it difficult to resist the temptation."

"Why would you work for the Venetian?" I tried to reason. "You said he had to blackmail you into helping so far."

"Yes, but I do not want this information to hand it over to that *stronzo*. I want it for myself. The Venetian can have Raffa's kingdom if he can steal it. All I want is his life."

"No." The word exploded from me like a bullet.

I wished it was one.

If someone had put a gun into my hand that second, I would have raised it without hesitation to put lead between my grandfather's eyes.

The thought should have chilled me.

That the idea of killing could be so immediate in my fantasies. That I could almost feel the weight of the gun and the cool of the metal in my hand, my index finger twitching like it was hungry for the pull of a trigger.

But I had already had my existential crisis about killing someone. The man on the top of the Impruneta bell tower.

Now, instead of the blare of panic trilling through my head, I heard only the cool, calm tones of Raffa.

Non sei un'assassina; sei una cacciatrice.

You are not a killer; you are a huntress.

And I felt it was true in that moment, staring at a stranger who shared my blood and feeling certain I would end him if he so much as laid a finger on Raffa or Martina or Renzo, Ludo, or Carm. On any of the Romanos who had taken me into their home.

Far from horrifying me, the idea sang through my blood like a macabre song.

"The Venetian doesn't want him dead yet," Gaetano continued as if I hadn't spoken, and I had a feeling he did that often, especially with women. "He doesn't have what he needs from Raffaele, and until he does, he can't secure the empire. But it is too good an opportunity to pass up. So I have made my own little plan. Unfortunately, it involves your cooperation.

"*Tu sei mia nipote. Il mio sangue*," he said in Italian, gesturing widely with one hand. "You are my granddaughter. My blood. Of course, even though the circumstances were not desirable, I was thrilled to discover your existence. It was wrong of your father to keep you hidden from us."

He paused for me to agree with him, and though I did take umbrage at Dad for keeping such a colossal secret, I couldn't very well blame him for keeping me from his family.

They were batshit crazy.

"I want to embrace you as my blood and, one day, maybe even my heir," he continued, dangling the last word like bait before a fish, hoping to hook me with its shiny promise. "What do you think about that?"

"I have no interest in being a mob boss," I said flatly, though that wasn't necessarily true anymore.

When Raffa came for me, I would never leave his side again. Not for meetings with Albanians, not to confer with other capos. Not when he could be in danger and not when he might be complicit in criminalities. I would go where he went—be it prison or the ER or any circle of Dante's hell. I would be his partner in all things.

The queen to his King Below.

He laughed. "That is a good thing. Men who want to be mob bosses only care about the money and the swagger. I have looked into you, Guinevere Stone, and you are a smart woman. First in your class at the University of Michigan for your MBA, a job at one of the best financial firms in the country. Doing what I do is much like running a giant corporation."

"Where people are killed if they don't follow company policy," I quipped.

A shadow passed over his face. "I do not appreciate jokes when talking about business, Guinevere."

"And I do not appreciate your threatening the man I love or my being kept hostage when I've asked to leave."

"We have welcomed you warmly," he started to say, but I cut him off with a harsh laugh.

"Warmly? My aunt drugged me on a train and dragged me here, and when I didn't immediately comply with your wishes, you had me locked in this room. I haven't met any other family members, and I haven't been allowed access to my phone. Is that considered warm in the Camorra?"

"Yes," he snapped. "A cold welcome would involve you strung up with the prosciutto in the barn, left to dry and rot until we deigned to slice you open. Would you rather the alternative?"

I swallowed thickly but gathered my bravado around me like a shield. "Which are you? The loving grandfather happy to meet his granddaughter for the first time, or the Mafia don wanting answers from me by any means necessary?"

"Can't I be both?" he asked, and it gave me chills because he was utterly sincere. "I do not want to hurt you, but I will if it means ending this mess once and for all."

"By killing me, you mean?"

"No, of course not. Why would I kill one of my only remaining blood relatives?" he asked, irritated with me enough that the thin, loose skin around his neck wobbled. "There are many stages between life and death, Guinevere. This is something I could teach you, if you consented to help us now."

"Help you how?"

The door creaked open, and Eduardo appeared holding two large ceramic pitchers and a pretty designer silk scarf, kind of like the one Raffa had used to tie my hair back on our ride out to Livorno.

"Tell me about Raffa Romano and his outfit," Gaetano suggested, flicking invisible lint off his suit pants.

I sat silently, letting the quiet stretch on and on.

"Eduardo," Gaetano said with a heavy sigh, gesturing toward me with a nod. "Perhaps you will have an easier time convincing her than I."

The whipcord-lean man stepped away from the middle of the cleared room, where he had placed the pitchers beside the chair, and came for me.

I don't know why I wasn't expecting the open hand slap that hit me over the ear. Pain and static erupted in my head, my vision fuzzy and white, my senses deafened by a loud ringing.

Vaguely, I was aware of Eduardo picking me up to carry me over to the chair in the center of the room and secure me with something by the ankles and wrists.

When my head cleared enough to make sense of things again, I was locked to the chair, with the end of my braid tied into the rope around my wrists so that my head was forced back at a painful angle.

"I am sorry for this, Guinevere," Gaetano murmured from his spot to my left. "But this is the only way to ensure Romano shows up in the piazza tomorrow. He needs to see how much you are suffering and imagine how much you will suffer still if he does not do as I've asked."

"*Vaffanculo*," I spat at him as Eduardo reached for the pitcher filled with water and draped the beautiful orange silk scarf over my face. "When Raffa comes for me, I hope he leaves killing you until last so I can be the one to put a bullet between your eyes."

Gaetano's laugh was muffled as Eduardo started to pour water over my face through the silk until I felt like I was drowning.

He's coming, I thought desperately as I struggled not to swallow water and fought to breathe.

He will always come for you.

"What is the security code for the palazzo in Firenze?" Gaetano raised his voice to be heard over the rush of water in my ears.

It was the first of many, many questions.

◆ ◆ ◆

Eduardo waterboarded me for a long time.

They interrogated me about Raffa, his business dealings and family, and then, when none of that proved fruitful, they asked me about my father.

My continued silence resulted in the questions devolving into threats.

Did I want to see Raffa tomorrow after he'd been killed?

Maybe they would place him in my bed while I slept so the blood would soak the sheets and wake me with a chill.

Maybe they would serve me his eyeballs, plucked intact from his head, on my breakfast tray Sunday morning.

Maybe they would hunt down my father all the way in Michigan so they could meet my mother and invite them for a friendly visit. Would that properly motivate me?

At some point, I couldn't even hear them anymore. Every single one of my senses and every atom of my being was focused on not asphyxiating. If I'd had the wherewithal to think beyond that, I might have criticized the torture technique. How could anyone focus enough to answer questions when they were fighting for every breath?

The sunlight spilling through the one window in the room was thick and syrupy with midday heat by the time he peeled the silk from my face for the last time and swept out of the room without untying me.

Gaetano had left a while ago.

He said it distressed him to see me suffer.

I would've laughed at the memory, but I was still struggling to drag air into my waterlogged lungs. My desperate gasps rasped too loudly in my ears, panic making the laborious act even more difficult.

It felt like I might never breathe properly again.

I coughed up water until I felt sick and then vomited the meager amounts of breakfast I'd eaten onto the wood floor beside my feet.

This was why Dad hadn't wanted me involved with his family.

This was why Raffa had kept his camorrista secret for so long.

There was nothing glamorous or comforting about life in the Mafia.

I was not even a mafioso, not even legally bound to one, and yet there I sat, tied to a chair, dripping with water and sweat, gasping like a fish out of water.

My mind had taken me to a place in the subterranean depths of my psyche, a kind of mind palace or safe harbor away from the horrors of what Eduardo was doing to me.

I found myself in a dark wood, the very same one as Dante in the opening line of *The Divine Comedy*. Virgil was there, as he was for the poet, greeting me solemnly and offering me a skeletal hand.

He promised to take me to my lover, but first, I had to journey through hell to reach him.

Now, sitting listlessly in the chair, the heavy drip of water leaching off my hair and clothes and the harsh rattle of my breath a soundtrack to the revelation, I understood something vital.

If this was hell, I would cross it over and over if it meant being with Raffa.

Even more importantly, I acknowledged that this wasn't just a once-in-a-lifetime scenario. Maybe I would never be waterboarded through a designer silk scarf again, but there would be other times when I would be in danger because of Raffa and what he was.

Loving the *capo dei capi* was not without its risks.

I had firsthand accounting of that.

But God, it was also not without its rewards.

As I dripped dry, a chill settling into my bones, I warmed myself by thinking about all the ways Raffa had loved me.

Buying me an entire new wardrobe, taking care of me when I was ill, letting me drive his Ferrari Spyder, buying me a *cornicello* to counteract my bad luck.

Trying to save me from himself, even though it hurt him.

It took me a long time to realize I was crying, because my face was already wet.

At some point, miraculously, I must have fallen asleep, because the next thing I knew, I was jerking awake so strongly I almost upended the chair.

A flurry of Italian shouts echoed throughout the usually quiet house, along with a sound that made my heart take off racing in my chest.

Gunfire.

I never thought I would be so happy to hear that tat-tat-tat of semiautomatic weapons.

When the door flung open, Ginevra was there in what looked like gardening clothes, dirt streaked across her cheek and a huge gun in one hand. Something in her expression flickered with relief at the sight of me before passing into horror and arriving at resolution.

"He's here."

I thought it was a sob crawling up my throat like a rat through a pipe, a sensation that almost made me gag, but when it emerged, it was laughter.

Bright, hysterical laughter.

Ginevra stared at me for a moment until a crash reverberated through the house, shaking the walls so that dust spiraled through the air.

"*Cazzo*," Ginevra cursed as she hurried to my side and bent to work at the ropes around my ankles.

"Something rammed the house," I said, smiling so wide it hurt my wet, aching face.

"Crazy man," she muttered before clamping the gun between her thighs to reach for a knife in her gum boot, cutting through the ropes to free me. "Attacking the Pietra compound in broad daylight."

I laughed again. In the wake of surviving this horror on my own, giving Gaetano and Eduardo nothing, and knowing that Raffa was not riding in on his noble steed as my Prince Charming but cracking open the very earth to find me, as Pluto had to reach Proserpina, I felt freer than I ever had before.

"He wanted to make a spectacle of it," I said, even though she hadn't asked a question. "He wants them to know he can come for them at home in broad daylight, with the house full of *soldati*, and still win."

"He won't win," Ginevra said as the last of my bonds fell away. "Not unless he has an army. This is a *castello*, Guinevere. It was made to withstand a siege."

I only grinned as she tugged me toward the door. My legs were gummy, but I forced them to move with minimal grace.

"Where are you taking me?" I asked.

Following her seemed like the best option regardless. I was a sitting duck in that room, especially given everyone in the house knew that was where I had been kept. I had no idea of the layout, but emerging from the basement seemed like getting a step closer to Raffa.

"The safe room," Ginevra declared, pausing at the threshold of a staircase to peek around the corner with her gun drawn.

"I'm surprised you'd bother," I admitted as I ran up the stairs behind her and followed her into a room hidden in the concave wall of the staircase.

Inside, an older woman sat on a chartreuse velvet love seat with two boys.

I recognized her instantly as the confused woman from the Duomo.

She blinked at me, pushing aside one of the boys gently as she stood up and then reached out her hand toward me.

"*Io ti conosco*," she said.

"You do," I agreed in Italian, stepping forward to take her hand and press it to my cheek. "I am your granddaughter."

Tears pooled in her lower lids, catching on the wrinkles beneath as they spilled.

"She has dementia," Ginevra explained quietly. "She often gets confused. Gaetano does not let her out in public much."

"I saw her in Firenze the day you took me from the train," I mentioned without looking away from my grandmother's beautifully aged face. "She recognized me then too."

"You have the eyes of your father," my aunt said. "Of your grandmother."

"What's your name?" I asked the elderly woman, who was still cupping my face, her thumb rubbing back and forth along my cheekbone.

"Giulia," she said with a tremulous smile.

"Hi, Giulia," I replied, pressing a kiss to each of her silken cheeks.

She beamed at me.

"And these are my sons, Circo and Ottavio," Ginevra introduced the two preteen boys, one of whom I'd also seen at the church with Giulia.

"I'm glad you broke the *G* naming tradition," I said, which prompted my aunt to laugh. "It was a bit much."

Behind me the door opened, Gaetano ushered in by a *soldato* I didn't recognize. He stopped in his tracks when he saw me there, face screwing up with distaste.

"What is she doing in here?"

"She is family," Ginevra pointed out. "Just because you do not trust her yet does not mean she shouldn't be kept safe."

"I am safer out there than you are," I countered. "They're here for me."

"To take you away again and *use* you against us," Gaetano said, his brows so knit together they were one thick black squiggle from a marker drawn across his face. "We will not give you up to be manipulated again."

I looked at the man who had raised my father and wondered how Dad could have become the kind of man I knew today. There were shades of the iron will and stubbornness that must have come as a product of this life, but John Stone was otherwise kind, caring, and thoughtful.

This paranoid creature who would waterboard his own granddaughter while claiming to want to welcome her into the family was the kind of monster Raffa had claimed to be. Two faced, violent as a baseline, convinced always that his way was the best.

It was ironic that this kind of man was exactly whom Dad and Raffa had warned me against, thinking themselves inherently monstrous too.

I could say with a clear heart that they were not.

And neither was I.

But that did not mean I wouldn't do something monstrous when my loved ones were threatened. Or when I was.

So I fixed a trembling pout to my mouth, ran to Gaetano, and threw my arms around his neck to sniff into his shoulder.

"I'm so sorry," I gasped. "I was afraid and confused, but I just want it all to go away. Please, make it all go away."

Gaetano was stiff in my embrace for a moment before the hand holding his cane came up to thump me gently on the back.

"Hush now. Do not worry. Your *nonno* will take care of it."

I lifted my head from his suit jacket just enough to peer around his arm at the *soldato* who had come inside with him. He stood close, a personal bodyguard.

Close enough that if I shoved Gaetano just a little bit as I nuzzled closer for comfort, I could snag the gun dangling from his right hand . . .

Gaetano stumbled back a step as I pushed forward, the guard reaching to steady him with his left hand. He was distracted by the movement, lulled into a false sense of security behind the locked door of the panic room with only the Pietra family inside.

So it was almost too easy to grab the gun and wrench it to the side, twisting his wrist to such an extreme angle he barked out a curse. Gaetano was between us, so it was impossible for him to get a good grip on me as I took the gun for myself.

Shuffling so that my back was to the side wall, I leveled the gun at Gaetano, then swept it across the room.

Ginevra sat with Giulia and her sons on the love seat, staring at me with more curiosity than fear.

Gaetano's gaze was one of indignant fury.

"You will not shoot us," he proclaimed. "This is your first time holding a gun, if I had to bet."

It wasn't.

I'd held one at the Beaumont Building what felt like years ago but was only weeks prior in Michigan, when those thugs had tried to take me away.

But he was right in that I had never fired one before.

I raised a brow at my grandfather and smiled, all teeth and peeled-back lips. "I know enough to hit a target four feet from me."

Gaetano shifted quickly for a man of his age, snapping his cane up with one hand to knock it against my wrist. The impact smarted, the weapon swerving to the right.

To the *soldato*, who used Gaetano's distraction to lunge for me.

Without a second's hesitation, I pulled the trigger.

The bullet caught him in the upper shoulder and hardly slowed him down.

So I fired again, his torso only a foot from mine. The kickback from the gun bit into my hand, but I hardly felt it through the adrenaline.

This time, the bullet blasted through his chest cavity, the force so much greater because it was at point-blank range.

When he hit me, it was in a stumble, his breath a thin thread of air whistling through his throat. I shoved him off me, and his body fell to the side against the wall, alive but not for long.

Gaetano stared at me as if he had never seen me before.

Which was funny, in a way, because I had never felt more myself.

There was a loud bang at the door, not as if someone knocked but as if a body was crushed against it. Gaetano pulled his own silver handgun out of its shoulder holster and shuffled back away from the door.

"It will hold," Ginevra reassured him. "It's reinforced. No one will get in using force."

All of us waited with eyes on the door, only the dying man's gurgling breaths to punctuate the silence.

"Guinevere, get back here," Ginevra hissed as a mechanical whirr sounded.

"I'm fine here," I insisted, but one glance behind me showed my aunt standing before Giulia and her sons, fierce and proud like a female warrior staring down the barrel of her gun.

"They must be friendly if they know the code," Circo whispered. "Right, Mamma?"

The whirr continued until there was a loud beep and the heavy door began to swing open.

Gaetano fired into the narrow gap, once, twice, three times.

"*Non sparate*," someone called out from the other side.

Hold fire!

My grandfather froze, his mouth puckering in tart surprise, while behind me Ginevra gasped.

Then again, I did too.

Because I would have known that voice anywhere. It had read to me before bed, soothed me through multiple hospital visits, and bantered with me my entire life.

The door pushed open farther, and John Stone, born Mariano Giovanni Pietra, stepped into the room wearing a bulletproof vest over his dress shirt, a semiautomatic rifle strapped across his chest as casually as a fanny pack.

"*Ciao, papà*," he said. "Are you happy to see me?"

Behind him, Raffa emerged in his own bulletproof vest, blood from a shallow cut weeping down his neck. His eyes immediately found mine, darkening as they took in my damp clothes and hair, the blood spatter from the fallen *soldato* at my feet.

Without hesitation, he stepped around Dad and pistol-whipped Gaetano, who fell to his knees with a sharp cry.

"Did you do this to her?" Raffa asked, his words as clear and cold as ice carved from an Arctic glacier.

Gaetano spat a wad of blood at his feet. "She was defending the man who killed my sons."

Raffa arrested completely before a snarl retook his features. He looked utterly feral in that moment, filled with animal fury and a base sense of right and wrong that was entirely founded on his own skewed code.

It was magnificent to behold.

Especially knowing that a crime against *me* had inspired it.

"What did he do to you?" Dad asked, staring at me in anguish. He looked simultaneously older than his years and younger. I could see the old version of himself transposed against the man he was now like a palimpsest.

"They filmed it to send to you," I said, surprised that my voice did not waver even though it was rough from choking on water and crying out with distress. "They waterboarded me for information about Raffa. About you."

Raffa cursed viciously in Italian, but it was my dad who shocked me.

John Stone, the same man who was a leading financial adviser and owner of the largest investment firm in the Midwest, the man who followed his routines like gospel, without deviation, who volunteered at the local homeless shelter and held me every single time I cried, stepped up to his father's kneeling form and put a bullet straight through his head.

CHAPTER TWENTY

Guinevere

Ginevra, the boys, and I screamed as his body hit the floor with a dull thwack, his cane clattering to the stone beside him. Gaetano's brains painted the wall, the floor, and an old leather chair the same color as the blood dripping from its upholstery.

"Mariano!" Ginevra snapped, stepping forward only to pause when Raffa pointed his gun at her. "*Che diavolo*?"

What the hell?

"Ginnie," Dad murmured, studying her with mild shock and warmth before he realized that she was exclaiming about their father's death. "If anyone knows how much he deserved it, you do."

My aunt stared at him for a long moment before her face crumpled. "I've wanted to do that for years."

I was pulled from their exchange by the fact that Raffa had crossed the room to my side and was cupping my cheeks tenderly to tip my face to his gaze.

"*La preda diventa la cacciatrice*," he murmured, his thumb rubbing through the blood under my eye.

The prey becomes the huntress.

"I knew you would find me," I told him, clutching at his wrists, the gun still held in one hand as I did so. To my mild horror, tears pricked the backs of my eyes. "Even when they hurt me, I thought of you, and I knew it would be okay."

I had never before now seen the expression that seized Raffa's face, a softening of every feature except for his eyes, those pale-copper orbs burning like firelight as they stared down into mine.

"I will always come for you," he swore. "Across oceans and any degree of space or time, I will come for you."

"*Me lo prometti?*" I asked, suddenly desperate to hear it. "Promise me."

"*Te lo giuro,*" he said solemnly.

I swear it.

"I'm sorry," I whispered, tipping my head forward to rest my bloody forehead against his chin. My fingers curled into the straps of his bulletproof vest and tugged him closer.

"Hush," he ordered, kissing my chin. "I am just happy to have you alive and in my arms once again."

I pulled back to look up at him, a stranger's blood on his lips, which I had transferred to him like a lipstick mark. The force of the love I had for him momentarily overwhelmed me, robbing me of my voice, stripping reality away to nothing but the gorgeous man holding me like a treasure even though I had hurt him, even though I was damp and bloody.

I thought of Petrarch's quote "To be able to say how much love, is love but little," and I understood it. There would never be enough language to harness the power of that singular sensation in my chest that existed just for Raffaele Romano.

As I opened my mouth to say something to that effect, I heard Dad say, "Jinx?"

And I was returned to myself jarringly, suddenly back in a safe room in the Pietra compound with a dead man to my right and an estranged family to my left.

"Dad," I said, choking on the word.

Raffa reluctantly dropped his hands and stepped away so I could move toward my dad, who had his arms spread, waiting for me. I threw myself into them without thought, taking the comfort he had offered me most of my life.

"Guinevere," he whispered, a sorrowful orchestra of pain in those three syllables. "My sweet girl, I thought I might have lost you."

I didn't know if he meant physically or emotionally, because both had been real possibilities. In the end it didn't matter.

I could now understand how much he hated this life and everything it had stood for in his memories, so it meant everything to know he had crossed the Atlantic to make sure I was safe.

"I love you," I told him, because somehow it was so much easier to say those words to him than to Raffa. Maybe because I had spent my whole life loving Dad already. "I'm sorry you had to grow up in this crazy family. Thanks for giving me a normal childhood."

Dad's laugh was wet in my hair as he held me close. "It was the only option acceptable for you. Your mother and I never wanted this life for you and Gemma."

I laughed a little. "Well, it seems I was destined for it anyway."

He pulled away to search my face with dark eyes. I kept my expression open, letting him read whatever was written there.

No more secrets between us.

"I suppose you were," he murmured, both proud and disappointed.

"What have you done with the rest of the crew?" Ginevra asked Raffa, standing behind Dad with her hands on her hips.

Across from her, Raffa stood with his feet braced and arms crossed, appraising her coolly. "Many have been killed. Though having John with us spared us the necessity of killing everyone. You really should update your security more often."

Ginevra scoffed. "We hardly imagined Mariano—John—would ever show his face again. Let alone to help Romanos break into our home."

"You kidnapped my daughter," Dad snapped, stepping away to face her with me tucked under his arm. "You gave me no choice."

"To be fair, we thought we were saving her," she insisted. "The Venetian told us Raffaele was keeping her hostage to stop us from turning on him."

Behind her, Giulia got to her feet and moved gingerly toward Dad.

"Mariano?" she whispered, trembling hands lifting to him as she approached. "*Bambino mio?*"

"*Si, Mamma,*" Dad said softly, bending so she could put her hands on his face. "I'm here."

I watched as Giulia, completely uninterested in the body of her dead husband, took her missing son's face in her hands and started to weep. And I wondered if more good things than bad had come out of being kidnapped by my father's family.

◆ ◆ ◆

It took hours to resolve the chaos.

Raffa had called in the Burette family, which include Stefania, the woman who insulted me at a gala my first time in Florence, and enlisted the reluctant help of the Albanians, who disappeared as soon as the compound was taken. There were bodies littered like festive decor around the grounds, a line of seven fallen soldiers on the front gravel drive like toppled GI Joes, two floating belly-up in the pool, another at the bottom of one staircase, limbs akimbo.

Raffa's men hauled them in wheelbarrows down the hill to the incinerator the Pietras kept to cremate their horses and sheep when they died, feeding them into the machine until black plumes of smoke drifted over the triangular treetops.

Inside, Ginevra corralled Giulia into her room for a rest, and then transferred her sons to a recreation room that was unharmed in the attack so they could lose themselves in video games while the adults talked.

We adjourned to the front living space because Carmine had driven a reclaimed military G-Wagon into the back of the *castello*, right through the wall of windows.

Raffa did not leave my side.

Even when Martina rushed me and lifted me from my feet in a bone-crushing hug that said everything she could not find the words to express.

I missed you. Thank God, you are safe. Don't do that to me again. I love you.

"I love you too," I murmured into her hair only to have her drop me unceremoniously on my feet and push me lightly in mock distaste.

I was still grinning when Renzo clamped both hands on my shoulders to give me a gentle shake of recognition and admiration.

"Good work in there," he said, jerking his head to indicate the panic room. "Got him right through the heart."

"Yay for me," I joked a little woodenly.

Now that the adrenaline was leaching away, I felt off balance and vaguely nauseated.

He cuffed me gently on the chin to reprimand my self-deprecation and shifted away so Carmine could come through and kiss my cheek.

"*A mali estremi, estremi rimedi*," he told me.

Desperate times call for desperate measures.

"You did well, Vera," he promised. "A woman worthy of a crown."

The way he waggled his eyebrows and slid his gaze to Raffa, it was obvious he meant the kind of crown worn by the queen of the underworld.

But it was Ludo who made me cry.

He gathered me up in his arms, uncaring of his still-healing wound, and hugged me with his whole body, even though it was unbearably gentle.

"I would not have smiled for a long time if you had died," he told me somberly in English. "You have brought joy to more than just the boss. I hope you know."

I had to swallow past the tears twice to say, "I hope you know he is not the only one I have fallen in love with."

He didn't smile when we parted, but the nod he gave me felt like an initiation into the inner sanctum I hadn't had until that day.

Raffa's crew had always enjoyed me, cared for me, but I had not been a part of their group, merely a visitor passing through. After this, I felt officially cemented.

It should have alarmed me, and in a way it did.

Raffa had made it clear you became a member of their crew by vows written in blood, and once you were inducted, there was no turning back.

But I had erased the tracks behind me in the dark woods a long time ago and had no desire to find my way back down the path I'd traveled, even if I could find it again.

When Ginevra reappeared with a middle-aged man who had survived the attack, she introduced him as her bodyguard and friend, Raul.

"So I suppose the question now is what to do with us?" Ginevra asked wearily as she took a seat near the wooden coffee table the rest of us were arrayed around.

"That is one of the issues we have at hand," Raffa agreed.

Dad had taken a love seat and pulled me down beside him so I couldn't sit with Raffa, but my capo had taken the chair perpendicular to mine and dragged it even closer so the toe of his shoe, stained with blood, kissed my socked foot. He had pressed Ginevra into sharing some of her clothes so I didn't catch a chill, and even when I was wrapped in a cashmere sweater, soft lounge pants, and socks, he had still given me the jacket from the back of his car.

I tipped my nose into the collar to enjoy the fragrance of woodsmoke and cedar.

"Part of me thinks it would be best to raze the entire family to the ground," Raffa continued casually, as if talking about mass murder was normal. "But you are lucky to be related to my *cacciatrice*, so I will spare you that."

"Thank you," Ginevra said with a nasty smile.

He ignored her. "The optics are not ideal, though. People know you worked with the Grecos and the Venetian against me—"

"Because we thought you had Guin—"

"Regardless," he interrupted with a cool look. "Killing Gaetano was not enough."

Ginevra didn't flinch, but she did look at her hands in her lap for a moment. "He was not a good man. You would not understand, but you should not hold his actions against myself, my children, or the men who were loyal to the family but unhappy with his leadership."

"You will make a list of the ones who were loyal to you," Raffa instructed, leaning back in his chair and crossing one ankle over his knee. He looked like a jungle cat trapped indoors, too wild to be tamed but pretending at it. "And I know about unworthy fathers, Ginevra Pietra. Be grateful John Stone is not one of them. If Guinevere had been any more the worse for wear, we would not be talking at all."

The threat was clear, sending a tiny thrill down my spine.

I would kill for you again until the streets of Florence ran red with the blood of your enemies, Raffa had told me, but it was only now I could see how truly he meant it.

How much I liked that he did.

"What do you propose, then?" Raul asked from his spot standing beside her chair.

"Reparations, to begin with," Raffa replied, nodding at Renzo, who said, "Sixty percent of any take for the first year, with ten percent off every year after that until you reach the original twenty."

Raul scowled. "That's highway robbery."

Raffa cocked his head to the side, considering the other man with lowered lids, an almost lazy insolence. "Would you rather have robbery or death?"

"And?" Ginevra prompted with a tired sigh.

"We need a public display of support," Martina explained. "Something profound. The Pietras are one of the oldest, most respected families in the Camorra. If we are going to fight off the Venetian's insurrection, we need visible support."

"Would you like us to take out an ad in the paper?" my aunt drawled, and despite myself, I grinned at her drollness.

"She could attend public functions as your date?" Raul suggested.

The air went flat like stale pop.

"No," I said, sitting forward for the first time. "That is not an acceptable option."

"Guinevere," Dad said, taking my hand. "Be reasonable."

"I've been reasonable all my life," I countered. "It hasn't worked well for me. And I won't be *reasonable* about this. Raffa should not have to pretend to date my *aunt* for political gain."

I tried to ignore the little arrogant smirk on Raffa's face, but it was hard not to match the grin with one of my own.

How was it possible that on one of the worst days of my life, I was also almost giddy with happiness? To have my dad here with me, no secrets between us, to have Raffa come for me even when I had taken away his hope, felt like gifts I had never dreamed of receiving.

"No," Martina agreed slowly, eyes bright as she looked between Raffa and me. "But there is another option that could work very well."

"Martina . . ." Raffa warned, grin collapsing into a dark look. "Do not."

"What is it?" I asked.

"It would only work if people knew about her heritage," Ginevra cut in. "It would expose her even more than she already is."

"Absolutely not," Dad said, shooting to his feet to point a vibrating finger at Raffa. "No *fucking* way, Romano. I agreed to work with you to help my daughter, but I do not approve. Not one fucking bit."

"*Che cavolo*?" I demanded. What the hell? "What are you talking about?"

Raffa dropped his foot to the floor and braced his forearms on his thighs to bring his face closer to mine. There was dried blood on the corner of his mouth that I shocked myself by wanting to lick clean.

"Marriage, Vera," he said quietly, but the words seemed to reverberate like a struck bell. "They are speaking of marriage."

Rage struck me in the gut, the breath leaving my body in a long whoosh.

"Excuse me?" I demanded after sucking in a lungful of air, the words sharp enough to cut. "Are you serious? You would marry my aunt?"

I knew arranged marriages were a thing in Mafia culture, even in Italian culture, but I could not even begin to fathom such a thing between Ginevra and Raffa.

Someone—Martina and Carmine, I thought—laughed a little.

"No, *stella cadente*," Raffa murmured, even more softly than before, so I had to lean closer to hear him. "I would not. That was not what Martina was suggesting."

I swallowed the bitter triumph at his words. "Then who?"

His mouth twisted into an approximation of a wry smile. "You are not usually so slow to understand. You must still have water in your ears." A grin tugged at my mouth at his teasing, but before I could jibe back, he continued, "The only eligible Pietra left to marry, Guinevere. *You.*"

I gasped so deeply, I almost choked on the breath.

"She is not *marrying* you, Romano. Guinevere is going back to Michigan as soon as we can get a flight out of this place. She is not staying in Italy, and she is certainly not marrying a known felon."

"Her father is one, so I don't see why it should matter," Ludo said.

"*Vaffanculo*," Dad spat.

Fuck off.

Ludo merely shrugged.

"It's not a bad idea," Raul said. "We could introduce Guinevere to society as Gaetano's love child, make it clear the line of succession is still strong, especially if she unites with the Romanos."

"It would be a blow to the Venetian too," Renzo added. "First the Grecos are incarcerated in a sting with the DIA, and then the Pietras are made loyal through marriage? It is very tidy."

"It's hardly tidy," Dad argued. "Guinevere is not staying in Italy."

"Dad," I said, reaching forward to grab his hand and tug him reluctantly back into his seat. "I am staying."

He blinked at me, the color draining from his face. "Guinevere, don't be ridiculous."

"I've never been less ridiculous in my life," I deadpanned.

"For a boy?" he stressed. "Your mother and I raised you better than that."

"You did," I agreed. "But I want to stay in Italy regardless of Raffa. For the first time in my life, I feel settled, like this is where I belong. You cannot deny that it had to be the hand of fate that threw me into Raffa's path on my vacation. I know you never wanted me to discover this place, but in doing so, I discovered the true me. I'm not willing to give that up for any man. Even my dad."

I had never seen heartbreak up close before, but it felt like a horror film played in slow motion. Each feature crumpled, his mouth downturned with the force of his grief, eyes squeezing shut like he could block out everything that had just happened, if only for a second.

"Damn it, Guinevere," he said with a quiet croak. "You are all we have left."

"I know, but I can't live for you and Mom. I have to live for myself. I'm twenty-three years old, and I want the life I've started to make here."

"With murders and mafiosi?" he asked, exasperated.

"With friends." *And my lover,* I thought but didn't say because there was still so much Raffa and I had to discuss. "Besides, you have to know we can't just go back to Michigan. People here know that's where I live, and even if I'm never with Raffa again"—I paused to breathe through the pain of that possibility—"I'm associated with him. I would much rather stay here with friends who can protect me and teach me to protect myself."

"Even if you stay, you won't marry him," Dad declared, but there was a wild desperation in his gaze that begged me to agree with him.

"I won't marry for Mafia politics," I agreed. "And I won't marry anyone who doesn't ask me."

It wasn't a good enough response, I could see in his huff of frustration, but it would have to do for now.

"Let's table that idea for the moment," Renzo suggested. "And focus on some practicalities."

CHAPTER TWENTY-ONE

Raffa

Practicalities included what to do with Philippe Morrone, the *bastardo* who had turned on me and mine.

He was not at the Pietra *castello*, but two of my men found him heading east through San Bavello, probably en route to Venice.

They had him ready for us when we returned to Villa Romano.

He was suspended in the barn like a leg of pork hung to dry and mold slowly in the dank, cool dark.

But I would not leave him to die in such a way.

I was too impatient. The rage that had been cancerously building in my gut since the moment Guinevere was taken had infected every inch of my tissues. The only way to combat this sick fury was to take it out on Philippe.

He was not even a man to me anymore.

He was a slab of meat, a carcass I had to prepare like a butcher into ordered pieces I could make sense of.

Fortunately, Philippe had witnessed my methods of interrogation before, so he had a taste for exactly what I could do to him if he did not answer my questions clearly and promptly.

Unfortunately, whoever had convinced him to flip on me was a powerful enough influence that he refused to give up the identity of the Venetian even when I asked . . . repeatedly.

"This is the last finger you have left on this hand," I told him conversationally as I wiped sweat from my brow and adjusted the cigar cutter around his index finger. "Do you really want to lose it and be left with only a thumb?"

Philippe let out an animal groan like a heifer. "*Per favore, capo, no.* You must understand! If I tell you, many will die. You do not want their deaths on your head."

"Do I not?" I mused, scratching at the stubble growing thick across my chin. "Should I not be the judge of that? You have proven a useless one yourself."

"*Lui è spietato*," he groaned as blood pulsed from the stubs of his lost fingers, dripping to the ground in a steady rainfall. "He is a savage. He has looked into your eyes, Raffa, and lied. He has watched you find love, and he wants nothing more than to rip it away. It is an envy that goes beyond hatred. He wants everything you have."

"My Guinevere?" I asked darkly, the cigar cutter biting into his flesh in a neat circle.

His cry echoed through the barn. "No, no, not her. But your life. Everything you own."

"Even if he had all the businesses, all my money and connections, he could not keep them. Do you know why, *pezzo di merda*?" I leaned close to smile in his face, the expression so cruel it hurt my face to make it. "Because the most important thing I own is the loyalty of my people." I sighed. "People unlike you."

"I am not as disloyal as you think," he cried out as I compressed the blades harder, the metal hitting bone. "All I ever wanted was to be part of this family. Even working with him, I tried to help you and Guinevere."

"Do not speak her name," I hissed. "You are unworthy of it. You will not tell me what I need to hear, and I am a man of my word, Philippe. Let me teach you what that looks like."

His scream tore through the air, beyond the wood slats of the barn, out into the cold autumn night.

He passed out from the pain, hand a bloody stump at his side.

I stood up and moved away to the table set up in the corner to retrieve a handkerchief to wipe my hands.

"He did say the Venetian is based in Tuscany," Renzo muttered, wearing spectacles as he bent to take meticulous notes of the interrogation.

Ludo sat beside him with his computer and tablet open, the screen of the former running a search for any bank accounts, addresses, and business affiliations linked to Philippe.

Carmine sat beside him drinking sambuca straight from the bottle.

Martina was in the great house, debriefing the *soldati* about the new turn of events and sending away any of the men who did not meet our exacting qualifications. I would have a skeleton crew at the villa before I housed another traitor close to my family. Only the men who had lived under our roof or Tonio's would be kept on until we discovered exactly where the treachery lay.

"So he is not working with Donatella Verdi," Carmine said.

"Not necessarily."

"She owes you her position and her life," he noted. "She would not have survived the coup against her brother without your support."

"Loyalty, as Philippe has proven, is not always evergreen," I drawled. "Get her to Firenze for the Ognissanti and the Giorno dei Morti celebrations. I want her to look me in the eye as she accounts for the actions of the people associated with her territory, even if she is not directly responsible."

"You plan to throw the Day of the Dead dinner even in light of this atrocity against our family?" Tonio asked from his post on a stool on the other side of the barn from the others.

They had never liked my uncle, and my uncle had never warmed to them. They were the old guard and the new, the differences between them never starker than in situations like this. Leo, seated with his adoptive father, often provided the bridge between the two. He had been raised just as much by Aldo Romano as by Tonio, even more so than me in many ways because he had lived at the villa during those eight years I was in London. He understood both sides of the coin in a way I could not.

"It is important to keep up appearances," Leo soothed. "We do not need people to think the Romano empire is crumbling under the stress of a few errant *stronzi*."

Tonio slammed his fist to the wall beside him. "We do not need to waste time on such niceties. Where are your balls, Raffaele? Your father would have killed every last Pietra standing, including that American girl and her cowardly father who fled our country. He would have put a bullet between the eyes of that traitor hanging there, giving you nothing but platitudes, and ended this bullshit."

"I am not my father, *zio*," I reminded him coldly. "Why would I kill men who could give me the answers I need to truly end this subversive war, hmm?"

"It is like wringing blood from a stone." Tonio spat, shoving to his feet, his stool thudding against the wall. His gun was in his hand a moment later as he stormed toward Philippe's hanging body. "Let me end this if you will not."

The moment his gun hit Philippe's cheek, I was behind Tonio with my own weapon pressed to the base of his neck.

"When will you learn, *vecchio*, that it is I who am in charge here? Not you. Stand down and get the fuck out before you push me any further," I warned.

"You would not harm your own family," he countered, holding firm.

"I would kill anyone willing to stand between me and the answers I need to protect my loved ones," I said, hissing the words into his ear just to see the way it sent a shiver over his skin. "Do not opt to learn that the painful way, Uncle."

"So soft." He clucked his tongue but dropped the gun and stormed toward the exit, then pulled open the barn door with a metallic gurgle.

"It is your determination not to listen to my advice that has put this family in such a mess in the first place. Did I not tell you leaving the arms trade would result in a loss of status and open us to rivals? Did I not tell you fucking an American girl instead of marrying Stefania Burette was unwise? You proud idiot, Raffa. You will get this family you are so eager to protect killed."

"Ignore him," Leo said in the silence that followed Tonio's dramatic exit. "He was worried about you today, that's all."

I scoffed lightly because while Tonio had always encouraged me to forge my own path, he had done nothing to curb the crueler impulses of my father, both in business and in regard to his family. He had stood by one too many times when Aldo hit me for me to believe he prized my well-being anywhere near as much as his own. When I took over as *capo dei capi*, he had the strange notion that I would defer to him in all things. He did not understand why I did not seek his counsel because he did not understand my most basic principle: not to rule like my father.

"Wake him up," I ordered Carmine, who stood to retrieve a bucket of cold water before promptly dumping it over Philippe.

He came awake with a splutter, thrashing like a fish hooked on a tight line.

"Raffa," he gasped. "You have to listen to me. I took Guinevere to help her. To help you both."

My laugh felt like a death rattle in my throat. "I tire of your games, Philippe. Be blunt or lose the fingers on your other hand."

"The Venetian was using Guinevere against you with the Pietras, trying to motivate them to join his cause by convincing them you had abducted her knowing she was a member of their family," he explained in a slurred rush.

"That's true."

The voice that spoke was so incongruent with the situation that, at first, I thought I had imagined it.

But when I turned to the source, it was Guinevere who stood beside the open barn door Tonio had left ajar. Her wavy hair was loose down her front, obscuring the long white silk nightgown I'd bought for her in Firenze that summer and an old Oxford hoodie of mine she wore unzipped over the top. There was something surreal about her fresh-faced, youthful beauty in the dark barn we used to string up men and strip them of their secrets. It did not feel wrong, exactly, but wild, as if a fey creature from the night had come to observe our wrongdoings with eager eyes.

"What are you doing here?" I asked when I found my voice.

I knew I made quite the vision, standing in the same trousers and shirt I'd worn for the raid, dried blood from a wound on my neck, Philippe's blood on my hands and splattered like polka-dot print along my front.

The violence of the moment and the relief at having her back were a potent, dangerous cocktail roiling through me. I wanted to throw her to the ground and fuck her in the dirt. I wanted to carve my name into her flesh so everyone would know whom she belonged to and fear the repercussions if they tried to harm her or take her ever again. I wanted to paint her in cum until she looked like mine, smelled like mine, wept my name with every breath from her lips.

She ignored me entirely, moving forward on bare feet across the cold, stained concrete floor, the hem of her silk nightgown *shushing* softly in the silence.

"What Philippe said is true. The Venetian tried to blackmail the Pietras into helping by telling them Raffa was holding me hostage," she explained, stopping beside me so the tips of her bare toes touched the blood on the floor.

When she looked at me, her eyes were filled with shadows.

"That does not mean he was trying to help us," I noted.

"No," she agreed. "But I think it means he is conflicted. Aren't you, Philippe?"

He blinked the sweat from his lashes as he looked at her, wary suddenly as if he sensed the same coiled, dark energy inside her that made my skin buzz with electricity.

"Yes," he whispered, gaze darting to the table filled with my crew and then over to Leo. "I did not want to betray you, Raffa. We have been friends since we were boys. But I owed it to the Venetian to help him when he asked for aid."

"Why?" I demanded, stepping forward before I reminded myself that Guinevere was beside me and she did not want to see more violence from me.

"It's okay," she whispered as if in answer, her fingers extending to brush against my fist. "I want to see what you would do if I wasn't here. I'm not afraid."

When I did not move, she pressed herself into my back.

"I am not afraid of you," she confirmed.

I swallowed the tangle of emotions clogging my throat and nodded curtly, stepping forward as I had intended with the cigar cutter in hand.

"Please, don't," Philippe begged. "I cannot tell you more. You have to believe me. Someone you love will die if I tell you more."

"The Venetian cannot hear you here," I reminded him. "I am your only judge, your only jury, and your eventual executioner."

His gaze darted to Renzo, who usually exacted such violence for me, but I grabbed his face to force him to look at me.

"No, no, I am the one who will end your life if you insist on keeping his secrets," I said, and my voice came up like smoke from an active volcano. "It was my woman you took, so I will be the one to watch the light go out in your eyes as the hope would have gone out of mine if something worse had happened to her."

Behind me, Guinevere shifted, but I tried not to think of her.

Instead I focused on Philippe, cutting his finger down knuckle by knuckle as he cried and shouted his innocent intentions.

After another half hour, it was clear he would not give up the identity of the Venetian. The only further thing of interest he admitted was that the Venetian was keeping an eye not just on my family in the villa but also on my companies, implying he had spies in both the Romano Group and Lupo Nero Investments.

I had long ago forgotten about Guinevere bearing witness to my interrogation, lost to the darkness that rushed up to meet me when I fell headlong into my birthright. So I thought nothing of the intensity with which I beat into Philippe's face after losing his fingers did not perturb him, slaking some of my rage on his body, and then nothing still of the knife I punched between his ribs and twisted until his body gave one last, pitiable sigh.

When I stepped back from the dead meat swinging from the ceiling, I was panting roughly, splattered in blood and limned in sweat.

"Take him down and feed him to the pigs," I told Renzo.

"Literally or figuratively?"

I startled like a spooked horse at the sweet tones of Guinevere's voice, snapping my head around to see her sitting at the table with Renzo, Carmine, and Ludo, holding a fingermark-fogged glass filled with Carm's sambuca. She sat so primly on the stool, back straight, legs crossed like a lady's in the pristine white nightgown.

But there was cool, quiet rage in those black-velvet eyes and a tiny curl to her red-ribbon lips.

"Literally," Ludo supplied. "We keep pigs a few fields over. Sheep, too, but for different reasons." When Guinevere raised an eyebrow, he shrugged. "Angela and Carlotta make their own yarn to knit."

"Of course," she murmured, that sharp-edged smile deepening.

Renzo got up to do as I had asked, cranking the lever on the chains attaching Philippe to the ceiling so that he fell to the ground with a wet thump.

Guinevere's gaze darted over before she looked back at me, utterly composed.

"Come sit," she suggested, waiting for me to do so before she handed me the glass of sambuca. After I tipped it back in one swallow, she took my hands to lay them palms up on the table and methodically began to clean them as best she could with the already-stained handkerchief on the table.

"Have you considered that the mole might be in the Romano Group and not necessarily a man in your outfit?" she asked conversationally, the way one would inquire about the weather.

Small talk.

I blinked at her, too exhausted and wrung out emotionally to wonder if her composure was a good thing or bad.

"Not really," I confessed, slumping slightly against the table. At this point, I'd had about ten hours of sleep in the last four days. "There is almost no way someone outside the life would know the inner workings of the Camorra the way they would have had to in order to strike at the heart of my operations."

"Fair," she acknowledged as she finished cleaning my hands as well as she could with the soiled fabric. She tossed it aside to begin a slow massage of my palm that wrenched a low moan of relief from my throat. "But I still think it is something to consider. You don't have much to do with the Romano Group, right? You even admitted that you don't sit on the board. It just seems like if there was going to be a mole, it would be a good place for them to hide."

"Philippe clearly is not the only one," Renzo agreed. "And Guinevere has a point. Apart from Tonio and Leo, we do not have many men we trust overseeing operations there."

"Because it isn't affiliated with the criminal activities of the outfit anymore," I said. "But I agree. It is the weak link."

"Are you saying I don't have a handle on things with the Romano Group?" Leo asked over my shoulder as he placed his stool beside Renzo at the table.

"I am saying everything in my life is unstable," I admitted with a twisted grin. "It is not a reflection on you, but on me, *amico mio*."

Guinevere made a noise in her throat and slid her fingers through mine. "I am afraid my bad luck has rubbed off on you."

"No, it is not luck but the history Aldo sowed finally cropping up in my life," I corrected.

"It isn't your fault," Leo said, but he seemed just as dejected as me, maybe even more exhausted, his shoulders slumped as he swayed to bump into me. "Sins of the father and all that."

I laughed, but it was more an exhalation of breath. "I think that deserves a toast." After pouring another finger of sambuca for myself and then refilling everyone's glasses, I raised the drink in the air. "To the sins of our fathers and grinding them into dust."

"*Cin cin*," my men echoed.

Guinevere did not say a word, but then again, she did not have a drink to toast with. Instead, she squeezed my hand and watched with low-lidded eyes as I swallowed down the harsh alcohol.

"I think that's enough for the night," she said with cool authority. "Leave us, will you?"

Leo hesitated, gaze darting between Guinevere and me, but Carmine got up with a burp and helped Ludo collect his various tech, and Renzo clapped me on the back before going to lever the dead body into a wheelbarrow.

I stared at my American girl through the commotion, trying to understand the intent in those night-dark eyes. She seemed more grounded than she had been since returning to Italy, a confident atavism that was utterly beguiling.

What might she do if she got me alone as she wanted?

Kiss me or kill me, I thought, sure of either answer.

"Leo," I said when he was the last one lingering. My voice was gruff, scraped raw by exhaustion and emotional rawness. "*Vai via*."

Leave, now.

His sigh was loud in the cavernous barn, but he did as I asked, dragging himself off the stool and shutting the sliding door behind him with a bang.

We were alone at last.

"Guinevere," I said to fill the silence, strangely unsure of myself and where we stood. "I am sorry—"

"No," she said, pressing her entire palm over my mouth to stop me from speaking. "No, tonight neither of us is sorry for anything."

She pushed out of her chair to climb into my lap, straddling my hips, hands digging into the sides of my hair so she could tip my head back to hold her intense gaze.

"Tonight, I want to fuck the man *and* the monster," she whispered against my lips. "I want the devil's hand on me, sending me straight to heaven."

"Why, Guinevere," I growled, nipping at her pouting lower lip as arousal burned away the edges of my fatigue. "That is blasphemous talk."

"Yes," she agreed, sliding her tongue over my upper lip. "I've discovered I like to sin when it's done with you."

Her mouth closed over mine, ending the conversation with an assertive kiss that demanded I cave to her impulses.

I was more than happy to.

After believing I would never have her like this again and then knowing she was in enemy hands, perhaps never to be seen again, kissing her seemed like the only possible thing to do. I could worry about the Venetian, the Pietras, Guinevere's parents asleep in my family house just meters from where we sat, and the emotional aftermath of having her in my arms one last time tomorrow.

For now, there was only this.

This sprite of a creature made of earth and firelight writhing in my lap and taking her pleasure from me like it was owed to her.

I growled as she rubbed herself over my erection, back and forth in a sinuous rhythm that made my brain fizz between my ears.

"I want you to fuck me right here," she said. "I want to take you inside me in the very place you feel like your worst self, knowing that I can handle it."

The fierce words broke the leash on my control, and I surged forward, consuming her mouth with mine, pushing the hoodie off her shoulders before lifting the hem of her silk gown up to her hips so I could cup her pussy in one palm. She was not wearing underwear, so the heat and damp of her arousal pressed intimately into my skin.

"You came out here wanting this," I noted in a rough rasp.

Her head tipped back between her shoulders, exposing the pale column of her neck to my teeth and tongue.

"Yes," she said with a little shiver, hands dropping to my waistband to deftly undo the belt, the button, the zipper so she could pull my rigid cock out into her hot fingers. Without hesitation, she curled her hand around my shaft and slotted me against her wet opening. "*Scopami forte*, Raffa."

Fuck me hard.

"Anything you wish." I reminded her of the promise I had made as I thrust forward, seating myself inside her velvet pussy.

She convulsed at the fullness, a moan unspooling from her open pink mouth.

When I pulled out slowly, she groaned in protest, winding her arms and legs around me like vines.

"Fuck me, please," she said, an edge of true desperation in her words. "I want to feel you for days like this."

Because you mean to leave me, I thought as something twisted brutally in my chest. I shot the thought dead, determined to enjoy this moment, this glorious shooting star of a woman, while I could.

So I fucked her.

Rabidly, ferally, like an animal that had been touch starved and alone too long.

The sounds of our coupling echoed through the barn, the wet slap of my balls against her ass, the wooden creak of the table as it shuddered under my driving hips, the high whine of Guinevere's pleasured groans and gasps, and the rough huff of my breath as I fought to control the orgasm already nipping at my heels.

One of my bloodstained hands found her swanlike neck, the red stark against her paleness, smearing pink into the skin and the lace of her once-pristine white nightgown.

"Dirtying you up," I grunted as I clasped her ass tight in my other hand, canting her hips to take me even deeper. "Love seeing all this innocence lost to me."

Something flashed in her dark eyes as she reared up to nip hard at my lower lip, leaving a rent in the skin that beaded blood. With a lash of her tongue, she licked it clean, blood on her lips as she grinned at me, her cunt rippling around me as if she was aroused by the violent act.

By the metallic taste of my essence in her mouth.

"I was never innocent," she argued with a smoky purr. "I was always yearning for this. Just waiting for you to teach me how to fuck and live and love in the dark."

I gritted my teeth as her words poured gasoline on the flames in my gut. Pushing her down by the throat, I pinned her torso to the table, then watched her small breasts heave as I collected her legs over my arms and hoisted them to my shoulders.

Like this she was supine beneath me, splayed for my pleasure.

She hissed, arching off the table as my initial thrust hit the end of her and sparked the first quake of her orgasm.

"There it is," I encouraged, driving into her harder. "You look so pretty coming apart around my cock, Vera. Not going to stop fucking you until you beg me to stop. You wanted the monster—here I am."

She gasped as my hand tightened on her throat, cutting off just enough of her air to send the pleasure spiraling to another level. With my free hand, I pushed the nightgown even higher and started to play with her clit, rolling it like a slippery bead between my fingers.

"I-I can't," she struggled, thrashing against my hips as I drilled her into the table and forced her to take more and more pleasure.

"You can and you will," I ordered in that blade-sharp voice that always made her shiver. "You have to earn my seed, Guinevere. Do you want it? Hmmm? Do you want my cum filling up this tight, hot little *fica*?"

Her mouth parted in a silent scream, every muscle in her lithe form tightening into stone.

I plucked once more at her swollen clit and watched as she transformed from solid into liquid, her limbs trembling into softness, her pussy pulsing wet and smooth around my still-thrusting cock.

She was a vision of ecstasy, a gorgeous woman turned into a masterpiece of pleasure.

All for me.

"Again," I growled, almost mindless with the need to brand her inside and out with my essence.

"Raffa!" she gasped in protest as I hauled her up and into my arms so her full weight forced her down on my cock.

I sank my teeth into the side of her neck, licking up the salt-sweet taste of her skin as I started to shuttle her up and down my length. I had never been so hard, so desperate to sink deeper and fuck harder.

"*Vieni per me*," she begged, loose as a rag doll in my hold but for the iron grip she had on my shoulders, nails digging into the muscle in a way I knew would mark me for days. "Come for me, Raffa. Fill me up."

I fixed my teeth into the junction of her neck and shoulder, pinning her like an animal in place for me to fuck to completion. Her nails broke the skin beneath my shirt as she ground into me, peaking for the third time on an orgasm that ripped a war cry from her lips.

I followed her into the dark abysses of pleasure. The only thought in my head was of pumping her full of cum, marking her as mine in the most primal way I could.

When I finally drifted back into my right mind, I realized I had turned us to rest my hips against the table, Guinevere a heavy weight in my arms, her breath warm against my neck.

"Vera?" I called softly, because I had held her in sleep before and knew the familiar laxity of her body against mine.

"Mmm," she mumbled, rubbing her nose into my throat as she settled even closer.

A smile pulled at my mouth.

After four days of dread and worry, my American girl was in my arms, trusting me enough to fuck her into a comatose state even with my bloodstained hands.

Even if she knew she would be leaving me again soon.

Careful not to disturb her, I tucked myself back into my pants and zipped them before draping the discarded hoodie over her shoulders and adjusting her weight in my hold. The barn was cool, but she was warm in my embrace as I carried her outside and up the hill to the house.

Someone had wisely kept the kitchen door off the terrace open for us even though the house inside was still and dark, most everyone in their beds.

I was carrying Guinevere through the open-plan kitchen and dining room when a cleared throat halted my progress.

My eyes adjusted easily to the dark, used to operating in the gloom, so it was not hard to detect John Stone sitting at the dining table with a glass of something alcoholic.

He stared back at me, eyes black pits like those of a skull in the night.

"She sleeps like the dead when she feels safe," he said finally, his voice coarse with emotion. "Though I still don't know how my sweet girl could trust someone like you, Romano."

I would have shrugged if she was not in my arms.

"You saw what I did to get her back from the Pietras," I said instead. "She trusts that there is nothing I would not do to make her safe and happy."

"Even if 'safe and happy' means letting her go?" he asked.

"I could ask you the same," I said, before continuing to the stairs. Only when I was about to ascend beyond his vision did I stop to add, "She will never be rid of me, Stone. Even if she wants to go back to America, I will watch her the rest of her life to make sure nothing gets in the way of her joy. Even if that thing is *you*."

John Stone said nothing as I carried his daughter to her bedroom and laid her carefully to rest, but I knew that was not the end of our feud.

Because John thought he was fighting for what was right for his daughter, thinking it was the same thing that was right for himself.

And I knew Guinevere was the only one who could make that decision.

As much as I wanted to use every ounce of my control and influence to make certain she made the only one I could live with.

Staying in the dark with me forever.

CHAPTER TWENTY-TWO

Guinevere

I dreamed that I was sitting at a café in Florence, waiting for Raffa to pick me up. When he pulled up in the red Ferrari Spyder, I hesitated, suddenly unsure about getting into the car with him even though I was desperate to join him. He watched me from the open window of the car with a patient smile on his lips, fingers drumming against the metal.

Just as I stood up to finally join him, the car blew up. A car bomb or something that completely eradicated the vehicle and everything inside it. Including Raffa.

I woke up crying.

As I blinked up at the ceiling with tears leaking down my cheeks, I knew I could no longer deny the truth.

There was only one path my life had been directing me down all these years, and it led through hell all the way to the throne of the devil himself.

A man who would break through the crust of the earth to find me. A man who had sacrificed again and again just to see me happy. A man who deserved the world and who somehow saw his happily ever after in *me*.

I didn't know where he was emotionally after last night in the barn, and I cursed myself for giving in to exhaustion instead of holding out to explain exactly how I felt, but I could still make amends this morning.

After a quick shower, where I was careful not to submerge my face beneath the spray because of the lingering nightmare of being waterboarded, and then the administration of my medicine, I went downstairs to grab something to eat. Four days without my meds wouldn't kill me, but I had to make up for the lack by drinking even more than my usual gallon of water a day and sticking strictly to my diet.

It was early enough that the kids were just gathering their bags to go off to school, so I paused to kiss them all on the head and give Zacheo a big hug.

"Are my parents still asleep?" I asked Angela.

"Yes. I expect they will sleep until lunch, so I am making something good."

"And Raffa? Is he up yet?" I grabbed an apple from the bowl on the island.

"He is meeting with Renzo. That is not a good breakfast, though, Vera!" Raffa's mother tutted at me in Italian. "Sit and let me make you something."

"No, thank you," I insisted, having caught sight of Ludo waiting for me outside as he had every morning before the Pietras took me. "I have a busy morning, but I promise to eat a big lunch."

"You are too skinny!" she called, but I was already slipping past Carlotta out the front door and jogging over to the side of the house, where Ludo was doing push-ups one handed to take the strain off his still-healing side.

Without hesitation, I sat cross-legged on his back.

"You think this makes it more difficult?" he grunted as he lowered himself again.

"It should." I chomped into my apple and took in the gorgeous fall morning over the Tuscan hills. "But it's mostly to prove that you absolutely should *not* be doing push-ups two weeks after getting shot."

"*Sto bene*," he said. "It was just a graze."

There were people in the vines, their voices carrying up the hill to the house, but after the first day of the harvest, the family didn't participate every day. On the last day, we would have another feast, but only as a family, to celebrate another successful year of grapes.

I didn't realize I had included myself in the family so easily until I was mid-swallow around a piece of apple, and I choked.

Ludo tossed me off his back to pound a hand between my shoulders until I coughed it out.

"*Grazie mille*," I rasped, waving him away as I stood up. "Well, now that I've almost choked to death, are you ready for our run?"

He nodded, staring at me a little harder than usual, probably because I was skipping in place. "You were just tortured and kept captive for days. Perhaps you want to take a break?"

"Pfft. I'm too energized this morning to take a break," I told him solemnly before shooting him a wide grin.

"You fucked Raffa in the barn yesterday," he countered.

I gasped, smacking him in the chest, and then darted off on the trail down the hill, yelling over my shoulder, "A lady never kisses and tells."

"You have a *succhiotto* on your neck. It goes without saying," he muttered as he caught up with me swiftly and fell into easy step beside me.

My hand flew up to my neck instinctively. I hadn't realized Raffa had left a hickey because I'd put my hair into a ponytail when I was in the kitchen and not in front of a mirror.

"So much for discretion," I bemoaned, but Ludo only bumped me with his shoulder in solidarity.

"Be careful with him," Ludo surprised me by saying. Unlike Martina or Carm, he was not usually one to speak about emotions. "Boss was in a bad way when you went back to America, but he nearly went mad when you were taken. He doesn't need much in life, but I think it is obvious that he needs you."

"I need him too," I offered simply. "When he's finished his meeting with Renzo, I intend to tell him just how much."

Ludo grunted, but I could see the faint curl of a smile at the end of his thin mouth.

"Softy," I teased him, which made him knock into me again and power forward even faster.

I laughed as I chased him.

After a moment, I heard voices through the cypress trees, and we rounded a corner to come up on Renzo and Raffa, who were both in their running gear, heading down the same trail. They were already sweaty, Raffa's tee tucked into the back of his black athletic shorts, his bare chest glistening in the new-day sun.

My mouth went impossibly dry, tongue adhered to the back of my teeth.

I deserved it, but Raffa's reserved look when he saw me over his shoulder panged in my gut.

"*Buongiorno*," I called over the crunch of gravel beneath our feet. "Isn't it a beautiful morning?"

Renzo blinked placidly back at me, but Raffa cocked his head, studying me for a hidden motive.

"It is," Ludo grunted, because he was a good friend and the silence was awkward.

"Your mother told me you and Zo were in a meeting," I told Raffa.

He waved between himself and his right-hand man. "We are multitasking."

"Do you mind if we join you?" I asked as we pulled abreast of the other two joggers. "Race to the bottom of the hill?"

"Will I have to carry you back up it?" Raffa finally said, and though his delivery was bland, there was a bend in his mouth that said he was teasing me.

Warmth blossomed in my chest. "If you want the extra workout, but I'm more than capable of running back up myself. Ludo and I do this circuit every morning."

Raffa lifted a brow as he looked to Ludo, who only grunted back.

"He gets more eloquent after the first two or three miles," I explained to Renzo and Raffa.

Even Renzo's mouth twitched this time.

"So," I drawled. *"Pronti?"*

Ready?

"*Partenza*," Ludo offered.

Set.

Raffa and I locked eyes as I waited for him to say the word. Instead, he reached out to put a hand on my shoulder. A smile was already forming on my lips when he slid his foot in front of mine so I tripped, and, using the hand on my shoulder, he controlled my fall to the ground.

Only when I was down and he was separated from me did he call out, "*Via!*"

Go!

"*Caspita*," I cursed in Italian as I heaved myself to my feet and took off after the men, who were still laughing as they sprinted down the winding road.

They were all taller than me and undoubtedly fitter than me, given that I had taken up serious exercise just in the last few months, but they only beat me by a handful of yards, which I took as its own accomplishment. Then I remembered that Ludo had a healing gunshot wound and still finished before me, and I felt a little less vindicated.

I bent over, gasping for breath with a hand to the stitch in my side, when I reached them where they were waiting at the bottom of the hill.

"*Bravissima*, Guinevere," Renzo praised me in that quiet way of his, stepping up beside me to squeeze my sweaty shoulder.

"Very impressive," Raffa agreed, staring at me from his habitual pose, arms crossed, legs spread like those of a fighter braced for combat. His sweaty hair curled around his forehead and ears, and there was that small, half-moon grin on his face he'd told me was made just for me.

"You should see her fight," Ludo added, stretching out his thickly muscled tree-trunk thighs. "She is weak, but very fast."

I rolled my eyes at my friend and flexed my minimal biceps. "Who're you calling weak?"

Raffa chuckled, reaching out to run rough fingertips over the thin-skinned underside of my arm. When I shivered, his smile turned predatory.

"You look stronger," he admitted. "You are certainly faster than when we ran together in Florence."

"I told you I took MMA classes and I started running a lot in Michigan."

"Why?" he asked, head cocked, something working behind those eyes the color of sun-bleached pennies.

It was a good question, and until that moment, I hadn't had a great answer for it. "I think," I said slowly, "I wanted to be prepared to defend myself in case I ever came back."

Raffa only leaned back a quarter of an inch, his expression hardly shifting, but I knew him well enough to know that he reeled away from my statement as if to protect himself. He stared at me, matte eyed and stern.

"Leave us," he said softly.

Renzo and Ludo were already turning to head back up the hill.

He waited until they were gone to ask, "Are you fucking with me, Guinevere?"

"No," I said calmly, stepping closer so the toes of our sneakers pressed together and I had to drop my head back to look up at him. "I've been scared. Chickenshit, my sister would have said. The truth is, even when I went home to my boring, respectable life, I felt like I was going insane. It wasn't . . . it wasn't *enough* for me anymore. Not just because it was a life without you, but also because it felt like I was forcing on an old coat that no longer fit right. I may have been raised a certain way, but I think I was born a little different. Obviously now that I know my dad was a mafioso, that makes more sense."

His expression was immovable.

I sighed, searching for the words that had been inscribed on my soul since before I had even met him. As I had often done in life when my own words failed, I found another way to give meaning to what lay inside me.

"Giovanni Boccaccio said, 'You must read, you must persevere, you must sit up nights, you must inquire, and exert the utmost power of your mind. If one way does not lead to the desired meaning, take another; if obstacles arise, then still another; until, if your strength holds out, you will find that clear which at first looked dark.'"

I took Raffa's hands in my own, rubbing my thumbs over knuckles I knew had bruised and split after fighting.

"I know he was a Renaissance humanist and probably didn't mean for me to interpret it this way, but that's what happened to me. I had this hunger inside me that no amount of reading or studying could quench. I thought I longed for Italy itself, the nation and the culture, but even though I love it here, how rich and warm it is, how unjudgmental, I know I was looking in the right place for the wrong thing. All along, every time I dreamed of fucking in the darkness, of villains and their cutting words and antiheroes with their tragic pasts, I was yearning for you. Preparing my mind and spirit to accept you for who you really are. My Raffa, but also, *capo dei capi, meus Rex Infernus*."

He stared me down with the brutal weight of his glare, an expression I knew had made men much larger and more powerful than me cower. I only blinked placidly back at him, waiting for him to accept my truth.

"What does this mean?" he asked finally, arms crossed so tightly—protectively—over his chest that the muscles in his arms bulged like coiled rope beneath his burnished skin.

"It means I love you, Raffa, and it changed my chemical makeup. Or exposed it, maybe. I want to be with you. I want to stay with you. And I want you to make me ready for anything that may come for us."

"You are prepared to sleep beside a man every night knowing exactly who he is? Criminal capo and all? That it won't stop, *ever*, the violence of this life. That there will never be a cap on the men who might die at my hands. Even God in Dante's *Divine Comedy* had to cast out rebel angels to protect his peace."

"Are you equating yourself with God?" I asked with a grin.

He shrugged, that quintessentially Latin expression that was oddly elegant. "God below, maybe. My point stands. We all do what we must to survive. We must be a little bit selfish to succeed. And my definition of success has always been looking after those who matter most to me. Nothing, not even your judgment, will stop me from doing what needs to be done in that regard."

"So you'd kill for me," I said, not a question this time because he had told me so before.

Already proven so again and again.

He peered at me the way a philosopher would study an ethical quandary, as if I was a fundamental question that would remain unanswered all his life and haunt him even in his sleep.

"I would die for you," he said softly.

I sucked in a sharp breath, somehow surprised by his answer.

To kill was one thing. It was aggressive, action oriented, something that left a moral stain on the heart.

But to die for someone?

That was wholly more complex. It took real courage to die knowingly and to do it protecting someone else. To place your life so literally before another's.

Knowing Raffa, it meant so much more that he would give up everything he had worked so hard for, worked to safeguard, for me.

Guinevere Stone, twenty-three-year-old Midwesterner with a chronic illness and some serious baggage.

In Raffa's eyes I was nothing so mundane. I was a shooting star across a dark night, a fairy-tale creature come to life, a fawn who was prepared to blossom under his tutelage into a predator worthy of hunting at his side.

It meant more, but it also terrified me.

The idea of a world without Raffaele seemed impossible. His presence had its own gravity, his smile, when it came, like a second sun. That he might *ever* not be around set off a series of responses inside me that mimicked a panic attack. Something I hadn't experienced since I was a teen.

My throat closed up, breath stoppered at the back of my mouth, lungs squeezed tight like stuck edges of cling wrap.

"Guinevere." Raffa's voice hit me like a slap, jarring me out of that horrified stasis into taking a shuddering breath. "Where did you go just then?"

"To a place where you don't exist," I whispered honestly, still deeply rattled by the idea. "I could handle my own death much easier than yours."

Raffa's mouth did a complicated pattern of moves—flexing into a grimace, curving into a pout—before edging into a shocked little smile and then flatlining entirely.

"You are so young, Vera. Do not even say that. You do not understand the weight of what that means."

"Don't tell me I don't understand the weight of death," I snapped, lunging forward with the force of the fire ignited in my belly, flaming up my throat. "Living with hyperoxaluria type 1, I've been aware of the possibility of my own death since before I was diagnosed as a child. My partner in the medical program died after her body rejected her liver transplant a year before I was set to have my own kidney transplant. Gemma, healthy, beautiful, vivacious Gemma, died when she was twenty-six of a heart attack one night, asleep in her bed. I *threw a man off a building* with my own two hands and watched him crack open in the piazza below me, knowing I would have to live with his death forever. And I killed again yesterday, knowing it was my life or his, and I did not hesitate. I woke up this morning, not from a nightmare of killing those men, but from one where you were killed instead. There were tears on my face when I opened my eyes."

Without my understanding why or filtering the urge, my hand lashed out to wrap around Raffa's throat, thumb digging into his carotid artery to feel the heavy tap of his pulse against my skin.

Then, rolling to my toes so I could speak that much closer to his bent head, I hissed, "I've danced with death my entire life, and it wasn't until I danced with you that first time in Florence that I started to understand what all that experience had prepared me for."

Raffa scoffed, but his hands found the curves of my hips, fitting there like they were handholds carved into my body just for him. "Falling for death incarnate in real life?"

"Falling for a man who would die before he let anything happen to me," I corrected. "You said you did not want a weak woman to hide behind you and turn a blind eye to what you do, and I won't. I want to know everything. But in exchange, you have to understand something too. You fell for a woman who would happily die before letting anything happen to you."

Almost before I had finished speaking, his hands were on me, digging into my ass to lift me into his arms, mouth already slanting down over my still-moving lips. Vaguely, I was aware of him shifting us as I slotted my hands into his sweat-damp hair and thrust my tongue back over his own, eating the groan out of his mouth like a glutton greedy for more.

A moment later my back was pressed to rough bark, and feathery leaves tickled the back of my head. The fragrance of dry wood and herbal, almost fruity greenery was heady in my nostrils as Raffa pressed me against an olive tree. Bracing me there, he moved back just enough to tug my spandex shorts down my thighs.

He broke our kiss to stare down between us at the bare skin he'd revealed at my groin.

"No underwear again?" he moaned before diving in for a wet, salacious kiss. "Such a good girl."

It was my turn to whine when he pulled away to spit on me, rubbing the wet into my pussy as if he was giving it a massage before doing it once, twice more.

Fuck, why was that so hot?

"My girl likes when I spit on her greedy cunt?" he asked me in a rumbly purr, eyes so dark they gobbled up the light.

"I like it when you do anything to my greedy cunt," I admitted.

His response was a predatory smile like a snarl. He sank two fingers inside me and used his other hand to tug down my workout top so it bunched below my breasts, plumping them up in the fabric trap. I had always been self-conscious about my lack of curves, but the way Raffa licked his lips at the sight of my sweat-glistening mounds and hard nipples made me warm with pride.

"*Sei così delizioso,*" he praised me before dipping down to bite at my left nipple, firm tweaks that connected to my pussy as in an electrical circuit. "So sweet even when you're salty. Especially then."

I reached for him, more desperate than I had any right to be, given we had fucked less than twelve hours before this, my cunt still tender from his ministrations then. But this was different.

Now, Raffa was *mine.*

Mine for as long as I would fight to have him.

"Mine," I rasped as I wrapped my hand around the thick heft of his erection through the thin weave of his athletic shorts. "*Sei mio.*"

"*Si, sono tuo. Qualsiasi cosa io sia, sono tuo,*" he growled against my breast.

Yes, yours. Whatever I am, it's yours.

I tugged the elastic waistband down to grip his hot flesh in one hand. The sheer weight of his heavy cock made me whimper.

"*Basta parlare,*" I cried out as his fingers curled inside me and sent pleasure pulsing through me like a strobe light. "Fuck me, now."

"So impatient to be impaled on my dick," he teased darkly, keeping his hips just far enough from where he had pressed down to the wood that I could only drag the head of his weeping cock against my wet crease. "*Sei affamata*. You are so hungry. Tell me how you want it."

"I want to feel you stretch me open on your thick cock," I said without an ounce of shame, canting my hips so the tip of him caught at my entrance. Hooking a leg around his hip, I leveraged my weight to impale myself just slightly. "Please, Raffa, don't tease me. Now that you are mine, I need you to claim me. Fuck me hard and paint me in your cum. Remind me why I never want to be without you."

A fierce snarl tore from his throat. "Hands on the branch. Do not let go."

I hastened to do as he asked, my hands trembling as I wound them around the thin branch over my head. The position lifted my breasts even more, so that they jiggled over the gathered fabric of my top. It also made me feel like I had no control, dangling from the limb like an ornament for Raffa to enjoy.

The moment I obeyed, he clutched my ass in both hands, tipped my hips up so that my thighs, trapped in the spandex, were pressed out and back between us, and then thrust himself to the root inside me. My head fell back between my shoulders on a shout as every synapse in my brain pinwheeled into fireworks.

"There you go." His praise was a litany of filth as he started to drive into me, his hands keeping my lower back carefully away from the rough bark so it wouldn't hurt but also so that he could haul me back into his every thrust. "Such a sweet, good girl taking my cock like this. You are going to let me fuck you whenever I want to, is that not right, *cerbiatta*?"

"Yes," I hissed, using my grip on the tree to swing myself into him, my teeth jarring at every thrust, my entire focus narrowed to the spot where he swelled and bucked inside me. "Yes, please."

"You just want to be used, *sì*?" he soothed, reaching up to pluck at each nipple, back and forth until I convulsed with each shock wave of sensation it evoked. "That is what you thought about so lonely in the dark those nights without me in your bed. You dreamed of me breaking in to take you in your sleep, waking you up with an orgasm."

"*Si, Raffa*," I panted as an epic climax loomed over me, threatening to crash over my head and drown me in sensation.

"Oh, you already want to come for me? Did I not give you enough pleasure last night?" he asked, a cold edge of displeasure in his tone even though the hand on my nipple arrowed down to my clit to thrum it with his thumb as if he were playing a slow note on the guitar. "Wait for permission."

"Please," I cried, my nails dipping into the wood, my hips juddering against his own as I fought off the impending orgasm. "Oh God, Raffa, please, I-I need to come for you."

"You look so pretty struggling for me." His mouth was at my chin, nipping along my jaw until he reached my ear, where he whispered, "Such a good, sweet girl. You can come for me now, Vera. *Vieni per me*."

When his teeth sealed over my neck, sucking hard at the bruise he had placed there yesterday as if he never wanted that claim of ownership to wane, the tension shattered and sent pleasure sluicing through me, touching each point of electricity, my pussy, my breasts, even my neck under his teeth, until I felt like one vibrant live wire.

Raffa grunted as I spasmed around him, his cock swelling even harder inside me moments before I felt the hot kick of cum flooding my pussy. The sensation made my walls flutter in the aftermath, almost a second, smaller orgasm on the heels of the first.

"I love the feel of your cum inside me," I murmured, grinding my hips back into his so little shudders of pleasure emanated from our connection.

Raffa pulled back from my neck to stare at me, his cheeks flushed, a lock of wavy dark hair hanging into his pupil-blown eyes. There was a wicked promise in that look that said he wasn't done with me yet.

I gasped when he pushed a finger inside me next to his slowly softening dick. He raised it, glistening with our combined cum, between us in offering.

Without hesitation, I leaned forward to suck it into my mouth, fellating it the way I would his shaft. From up close, I watched his flush deepen as he studied me.

"We taste so good," I murmured, chasing his finger when he pulled it from my mouth. "You don't even know."

"No?" he asked, a slow smile tugging his mouth. "Let me see, then, shall I?"

Before I could process his intent, Raffa was on one knee, his hands clasping my ass to tilt my wet pussy into his mouth. I gaped down at his dark head between my thighs, his tongue inside me and his groan a palpable vibration against my swollen folds.

"OhmyGod," I slurred, unbelievably aroused by the sight of him eating his cum out of me, humming as if the flavor of us together was the best taste in the world. "Fuck, Raffa, that is so hot."

He threw my legs over his shoulders to ease me down from the branch so he could have better access, and I curled over him, hands clutched in his silken hair to pin him close. His resulting groan urged me to hold him tighter, grinding down against his tongue as he fucked it inside me.

"*Dio mio*, you're going to make me come again," I said with a hitch of breath as the tension in my womb wrenched tighter and tighter.

Already I was so close to the breaking point, my thighs quaked.

Raffa's fingers dug almost painfully into my ass, the bite of hurt only sending me higher.

"*Vienimi sulla lingua*," he encouraged roughly before placing a wet, sucking kiss on my clit.

Come on my tongue.

I broke open like pottery dropped to the earth. Only Raffa's hands and mouth kept me from falling apart, the two points of contact like glue holding me together. I trembled around his tongue, the wet sound of his mouth sucking up my juices driving me higher.

"Oh God," I cried, and I meant him.

Raffa, the only god who mattered to me. King Below. The most powerful man I knew, on his knees for me again to bring me inconceivable levels of pleasure.

When I was just a shivering, oversensitized collection of atoms in his embrace, Raffa carefully stood up with me in his arms, my legs listless around his hips, my hands loosely wound around his neck.

"I think you killed me," I said softly. "When I said I would die for you, I didn't exactly mean at your own hands."

His chuckle moved over me like sunlight as he sat on the ground at the base of the tree with me in his lap. Once settled, he tugged my arms down so he could gently massage the stiffness out of my fingers.

"A good death, though, I think." His smile was small and wicked, lips still glossed with us.

I leaned forward to kiss him, wanting to taste us too.

He hummed with satisfaction, palming the back of my head as he let me slide my tongue over his lips and then between his teeth.

"We taste good together," I admitted when I pulled back. "I think that was the hottest thing that has ever happened to me."

He cocked a brow. "Even more so than when I fucked you in every one of your sweet holes that last night at the palazzo?"

I shivered at the memory even as a blush stamped its heat into my cheeks. "Okay, maybe not."

His laugh was a smug rumble. "I promise to give you many more salacious memories. Now that you are staying."

The last wasn't said as a question, but I could read the lingering tension in his body at the words. So I cupped his handsome face between my hands, thumbs rasping through the short beard he'd grown, the way I'd wanted to do since I'd first seen him in Ann Arbor again.

"I can't promise I won't ever be scared or need some time or space to process, but I can promise that space won't be the Atlantic Ocean and that time won't be two months."

"Seven weeks and five days," he corrected solemnly.

My heart expanded so large in my chest, it hurt to breathe. I dipped to press my forehead to his and whispered, "I love you no matter what comes, okay? *Te lo prometto.*"

I promise.

"*Te lo prometto, cerbiatta mia,*" he echoed.

"You keep teaching me about sex," I said, leaning back to look him in the eye. "I think it's time you taught me how to be *la tua cacciatrice.*"

The most beautiful smile I'd ever seen, full of love and laughter, claimed my kiss-swollen mouth. "*Bene.* The first lesson, Vera, is how to fire a gun so that the next time a man comes for you and you shoot him in the chest, it is not a fluke that puts the bullet there."

CHAPTER TWENTY-THREE

Guinevere

The woman standing by the edge of the vineyard just off the kitchen terrace looked so much like my sister Gemma, that for a moment I thought she was a ghost. Or worse, that she might still be alive, waiting for my touch to bring her back home.

She turned seconds later, sensing me, maybe, as I came up the path from the makeshift shooting range where Martina, Carmine, Raffa, and I had practiced shooting for the last two hours.

I was sweaty, still in the workout clothes Raffa had fucked me in hours earlier because he had taken me directly to the range to learn how to properly shoot pistols, rifles, and, just for fun, a vintage revolver that Tonio had once given him as a present.

This was how my mother saw me for the first time in my element: sweat-slicked, bruised at the neck by a love bite from my capo, walking with the men and woman who made up most of the family I'd found for myself in Italy.

It wasn't the worst image.

In fact, I found myself wishing Mom had a camera so I could ask her to capture the new me.

"Hi, Mom," I called instead, breaking into a jog when her response was to hold her arms open for me.

I threw myself into them, squeezing tight as I buried my face in her freesia-scented blond hair.

"Hi, sweetie," she murmured as she clutched me right back.

Even though I had spent a few hours with my parents when we'd returned to the villa after the rescue, there was still so much to resolve between us. There had been long-awaited explanations, tears shed, and some shouting, but the conversation had been like lancing an infected wound. It had hurt just as much as it had been necessary to heal.

We held each other for a long moment, and when I tried to step away, she pulled me in even closer with a broken whisper of "When you left without a word, I thought we might not see you again, but when Raffa called your father and told him you were in trouble? I couldn't stop thinking about all the things left unsaid between us. About how wrong we had been in keeping you from the truth. I wondered if losing you to this life was some kind of karma."

My heart ached at the worry she must have felt, even though she'd been complicit in lying to me too.

"You could have told me everything," I said when she finally loosened her hold enough to let me step back, even though she still held my hands. "You should have told Gemma and me all of it a long time ago."

Mom sighed, dropping one of my hands to usher me into the vines. I looked over my shoulder for Raffa, who watched me from the terrace over a cup of water and inclined his head as I walked away.

He was the one who had encouraged me to talk things through with my parents.

"You have already lost too much," he'd said. "All of you have."

I wondered what Gemma would have thought of the mess Mom, Dad, and I found ourselves in, and decided she would have loved it. Chaos was her happy place, and truth was her comfort.

"I told Gemma about my own life somewhat," Mom said as she trailed her fingers along the vines.

This section had already been harvested, so only leaves remained.

"I told her my people were winemakers," she continued. "I have always been proud of that. Albania is one of the oldest producers of wine in the world, did you know that?"

I smiled slightly. "You may have told me once or twice when Dad got cocky about his wine knowledge."

She laughed, and I realized I looked like her a bit when she did, in the lines beside her eyes and the scrunch of her nose. "It was much less dangerous for Gemma to go to Albania than it was for either of you to come here. My family did some work with the local Mafia when I was a girl, but we weren't powerful or well known. Not like your father and his family."

It still blew my mind that Dad was a Pietra. That he'd killed and stolen and lied, all elements he had raised his daughters to abhor.

"Again, if you'd told us, we might have made different decisions," I said.

"Yes," she agreed. "But we didn't realize you were so headstrong. Our mistake."

"Gemma was too," I reminded her. "I'm surprised she didn't visit Italy too."

It would have been just like her to go to the country our father hated just to prove she could do whatever the hell she wanted.

"She didn't, and she still died," Mom murmured, twisting a grapevine between her fingers.

I pressed into her side, so she lifted an arm to curl it around me.

"I miss her all the time," I confessed. "Being here . . . it makes me feel closer to her. She always encouraged me to break out of my shell and explore. She would be proud of me, I think."

Mom sighed again but pressed a kiss to the top of my head. "She would. As am I."

I frowned, tipping my head back to look up at her, and found her beautiful face was more solemn than I had seen it in years, since those months I'd spent so sick in the hospital.

"I know you don't understand why we kept all this from you, but we had our reasons, and they were justified, if a little misguided. Your life has already been so difficult, sweetheart. Unlucky as you've been in health, we thought to spare you from the dangers of your dad's past life."

I could understand that, even if I didn't like it. Not having children of my own, I could not begin to comprehend what it must be like to want to keep them safe.

I only know how I felt about Raffa. The lengths I would go to in order to protect him.

There was no limit on that, and so there must have been no limit on what my parents would do to protect Gemma and me.

"I get that," I told her. "But that doesn't change what's happened. I came to Italy, and I found myself here. I won't be going back with you."

Mom laughed a little, surrendering. "Yes, your father told me you'd said that. Even with the danger, Jinx? Is he really worth being . . . *tortured* as you were?" Her smooth, cool hand cupped my cheek. "Is it really worth knowing you could die because of him?"

"Yes," I said simply. "When life isn't worth living without him."

She sucked a breath in between her teeth, eyes shining. "Oh, damn. Why did you have to go and have your father's heart?"

"Dad's?" I asked, surprised. "I used to think we were so much alike, but now . . . it feels like we are strangers."

"Oh no," she corrected, taking my hand to walk along the vines again. "Your father fell in love with me when he started to travel to Albania to do business with the Mafia there. He told me it was love at first sight the day we met at my parents' vineyard, where he was having lunch. We both knew we could not be together, but your father didn't care. He told me he would move heaven and earth to be with me, and he did. When I found out I was pregnant with Gemma, he decided to give up everything he'd ever known to keep his new family safe. We left for the US two weeks after I handed him the pregnancy test. He never spoke to anyone from his old world again, but I knew it had to have pained him. He never seemed to regret it, and he never made me feel guilty for his sacrifice."

My chest hurt, filled like a balloon close to bursting.

"You are willing to give up everything you've ever known for your Raffa, just as your father was for me," she said softly, stopping to tuck a lock of hair behind my ear. "So I know nothing I say will stop you, even though I wish I could because I want you safe and close more than anything."

"He's not a bad man," I told her in a threadbare voice. "In fact, he's the best man I know."

"So is your father," she said. "I understand, honey. More than I can say. I won't stand between you and happiness."

"And Dad?"

Her sigh stirred my hair, and she held me close. "Your father will take some more convincing. We are going to stay here for a while, I think. If you mean to make a life here, we want to make sure it's a good one. I won't be able to drag him home until he sees with his own eyes that Raffa is good enough for you."

"You might be here forever, then," I quipped. "Dad doesn't seem inclined to like a Romano based on principle."

"The only time I've ever seen your father cry is for you girls," she said firmly, cupping my face so I had to look into her warm hazel eyes. "His number one priority in life is seeing you well. Give him a chance, and he'll give you and Raffa one."

"I can do that," I allowed, shifting to throw one of her arms around my shoulder so we could keep walking. "So, Mom, were you ever tortured for Dad? Maybe we can trade notes."

Her laugh rang out over the rows of grapevines and soared deep into the heart of the valley below us. I thought the sound suited this space, the marriage of my old family and new coming together in a way I had never believed possible.

◆ ◆ ◆

I was working in the office with Carmine later that afternoon after a lengthy shower and a slightly awkward lunch with the Romanos and my parents. My work for Dad's company was over, but I was transitioning into doing some things for Lupo Nero, Raffa's investment company, and I couldn't help but advise Carmine when he asked me for help on a problem.

Which was my current project.

A series of break-ins at some of Raffa's shell companies had been occurring over the last few months, but nothing seemed to have been stolen, and there was no discernible link between the companies that were targeted.

"Perhaps you can see something we haven't with that puzzling mind of yours," Carmine had suggested, handing me the flash drive with the information. "We believe it has something to do with the Venetian."

"I can take a look." I accepted the files. "But I'll need access to more information about Lupo Nero and the Romano Group."

"Why the latter? None of the companies are attached to the Romano Group."

"Call it a hunch," I'd said with a shrug, and Carmine hadn't hesitated to create an account for me in their software so I could access the necessary ledgers and financial documents for both companies.

Three hours later, the sun was a narrow neon-pink ribbon on the horizon, and my eyes were so dry they clicked when I blinked as I studied the files open on my computer screen.

It was no wonder I startled when a soft pressure bloomed on my bare shoulder.

Raffa's laugh was like smoke as his hands came down to settle on my clavicles, holding me still so he could plant another kiss on my neck over the bruise there.

"I thought you were done working for your father?" he asked, nosing into my hair in a way that made shivers erupt down my spine.

"I am, but Carm asked me for help with a problem. Is that okay?" It occurred to me it might not be. I'd never spoken to Raffa about the no doubt confidential information Carmine shared with me while we shared the office.

"Of course it is," he said, voice bright with pleased surprise. "If you would consider it, I would hire you right here and now to work with me."

"Really?" I shivered again as he nipped my earlobe.

"Why do you sound so shocked? You have already proved immeasurably helpful both with the Chinese wine fraud and with taking down the Grecos for their Albanian shipments."

"Well, I am looking for a job now that I plan to stay here . . ." I teased, leaning into his questing mouth at my jaw. "But it might be a conflict of interest, given I'm sleeping with the boss."

His growl was mostly a purr as his arms bracketed me on the chair from behind. "It is a good thing I make my own rules then, is it not, *cacciatrice*?"

"It is," I gasped as he sucked hard at my neck and blew cool air over the wet mark. "But I can't tell if you are joking or serious when you play with me like this."

He jerked the chair so it spun to face him and caged me in once more, lowering his face so that finely honed handsomeness was all I could see.

"Work with me, not for me, Vera. My partner in all things, remember?" He waited for me to nod. "I was not joking about that. Have you ever heard of the Roman empress Theodora? No? Well, she was married to Emperor Justinian, who loved and respected her so adamantly that he made her his equal on the throne. She was his greatest adviser and attended state council meetings, made both political and religious decisions, and became a well-known figure in her own right."

"You want me to be your Theodora?" I asked through the wide, jaw-aching smile on my face.

Raffa's pale-copper eyes gleamed. "*Mea Regina Inferna* is more apt, perhaps. But yes. Equal in all things. Why would I not want your brilliance working alongside me?"

"It's good to know you think I'm more than just a pretty face," I joked, and kissed his chin.

He gripped my chin in his hand, expression somber when he stated, "The prettiest face to house the most beautiful mind. I am in awe of you, Vera. Do not underestimate that."

"I couldn't," I promised, pushing my fingers into the short hair over his ears to bring him closer so I could speak against his mouth. "Because I feel the very same. There is an echo, I think, between our hearts. What you feel, I feel."

"What am I feeling right now?" he asked sinuously, licking my lower lip.

"Dinner," Angela bellowed from down the hall in the kitchen.

I grinned and punched a kiss to his pouting mouth. "Later, I promise."

"Having a house full of our kin is not conducive to how I feel about you agreeing to stay here and be with me," he groused, standing up to glare at the chaos of noise outside the door as feet stampeded to the kitchen.

I laughed. "No, but maybe we can stay at the palazzo soon, just the two of us?"

"Yes, that was actually what I came in here to say. This weekend is Giorno dei Morti, the Day of the Dead. Traditionally, I host a party at the palazzo, which begins in the private cemetery. Donatella Verdi, the *capo donna* in Venice, will be there, as will most of my other capos, to celebrate."

"And to be questioned about their loyalty?" I surmised.

"Exactly. I would like you there with me."

I blinked at him as a smile slowly broke over my face. "Yeah?"

He had not let me join him for the meeting with the Albanians because I had refused to be a part of his world, but now? Now, I would meet them all at his side.

The prospect should have worried me, maybe, but instead I felt suffused with pride that he wanted me beside him and a dark anticipation of watching my powerful man in his element.

"I'd love to," I told him.

A tenseness I hadn't noticed until it was gone faded from his frame, leaving behind a soft expression that took my breath away.

"*Bene*. We will leave a day early to have an evening alone in Firenze. I want to take you somewhere special."

"Okay," I whispered, a little dizzy with joy. "I'd like that too."

We stood looking at each other with silly smiles on our faces for a long moment before the bell clanged in the kitchen, Angela reminding the stragglers that dinner was on the table.

"Come, let us see if this meal is any less painful than the last," he joked, offering his hand to me.

I giggled but shook my head. "Distract your mom for me? I just want to finish up here—I think I was onto something."

Raffa bent to press a kiss to my forehead and then, unsatisfied, tipped my head to place a lingering one on my mouth.

"Do not be long," he implored before turning on his heel and leaving me to it.

I listened as he distracted his mother in the kitchen when she asked after me, and then bent over the keyboard again.

Because there was something in this mess of data that called to me, something about how each company that had been broken into hadn't noticed anything missing. Imelda's vineyard was one of them; then there were a textile factory outside Milan, a chain of pizza places across Europe Raffa had invested in at its source in Naples, a balsamic company in Bologna, and a turbine manufacturer in Turin.

All seemingly without connection, except . . .

The Romano Group had once been invested in that same pizzeria in Naples, but they'd removed funding before expansion over four years ago, when Raffa became capo.

There was an article in the *Corriere della Serra* about the Romano Group's lost bid on a huge green tech firm out of Rome last spring and a blog post from a popular food writer about the sale of Tenuta Romano from the Romano Group to a global subsidiary three years ago because of ethical differences between Delfina Romano at the winery and Romano Group CEO Tonio di Conte.

It seemed that every company that had been targeted was a missing piece in the fabric of the Romano Group's company.

It could have been a coincidence, but I wasn't the kind of girl to believe in coincidences.

I believed in data-based patterns and mathematics.

I believed in fate.

And something told me that I was right about the Romano Group being the crack in Raffa's armor. He had dismissed it too readily because of his issues with his father after he died, and it had been left too long unchecked.

I pushed out of my chair, wincing at the crick in my back, and went down the hall away from the kitchen, toward the office Leo kept at the back of the house.

The door was open, but the space was empty, Leo no doubt already gathered with the others for dinner.

I hesitated in the doorway, listening to the cacophony of dinner filtering in from outside, and stepped into the office.

There was nothing on the wide wooden desk but for a computer and a small red clock with, shockingly, a Leaning Tower of Pisa photo on its face. It was cheap and kitschy, so incongruous and unlike Leo that I frowned at it for a long moment before I started snooping.

The bottom two drawers were locked, but the top one opened beneath my hand and exposed a messy interior filled with sheaves of loose paper, notepads, pens, and a handful of notes in other denominations—American, British, Chinese, and Albanian.

I shifted through the papers with one eye on the door, so I almost missed it when my fingers pinched the edge of thicker card stock. My gaze flickered down to catch the edge of a postcard.

I frowned, tugging it out from under a notepad to reveal a photograph of the Ponte Vecchio in Florence. It was astoundingly familiar because I had bought the very same postcard of the bridge to write one of my many unsent, diary-like postcards to Gemma.

My fingers shook as I flipped the card over to see the back, and I sucked in such a sharp breath at the sight of the recognizable cramped handwriting that I nearly choked on it.

> Dearest Gemma,
> You would not believe the adventure I am having here, only because it seems like something that would happen to you and not me.
>
> I met a man.
>
> I know, shocking.
>
> Even more so? He hit me with his car before he basically saved my life. I was being chased by someone who was trying to molest me, and he just appeared in the road in this ridiculous red Ferrari. He blamed me for hurting the car, can you believe that?
>
> But then he helped me into his car and tied my broken sandal to my foot, and you know what I felt like?
>
> Cinderella.
>
> I've never felt that way before. Not like a damsel in distress, necessarily, because you know I've been sick and I've been dreaming all my life. But like . . . like magic is real. Like if I reached out to touch this man, he could change my world.

I've been staying at his palazzo (a.k.a. palace!) for ten days now, and I can confirm—he's doing just that.

Changing my life.

Changing me.

Through kindness and satiating my curiosity. By being the handsomest man I've ever seen and taking care of me so tenderly when I've been sick.

He says he isn't a good man, that he's helping me reluctantly, but I don't believe it.

There is a loneliness in his eyes, Gemma, and I want to be the one to vanquish it.

Wish me luck.

Your eternally unlucky sister,

Jinx

That was my writing. My postcard.

One of the ones that had been taken from the apartment I'd rented from Signora Verga in Florence.

What in the world was it doing in Leo's desk?

"Can I help you find something?"

I snapped my head up to see the man himself leaning against the doorframe. Unlike Raffa, with his habitual closed-off pose, his arms crossed and feet braced, Leo had his arms loosely at his sides, a small smile on his face.

As if I had not just been caught snooping in his office.

"I was searching for a notepad," I said, slipping my fingers off the postcard to the bound papers on top of it and then raising the notepad in the air for Leo to see. "Carmine and I are working on my written Italian, and I'm ashamed to admit it isn't going well. We ran out of paper."

"Ah," he said before a short pause. "Well, here, take as many as you want."

He crossed to me on those long legs before I could push the postcard back under the mess in the drawer. His fingers lingered along the edge of it, but I was not afraid to look up into his face to read his expression.

"It's a sweet note," he said finally, lifting the card and turning it over and back. "When I first found it, I didn't know who Gemma was, but now I can say I'm sorry for your loss."

I swallowed thickly and glanced up to find his countenance was one of real sorrow.

"Thank you," I said. "But how did you come to find this? I thought they'd all been stolen when the Venetian broke into my apartment."

"The rest were," he agreed with an easy shrug, dropping the postcard onto the desk and putting his hands in his pockets to rock back on his heels. It was a boyish gesture to match the slightly chagrined expression on his face. "I'm afraid I took that when I went looking into you after we met at Fattoria Casa Luna."

"Looking into me?"

"You have to understand, there have been many women in Raffa's life who sought to use him for their own designs. Then there you were, this American girl he ran into, suddenly living in his palazzo? Wearing designer clothes he bought for you and hanging out with his inner circle? It was alarming."

"So . . . you looked into me," I repeated. "You broke into my apartment and spied on me?"

He winced. "I didn't *spy*. But I had to check to make sure you were who you said you were. It's part of my job."

"Isn't Martina his consigliere?" I asked.

"Yes," he said with a wan smile. "And Renzo is his underboss. Ludo is his hacker, and Carmine is his second at Lupo Nero and helps to run the other companies."

"And you look into suspicious people?"

Raffa hadn't given Leo a title.

Leo? He does everything I need him to do, sometimes before I can even ask it of him.

"That and whatever else needs doing," he agreed. "I'm sorry for it, but it had to be done. Raffa protects us all, and in turn, I must protect Raffa."

There was something about the way he said it, defensive almost, aggressive definitely. Like his ability to protect had come into question, and he was determined to prove his worth.

"I want to protect him too," I said calmly, because I understood that looking into me had been the smart thing to do. "Though, obviously, you missed my connection to the Pietra clan. That would have been helpful to know."

He blinked at me, and his voice was very mild when he said, "Yes, it would have been. Though computer wiz Ludo didn't find it either, so I won't castigate myself too much."

I nodded, continuing to stare at him, because despite his open expression, I found him the hardest to read of all Raffa's mafiosi.

"Here," he said, pushing the postcard closer to me with his pinky. "You should have it back. I'm sorry I can't do more."

Without another word, he strode toward the door and back down the hall.

It took me a moment to wonder what more he could have done beyond giving me back my unsent letter to Gemma.

CHAPTER TWENTY-FOUR

Raffa

I waited for Guinevere in the lobby of the Florentine palazzo, studying the bowl of red flowers on the entryway table but remembering the black chrysanthemums that had been placed there during the San Lorenzo celebration in the summer.

The night everything had gone to hell, and the last time Guinevere and I had occupied this space together.

It was amazing what a difference three months could make.

She had fled the country and come back, my reluctant prisoner for her own safety, and now a blue-blooded Mafia princess in her own right, ready to take my side as my queen.

It was too good to be true for a man like me.

What had I done in all my years to deserve a woman who saw my darkness and understood its necessity just as much as she saw my light and nurtured it?

She was not the yin to my yang or the white to my black, nothing so stark and contrary.

There was no end or beginning to our connection, but a gradation from self to self, a blurring of lines between our souls that perfectly harmonized the dark she'd yearned for in her own life with the light I'd needed in my own.

I knew if I had the courage to show her all the parts of me that I did not love, she would find some way to love them too.

What kind of magic was that?

The kind that drove Dante to write about Beatrice all his life.

The kind that prompted Emperor Justinian to make Theodora an empress at his side.

Even though I was not the type of man to warrant a happily ever after, I thought that, with her at my side, we could fight together to win one.

Starting with what I had planned today.

I was uncharacteristically nervous as I waited for Guinevere to join me, my fingers itching to check the messages on my phone once again to make sure everything was in place, though I knew it already was.

A week of planning and very, very deep pockets could get you anywhere.

"Sorry it took me so long." Guinevere's lilting Italian floated down the curved staircase toward me.

When I glanced up, what breath was locked in my lungs evaporated at the sight of her.

She looked ethereal, Proserpina descending into the dark underworld to meet her dark groom. The gauzy white gown clung to her like condensation, a narrow panel over each breast that revealed acres of pale-gold skin to her navel, where another panel wrapped around her slim waist before giving way to a loose skirt that skimmed her legs all the way to the floor. With her long, heavy tresses brushed into gleaming waves and the heavy, square gold earrings I'd given her at her ears, she seemed every inch a Roman goddess.

"I don't think I've ever seen you speechless," she mused with a feminine smile as she finished climbing down the stairs and stopped in front of me. "Do I pass muster?"

"*Sei uno spettacolo*," I admitted. "*Mi togli il fiato*."

You are utterly beautiful. You take my breath away.

Guinevere blushed, pink heat streaking her cheeks and chest. I reached out with my thumb to trace the warmth over one side of her face.

"Thank you," she said simply. "You said to dress for something special, but the Day of the Dead celebration is tomorrow, right?"

"*Si*, tonight is just for the two of us."

She cocked her head slightly but nodded, taking my offered arm so I could lead her out the doors to the car that waited for us. Her laughter was bright when she caught sight of the Ferrari NART Spyder.

"If you let my dad drive this, he might actually start liking you," she teased as I opened the door for her.

I waited until she was ensconced in the car to smile, remembering my conversation with John Stone from the day before.

"Can I talk to you for a moment?" I had asked as I stopped beside the chair John was occupying while he watched Guinevere and her mother play in the pool with some of Carlotta's and Stacci's sons.

His lips thinned. "If you feel you must."

I bit back the edge of my smile and sat in the chair across from him, bracing my forearms on my thighs so I could lean closer. He eyed me suspiciously, rightly guessing that I was settling in for a serious conversation.

"You aren't marrying her, Romano," he said, startling me with his perceptiveness.

The smile I gave him was wolfish. "She wants to be with me, Stone. Forever."

"And you don't doubt that?" He scoffed. "She's a twenty-three-year-old girl who has been sheltered most of her life. She's blinded by your handsomeness and intrigue, but she doesn't truly know what she is getting into bed with, and when she does, she'll be gone quicker than you can act."

"Do not contradict how Guinevere has spoken of you and be condescending now," I said blandly. "I believe you were with me two days ago when we broke into your family's castello *and found they had tortured Guinevere. You saw she shot a man to save herself. Maybe you do not know about the man she pushed from a bell tower to save our friend Ludo, and*

maybe you have not seen how her curious, brilliant mind has seized on the intricacies of legal and illegal business dealings, but I have seen it all. I was once skeptical like you were, and it was a mistake I will not make again, not when she has told me repeatedly she does not see me as a monster, even when I do monstrous things. No one knows better than Guinevere what she wants, and I trust her enough to know she wants me."

"Pretty speech," John muttered, rubbing a hand over his downturned mouth. "You speak English very well, if formally."

"I went to Oxford," I supplied, just to watch him sigh.

I was not the thug he wanted me to be, the villain he could paint for his daughter, a beast who turned to violence because he was uneducated and brutish.

"I cannot have been the only who heard her say she would not marry anyone who did not ask her the other day in the castello*," I added.*

"No," he confessed, turning his head to watch as Guinevere tossed a squealing Mattia into the water and then Zacheo right after him. "I heard that."

"You believe I want to marry her just to solidify my power base," I said, and it was not a question, because I could see the suspicion in the way he had looked at me since the idea had come to light at the Pietra castello.

"It would work," he noted. "Joining two prominent families that have feuded for years would be a coup for you. Something to settle the worry and gossip about the Venetian. But my daughter is not some pawn."

"I call her mia stella cadente*," I told him, because there was no way Guinevere could ever be a pawn to me. "She brought such light to my life I was sure it could not last, even though I wished it would. Now I know she will stay even if I do not ask. I know she will fight for us even when I do not want her to. I think you know these things too, so let me tell you what you do not know because you do not know me."*

I breathed deeply. Being vulnerable with another person was not something I took lightly or did easily, but Guinevere's father deserved it despite sharing blood with Gaetano Pietra.

"You think I am the kind of man to end lives without thought, to amass fortunes because I am greedy, and to lie because I have no morals. You might be right. But the man I am will also kill anyone who so much as looks at Guinevere the wrong way. I am the man who will use every dollar I have to buy her whatever her heart desires, and I am the man who will lie without blinking if it means protecting her from harm. I have sacrificed many of my dreams to keep my loved ones safe, Stone. But I will sacrifice many more to keep Guinevere safe and by my side."

John stared at me for a long time, his deep-brown eyes so like his daughter's, though filled with sharp scrutiny. I let him look, leaning back in the chair with one ankle across my knee so I could enjoy the merriment of my family around me.

When Guinevere got out of the pool, dripping wet in only a tiny red bikini I wanted to undo with my teeth, and glanced over at me, I patted my thigh with one hand.

She bounded over without hesitation and plopped herself in my lap with a giggle as she soaked my clothes through to the skin.

"Sorry," she said with a sassy grin before kissing my cheek.

"Worth it," I assured her.

Instantly, she melted into me, curling up against my chest as if content to stay there, wet and cooling in the autumn air, forever. I leaned over to the towels waiting on a bench beside me and unfurled one to drape over her.

When I looked back, John was watching Guinevere with an expression of such intense sadness and love, it made me momentarily pause.

"I missed you," he said to her softly.

Guinevere reached a hand out to him from under the towel and waited until he grabbed hold before she said, "I missed you too, Dad."

The moment he stared at me with tears in his eyes, I knew I had his blessing. But it was not until Guinevere was dragged back to the pool by Zacheo, Mattia, Maximo, and Vitale that he reached over to grab me hard by the shoulder.

"You hurt her," he had said gruffly, "and I'll polish off my old brass knuckles and beat your stupidly handsome face in."

"You know," I told Guinevere as I slid into the driver's seat. "I think I will drive it back to the villa when we return and let him take it on a joyride."

She laughed. "Are you trying to suck up to my dad, Raffaele?"

I shrugged one shoulder. "I feel no shame about it. If I want to keep you in my life for a very, very long time, Vera, it is necessary for your father and me to be on good enough terms that he does not appear seconds away from shooting me at any given moment."

After a long beat of quiet, I glanced over to see her watching me with palpable tenderness. Her hand reached over to rest on my thigh, squeezing gently.

"I know you think you're mad, bad, and dangerous to know, Raffa," she said quietly. "But you are the best man I've ever known. And I know you think you corrupt me, but I honestly believe you make me a better me."

"*Sei la parte migliore di mei*," I told her. "You are the best part of me."

"Agree to disagree on that." She leaned over to kiss my suited shoulder. "But I appreciate the sentiment. So will you tell me where we are going?"

"No."

"Raffa!"

"Vera."

"Don't be a tease," she insisted.

"I know for a fact that you enjoy it when I tease you," I countered, sliding her a dark look. "If last night in bed was any indication . . ."

She pouted, but her eyes sparkled in the low light inside the car.

"Besides, you do not have to wait long," I said as I pulled up to the front of the Uffizi, where a valet was waiting for us.

If Guinevere was disappointed we were going to the famous gallery when she had already visited, she did not say a word as I helped her from the car and handed the keys to the valet, the same young man I had met outside Guinevere's apartment in the summer. He grinned at me as he took the keys, but a single cool glare reeled in his enthusiasm for driving my car.

"I recognize him," Guinevere murmured as we made our way inside the museum.

"He was one of the thugs outside your shoddy apartment beside Fortezza da Basso."

"That's a weird coincidence," she said, peering up at me because she knew it was not just that.

"He had the decency to look out for you while you lived there and keep the general riffraff from disturbing you, so I hired him for a few odd jobs." I shrugged.

"Sweet," she reminded me, as she had done so many times since we had met. "You are unbearably sweet, Raffa Romano, and there is no hiding it from me."

"I think your definition needs recalibrating if you think hiring a young thug to work for my criminal outfit is worthy of an altruism award."

She laughed, the sound echoing off the marble floors and pillared walkway as we made our way down the silent corridor toward the gallery I had selected for the night.

"Where is everyone?" she asked.

"It is past closing time," I told her as we stopped at the entrance to the temporary exhibition space. "And this special exhibition is only for you."

"What?" she gasped as I pushed the doors open to the hall.

The interior was decorated sublimely, given the short amount of time the curator, Amir Saleh, had had to bring everything together for me.

In the center of the room sat a small table draped in white linen and laid with fine silver and china, a bottle of prosecco and a bottle of sparkling juice sitting in a gold bucket beside the chairs. The floor was festooned with red petals, not from roses but from poppies, the same flowers I had imagined Guinevere twirling in the first time she'd tried on a red dress for me.

But it was the art in the room that stole the show.

Amir had brought in part of the Dante exhibit they had shown at the Ashmolean in Oxford a few years ago thanks to my connections there. Auguste Rodin's sculpture *The Kiss* dominated one corner, on loan from Paris, and art from Salvador Dalí, William Blake, and Dante Gabriel Rossetti flanked the walls.

Immediately before the table sat the most famous piece of art in the entire museum, though. Sandro Botticelli's *The Birth of Venus*, his goddess bearing a remarkable resemblance to his great love, Simonetta.

Next to that, Alessandro Allori's *The Abduction of Proserpine*.

Pavarotti's music played softly in the background as Guinevere clapped her hand to her chest as if to contain her wildly beating heart and swept around the room, staring at each piece.

I waited inside the doors, hands clasped behind my back, as I watched her look of unadulterated shock and wonder.

Finally, she stopped before the painting of Venus and turned to me with her mouth open in a soft O.

"This," she started, and then swallowed hard before trying again with an ineloquent wave of her hand. "This is a love letter written in art. You . . . you found all the stories we've likened our love to."

"I did," I agreed. "Though there is a mosaic in Ravenna of Theodora and Justinian that is adhered to the wall of a church, so I will just have to plan a trip there for you to see it."

"They're . . . God, Raffa. They're so beautiful," she whispered through the thickness of emotion in her throat.

Her eyes sparkled with unshed tears.

I stepped toward her and gathered her beautiful heart-shaped face in my hands so she could see the sincerity in my eyes when I said, "None of them come close to the beauty you bring to my life. Not one of these stories is as perfect to me as ours."

Her hands came up to clasp my wrists, holding me to her. "Even though I left you?"

I rubbed my thumb against the end of her pouting mouth to erase the frown.

"I am glad you left," I said. "It taught us both lessons we needed to learn."

Her laugh was wet. "That I am too stubborn for my own good?"

"That we cannot be fulfilled unless we are together."

"You know I won't leave you ever again, right?" she asked, her eyes wide with desperation as they searched my face. "When I promised you, I meant it. Nothing can take me from your side again."

"Let's not tempt fate," I encouraged, leaning to kiss the tip of her nose because she was adorable and I did not have to try to resist her temptation any longer. "You are not that proficient with a gun yet to ward off any enemy."

"Soon," she swore. "Just like with Empress Theodora, people will come to fear and respect me too."

"*La mia temibile cacciatrice*," I teased as I bit into her lower lip. "*La mia stella cadente*."

My fearsome huntress. My shooting star.

"*Meus Rex Infernus*," she said, rolling to the toes of her high heels to better kiss my mouth, sliding her tongue between my lips with a proprietary assertiveness that made my cock ache. "I want you."

"Dinner will get cold," I told her, but I was already lifting her into my arms, her legs wrapping around my hips as I walked over to the bench before *The Birth of Venus* and sat down on it.

"Cold is good," she murmured nonsensically. "I have this fire beneath my skin, and I need you to put it out."

"Is that right?" I asked roughly as her mouth trailed from mine to the corner of my jaw and then my neck. "I brought you here to admire the art, Guinevere."

"After," she suggested, biting into my earlobe as she moved sinuously over my lap, rubbing herself against the crest of my hardened cock beneath my trousers.

"Now," I insisted, clamping my hands over her hips to lift her off me and settle her between my legs, on her feet.

She pouted.

I ignored it, pushing her firmly away from me until she took a few steps back.

Only then did I brace my hands behind me on the bench and lean back to devour her greedily, lazily, with my eyes.

"Well?" I asked coolly. "I am here to admire the art, Guinevere. Undress and let me admire the most beautiful piece in the room."

Her nostrils flared as she took a startled breath, but I watched the way desire transformed her too, deepening the pink in her cheeks and lips, turning her eyes to hot, dark coals.

My sweet *cerbiatta* might have struggled to strip for me in a public place like the Uffizi, no matter that it was closed, the cameras off, but my fierce *cacciatrice* loved the challenge. Her chin tipped high as she slowly moved her hands up those narrow panels of fabric covering her breasts, molding the shape of them, pausing to pluck at her nipples until they were hard beads beneath the gauze. I could almost see the dusky rose of them through the slightly sheer chiffon.

"*Sei così bella*," I encouraged her as she slipped her fingers beneath the panel and edged it in tiny increments until it fell off one shoulder, exposing her right breast to my gaze.

Puckered pink nipple, high, pert swell.

My mouth watered.

A coy, feminine smile played at her mouth as she did the same little dance with the other strap until it fell, limp petals at her waist revealing that lean, slightly curved torso, bare but for the *cornicello* necklace I had given her at her neck.

"*Il tuo seno mi fa venire l'acquolina in bocca*," I growled.

Your breasts make my mouth water.

"Take out your cock for me," she asked, touching her tongue to her lower lip while she waited for me to obey her.

I pulled myself out through the zipper carefully so that I remained fully clothed, just the hard, weeping shaft of my dick exposed for her gaze.

"Do you want me to stroke myself while I watch you get naked?" I asked, my voice as deep and dark as the desire curling like my hand around my length.

"Yes," she hissed.

"Then continue," I demanded, wrapping my fingers around the base of my cock but not stroking.

I waited until she started to roll her hips, shimmying the tight fabric down them and then turning to show me the way it caught under her ass, plumping the cheeks beautifully above the fabric.

"*Sei la creatura più sensuale che abbia mai visto*," I praised. You are the most sensual creature I have ever seen. "Bend over and show me your sweet pussy."

She let the collected fabric drop to the marble floor in a pool of white like fallen moonbeams. Left only in her gold high heels and a tiny strip of white lace bisecting her cheeks and covering her mound, she looked like an angel fallen into the dark underworld, a morsel for me to devour.

"Take them off," I grunted, my civility sloughing off under the heat of the fire building between us.

She toyed with me, looking over her shoulder with her lower lip trapped between her teeth as she played a finger along the edge of the underwear. When she removed it, I could see how it glistened with her juices, and I groaned as she lifted it to her mouth to suck hard at the taste of herself.

"*Sei deliziosa, vero*?" I asked.

Delicious, isn't it?

She hummed her agreement.

But I was done with the anticipation.

"Come here," I said. I waited as she straightened and walked, slow as could be, between my legs.

Instead of pulling her into my lap, I snapped the side of her thong so the fabric fluttered to the floor and then lay back on the bench to tug her over my face. She gasped as I forced her to swing a leg over the bench so she was straddling me and then brought her pussy down to my mouth to feast.

She writhed on my tongue as I ate her ravenously. Already wet from the show of exhibitionism, Guinevere was swollen and ready to come in minutes. I kept her on the edge, thrumming her clit with my tongue and then fucking into her heat until her hands pulled my shirt out of my trousers and she carved her fingers into my abs.

"Raffa, please," she cried out, grinding into my tongue.

"Come for me and Venus," I told her before sucking her sweet clit into my mouth and humming around it.

She shattered so violently I had to clamp my hands over her thighs to keep her seated on my mouth. Her juices ran onto my tongue, nectar sweet.

She was still orgasming when I pushed her down my torso into my lap and sat up, swinging my legs over the bench so that we both faced Botticelli's famous painting, Guinevere's favorite artist and favorite work.

"You are more beautiful than the goddess of love could ever be," I said as I slid my cock through her drenched folds and then shuttled her down my shaft.

She threw her head back onto my shoulder, arms going behind her head to grab at my hair.

"Spread them wider," I demanded, and waited until she hooked her thighs over the outsides of mine, exposing herself to the room as if the painted audience was a real one. "Let them watch how well you take my cock in your little cunt."

"Oh my God," she whispered, eyes squeezed shut as she started to shiver apart with pleasure.

I moved one hand from her breasts down her flat belly to her wet, throbbing clit and rolled it under my thumb.

That was all it took for her to crest like a wave over my dick. I held her still with my other hand as I fucked up into her spasming grasp, her cum flooding my shaft and dripping down my balls.

"That's it," I gritted out through my teeth. "That's my good girl."

Moments later, I found my own release, grunting as I filled her up with cum, unable to stop the fantasy of one day breeding her, stuffing her full of cum again and again until she was pregnant with our child. Even knowing she was on the birth control shot, the idea of doing so now was incendiary.

The climax tore me apart, an atom-by-atom explosion that robbed me of sight, breath, and thought for a pure moment of ecstasy.

"Oh my God," Guinevere murmured, her voice a tether I followed back to earth.

She was slumped against my chest, head resting on my shoulder, nose tucked under my jaw, legs limp where they were splayed over mine.

I slid my hand over her belly and pressed there as I kissed her forehead.

"One day," I muttered, still half drunk on my orgasm. "I am going to fuck you without protection or birth control, fill you to leaking every single day until you get pregnant with our child."

A full-body shiver racked Guinevere's body, and a breathy little gasp followed her pussy spasming around my softening length.

"Oh, you like that idea," I noted with smug, masculine pride.

"I do," she admitted, leaning back to smile shyly at me. "It's unbelievably hot."

"It is," I agreed. "But first things first, I think."

She raised a brow at me, an expression I was happy to know she had adopted from me. I ignored it to shift her to the bench so I could get up and retrieve her dress. She sat still and pliant while I dressed her, slipping the fabric over her head, lifting her to her feet to tug it over her hips so it swished at her high-heeled feet. I got on my knees before her to kiss each knee before it disappeared beneath the material and the inside swell of each breast when I adjusted the panel just so over its curves.

By the time I finished tending to her, her lids were low over smoldering dark eyes. She smoothed her fingers into my hair, pushing the waves back from my forehead tenderly.

"I love you." She spoke softly, as if the words were a reverent prayer in a sacred temple. I was glad for it, because I had made this space as holy to us as possible, filled with symbols of the greatest love stories ever known, including our own. "All this is unspeakably wonderful," she said, gesturing to our surroundings. "But it's you I can't take my eyes off."

I smiled at her. "I read the letter you wrote in the Chiesa di Santa Margherita de' Cerchi." At her little gasp, I raised a cocky brow. "I had it retrieved from the bowl. It is better that the man who loves you and is capable of and *willing* to give you whatever you want knows the desires of your heart than some priest in a chapel, no?"

She frowned slightly, but did not stop me from continuing.

"'I want a life filled with fire, and I want to be courageous enough to stand the flames.' That is what you wrote before you told Beatrice, or God, or whoever you hoped might grant wishes, that what you desired most was love. Love of a man whose touch threatened to raze you to ash."

"Only so I could be reborn into something better," she murmured, smoothing a hand into my hair. "Something stronger."

"I told you once that maybe you were unlucky in life because you were saving all your fortune up for a truly epic love story," I said as I gathered her slim fingers in my calloused grip. "I did not understand at the time that the same thought could be applied to me. Whatever hell I have endured in this life, it was to earn the perfection of you at my side."

"Raffa," she breathed as I leaned forward to kiss the bared skin above her navel.

I was nervous, which was strange for me. But the stakes had never been so high. Not even when I had decided to take over as *capo dei capi* from my father to save my family.

This was a decision I was making for me. A selfish one, given the dangers Guinevere would have to endure by my side, but one I found I could live with because she had convinced me that she could handle the heat, enjoy it, even.

I had to believe, as she did, that fate had created us for each other and thrown us on an inevitable course toward this very moment, where I would cement our destiny for the rest of our lives as one of Italy's greatest love stories, even if ours was never told as widely as the ones that surrounded us in this room.

"So I hope you understand I am not doing this because you are suddenly a Mafia princess and uniting our families would shore up the power that our enemies have been trying to steal for months. I am doing this because you are the one dream I will allow myself to have without guilt or avarice. I am doing this because I had forgotten what joy was and connection could be until you jumped into the road and I hit you with my car." I paused as she let out a weak laugh. "I am doing this because I love you in any language across any span of time, and I will never stop, not even when my last breath leaves my body. So, Guinevere Stone, I am asking you to stay by my side forever as my wife because no one will ever love you as much as I do."

Fat tears pooled in the lower troughs of her lids like diamonds before rolling down her cheeks. One splattered over our joined hands, anointing us.

"We've only known each other for four months," Guinevere whispered thickly. "Most people would think we were crazy." A blinding smile streaked across her face like a shooting star. "It's a good thing then that my Infernus Rex taught me not to care what other people think. Yes, Raffaele, *si*, *sic*, *oui*, *po*, *ja*." Her bright laughter frothed over her lips, sparkling as champagne. "In any language, *yes*!"

I caught her as she threw herself to her knees and into my arms. Her mouth found mine unerringly, hot and firm over mine like a seal, a stamp of approval for our union.

I let myself dissolve into the sweet caress of her lips and tongue for a moment before I pulled back just enough to kiss the tears from her cheeks.

"So pretty when you cry," I murmured, cupping her face in both palms so I could stare at her beauty and know I could do so every day for the rest of our lives.

My chest ached with the brutality of my heart banging against its confines, eager to jump through the cage of my ribs into Guinevere's hands.

"I can't believe this," she said with another giddy laugh, peppering my face with kisses. "It feels too good to be true."

It would never fail to amaze me that this woman could think something involving me was too good to be true. I had always harbored a secret desire to be seen as good and worthy, above the writhing masses of immoral *soldati* and capos my father had ruled. I knew I was no better than them, not really, but to have Guinevere believe I was made a tremendous difference in the weight I had carried over my shoulders for much too long.

"Give me your hand," I told her, already taking her left hand in mine so I could place the ring I had chosen on her ring finger. I explained the significance of the choice as I slotted it over her narrow digit. "The first wedding rings have been attributed to ancient Rome. They were first cast in iron, but it rusted, so they moved to gold. They were called *fede*, and the Irish claddagh ring is based on a similar notion of two hands holding the same heart."

Guinevere gave a shivery exhale as the two hands framing an enormous black diamond fit into place at the base of her knuckle. The dark gem gleamed like her fathomless eyes as she stared at it in wonder and then back up at me.

"It's perfect," she breathed. "Of course it is."

I could not resist the proud smile that fixed between my cheeks. "Only the best for my Regina Inferna."

She tipped her head back to laugh at the ceiling. “I don’t know if I’m quite worthy of the title yet, but one day, I will be.”

This time pride for her sluiced through me. “Of that, I have no doubt, *cacciatrice mia*.”

With a devilish smile, she moved closer, straddling my bent knees so she was in my lap, her bare, cum-filled pussy against my trousers.

“Maybe you should teach me a little more about being wicked,” she suggested before fisting her hands in my hair and fixing her mouth to mine.

“Anything you wish,” I promised against her lips before toppling her onto her back to have my way with her once more.

This time as my fiancée.

CHAPTER TWENTY-FIVE

Guinevere

I could not stop staring at the six-carat black diamond surrounded by tiny white diamonds like stars around a depthless sky. It looked outrageous on my slim finger, a statement of such wealth and excess it should have been obscene.

But I loved it.

Because it was a statement of Raffa's love and possession.

A symbol of his trust in me and my ability to endure any of life's misfortunes that might befall me as his partner in crime.

To honor both the ring and the fact that it was the Day of the Dead in Italy, I was wearing a liquid black silk gown with a daring slit in the left side of the skirt that exposed my leg from hip to ankle. The fabric clung to my waist and breasts like an oil spill, revealing every inch of my shape even though it covered my chest completely. With my hair curled and half of it pulled back with antique gold combs studded with more black diamonds, I looked exactly like the kind of woman who might stand beside the King Below.

As if summoned by my thoughts, Raffa appeared in the bathroom mirror behind me dressed in his own finery, a black suit, shirt, and leather shoes. The starkness of the monotone outfit made his hair glow like burnished bronze, his eyes a pale echo, shining like sunlit amber with an inner happiness that had not ebbed since I had agreed to be his wife the night before.

He leaned against the doorframe with his arms crossed, face utterly expressionless but for the heat in his gaze as it swept over my body.

"Well?" I asked with a little smile as I finished applying the gloss over my bloodred lips. "What will your criminal colleagues think of your American fiancée?"

"I do not care what they think," he said disdainfully, as if the very idea was ridiculous. It made my grin widen. "Not when I know without a single doubt I have the most beautiful woman in Tuscany on my arm tonight."

"Just Tuscany?" I joked.

"The world," he corrected, stalking over the marble tiles of the palazzo bathroom to cage me in with his arms on the counter to either side of me.

We made a striking couple in the reflection of the wide antique mirror. My hair and eyes were darker, almost black in the golden light from the sconces, but my skin was still fairly pale from my autumn in Michigan, whereas Raffa had light, almost fire-kissed brown hair and eyes and a rich tan. The harsh lines of his angular, masculine beauty complemented the delicacy of my own features and slightness.

I watched as a faint flush of arousal bloomed in my cheeks and seeped down my neck.

"We are a perfect match," he murmured as if reading my mind, holding my gaze before pressing a warm kiss to my exposed shoulder. He moved my hair to plant another one on my neck. "*Come due gocce d'acqua.*"

Like two drops of water. Made of the very same substance.

"I have something more for you," he admitted, pulling a glistening chain from his pocket.

My sister's cross dangled from his fingers as he lifted it to fasten the necklace around my throat. My fingers trembled as I touched the intricate metalwork.

"I recovered it from the body," he explained before I could ask. "It was your sister's, and you should have it."

The cross settled perfectly in the expanse of skin above the neckline of my dress, a beautiful addition to the outfit. I was not religious, but I appreciated the history of the church in this country, and it felt right to wear what was clearly a Pietra family heirloom.

"If I wear it, will people know where it came from?" Where I came from.

"Maybe," he allowed. "You do not have to wear it tonight if it makes you uncomfortable to be associated with the Pietras. I would rather you be associated with me anyway."

I smiled slightly. "Heathen. You know I am yours first and foremost. I would like to wear it. It would be good for your *soldati* to see the connection."

Raffa didn't disagree.

"I wish I knew why that man had her necklace," I admitted. "It doesn't add up. She may have been dating the Albanian gangster, but how did it end up in the hands of an Italian mafioso?"

"We might never know," Raffa warned. "But the Albanians will be here tonight. Drita's brother was the one who dated Gemma. You can ask her some questions, though she may be reluctant to share."

"Why?"

"I killed her brother when she tried to play games with me after you were taken."

I blinked at him in the reflection, but he was utterly calm and sincere. For some reason, it made me want to laugh. Standing in all our designer finery, with thousands of euros' worth of jewels on my person, and we were talking easy as you please about murder.

It was fitting somehow.

"Well, that's understandable but inconvenient," I said with a small sigh.

Raffa let out a guffaw of surprised laughter, his arms wrapping me up like a present. "*Sei magnifica*. You never fail to surprise me."

Warmth flooded me. I wondered if it would always be like this between us, even as I knew it would be. For exactly the reason Raffa had just proclaimed, we would never fail to surprise each other.

"Let's get married tomorrow," I said suddenly, and I could tell he was surprised by the split second he froze with his lips against my throat. "I don't want to wait."

"We have nothing but time, Vera," he cautioned, wrapping one arm around my waist to bring me tight against his front. "I am not marrying you for political reasons. We can wait as long as we wish."

"Then why did you propose now?" I countered with an arched brow.

He matched the expression. "Because I had just lived through four days believing you might be dead. I did not want to live another twenty-four hours without telling you how ardently I love you and want you beside me for the rest of time."

"For a mafioso," I said somewhat breathlessly, "you are the sweetest man I've ever known."

"Do not mention that to the people waiting at the Cimitero delle Porte Sante," he suggested dryly, referring to the cemetery where he was hosting the gathering. "It would ruin a reputation I have spent considerable time cultivating."

I bit the edge of my grin. "No, it is my secret gift, and I intend to keep it that way. But Raffa, I still want to get married soon. I know it has only been a few months, but I feel as if I have waited my whole life to be here in this place with you as my person. I want us to own each other in every way we can."

His copper-coin eyes flashed with delight. "It is not enough that you have my ring on your finger and fresh cum leaking down your thighs?"

I squirmed, hyperaware of the dampness of my underwear. Raffa had requested I not clean up before the party. He wanted to know that his cum was inside me while I spoke with men who would covet me for my beauty and spirit.

"It's enough for now," I allowed. "But you do call me your greedy girl sometimes. Let me be greedy in this. I wasted so much of my life being afraid to go after what I wanted, and now I know what I want. You."

"How soon?" he asked with a sigh, but he could not quite hide the edge of his smile.

"Before my parents leave?" I suggested. "Mom said they might as well stay for Christmas. I would love to have a winter wedding at the villa."

"As you wish, *stella cadente mia*." He turned me around by the hips to seal the words with a kiss.

I laughed when he pulled away with my red gloss on his mouth and cleaned it with my thumb.

"Red is much more your color than mine," he agreed drolly.

I beamed at him. "I wear it for you, though."

"I know." His features softened for a moment as he pushed my hair back and framed my neck in his hands. "Now, your sweet Raffa is gone for the rest of the night, and in his place, your King Below. Are you ready to embrace my dark kingdom?"

"Lead the way."

◆ ◆ ◆

This party was not like the San Lorenzo celebration Raffa had hosted at the palazzo for our collective friends.

For one, Raffa hosted his annual Day of the Dead party in the Cimitero delle Porte Sante, the Sacred Gates Cemetery, just behind Piazzale Michelangelo in the fortified bastion of the Basilica of San Miniato al Monte. It was a public resting place of famous Italian figures, such as the author of *Pinocchio*, but thanks to his connections with local officials, like the mayor, Raffa was granted private access after hours.

It should have been macabre, maybe, but Italians' Day of the Dead on November 2 was not like Halloween in the US. It was a time of reflection and a reminder that we continued to love our family and friends even when they passed beyond the veil.

The tombs themselves were works of art, statues and mausoleums gleaming in the light of dozens of standing candelabras erected throughout the space. Everyone had come bearing flowers to place on graves out of respect, but Raffa had ordered countless more, so the very air was thick with fragrance.

Everyone was dressed to impress, flaunting their wealth in designer suits and gowns, both men and women decked out in gems. Raffa and I had stood at the entry to the cemetery for over an hour greeting the guests, and I was surprised that most of them handed us baskets of cookies, sweets, and wine.

Raffa had explained it was custom in the south, where his mother was from, to give a *cannistru*, or basket of sweets, to celebrate the dead, and it was a fitting hostess gift for the celebration.

There were also black chrysanthemums everywhere, throwing me back to that last night in the palazzo when the Venetian had sent an assassin to take us out.

"You are safe here," Raffa murmured into my ear as if sensing my disquiet. "I have men crawling every inch of the perimeter. No one will get to you tonight. Or ever again."

"Even you can't promise that."

"I can and I will. You saw how I killed Philippe. But you did not know they call me Il Gentiluomo because I leave notes on my corpses, little life lessons to warn my enemies."

"What did you leave on Philippe?" I asked softly in the lull we had between conversations with endless mafiosi and their dates. "I thought you were going to feed him to the pigs?"

Raffa's expression could not have been called a smile, though his mouth flexed. It was a dark, sinister twist of his lip that made me shiver in places I probably shouldn't have. "He did not deserve such a subtle ending."

"He strung him up in the Square of Miracles in Pisa, in the very same place Gaetano had told him to come if he ever wanted to see you alive again," Martina said, appearing at our side with a martini, a skewer of olives raised to her lips. She ate one before finishing. "It was quite the spectacle. It was even in the papers."

"The note read 'Touch her and die,'" Carmine added, plucking the olives from Martina's hand to swallow the last two down himself. "He has always been dramatic."

"Says you," Renzo said, pushing his brother away from Martina, either to punish him for stealing from her or to stop Martina from stabbing him in the eye with the skewer, as she looked very ready to do.

"Raffa," I murmured, sliding my hand down his arm to squeeze his hand. "Why do I have a feeling that is about as romantic as mafiosi get?"

Martina laughed. "Because that's probably true."

"Well, he did fill an entire Uffizi exhibition with art that symbolized our love story last night," I said slyly, because Raffa had left it to me to tell his inner circle—*our* friends—about our engagement. When I questioned why he had kept it from them, he said he wanted me to be the first person who knew, outside of my father, whom he had actually asked for his blessing.

I still could not believe he had given it.

But it gave me hope that the recent chasm between my father and me could be breached by the honesty and trust we were finally trying to communicate to each other.

"*Cazzo*, Raffa," Carmine said as Ludo wandered over with a napkin piled with *dolci dei morti*, little cookies shaped like bones. "What was the occasion?"

"Maybe the fact that Guinevere survived being abducted?" Renzo asked dryly.

"Or the fact that she's decided to stay with us?" Ludo added, flashing a brief smile, his mouth still filled with food.

"I had a very good reason," Raffa agreed, lifting my ringed hand to his lips to kiss it.

"He asked me to marry him," I admitted as my ring flashed in the candlelight.

"*Dio mio*," Martina gasped, snagging my hand to raise it to her face.

"*Merda*," Carmine muttered, bending over next to her.

"That's quite the rock," Renzo said, thumping Raffa on the back with such a broad grin, I almost didn't recognize the taciturn man. *"Congratulazioni."*

"Congratulations," Martina crowed, throwing my hand in the air to practically suffocate me with a tight hug. "I am so fucking glad we get to keep you."

"Me too," I croaked as she tightened her hold.

"Try not to break my fiancée's ribs, Tina," Raffa drawled. "Her father will take back his blessing if one of my *soldati* starts breaking her bones."

"Sorry," she said with an unrepentant grin. "I am just so thrilled."

"Me too," Ludo declared, shoving Martina aside with a hip to encompass me in his wide, bulky arms. His hug was achingly gentle, those man-killing arms barely contacting my skin. "Happy for you. And me. I like my workout buddy."

I laughed and kissed his cheek. "Me too."

"Waiter," Carmine called to the server handing out prosecco from a silver tray. "Bring us the bottle!"

"Obviously I'll be your bridesmaid," Martina told me. "But don't you dare put me in a dress."

"Deal," I agreed, surprised and happy she would want to stand up with me instead of Raffa.

"We have to stick together as the only women." She winked at me.

"I have three sisters and a mother, as you well know," Raffa noted.

"Yes, but I meant in the outfit. Now I have Guinevere to help me keep you *idioti* in line."

Raffa rolled his eyes at her, but he was too happy to pull it off with his usual disdain.

"To Raffa and Guinevere," Carmine saluted with his glass after handing them out to everyone else.

"Raffa and Guinevere," our friends echoed.

My sip of champagne mimicked the bubbly, ethereal feeling in my belly that I had never experienced before. Something like an excess of happiness.

"As much as I want to celebrate, I came over to collect you for Capo Burette. He wants to speak about the textile factories outside Milan," Renzo admitted.

Raffa nodded, turning to press a kiss to my cheek before he stalked off between the elaborate tombstones to meet with Stefania's father. Happily, the woman herself wasn't present, and Raffa informed me her father had arranged a marriage with a camorrista in the south to get her away from his territory.

I couldn't say I wasn't pleased by the idea.

Left to my own devices as the others followed Raffa, I wandered through the cemetery, admiring the sculptures until I found one of the most famous ones I had read about. The tomb of the Mazzones, which depicted two siblings dancing on their grave, reunited in death after dying shortly after each other. It was a beautiful display, the symbolism reaching down inside my chest to clutch at my heart.

"Italians are the best storytellers," a female voice said from over my shoulder. "If I do say so myself."

Her English was flawless, hardly accented.

She was an older woman, but it was hard to pinpoint her age in the flickering light and shadows cast by the candle flames, and she was perfectly groomed, not a hair out of place. In a golden dress that dripped with crystals, she seemed to dance like the inside of one of those flames, dangerous yet intangible.

"I am Donatella," she said, extending her heavily bejeweled hand to me. "And you are Raffa's American."

I took her cool, dry hand in mine for a firm shake.

Her gaze flickered down to the large cross at my throat, and her brow quirked. "Not as American as I thought, perhaps. Where did you get that from?"

"It was my sister's. My father's family is from the region," I allowed, unsure about how to proceed because I recognized her name.

Donatella was the female capo in Venice. The woman Raffa and his men felt sure would not have turned on him, because he'd helped her take power from her brother years ago.

"Near Pisa, correct?" she surmised with a thin smile. "I have never much liked the Pietra clan. They always felt they should have been in charge of the north just because one man many generations ago was a famous corrupt politician. Who cares about the past, hmm? It is the present that determines the future."

I cocked my head. "I'll have to disagree with you, *capo donna*. I believe by looking to the past you can see the pattern of human behavior and human error."

Donatella pursed her lips. "Yes, perhaps this is true. And in your past? Secrets and lies, I'm sure."

"Some," I agreed, feeling as if I was playing a game with an apex predator. "And in yours? Betrayal and subterfuge. Does that mean you would be willing to act similarly now?"

"You speak of the coup against my brother," she said flatly, amusement dying.

"And you speak about the fact the Pietras abducted me last week," I returned. "We both seem to know a lot about each other."

"Yet we only just met. How interesting."

"Tell me, Donatella," I asked, studying the way the light hit the champagne in my glass. I wouldn't drink it, given my illness, but it was a great social prop. "Would you work against Raffa the same way you once worked against your brother?"

"Who are you to dare ask me that?" she hissed, stepping closer. "Some American *puttana*?"

I stepped closer too, my free hand falling to the slit in my dress, ready to grab the knife strapped to the inside of my other thigh. Ludo had been teaching me about wielding a dagger for the last few weeks, and I was getting good enough that with the element of surprise, I was sure I could take Donatella.

"I am Raffa's fiancée," I said calmly. "And a member of Clan Romano. I am free to ask you anything I want, and you are free to answer, unless you want to witness his fury when I tell him what you just called me." My smile cut into my cheeks like knifepoints. "He is so protective of those he loves."

Donatella's laugh was brittle. "You think he loves you, *ragazza*? Your sister believed the same of such a man, and look what happened to her."

I felt as if I had run headlong into a brick wall.

"Excuse me?"

Donatella's sneer glowed orange in the firelight. "Her name was Gemma, wasn't it? I recognize the cross. I saw it last summer when they stayed with me in Venice."

My heart had slowed to a crawl, my blood like wet cement churning thickly through my veins. "You knew Gemma?"

"Keep up, child. Of course I did. I was the one who introduced them. The Albanians work through the port of Venice, and I transport the goods for Raffa and those eastern European gangsters in the east. With his ties to Venice, it made sense for Raffa to make him a liaison to my outfit, just as Carmine is with the Albanians and Renzo is for those scum in the south."

"Who?" I whispered.

She waved her hand, gold bangles clanging together. "Who? I am surprised you don't know, given you have been living with him for some time. You are staying at Villa Romano, no?"

Dread poisoned every breath I struggled to take into my suddenly weak lungs.

"Who?" I repeated.

But I knew.

I knew.

"Are you Italian?"

"What is your last name?"

"So you did not know who Raffa was before you ran into him?"

"I am sorry. You just look like someone I once knew . . ."

And then . . .

"I was rude when we first met. It didn't have anything to do with you. Not really."

"I fell in love with a foreigner once too. She was charming and beautiful, and I thought at the time that I would give up anything for her."

"It didn't end well."

Leonardo di Conte.

The postcard I had written to Gemma was in his desk.

He was the one living at the villa with Philippe, taking charge of the compound while Raffa and the rest of his crew stayed in Florence. I thought about the curve of dark ink peeking out of his opened shirt when we danced at *la vendemmia* and decided it could have been the curl of a *G*.

Gemma had always thought it would be so romantic if her boyfriend got her name tattooed on him somewhere.

My breath burst out of me like a bullet from the chamber of a gun.

"Did he kill her?" I asked Donatella, seizing her arm like a life raft.

She shrugged delicately, completely unperturbed by the chaos roiling inside me. "I was never sure. He seemed to love her, but you can never really trust a man." Something dark flickered over her face. "You should have left Italy behind when you had the chance."

I snarled at her. "You should have told Raffa about this."

She laughed. "I do not report on the sex lives of camorristi, nor would Raffaele want me to."

"I hope you are willing to bet your life on that, because he is about to find out," I snapped in vicious Italian before I gathered my skirt and ran through the cemetery in search of him.

"Raffa!" I called out.

"Guinevere?" He was not panicked, but his response was immediate.

I only had to round one more corner, and there he was, jogging toward me, arms open for me to throw myself into.

"It's Leo," I panted, my nails curling over his shoulders. "Leo was Gemma's mysterious Italian boyfriend. Leo was the one doing business with the Albanians and, I think you'll find, the Grecos and the Pietras. It was Leo all along."

"How do you know this?" Raffa demanded, eyes flashing, already moving, with me tucked into his side, back into the fray of *soldati*.

"Donatella Verdi told me."

"Renzo," he bit out as soon as we approached his clutch of friends. "Bring me Donatella Verdi, and get Leo on the phone immediately."

CHAPTER TWENTY-SIX

Raffa

It was my worst fear.

The reason I had descended into hell and taken up the dark crown of my father.

My family meant everything to me, my heart beating outside my chest.

And now they were in jeopardy from the very man I had considered a part of my family since I was a boy.

Everyone was on lockdown. The capos and soldiers at the party were to remain there under Burette's watch until I called in to say we had arrived at the villa safely. Their phones had been confiscated before they had entered the cemetery—a matter of protocol—and I did not want to risk anyone calling out to Leo to warn him of our arrival or our knowledge that he was a *che schifoso voltafaccia*, a filthy fucking traitor.

I simply could not believe it even as I sped toward Villa Romano with Guinevere beside me, the nightscape a streaky blur as I raced home through the Tuscan hills, praying to God or whoever might listen to an immoral man like me to keep them safe from harm.

Leo had been my best friend since the cradle.

I had taken my first steps with him, shared his first day of school and last, laughed when he got drunk for the first time on Aldo's sambuca and threw up in the vines outside the kitchen terrace, and stood shoulder to shoulder with him when my father died.

What could I have done to deserve such faithlessness from a man I had believed was my steadfast friend? No, more than friend—brother.

Family, but chosen.

And somehow that was worse.

That my judgment was clearly so poor I had not seen the sheep through the wolf's clothing.

The moment Guinevere had accused him, my thoughts had fallen like dominos toward the inevitable conclusion.

Leo was my liaison in the northeast with the Venetians. It had made sense, when I came to power, to keep him there because he and Donatella were distantly related. The di Contes were a prestigious family line in the region all the way back to Venetian aristocracy.

He was, as Guinevere had guessed, a crucial part of the Romano Group, seeking to shift his power back into the company the way my father had once done.

"Aldo spoke of adopting him," I ground out as we took a hairpin turn and Guinevere veered into my shoulder, not complaining, just holding tight to her seat. "Could he have been so bitter about it that he would do this?"

"I don't know," she admitted immediately, and it was clear her brilliant mind was puzzling over it too. "Has he always been particularly power hungry?"

I checked the rearview mirror for Carmine, who was driving the Lamborghini behind me with Martina, Renzo, Ludo, and a few other trusted *soldati* from the party.

"He was always the obedient soldier, never talking back, always eager to help Aldo and Tonio with whatever they needed. He had killed a dozen people by the time I was made to kill my first. But . . . no. He seemed fine with his lot, my best friend, a key part of the organization. He never once complained or asked for more."

The steering wheel made a horrible sound as my grip tightened painfully around it.

"He is a second son to my mother, a brother to my sisters, uncle to my nephews. Tell me, how could he turn against us? What the fuck could I have done to make him try to kill me and mine? *Cazzo*!"

"I don't think you can rationalize this," Guinevere said softly, placing her hand on my tensed thigh. "He is clearly a psychopath. My—my sister loved him, and he killed her . . . There is no other reason to do something like that but psychopathy."

"If he has hurt any of them," I whispered, as if the words might become reality if spoken too loudly. "I will rip the world apart to find him and spend the rest of my life killing him day by day, little by little."

"Yes," Guinevere agreed. "You will. But let's try not to think that way. He has no reason to know that we've discovered what he's done."

I swallowed thickly, desperately clinging to the feel of her hand on my thigh, the scent of her feminine fragrance in my nose, and her soft presence in the small space with me. Without her anchoring me, I might have crashed the car, fury overloading my system.

"They have to be okay," she murmured, as if it was a prayer.

I tried to manifest the same thing, but though we should have had surprise on our side, there was a sinking in my gut that told me we were about to meet more of our signature misfortune.

Which was why, when we crested the hill across from the one Villa Romano rested atop, I was not shocked to see smoke billowing from the far side of the house.

"*Merda*," I cursed, slamming my foot down on the pedal so we went careening around the first loop in the circular driveway that carved its way up the hill.

"How would he know?" Guinevere demanded.

Either someone at the party had broken through Burette's watch, or, more likely, something else had given us away.

It did not matter now.

All that I cared about was making sure no one had been hurt.

When we turned the corner toward the olive grove, we hit a wall of flames. The orange-and-gold fire licked at the end of the gravel, consuming the dry olive trees in snapping, voracious bites down the hillside.

"Someone started it up at the side of the house," Guinevere whispered, peering out the window.

Cazzo.

Behind me, the SUV swerved hard in the gravel and nearly veered off the road, but I deftly maneuvered the Ferrari up the last curve and swung to a stop in the circular drive, leaving the car running as I sprinted into the house.

"Mamma!" I shouted through the smoke curling in from the opened windows and kitchen door. "Carlotta, Stacci!"

"Raffa." Stacci appeared at the base of the stairs with Nico on her hip and a weeping Mattia holding her hand. "Thank God."

"What the fuck happened?" I asked as I swung Mattia into my arms and hustled them out the doors.

"The others are at the other side of the house," she said after coughing roughly. "John was the one to smell the smoke about fifteen minutes ago, but by then the grove was already well lit."

"Where are the *soldati*?" I demanded.

"Fighting the fire," she explained as we rounded the house to see Emiliano comforting a sobbing Maximo, Carlotta cradling Vitale, John and Elizabeth Stone clutching each other, and Mamma with her arm around Lando, who was sporting a vicious burn on his forearm.

"Did you call the firemen?"

In answer, the distant sound of sirens echoed through the valley over the crackling of splintering, overheated wood.

"Where is Zacheo?" Carlotta asked Stacci, standing up with Vitale in her arms. "He should have been in the house."

"I checked," our sister said, going pale. "No one was left inside."

"Where is Leo?" I asked, a shiver ripping like torn Velcro from my spine.

"He was inside when the fire started, but he went out to help Lando and the others keep the fire from the house," Stacci explained.

"Do you think he has Zacheo?" Carlotta asked, eyes wide and dark, the same color as the soot raining down around us.

"Maybe," I allowed, taking one of my guns from the holster at my ankle and pressing it into Stacci's hand. "If he comes back here, shoot him."

"What?!"

"Do it, Stacci," I ordered, holding my hands firmly over hers on the weapon. "Trust me. Shoot first and ask questions later."

"I will look out for them," John said, coming up to me with a soot-streaked face and a grave expression. There was a gun tucked in his waistband, one he must have been given by a foot soldier.

I did not take it from him. He had killed enough people in his time as a mafioso to have become an expert with it, even if it had been years. I gave him a solemn nod, thanking him for the offer to protect my family.

God knew I would always protect his.

"Will you find Zacheo?" Carlotta begged, her gaze reflecting the smoke curling over the top of the house. "Please, Raffa."

"Of course I will," I promised, turning to leave as Renzo, Carmine, and Martina joined us. "Martina, stay with them. Carm, Zo, help me find Leo and Zacheo."

I sprinted around the house to the flaming olive grove, where some of my men had laid sandbags to stop the progress of the fire and were currently aiming two garden hoses at the burning edge of the trees.

"Where is Leo?" I asked them, already moving toward the fire.

How had he lit the fire if he was inside when the family noticed it? Had he set a device to go off to give himself an alibi? Was he using the cover of flame to get away undetected?

"He went in to find Zacheo," Michele shouted over the loud roar. "So did she."

She.

Panic tore into me with brutal, blunt-edged teeth.

"She?" I echoed, looking around for Guinevere.

"Your American," he said, confirming my worst fears. "She heard Aio barking in another direction and ran into the fire before we could stop her."

I stormed toward him, gathering his shirt in my fist to heave him to his toes so I could snarl in his face. "And you did not think to go after her to make sure she—*they*—were safe?"

"Leo told us to keep the fire back," he explained, but he had lost all color as he stared into the ferocity of my fury.

"Hope she is unharmed, or I will make sure you regret that decision for the rest of your life," I snapped, dropping my hold to study the olive grove. "Ludo, can you get to your drone?"

Without responding, my friend turned and raced for the house, where he kept the machine.

"There are acres of groves, Raffa," Renzo said quietly. "We have no idea where they could be or how far the flames stretch after we lose sight of them down the hill."

"Michele, where did Leo and Guinevere go?" I asked the cowed man beside me.

He pointed at two rows, one to the left and one to the far right.

Cazzo.

"We need to get to Leo before he disappears." Carmine said the words I had been thinking. "If you confront him, he might stand down. I have to believe at least some part of him still thinks of you as his brother."

"I'll go after Guinevere," Renzo promised. "I'll find her and Zacheo, Raffa. I promise you."

Fear soured the back of my tongue and made me want to gag, but I forced it back with a hard nod and looked to Carm, who gave me a grim smile before we both threw ourselves into a break in the fire.

Smoke enclosed us instantly, a thick, choking haze that burned my lungs each time I was forced to draw breath. We stayed as low as we could, making our way deeper into the fire, where whole sections of olive trees had been razed to blackened matchsticks.

My phone buzzed in my pocket, Ludo's name on the screen.

"I got him, boss," he declared, and I thought I could hear the faint whirr of the drone somewhere above me. "He's ten rows to the left and three klicks down from you. It's hard to keep a lock on him through the smoke, but I don't think he's alone."

I covered my mouth with the collar of my jacket and indicated at Carm over my shoulder to head left. A smoldering branch broke off with a brutal crack as I raced by, and I turned just in time to see it fall straight for Carmine.

Without thinking, I dove, smacking him out of the way.

The branch landed on the edge of my leg, burning through to my ankle. I hissed at the pain, kicking it off and rolling away from it. Carm helped me to my feet, coughing into his jacket sleeve and patting me on the back in thanks as we started moving again.

As we continued moving east, I heard the faint sound of voices.

I picked up my pace, holding my breath as much as I could through the smoke and wishing fervently that Renzo had already found Guinevere and Zacheo.

We left the fire behind us and exploded into a clearing. A man lay prone on the ground, a visible gash bleeding profusely from his head.

It was Uncle Tonio, passed out in a pool of warm blood.

In the distance, there was the roar of an engine starting.

My predatory instincts raged at me, insisting it was Leo who had attacked Tonio and started a nearby car to race away into the dark.

"Go," I ordered Carmine in a rough bark as I slapped at Tonio's face. "Call Ludo and get him tracking the car by drone."

Tonio came to with a gasp as Carmine disappeared down the hill.

"Leo," he cried with a broken sob, clutching at my shirt. "My son."

More blood sluiced down his shirtfront, and I realized he had been shot.

"Did Leo do this to you?" I asked as I pulled his shirt apart to examine the wound.

"He told me he didn't want to hurt me, but I couldn't just let him walk away from this betrayal," he panted through the pain. "I can't truly believe it. My boy . . . why would he do this?"

I helped Tonio to his feet, putting pressure on the wound with one hand and taking most of his weight over my other shoulder so I could walk us back up the hill to the house outside the flames flickering to our right.

"You had no idea?" I asked, taking advantage of Tonio's delirium to push for the truth.

It seemed wildly unlikely that he had been in on Leo's plan, given that Leo had shot Tonio and left him to burn in the olive grove, but I would never take trust for granted again.

"I caught him in Carmine's office, going through Guinevere's computer. Something seemed to spook him, and I followed him out to the grove only to find it on fire. I confronted him about his deception, and he told me he was just taking back what was owed to him." He sucked in a rattling, wet breath. "Apparently, your father promised to make him his heir."

"To keep him in line," I concluded in a bitter mutter. "*Cazzo*, he was a bastard."

"Leo has been organizing this for some time." Tonio coughed so hard, blood splattered his lips, and I had to take more of his weight for the steeper incline before the house. "He was being cagey at work. I should have been more suspicious, but . . . he is my son."

Yes. Family ties could blind someone to the truth too easily. I had let my same love of Leo veil me from his deception for too long, putting myself and my loved ones in jeopardy.

"What happened?" Martina asked as she caught us coming over the ridge onto the terrace, rushing forward to help me lead Tonio to a chair.

"Leo," I said like a curse. "Where is Guinevere? Is Renzo back with her?"

Martina's concerned expression was answer enough.

I was just about to plunge back into the flaming grove when I heard a familiar bark.

A moment later, Aio appeared, with Guinevere stumbling after him through the smoke, Zacheo clinging to her front like a spider monkey, Renzo at their back, curving over them both like a shield.

Her hair was a wild tangle, ash glittering dully in the murky red light cast from the flames, and her cheeks were burnt crimson from the heat, the hem of her silk dress torn and charred. She looked like a queen emerging from hell triumphant, and I was certain there had never been a more beautiful sight than Guinevere alive and heroic in that moment.

To think I had doubted she could handle this life.

She was clearly born for it.

I was on them before I could think to move, gathering Guinevere and Zacheo in my arms, peppering their sweat-slicked, sooty faces with kisses.

"My huntress," I breathed against her cheek before taking her mouth in a kiss. "What were you thinking?"

"I was thinking I needed to get to Zacheo," she croaked, leaning her forehead against mine. "He's taken to wandering off into the grove to search for fairies lately. I knew where he might be."

"So you risked yourself?" I demanded, holding her face in my hands, smoothing the ash from her cheeks.

Her bloodshot eyes were defiant as they stared up into mine. "You aren't the only one who would risk their life for this family."

The foundation of my heart shook like tectonic plates, shifting to make room for even more love to take root inside me.

"You are the fiercest, bravest woman I have ever known," I whispered through my thick, heat-scorched throat.

Guinevere gave me a tremulous smile as Zacheo nuzzled into her neck with a whimper.

"But do not ever scare me like that again," I demanded. "Now that I have you, I refuse to live without you. Is that understood?"

"*Si, Raffa, lo capisco*," she agreed, leaning heavily into my side as Carlotta came racing around the corner yelling for Zacheo.

He squirmed from Guinevere's arms, dropping down to the ground with a cry as he ran for his mother. I watched them reunite, mother and son sobbing as they held each other. Behind them, the rest of my family—our family—appeared, walking to the edge of the terrace beside us to watch the flames eat away the side of my family's centuries-old olive grove.

"I'm sorry," Guinevere whispered as we watched it disappear.

The sirens were louder now, the fire trucks winding up the hill toward us.

"It's just a grove and just a house," I murmured back as I pressed her into my side and gathered my mother under my other arm when she wandered close. "It is these people that make it a home."

"I'm sorry about Leo," she amended. "I can't imagine how much that must hurt. Gemma lied to me, and it wasn't even maliciously done, but it still aches in me like a bruise."

The pain of Leo's betrayal was like a lance through my sternum, something impossible to breathe around without pain.

But I knew the antidote to pain like this.

I had been a made man for long enough to know the only thing that could quell this hurt was good, old-fashioned revenge.

And I intended to have it.

CHAPTER TWENTY-SEVEN

Raffa

Ludo tracked the car with the drone as far as distance would allow, which gave us just enough time to jump into our own car and gun after him.

I did not want to leave Guinevere or the rest of my family, not when my fiancée and nephew were being treated for smoke inhalation, not when the house was uninhabitable because of lingering smoke as the firefighters put out the raging olive grove fire.

But these were the choices I was faced with as *capo dei capi*.

Their safety came before their comfort, as much as I would have loved to be there to tend to them.

As long as Leo remained at large, he would come for me and mine.

And that was unacceptable.

We stopped just long enough to visit the armory in the barn, thankfully on the other side of the fire. Equipped with guns, ammo, bulletproof vests, a smoke bomb, and a handful of grenades, Renzo, Carmine, and I went after the man who had once been one of us.

Three cars followed in a procession behind us, unmarked black SUVs filled with loyal *soldati*. Burette had sent his men down from Florence to fortify the villa while we were absent.

I trusted the man because he had proven himself again and again to me, even when I had publicly set down his daughter at the fundraiser in Firenze in the summer. He was a seasoned capo who would guard my family like a dragon its treasure hoard.

Leo had headed north, which was no surprise. I had already alerted Damiano, the *capo dei capi* in the south, to be on the lookout for Leo, and the region was filled with many more camorristi than the north.

We found his car abandoned in Pistoia, the doors open, a fire crackling in the interior where it was parked in a narrow alley on the outskirts of town. Dawn was starting to turn everything from black to grayscale.

"Ludo, can you check surveillance in the area? I have to believe he headed this way for a reason. Even if he stole a new car, his center of operations has to be somewhere here in the north."

"Yes," Ludo said, his computer in his lap, fingers flying. "But it will take me a minute."

I did not tell him we did not have a minute to spare. Instead, I drove us down the street to an all-night café where we could regroup. As Carmine ordered us coffees and Renzo argued with Ludo about which intersections to check out first, I tried to think about what I knew of my best friend.

His parents had died when he was just a baby, leaving him in Tonio's care, but I thought they might have lived somewhere close.

I pulled out my phone to search the shared family album Mamma had made a few years ago, filled with old, scanned photos, until I came across what I was looking for.

"Maria, Cristo, and Leo Rizzo," it read on the bottom of the yellowed photograph that depicted the couple smiling in front of a tiny house.

"Can you run a search on that house?" I asked Ludo, sliding my phone across the counter to him.

He nodded, mouth tight as his fingers worked and his eyes swept the screen.

"Leo stole a car near the train station," he said a moment later. "But he started heading east, not north."

"Toward Venice, maybe?" Carmine suggested, setting the coffees down for us. "Donatella's people might harbor him."

I moved over Ludo's shoulder to watch in real time as he ran a search for the little house from the photograph. Images opened and collapsed across an open map until finally it pinged somewhere on the edge of Tuscany and Umbria.

Right near Fattoria Casa Luna.

I thought of running into Leo at Imelda's winery even though he had no reason to be there, of the break-in they'd experienced in the summer.

"Do you think Imelda's involved?" Carmine asked, shocked.

"No." Of that I had little doubt. Imelda was one of the women who had benefited most from my takeover after Aldo, who had notoriously felt a woman's place was in the kitchen or the bedroom. "But call her. Tell her we are on the way and to look out for Leo."

She was waiting outside the main building of the vineyard when we arrived, arms crossed and brow furrowed.

"He hasn't been here," she said as soon as I alighted from the car. "But I checked the security tapes, and he's been visiting a few times a month for the past year. Sometimes he meets with Wyatt."

The British *stronzo* who had not noticed we were being defrauded by the Chinese import company. Not noticed or, more likely now, colluded with them to steal from me to fill Leo's pockets.

"No one lives in the house," she told us as we walked en masse around the building to the back garden and the path that led around the outside of the vines to the little yellow house fifteen minutes from the main cluster of buildings. "Cristo and my husband were cousins, so we gave them the house when Tonio cast Maria out for marrying beneath her."

"Tonio kicked her out?" I frowned because I had never known that. "He always told Leo about how much he loved his sister."

Imelda scoffed. "That old fart is cold as ice. He told Maria he wouldn't support her if she went through with marrying a common vintner."

It was not uncommon for the patriarch to use his unmarried family to strengthen ties with other clans and mafiosi, but I had not known Tonio had tried to do that.

"He wanted her to marry Alfonso Greco," Imelda added.

Alfonso Greco.

The man who had banded together with the Venetian to come after me. That history explained why Leo might have thought to join forces behind my back.

As we came up on the house, I pressed a hand to Imelda's hip. "Wait here. Do you need a gun?"

She quirked a dark eyebrow and pulled out a pistol.

I nodded, then directed Carmine, Renzo, and my other *soldati* to surround the house and close in.

As I approached the front door through the vines, I noticed a man patrolling outside, his dark clothes blending in with the shadows. I lifted my gun and popped off two quick shots, the silencer muffling the sound of each bullet. I crept forward and bent to check his pulse to ensure he was dead, then approached the front door, pausing beside it to listen for any noises inside the house. There was a low murmur of voices, but not many.

I peeked through the gap in the curtains of the front window and glimpsed three men around a dining room table, playing cards. They wore gun holsters at their sides and radios hooked over their ears.

What could they possibly be there to protect?

"*Andiamo*," I whispered into my own comm, and then shot out the mechanism on the front door before kicking it in.

The men were scrambling when I went inside, cards spiraling through the air as they fumbled to pull out their weapons.

Pop. Pop.

More shots fired from the back of the house.

I squeezed off three more myself, hitting the closest man in the neck and chest, taking him down for the count. The other two dove behind the table, overturning it to hide behind the marble top.

Renzo appeared at the other end of the kitchen, moving toward me quietly.

I let my foot crack over a splinter of wood so they would be focused on my approach. One of them lifted his head to fire at me.

I ducked just as Renzo took aim at that raised head and splattered it across the back wall with a bullet.

On another day, when I did not feel emotionally flayed alive, Renzo and I might have competed for who could get the last man standing.

The man surprised me by shooting the mirror to my left, distracting me for long enough to jump over the table and hurl himself at me. We fell to the floor, my gun skittering from my hold. I used his leftover momentum to flip him onto his back, sliding a knife from its sheath at his waist as I evaded a left hook and then reared up to slash the blade across his neck. He ducked my swing, snapping a big hand up to grip my neck in a vise that had me seeing stars. But I still had the blade in my hand, so I switched grips and slid the sharp edge from the end of his forearm to his wrist on the arm grasping my throat.

Warm blood sluiced over us both as if poured from a basin.

A moment later, his hand dropped dully to the carpet, and he focused on breathing through the wet gurgle of blood filling his throat.

I climbed off him and retrieved my gun to find Carmine had joined Renzo.

"All clear up here. No sign of Leo," he told me. "But the basement is locked tight and coded with a high-tech alarm. Ludo's working on it now."

"What the hell could they have been hiding here?" I questioned. "And why the hell go to so much trouble? I cannot image Leo *hiding* behind a locked door."

I rounded the corner and moved through the handful of men waiting for Ludo to hack into the alarm panel.

"It's top tier," he grunted, two sharp tools in his mouth and another in his hands as he parted various wires behind the panel. "Digital access wasn't cutting it."

"Do you know which wire to cut?" Carm asked doubtfully.

"I should."

"Wow, that instills confidence," Carmine muttered.

I ignored their banter to go down the hallway, checking each door until I found what I was looking for in the back of a closet. A moment later, the lights flickered and went dead.

Thankfully the sun was cresting over the hills, spilling pale, honeyed light through the windows so we could see some of what we were doing.

"What did you do?" Carm asked as I returned.

"I cut the power," I muttered, grabbing the bolt cutters from my backpack to snip the lock on the door to the basement.

When the door still would not budge, I told everyone to stand back and fired at the opposite side of the panel, aiming for the hinges. After a round of bullets, the wood creaked and split apart.

I pushed it open so powerfully, it banged against the opposite wall.

"Let me go first," Renzo insisted, but I was already going down the wood treads, the smell of piss and damp cellar rising in my nostrils.

Nothing shot at my feet as I descended, and I had no idea what I might find waiting for me in the basement.

But nothing could have prepared me for the sight of an emaciated girl tied to a chair and gagged with a stained rag. There was a Colombina Venetian mask over the upper half of her face.

"*Che cazzo?*" I muttered as I moved to her, Renzo and Carmine checking the rest of the basement as I approached, the other soldiers at my back.

She was young, her matted, unwashed blond hair hanging in her face where it was slumped against her shoulder. Even though she was clearly captive and bound, there was no other sign of injury.

I had tipped her face up to further examine her when her eyes popped open.

They were not the same rich brown of freshly tilled earth like my Vera's, but the shape was the same, doe eyes topped with delicately arched brows in a heart-shaped face.

"Gemma?" I whispered, recognizing her from the photo I had seen in Guinevere's apartment.

She jerked against the ties, shouting something behind her gag.

"Boss!" Carmine yelled.

I deftly untied the back of the gag so Gemma could speak to me, the fabric falling away at the same time Carmine called, "There's a fucking bomb down here."

"Get out!" Gemma screamed in English, voice hoarse, eyes rolling wildly in her head like those of a feral horse. "H-he called ahead and knew you were coming. It's a trap."

A moment later, the first explosive detonated.

CHAPTER TWENTY-EIGHT

Guinevere

The entire family had moved to Stacci's house down the road from the main villa to sleep what was left of the night. It was an enormous house built for their ever-expanding family, with enough rooms for the adult couples to each have one and for the kids, frightened out of their minds, to share one, where we'd laid mattresses down so they could all cuddle together.

Only Zacheo had refused to leave my side, clinging to me so tightly his little nails had left crescent-moon shapes in my thighs. I'd told Carlotta and Emiliano that it was fine if he slept with me and took him up the stairs to the small bedroom at the back of the house, where he had immediately curled into me, tucked up like a bug in a rug, and fallen asleep.

He was twitching beside me, nightmares plaguing his slumber, but he eased when I smoothed a hand down his freshly washed hair. It soothed me too.

When I had first seen Leo at the edge of the fiery tree line, my only thought had been of revenge. I was going to tackle him to the ground and beat his head in for what he had possibly done to my sister and had attempted to do to Raffa. But when I overheard his conversation with a *soldato* about Zacheo lost somewhere in the grove, I felt my soul cleave in two.

Did I go after Leo and appease the fury wrapped around my heart like an iron vise, or did I go after sweet Zacheo, who had taken such a shine to me the last month he had been my constant shadow at the villa?

In the end, of course, it was not even a question.

I followed Aio's barking entreaty farther along the trees before I dived into the curling black smoke.

Until the day I died, I would remember the feel of the scorched soot in my lungs, the heat pressing into every side of my body like ghostly hands threatening to drag me into the depths of hell. I called for Zacheo until my voice ripped up my throat; I'd headed to the copse of trees that we had played in many times before, where there was a trunk that looked like a throne. We liked to play make-believe there and had even erected a little fairy house in one of the trees. It was disorienting with the smoke, and I was completely lost until one of my croaky cries was met with the sweetest voice I thought I had ever heard.

"Vera?"

He had hidden against the lip of a well just beyond where we played, wet from the bucket of water he'd thrown over his head to cool himself.

"*Che ragazzo sveglio che sei*," I'd praised him as I collected his steaming body in my arms, tucking his face into the gathered fabric of my dress so he might breathe through it.

Clever boy.

The weight and warmth of him curled under my arm kept the residual panic at bay even though I was too agitated to find sleep myself.

I could not believe Leo had done something like this.

The more I thought about it, the more I remembered the aching despair on his face when he had talked about the foreigner he had fallen in love with. The sincerity and protectiveness he'd exhibited when he told me I was basically a coward for giving Raffa up just because I did not like the nature of the truth I had begged him to reveal.

How could someone who had been born and raised in the warmth of the Romano family end up this way?

I knew Aldo Romano was not like Angela, Carlotta, Stacci, and Delfina. I knew he had been a tyrant who ignored his daughters, manipulated his son, and loved his wife but expected her to warm his bed, raise his children, and look the other way from his transgressions, but he had raised Raffa as much as Leo. How could they have ended up so different?

Even more, how could sweet, charming, and shrewd Gemma have fallen in love with such a psychopath?

She had been drawn to bad boys in the past, but there was a difference between her pot-smoking older college boyfriend and a murdering mafioso. Even the Albanian gangster would have been better than this.

Could Leo have killed her? Someone who was made of sunshine and wickedness and such fun her smile alone could make you laugh?

Could he have been looking me in the eye all this time knowing he had killed her and somehow covered it up?

Raffa might have told me I always wanted to believe the best of people. That I had a tendency, as I had with him, to romanticize the villain.

But as the dark hours passed into the pale tendrils of dawn, I became more and more convinced that I was missing something.

The pattern did not fit.

I needed to know *why*.

It had to be more than rivalry and the desire to be *capo dei capi* over Raffa. I had read once that the biggest motives for murder were greed and love.

Didn't Leo already have enough money and power as COO to the Romano Group and underboss to Raffa's criminal syndicate?

The bedroom door creaked open.

I was up, gun in hand and trained on the dark mouth of the doorframe in less than a heartbeat, one hand on Zacheo's shoulder.

"It's just me," Carlotta said softly in Italian. "I am sorry to scare you. I couldn't sleep, and I wanted to check on him."

My aching muscles softened. "Of course. Why don't you come sleep here with him? It will bring you both comfort, and I have given up on sleep myself anyway."

She hesitated, but I could tell she wanted to hold her son. "Are you sure?"

In answer, I got out of bed and walked toward her, kissing her on the cheek as I made to move into the hall.

Her hand caught mine before I could.

Those eyes, almost as pale a brown as Raffa's, glowed in the low light. "Thank you, Guinevere. I cannot thank you enough. Not just for saving Zacheo, but also for bringing joy to Raffa. He has sacrificed everything for this family. I am happy he has someone willing to sacrifice for him too."

I squeezed her hand but could not find a way to fit words to the emotions tangling up my throat.

She smiled, released me, and hurried across the wooden floor to the bed.

I closed the door on them and headed down the hall to the stairs.

The lower level was dark, but I caught sight of a sentry near the front door, and Martina sat in the kitchen, staring into a glass of amber liquor.

"Couldn't sleep?" she asked without looking up.

"No."

"I can't stop thinking about Leo," she admitted, turning haunted eyes to me as I sat across from her. "I am going back through everything we have ever done together. When you first arrived, I had heard a rumor that the Pietra clan was being blackmailed by the Venetian into helping his cause. I told Raffa I had to speak to him about it, but Leo told me it was idle gossip. That the Pietra family had nothing more to lose they could be blackmailed with."

"He knew who I was the whole time I've been here," I agreed. "Donatella told me he dated Gemma when she was living in Albania before she died." My fingers found the warm metal of the cross around my neck. "He gave this to the man on the bell tower to try to convince me to go away with him."

"So he could use you against Raffa," Martina concluded with a heavy sigh before downing the rest of the booze. "*Merda.* Even if the boys find him, we will have to completely overhaul all our systems. Who knows how much he has infiltrated and redirected for his own gain."

"I can help with that," I offered, invigorated by the idea of doing *something.* I knew I would have done more harm than good, slowing them down, but it physically pained me to stay behind while Raffa, Renzo, Carm, and Ludo hunted down Leo. "You know I'm good at finding patterns and discrepancies."

"True. I'm sure Raffa will want your help."

"I could start now," I suggested. Now that the thought was planted, I could not ignore it. My knee jumped restlessly under the table. "Maybe I could find something to help the guys hunt him down now."

Martina's mouth flexed into a thin line. "It's four in the morning, Vera. You can take a look tomorrow."

"It's four in the morning, but there's no time to waste, right?" I pushed. "C'mon, Tina. I have everything I need at the office in the main house. Walk me over?"

"Ah, what the hell," she said with a heavy exhale. "I wasn't going to sleep for shit anyway."

"That's the spirit," I agreed, jumping out of my chair, landing hard on the blistered soles of my feet, the pain bright even through the soft slippers and gauze Stacci had helped me wrap them in. Running through a burning olive grove in bare feet had not been one of my smartest decisions.

Martina nodded to the two men standing guard at the rear entrance of the house as we passed by them and started along the path to the main house. The way was lit with twinkling lights that mimicked the stars overhead.

"I could spend my whole life here happily," I said, staying close to Martina, who had her gun drawn even though we were surrounded by soldiers on the property. "And I intend to."

A little smile flickered at the end of her mouth. "I am glad for you and Raffa both. For myself too. I do not like many people, and when I find a decent one, I like to keep them."

I laughed a little even though it hurt my throat. "Thanks."

"If Raffa and I can make it work, I don't see why you and Renzo can't too," I added, knocking my shoulder into her.

Martina rolled her eyes at me, but she was quiet for the rest of the walk, and I had to wonder if she was really considering my words. Life was too unpredictable to waste a moment of it on indecision when what you wanted was within your grasp.

The villa looked like a broken, empty shell when we arrived. The windows and doors were all wide open to clear the space of lingering smoke, and the entire back side was smudged with soot. It was cold enough in early November that I pulled on a coat at the entrance, a large black barn coat that smelled of Raffa.

I chafed my hands together, breath white in the frigid air as we entered the office, and I hustled over to my workstation. The neat pile of papers I'd had at my desk was strewn across the tabletop and floor, probably because of a breeze from the opened window.

But when I went to type in my password, I realized the computer was already unlocked.

I frowned at the documents open on the screen, layer upon layer of open tabs. The financial documents, notes I'd taken, and even the websites I had searched to delve deeper into each business the Romano Group and Lupo Nero owned and operated.

"I didn't leave this like this," I whispered to Martina, though we were the only ones in the office.

"What do you mean?" she asked, leaning over my shoulder.

It was then I noticed the little flash drive stuck into the side of my laptop.

"What is this?"

Martina froze behind me, then cursed softly. "It's a spyware flash drive. Ludo programs them and gives them to us when we need to break into someone's hard drive or spy on their online activities."

"Someone wanted to see what I was working on."

Which meant someone knew I was combing through the Romano Group's financials.

"This is why he set the fire," I realized. "He looked into what I was doing for Carmine and discovered I was onto him."

"*Merda*," she spat. "I cannot believe that piece of shit."

Guilt sucker punched me. If I had been more discreet, none of the family would have been at risk. Everyone was going to be fine, but the kids, Zacheo especially, were probably going to be traumatized for life.

"Don't blame yourself," Martina said. "It's that *figlio di puttana* who deserves all the guilt for this and everything else he has done."

"True." I straightened my shoulders and chafed my cold hands together again. "Okay, well as a royal fuck-you to Leo, I am going to spend the next few hours discovering exactly how deep his conspiracy goes. Pull up a chair and make some coffee, would you? We'll be here awhile."

Martina snorted but drifted away, hopefully to the kitchen to make coffee while I got to work.

It only took me twenty minutes to realize I didn't have the full picture from the Romano Group. Whatever had been sent to Carmine had been doctored, because there were huge gaps in their financial statements. I studied the little flash drive beside my computer and sucked on my teeth before pocketing it and creeping down the hallway to Leo's office.

The early-morning light warmed my sore feet as I crossed the study to the desk and sat at the multimonitor computer. It took me a moment to find the USB port and then another to figure out how to use it to crack Leo's password protection.

I gained access to the computer, but his files were encrypted with a password too.

My dad and I used to play encryption games and solve riddles, so I figured I had just as good a shot as anyone at guessing what Leo's password could be. I tried a variation of his birthday and the first nine numerical digits because I knew those were the most common password choices, but I was still locked out, with a warning that I only had three attempts left.

So I tried to think about Leo as a man instead of a stranger. The conversations he had been a part of at the dinner table, the jokes he had shared with Raffa and the crew, the proclivities he'd shown without meaning to.

But nothing particularly stood out except for his betrayal and the surreal fact that he had been dating my sister.

My sister.

I loved a foreigner once . . .

I chewed on my lower lip as I considered the possibility that Leo, despite having betrayed his best friend and pseudo family, might have enough of a heart to give it over to another person.

Gemma.

My fingers trembled lightly as I used one finger to type the letters and numbers into the keyboard.

G-E-M-M-A-1-9-9-7.

Files exploded open on my screen: building plans, construction codes, green tech development specs, and financial projections for countless agricultural businesses. I recognized many of the names from the shipping manifests and many more from the files Carm had given me from the Romano Group.

But there were even a few for holdings I knew Raffa owned under Lupo Nero, like Imelda's Fattoria Casa Luna.

Obviously, Leo had stolen information about them to use for his own gain.

I pulled up Leo's banking application, my heart knocking so hard against my chest it bruised my ribs. It was the way I always felt when I was onto something.

The application was blocked by another password protection, and this one would not respond to the same Gemma password.

I'd sighed, ready to find Martina to ask for her help, when a masculine noise came from the door, startling me so badly I shot out of my chair, banging it hard against the wall behind me.

"I'm sorry," Dad said, hands open palms up as if in surrender. "I didn't mean to startle you, Jinx. I saw you walking over out the bedroom window and I just . . . I wanted to make sure you were okay." He huffed out a bitter breath and scrubbed a hand over his face. "Of course you aren't okay. It's been one thing after another since you got to this fucking hellhole."

"Dad." I sank back into my chair, feeling suddenly so exhausted that each of my bones was too heavy to hold upright. "This place is not a hellhole. I hope you know that by saying that, you are insulting my love for it and the peace I've found here."

"Peace?" he scoffed, eating up the space between us on long legs to reach over the desk for my hands. When I did not give them to him, his fingers curled into loose fists. "Guinevere, how can this violent series of unfortunate events have brought you anything close to peace?"

"I found love here, and community. A sense of belonging that I never had back in Michigan. For the first time in my life, I know who I am, and I like *it*. To me, that is the definition of peace," I explained as I turned my attention back to the computer.

I could feel Dad's gaze on me, heavy as a brand, as I entered Leo's full legal name and sent a "forgot password" notification to his email, which I had access to through his main account.

"You almost died again yesterday," Dad said softly.

"I'm fine."

"You could have ended up not fine at all," he pushed. "I know this is the life you've chosen, and I wish you hadn't—God, do I wish you hadn't. Believe it or not, though, I am trying to be understanding. I just need you to understand that you are my baby, Jinx. The moment I held you in my arms, I knew we would have a special bond, and that bond has been tested by terrifying trips to the emergency room and kidney transplants, by my secrets and lies, and by your choices here in Italy. It's been tested because I have never been more afraid to lose someone than I have been to lose you, especially after your sister's death."

I looked up from the prompts for resetting Leo's banking password to see Dad's dark eyes limned with tears, almost silver in the heavy morning shadows. It was hard to breathe through the emotion his speech evoked, through the tension that had been stretched between us for the last few months when all my life, he had been the person I'd felt most myself and safest with.

"I'm just asking for you to understand me as I try to understand you," he finished with a limp shrug. "I want to support you—I *will* support you—but I just have to get out of the way of my own fears first."

"Okay," I said immediately, finally reaching across the desktop for his hand. It was warm and thick with muscle in my grip. "I can do that. If anyone can understand taking some time to digest all *this*, it's me. I didn't exactly decide this was the life for me overnight, Dad. I am not that impulsive. I've spent many, many sleepless nights weighing the pros and cons."

"And the pros outweigh the laundry list of cons?" he asked with a wry smirk.

"Raffa alone would tip the scales," I admitted. "And that's not factoring in his family and our friends."

Dad rubbed his free hand over his mouth and nodded. "Okay then. I know your mother told you we plan to stay for some time, and she meant it. I can do most of my work from here and schedule videoconferences according to the time difference. I won't leave you until I'm sure you're settled. Until we feel good about our relationship again."

My heart tripped lightly, suddenly unburdened of the weight of my father's disappointment.

"I love you," I told him, squeezing his hand. "I know you thought I would judge you for your past in the Mafia, but even if I hadn't had my own experiences with it, I could never think you were anything less than the best dad in the world. You taught me how to take the true measure of a man, and it has everything to do with his heart and mind and very little to do with his social conformity."

Dad laughed, and the exhaustion that had sandblasted his face broke open to reveal his handsomeness. "I tried to conform for almost thirty years, and look where it got me!"

I smiled at him. "Right back where you started. Which means maybe you want to help me with this?"

He got up from the chair and rounded the desk to peer over my shoulder as I finished resetting Leo's password.

"How did you do that?" he asked.

"I had all his personal information right here," I said, indicating the computer. "And the Romano Group's information from Carmine. It was easy."

Pride suffused Dad's face as he smiled at me. "I never knew, all those hours we spent playing math and pattern-recognition games, that I was preparing you for a life of crime . . . but whatever you do in the future, I am very proud to be your father. You are quite the woman, Guinevere."

"I was taught by the best," I quipped. "Now, pull up a chair and help me determine exactly where the money he's been siphoning from the Romano Group and stealing from Lupo Nero's companies is going."

◆ ◆ ◆

We worked in silence for an hour, long after Martina had brought in steaming mugs of coffee and curled up in the chair across from the desk with another laptop to help us in our mission. She wasn't as familiar with financial forensics, but she provided invaluable context.

Still, I could not find any evidence that the money Leo had been channeling away from Raffa's enterprises was going into Leo's own pockets.

Until I decided to stop looking for it in Leo's coffers and just follow the trail of money.

My mind snagged on a pattern I vaguely recognized from having gone through the shipping manifests when Raffa was trying to figure out who was smuggling the Albanians' drugs through Livorno.

A bastardized anagram, but this time with an affine cipher instead of a Caesar.

It took Dad and me a long time to work out the mathematical equations for the businesses in the Romano Group's holdings, but eventually I used frequency analysis of all the company names to come up with the numbers needed to solve the simultaneous equation.

And thereby crack the code of where exactly Leo had hidden the money.

Only, the main holding company that was the pot of gold at the end of a very long rainbow, Nobiliaire, was not owned by Leonardo di Conte.

It was in a trust for a Maria Rizzo, his deceased mother, held by Antonio di Conte.

I was familiar enough with trust law to know that only the holder of the account could access the funds, and after a quick internet search, I found the same was true in Italy. So why would Leo funnel all his hard-won dirty money into an account he could not access?

Unless Leo was not the puppeteer but, instead, the puppet pulled by someone else's hands.

The account holder: Antonio di Conte.

Uncle Tonio.

I blinked at the financial records, wondering if my sleep-deprived brain was imagining things.

We had not been suspicious of Tonio at all.

He was a seventy-year-old man, for one thing, and the Venetian was said to be a tall, fit young man.

But if Leo was working with him, then perhaps Leo had been the one to don the mask and do Tonio's more aggressive legwork.

For another, he was already head of the Romano Group, with what had to be an incredible salary and a lot of sway in Florentine society as its CEO.

So *why*?

Why would he and Leo decide to cut off the hand that fed them and go after the whole enterprise for themselves?

Why would Tonio go to such lengths—getting Leo to shoot him!—to make us believe he was free of guilt? What did he need before he got rid of the Romano family entirely?

"Where is Tonio?" I whispered.

Martina straightened out of her slump at my tone. "He was taken to the hospital for his injuries. Why?"

"Are there any *soldati* with him?"

"Just his usual bodyguards, Ernesto and Michele."

I blinked slowly as the name Michele swam up from the depths of my memories.

"Michele and Philippe were brothers, right?"

"No, just friends. They grew up in the same village, and Tonio practically fostered them. Michele's father was a drunk, and Philippe had to take care of his single mother. She was very sickly. Aldo gave them work."

Not Aldo, I corrected mentally, but Tonio. The grumpy but sweet older man who was known for taking in strays like Leo. Only, he had been doing it not out of the goodness of his own heart but out of greed, in order to build his own internal army to take control of the outfit from Aldo—or Raffa—one day.

Had he been working against the family for that long?

Was his problem with the Romanos about the sins of the father and not the son?

"It was Tonio," I said. "Tonio was the one pulling all the strings. Leo might have helped him, but they did it together."

"You're saying Tonio shot himself and stayed in the burning olive grove by choice?" Martina asked, but she wasn't skeptical, just working it out aloud.

"It would be clever," Dad said darkly.

Martina was already on her phone, fingers flying as she shot off texts.

"Leo could have been the one to shoot him," I allowed. "But it was a setup to take suspicion off him and put it firmly onto Leo, who we already suspected. This way Tonio could stay close."

"But why not just kill Raffa and be done with it? I'm sure being so close to the family, to Raffa, he would have had the opportunity," Dad noted.

"Not really," Martina said. "Raffa is rarely truly alone. Either Renzo, Carm, Ludo, or me is always with him or in the vicinity. If he'd killed Raffa outright, we would have taken him down."

"Exactly." Adrenaline transformed my blood to battery acid. "Whereas if the Grecos or Pietras were the ones to kill Raffa, Tonio could step in like the hero to take over and then wipe out his accomplices in the name of revenge."

"Bravo, Guinevere," someone said from the doorway.

I looked up just in time to see Tonio, dressed impeccably in a three-piece suit, looking every inch the strong, deadly mafioso even with his recent gunshot wound, lift his gun and fire.

The scream that tore from my smoke-ravished throat tasted like blood.

Because the bullet had been meant not for me but for Martina, who didn't even have time to fully turn toward the threat before the shot punctured through the back of her chair straight into her torso. I watched as her eyes went wide and breath punched out of her lungs. Clasping a hand over the blood bubbling up behind her shirt, she tried to stand up only for her legs to give out, falling back into the chair with a shuddering moan.

"Stay there, Pietra scum," Tonio coolly ordered my father, who had stood to go to Martina. "Do not even blink, or I will shoot you too."

Dad opened his palms innocently and remained where he stood.

"On the other hand," Tonio mused, cocking his head to consider my dad. "I do not have any need of you."

"Wait," I demanded, stepping in front of Dad. "If you need me, you need him. I won't do anything for you if you kill my father."

Tonio sighed as if I were a particularly petulant child. "You are hardly in a position to make demands."

"Raffa will eviscerate you for this," I said, hoping that dragging him into conversation might give some of the *soldati* on the property the opportunity to come looking for us, especially if Martina had had time to text Raffa or any of the others about our revelations.

Tonio moved farther into the room, and I realized he was holding his torso stiffly, so the gunshot must have been bothering him, even if he was trying to hide it.

I filed that away for future use.

"Raffa won't be doing anything any longer," Tonio told me with a kind, almost grandfatherly smile that nonetheless froze the blood in my veins. "He's dead."

For a moment, everything stopped.

Sound fell into silence; colors faded to white static.

My heart ceased beating.

And then the pain rushed in, as if Tonio had shot me straight through the chest instead of Martina, who sat slumped over and unconscious in her chair, slowly bleeding out.

It was as if Tonio had declared my own death too.

Because if Raffa was truly gone . . .

"How?" I asked, surprised by the vicious strength of my tone when I felt my internal organs shutting down.

"You like patterns, don't you?" he mused as he walked over to Martina and callously shoved her out of the chair.

She fell to the floor limply with a sickening thump.

Tonio sat in the empty, bloodstained seat with his gun resting on one thigh, trained at Dad and me.

Maybe, if it had only been me at risk, I would have hazarded an attempt to attack him. After all, he was an elderly man, and I was young, with some degree of training. If I could just get close enough with the element of surprise, I had no doubt I could disarm him.

And if Raffa was dead . . .

Then no one was coming to save us.

Before I went to pieces, I had to get Dad out of this situation.

"Well, you are all unbearably predictable," Tonio continued, adjusting his tie so it lay flat down his chest. "Of course Raffa would never suspect his old uncle, left bleeding in the grove, of being complicit in his demise. Of course my *stronzo* of a 'son' would take the first opportunity I was compromised to go after his girlfriend, and *certo*, Raffa and his band of unmerry men would follow. It was just a matter of setting up a neat little trap to take them all out in one fell swoop."

"Why would you want to kill your own son?" my dad asked, slowly trying to tug me back so he could step in front of me.

When I did not move, he sighed and stepped up shoulder to shoulder. The weight and warmth of him beside me provided me safe harbor in the maelstrom of horror, despair, and panic wreaking havoc within me.

"Leo was always such a good little soldier," he said, reminiscing like we were old friends around a coffee table and not in a quasi hostage situation. "He had to be, as the only child I decided to adopt for my own. There were always other boys that could have taken his position whom I found over the years and groomed into service of the Romano empire. He knew if he was not exemplary, another could fill his very coveted shoes. But then he met your daughter." His pleasant face twisted into an awful sneer, a gold filling winking in the brightening morning light. "It seems the Pietra girls have the ability to corrupt good men from their true path."

My laugh was coarse like tearing fabric. "That's rich, coming from you."

He leveled me with a flat look, adjusting the barrel of the gun so it was clearly aimed at my father. The threat was obvious yet clever. I was much more likely to be obedient if Dad was in danger rather than me.

Especially if Raffa was gone.

"He tried to keep her a secret, but I knew he was going soft. Traveling to Albania more than was necessary, suddenly questioning why we had to destroy the Romanos to take what should always have been mine."

Mine, not *ours*.

A slip that revealed his dangerous narcissism.

"Why should it have been yours?" I demanded. "The Romano clan has held this territory for generations."

"And for generations the di Conte family has supported them," Tonio snarled. "We used to be princes of Italy, and now we are reduced to common foot soldiers. I thought when Raffa refused to enter the family business, when my continued efforts to lead him to university and civility paid off, that we would finally have our opportunity. Aldo swore an oath to make Leo his heir."

A muscle under his eye twitched manically as he looked into old, sour memories.

"He lied," I surmised.

"He lied," Tonio agreed. "In fact, he made fun of me one night when we were in Pisa to confer with the Pietras. The first day's meeting had ended, and Aldo had too much grappa. When I spoke of Leo joining us on the tour of the territory we took each year, he *laughed*." There was a pause riddled with the palpable electric energy of his rage. "He told me Raffa would be his heir if he had to drag him back from that British isle kicking and screaming. He had a willing, capable man who wanted the throne, and he still refused to see beyond his own nepotism."

"You were the one who killed him," Dad said slowly as he put the pieces together. "You always blamed the family for what happened to him, but Ginevra told me Gaetano swore he never touched the capo, even though he was the one accused of murdering Aldo Romano. It was you, wasn't it?"

Tonio flicked an invisible piece of lint off his thigh. "It was an accident, really. Grappa always brings out my baser urges, and I could not stand to look a minute more on that smug Romano laughing at me. Luckily, it was fairly easy to lay the blame at the door of the Pietras, given the history of distrust between the two families over the centuries. The two most powerful Northern Mafia families at war? It was too salacious not to be believed."

There was a flicker of shadow in the light pooling in from the open door to the hall. I tried not to pin my gaze obviously over Tonio's shoulder, but I kept track in my periphery as the shadow detached from the wall and loomed just beyond the frame.

Someone had come.

My heart leaped into my throat, hope so bright behind my eyes it threatened to blind me.

Raffa.

But the man who slipped into the room with a silver handgun in his grip, trained on the back of Tonio's head, was not the man I hoped to see.

Leo di Conte looked terrible.

Heavy bags drooped beneath his eyes, and his normally golden hair was covered in a fine layer of soot that stained his white dress shirt and trousers as well. His gaze flicked up to mine, a warning to stay quiet implicit in his gaze as he tried to angle himself behind his father.

Something in my expression must have given him away, because before he could shoot, Tonio was lurching out of his chair, grabbing for me where I stood beside the desk and wrapping his arms around me in a tight bear hug. I'd been so focused on Leo, I didn't have time to counter Tonio's attack, and before I could think to move, I was caught in his grip, the cold kiss of a gun at my temple.

"Ah," Tonio sighed sadly, breath moist against my cheek. "I see the explosion did not take you with it."

Leo bared his teeth. "You fucking bastard. Gemma didn't deserve that."

Beside us, Dad lunged for me, but Tonio clicked his tongue and shuffled us away from him, grinding the gun into my head.

"Not so quick, Pietra. You only have one daughter left now. You wouldn't want to lose her too."

"Gemma was alive?" I whispered, looking at Leo. "All this time?"

Those devastated blue eyes flickered to mine, then back to his father. "Yes," he ground out. "It was how Tonio was keeping me in line. Gemma was the one who sent the man at the bell tower in Impruneta with her necklace. She was trying to get you to help her without putting you in danger. If either of us had tried to tell you what was going on, Tonio had the house he was keeping her in rigged to explode."

People will die if I tell you, Philippe had sobbed before Raffa killed him.

Gemma.

Tonio had staged her death and kept her locked up for over a year to use her as a tool against his own son, to take down Raffa in his quest to become *capo dei capi* himself.

And now, because of him, both my beautiful sister and the love of my life were dead.

"He died with her?" I asked with the rest of the breath left in my body.

Leo nodded tersely. "When I arrived, they must have been in the basement with her. The car was outside, and the tripwire for the bombs was at the top of the stairs."

I closed my eyes against the brutal wave of pain that wrapped me in its viselike hold, crushing me from the inside out, bones and sinew ground to dust, veins bursting open.

"I didn't want to hurt him," Leo said quietly, and when I opened my eyes to look at him, tears were rolling through the dirt on his cheeks. "But Tonio had me by the balls."

Tonio's chuckle filled my ear. "You and Raffa were never very good at chess."

"So what now, *vecchio*?" Leo demanded. "Raffa's dead, but here we are, and I do not intend to let you out of this house alive."

"You're a wanted man, Leo. All I have to do is call the *soldati* to us, and they'll come running to end your life," Tonio replied calmly.

"Even with you holding Raffa's fiancée at gunpoint?" he countered.

Tonio was quiet for a moment. "Pietra, move to the side wall and stand still."

I watched from the corner of my eye as Dad obeyed, his gaze fixed on mine. It was calculating, and I was reminded that he had been born a mafioso, not a financial adviser, and he might be able to see a way out of this better than me.

"Sit," Tonio ordered seconds before shoving me into the desk chair. "You have access to Romanos' accounts through Lupo Nero and the outfit. I want you to transfer funds to me. I know I do not have to tell you my banking information because you were stupid enough to go snooping where you do not belong."

"No," I snapped.

Tonio's response was to shoot at my dad.

The bullet embedded itself in the wall an inch from his head.

Dad didn't even flinch, but I did.

"At least let Dad check on Martina?" I asked quietly. "Then I promise I'll do what you want."

After a brief hesitation, Tonio agreed, and Dad bent to check Martina's pulse.

"It's there but slow and weak," he announced.

Fuck.

"Get to work," Tonio urged me, sticking the gun against the swell of my skull.

Slowly, my fingers moved on the keys.

"Don't think about it," Tonio said a moment later, and I looked up to see that Leo had inched forward, probably to take a shot at his dad.

Tonio crouched behind my chair so only his head was visible, still too close to mine for a clean shot.

Leo gritted his teeth, but when I locked eyes with him, he shuttled his gaze toward the window on the wall to my right. I followed it, maneuvering the cursor across the screen to scroll through records as I wasted time, and studied the vista outside. The hill sloped up slightly before falling into the vineyard, and out among the greenery I caught a metallic glimmer.

The dead weight of my heart stuttered like a failing engine as I narrowed my eyes and looked closer through the leaves.

There.

Hair that shone like burnished copper in the sunshine.

Raffa.

As if sensing my gaze, he crept forward through the vines until he was just visible through the window.

If Tonio looked up and over, he would see him.

"So you got your best friend and your love killed," I said to Leo, letting the echo of my pain suffuse my voice. "Your cowardice took my fiancé and my sister from me."

"I'm sorry," Leo said, and there was true agony and contrition in his voice, a wealth of it I could not even begin to process.

He had done so much wrong, all in a bid to save Gemma.

Could I blame him?

Wouldn't I do the same thing for Raffa in a heartbeat?

Our conversation successfully distracted Tonio, who laughed cruelly. "Love makes idiots of everyone."

My gaze clung to Raffa as he approached out the window. He was covered in soot like Leo, but his shirt was torn open along one side, bandages evident over his ribs. Something had torn through his eyebrow, blood crusted along his nose and cheek.

It was obvious he *had* been in the explosion Tonio had set, but somehow he'd escaped relatively unharmed.

I just had to hope the others—*Gemma!*—had too.

"For love, a fawn can become a huntress," I told Tonio before I shoved the rolling desk chair back hard into his legs and dropped beneath the shelter of the desk.

A moment later, a violent crack pierced the air, followed by the shattering of glass and a heavy thwack. I spun around to witness Tonio slipping down the wall with a slack, open mouth, a bullet drilled through the center of his brow, his brain blasted across the red walls behind him.

Glass tinkled as more fell, and then the crunch of boots on the debris-strewn floor.

Raffa had climbed through the window, stalking toward us with his huge gun trained on Tonio.

Pop. Pop. Pop.

I watched as he drilled three more rounds into Tonio's already-dead body, the corpse jumping from the impact.

Blood sprayed my front from my close proximity.

If Raffa had miscalculated the shot by even two inches, I would have been dead instead of his uncle.

But then again, we both could have died today, and the thought of that, of the life-ending anguish I'd felt believing he was dead, rocked through me like an earthquake.

"Raffa," I said, standing tall to face him.

The predatory expression that had turned his face to marble wavered, as if the sound of his name in my mouth called him back from a berserker rage. A moment later, his gaze turned from Tonio to me, and the last of that hardness shattered into unfiltered relief.

"*Vera*," he breathed like a dying man's last wish.

And then we were crashing into each other despite his injuries, my hands fisting in his hair, his gripping my ass to leverage me up into his arms, our mouths connected like a watertight seal for our plundering tongues. We kissed so desperately I could not breathe and didn't care to ever again so long as I could stay safe in his embrace for the rest of my life.

"*Meus Rex Infernus*," I said against his mouth. "Come to save me."

Because he was no one's Prince Charming, but he was my King Below. And no matter the enemy at the gates, I knew in my bones we would find a way to conquer them and live the rest of our lives in our kind of dark ever after.

"My huntress," he whispered as he kissed my lids, my nose, the point of my chin, anointing me in his love. "You are so fucking brave. I am so sorry."

"Don't be sorry," I insisted, holding him away from me by tightening my fingers in his hair. "This wasn't your fault. It was Tonio and . . ."

I hesitated.

Because it was also Leo's fault, even if he had been the reluctant villain to Raffa's reluctant mafioso.

Which reminded me . . .

"Gemma," I gasped, almost choking on the hope ballooning inside me. "Is she . . . ?"

Raffa smoothed a hand down the back of my hair. "She is."

He turned so that I could face the room again and notice what had taken place in the few moments we had taken to reunite and reaffirm we were alive.

Renzo knelt at Martina's side, his hands wet with her blood as he stanched her wounds. She loosely held on to his shirt, lids fluttering as she struggled to breathe, but she was alive.

And beyond that, Leo was on his knees holding on to a figure in a dirty gray dress, with blond hair I recognized even under the grime of soot and ash.

"*Gemma*," I mouthed because the air had been ripped from my lungs. I tried again after sucking in more oxygen, which burned going down. "Gemma."

Leo's hands spasmed on her back before reluctantly loosening so that she could pull away and twist to look at me.

"*Dio mio*," Dad said from beside the left wall, his hand at his neck as if his shock and joy were strangling him. "Gemstone."

His nickname for her all our lives.

Gemma's big blue eyes, bloodshot and weary, filled with tears.

"Hi, Dad. Hi, Jinxy." Her voice, rough as it was, sounded like a gospel chorus, something heralding hallelujah.

Together, Dad and I took a first running step and sprinted to her, falling to our knees in order to tackle her into a group hug. We were all crying, sobbing so hard I thought I might go on crying forever. It felt too surreal, too precious to stop touching her for even a moment, as if she might disintegrate, lost to us but for our memories once more.

Vaguely I was aware of Raffa and Leo speaking over us, the tension radiating off my fiancé, who stood at my back like a shield.

"You can't say you wouldn't have done the same for Guinevere," Leo was saying.

"I would have," Raffa agreed instantly. "But I would have fucking *told* you."

"He would have killed you, do you get that? He monitored me all the time. He owned Philippe and Michele and Bruno. All soldiers close enough to track your every movement too. If I made one mistake, he took it out on Gemma. That night in the bell tower, Gemma sent one of the guards she had persuaded over to her side to Impruneta to make contact with Guinevere. Unfortunately, Guinevere spooked and killed him, and Tonio witnessed the entire mess. He didn't feed Gemma for a week after that, and he beat her each one of those days. We did not try again."

Gemma whimpered slightly in response, pulling away from us just enough to lift her hands between us. Each finger was tipped with raw skin, the nails removed. Three fingers on her right hand had clearly been broken and not reset, and she was missing the entire pinky on her left hand.

"Oh, honey," Dad said, the words torn from him as he gently pulled her hands into his and pressed his mouth to the back of her mangled hand. "My sweet girl."

I cupped my hand over my mouth as if I could contain the brutal sob carving out my throat. Dad sensed it, slipping one of his arms around me to tug us both into his side as if he could physically shield us from the trauma of our past and future.

Gemma curled into him, reaching out to hold on to me so tightly I knew it had to hurt her brutalized hands.

"What are you going to do with me now?" Leo asked, utterly resigned to his fate, almost eager for it, as if it could rectify the utter chaos he'd helped to bring to our door.

"Kill him," Renzo snarled from where he was still tending to Martina.

Soldati had entered the room, lingering in the doorway, one of them crouched beside Martina with an impressive first-aid kit.

But the only people who existed for me in the room were my dad and my sister, and the two men who had changed the course of the Stone women's lives forever.

I wanted to beg Raffa to spare Leo just for Gemma's sake as much as I wanted to order him to tear Leo apart with his bare hands and burn the pieces, so I stayed silent, muted by the force of the opposing desires.

"He was the only thing that got me through this hell," Gemma said quietly, in such a raspy voice I felt sympathy pains for her in my throat.

The words seemed to resonate with Raffa, though. We all understood about going through hell to get to the other side. I'd led him through the deepest, darkest circles of hell just as Beatrice had done for Dante, and apparently Leo had done the same for Gemma.

Raffa's precious-metal eyes fell on me, their warmth softened with love even while his mouth twisted with lingering fury and indecision.

It wasn't just Gemma who loved Leo.

Raffa had related to him as a brother for every one of his thirty-four years, and to kill him now. when he understood his motivations for helping Tonio under duress . . . I did not think the monster in Raffa would win out.

The man beneath the predator had too big a heart.

"We will sort it out," he said finally, staring Leo down even as he staved off his execution. "But you will account for your actions, Leo."

His friend swayed slightly on his feet as if relief had made him dizzy.

"Thank you, *fratello*," he whispered.

"You will spend the rest of your life earning back my friendship, if it can be done at all," Raffa declared coldly, but his hand found my shoulder and moved up my neck to tip my chin back so he could look into my eyes. "Consider it a wedding present, *cacciatrice*."

The smile that overtook my face ached in my cheeks. I pulled him down to the floor beside me, where he naturally shifted me half into his lap, even though I was still partially under my dad's arm.

"Gemma," I told my sister in a waterlogged voice, "this is Raffaele, my fiancé."

A glimmer of her previous coquettishness sparked in Gemma's eyes as she glanced between us. "I met him when he saved my life. When the first explosion went off, he shielded me from the blast before Leo arrived and got us out through the bunker exit."

I felt oversaturated with relief and joy, as if every atom of me was filled with enough light to burst like a supernova. In the wake of terror, joy was so much sweeter.

"He saved mine too," I said, and I meant so much more than just today.

He had been saving me since the day he'd hit me with his Ferrari in the middle of an empty Tuscan road, but the truth was, I knew I had been saving him too.

It might have been silly to some, but as I sat there holding my man, my dad, and my sister, and my mom came running into the room with a loud sob before throwing herself at all of us, I said a prayer of thanks to Italy.

"It is fate that I am here," E. M. Forster once said, "but you can call it Italy if it makes you less unhappy."

And I knew it was here in this forbidden country that I had finally found myself and the life I was meant to live.

EPILOGUE

Raffa

Christmas morning arrived in a wash of white. The hills and valleys extending from the villa were layered in crystalline powder that glittered in the colorless light filtering in through low, pale clouds. It seemed like something from a dreamscape, a landscape so pristine it could not exist anywhere outside the mind.

It was the perfect day to marry the girl of my dreams.

The woman who had taken my hand and led me out of my own personal hell into a future I had never dared to envision for myself.

Only seven weeks had passed since I had killed Tonio and Gemma had been returned to her family. Seven weeks of incandescent joy and grueling trials as I purged my organization of Tonio's influence and Guinevere adjusted to life as a capo's bride.

John and Elizabeth had stayed in Tuscany to oversee both their daughters, given that neither of them consented to return to Michigan. Understandably, the Stone parents would not be parted from either child after what they had all been through, even with John's long-standing hatred of this country and my lifestyle. Clearly, I had underestimated the lengths the man would go to for his family.

It made for some interesting family dinners, merging the Stones with my wild, warm Romano clan and my found family of Renzo,

Carmine, Ludo, and Martina, but after a few weeks, the Stones started to unwind and soften toward everyone.

It was largely due to Gemma, who was so fragile and, apparently, wildly unlike how she had been before her abduction that any conflict sent her into a blind panic only Leo could bring her back from.

But it was also because of my Vera.

After everything she had been through to be with me, it would have been reasonable for her to be bitter or afraid, spooked by the creak of a closing door or the shout of one of the children in the yard. Instead, there was a strength and vibrancy in her that had lain half hidden beneath the sand, like treasure yearning to be dug up and exposed, when she had first arrived in Italy. She moved through the world bravely, boldly, with an elegance and inner peace that transfixed me whenever I had the opportunity to observe her cooking with Mamma, Stacci, Delfina, and Carlotta or playing with the children or walking quietly with Gemma among the vines.

Guinevere was at peace. With *me*.

It was a conclusion I drew again and again each day I spent with her at my side, and yet it had not once lost its wonder.

As a boy, I had yearned for a different kind of life than my father or uncle had wanted for me and assumed that when I was forced to take up their mantle, I would lose a part of my soul in the process. But Guinevere had proved me wrong. She had shown me I was still capable of goodness, even when the decision was hard, such as pardoning Leo for allowing himself to be blackmailed by Tonio. She had shown me that even though I had blood on my hands and sin on my mind, I was still capable of the kind of profound love that artists and poets had written about throughout history.

Sometimes, in the darkest hours of the night, I lay awake beside her in our bed and trailed my fingers down the knobs of her spine, over the arch of her buttocks and the curve of her thigh, just to make sure she was real. Just to know she was mine.

All that sweet curiosity and keen intelligence, that steadfast loyalty and passionate fervor, wrapped up in that slim, doe-eyed frame.

In those night hours when the familiar specters of self-hatred and self-doubt visited my bedside, it helped to touch her like that and remember that she was strong enough to survive this life. To survive me.

Not only survive it, but also thrive in it.

My huntress had started working at the Romano Group, cleaning up the mess Tonio had made of the previously entirely legal enterprise so that it would not draw the attention of Sansone Pucci's DIA. She did not want to be CEO, because she was curious about the criminal side of my businesses too, intrigued by the loopholes and schemes we had constructed to take advantage of the government and twist their profits for our own.

"I think I have a knack for this," she had said one afternoon, sitting in my lap in the office Carmine and I used. I had been working when she came into the room and folded herself into my lap without hesitation, clicking through the proposal I was reading as if it was her right to do so.

It was a little intimacy that took my breath away, her comfort with me and her confidence in the fact that she belonged, with me, in this house, in the Camorra and this dark world of mine.

It never failed to arouse and wow me.

So I had proceeded to show her that I had a knack too, one involving my tongue and the sweet-slick apex of her thighs.

We were both busy in the wake of Day of the Dead, Guinevere with her new work and tending to Gemma, John, and Elizabeth, but also to my nephews, who had varying degrees of trauma from the night of the fire. Zacheo in particular had imprinted on her and monopolized her time whenever he could.

Guinevere did not protest.

In fact, one night only two weeks after our confrontation with Tonio, when I was seated to the root inside her as she rode me in a sinuous, rocking rhythm like the waves rushing to shore at Livorno, she had bent to me and whispered, "I want children with you more than my next breath."

She was still young, and we had not been together for a full year, but I knew that was in our future, filling this house with even more children to love and cherish as we did Stacci's and Carlotta's.

Children.

A concept I had never thought of for myself.

One that I had written in invisible ink on the inside of my heart.

Of course, my Vera could see that and offer it to me, yet another gift I would never be able to repay her for, though I would spend the rest of my life trying.

"Can I speak to you for a moment?"

I was pulled from my contemplation by John standing at the door to my office in a custom tux I had insisted on buying for him for the wedding. He had grumbled, but when Elizabeth had seen him in it and practically cooed her praise, he had actually blushed.

My imminent father-in-law and I had not magically become close over the last month and a half. Guinevere was his treasure, and I was the villain taking her away from her life in Michigan to an Italian life of crime.

But he had softened, almost imperceptibly.

I had caught him with a smile at the edges of his mouth when he watched Guinevere laugh with me, when he saw the way I treated my mother and sisters. He might have wanted to hate me, but I was the choice his daughter had made, and he respected her enough to treat me courteously.

"*Certo*," I said, indicating the couch along one wall.

I took the chair across from him and waited.

The wedding would start in half an hour, and I had been relegated to my office when I had arrived this morning from Stacci's house because I was not allowed to see the bride before the wedding.

"I understand you still haven't decided what to do with Leo," John said, surprising me.

We did not try to keep business discussions from John and Elizabeth, just as we did not from my family, but we mostly spoke about outfit affairs in my office. Though it was not exactly hard to discern that I did not know what to do about Leo di Conte.

He had been my best friend all my life only to betray me in order to save the life of the girl he loved. A girl who happened to be the sister of my own beloved.

I could not exactly murder him for his crimes when doing so would hurt Gemma and therefore Guinevere.

When, if I was deeply honest with myself, it would hurt me.

The problem was, I did not trust him with my business anymore, and I did not trust him in my life. He remained on the property—he and Gemma stayed in the guesthouse down the road, near Carlotta's house, because Guinevere needed her family close—but he was not welcome in my orbit.

Nor was he particularly welcome in Guinevere's, though she tried to be cordial for Gemma's sake.

Even though I did not want him near, he also knew too much about my dealings for me to let him go off on his own.

"I think I have a solution," John continued, scowling at his hands as though they had wronged him.

"I would like to hear it," I said, leaning back comfortably in the chair so he would know he had the floor.

He rubbed a hand over his mouth, then fixed his gaze on mine, dark eyes hard with resolve. "The Pietras are in disarray since you killed Gaetano. My sister's boys are too young to take over, and there is no clear line of succession. But Gemma is a Pietra, and Leo is a seasoned mafioso with knowledge of the clan." He did not mention that Leo's intimate knowledge of the clan came from Tonio's attempt to onboard the Pietras for his attempted coup. "I am willing to stay for six months to stabilize the family and teach Leo and Gemma the ropes, as it were, before I go back to Michigan."

My brows rose of their own volition. "This is a surprise from someone who once threatened to cut out his daughter for merely visiting the country. You are now willing to stay and dirty your hands once more? Why?"

John looked out the window as if the answer was written on the windowpane.

"You don't have children yet, but one day I imagine you'll understand exactly why I am offering this. I've made no bones about the fact I did not want this life for either of my girls, but it is the life they both chose. Gemma is not happy with me and the lies I told that kept her from her heritage. All she wants is a life with Leo, and all Leo knows is this life." He opened his hands wide. "I thought she was *dead*, Raffaele. I mourned her. I organized her funeral. Second chances are so rare, and I have one. If I can help my daughters in any way, I will, even if it goes against my own grain."

"You would have done what Leo did for Elizabeth," I concluded, because John Stone might have anglicized his name and put on a suit to make money for other men, but he had been born Mariano Giovanni Pietra and raised as a camorrista.

Any man with a heart like ours would burn down the world for the woman he loved, consequences be damned.

"I would do it still," he agreed. "And I would do it for my girls too. This doesn't just help Gemma. Guinevere will be happy to see the back of the man who tried to kill you, even if he did not want to, but she will be happier still that it means Gemma is only a short train ride away."

Guinevere would never ride a damn train again as far as I was concerned. It was only one of the reasons one of her wedding presents waited outside in the garage, a gleaming red Ferrari 458 Speciale I knew she would love.

"Does it solve your problem with the Pietra clan and Leo?" John asked.

I hesitated before nodding. "It would. I would send Carmine with you too. He knows the area well, and he can oversee Leo."

"You don't trust him."

"Would you?" I demanded. "He colluded to kill my soon-to-be wife. If he had not had the good luck to earn the love of a Stone woman, he would be in the ground with the worms."

John nodded as if he understood and even agreed with that sentiment.

"I will watch him closely," he promised. "I have as much of an investment in his success as he does, because of Gemma."

"You think he is good enough for her?" I asked, successfully keeping the scoff from my tone.

John's grin was sharklike. "No more than you are for Guinevere. Unfortunately, they did not put it to a vote before they went and lost their hearts to made men."

"Thank God for that," I said dryly, and was surprised when John chuckled.

"You'll take care of her," he said, leaning back and opening his posture up to me deliberately. "The only reason I am okay with any of this is the way you look at her."

"And how is that?" I asked, even though I knew.

"You look at her like she is your private church, something holy and safe and entirely yours. Like you will spend the rest of your life worshipping her. Sometimes, when you say her name, it's like a prayer." He shook his head ruefully. "I do not need to ask if a man like you believes in God, yet that's the way you look at her? No, Raffa, I have no doubt you live for her and you would die for her. A father would be greedy to ask for more."

I did not say a word, because he was right.

There was nothing in this world I loved so much as my Guinevere. But it felt good to hear it and know that he trusted me with one of his most precious gifts.

"*Grazie mille*," I said quietly, standing up to offer my hand. "I am grateful that you raised such an incredible woman, and I am grateful that you are willing to do this for her, for all of us."

He clasped my hand strongly, squeezing tight and pumping it up and down a few times before he leaned over our hands to clap me on the shoulder.

"Anytime," he said.

I nodded, my voice stuck behind the lump in my throat, because something about the look in his eyes and the gesture hinted that one day, he might do anything for me too.

After being raised by a man like Aldo and then mentored by one like Tonio, it felt almost painfully good to be in the presence of a man like John.

"Sorry, are we interrupting?" Carmine asked as he swanned into the room with a bottle of prosecco and a handful of glasses. "Good. Raffa is about to marry a woman who is entirely too good for him, and we must have a toast to his good luck."

John and I both laughed, dropping our hands to gather near the desk with Ludo, Renzo bringing up the rear with Martina on his arm. Since she had been shot, he had not left her side for anything. When Guinevere asked if they were finally dating, Martina had tried to prevaricate, but Renzo had leaned over to kiss her silent at the dinner table.

Guinevere had started a round of applause.

"I am happy to toast to my own good luck," I allowed, accepting a glass of fizzing sparkling wine.

"Did you ever think this day would come?" Martina asked with a wink.

"No," I said honestly, even a little hoarse. "No, I did not."

"Well, we did," she insisted. "You deserve the best, boss."

I might have argued, but Guinevere *was* the best, so instead I raised my glass to my best friends and my future father-in-law and said, "To family, old and new."

John bit back his smile but joined the others when they echoed my sentiment.

◆ ◆ ◆

I stood before an arbor of cedar boughs that perfumed the air with their pungent, earth-sweet scent, waiting for my bride to walk down the aisle Ludo had shoveled in the snow and laid with black rock. It had been Guinevere's idea to walk on the dark stone.

"We walked through hell together," she said. "I want this to symbolize that."

Our families sat on rustic wooden benches, bundled up in furs and opulent coats to stave off the winter chill, their breaths clouding the air as they waited for the last addition to our party. Mamma wept softly next to Stacci, already overcome with happiness, and all the kids sat very patiently in their finery except for baby Nico, who had fallen asleep in his father's arms. The only one missing was Zacheo, who was our ring bearer, walking down the aisle as the string quartet played Pavarotti.

Delfina stood at my side in a black suit as my attendant, and Gemma had already walked down the aisle with Elizabeth as Guinevere's bridesmaid. Gemma watched Leo where he sat in the second row as if he was a midnight eclipse, something profound and magical she could not break from.

The music swelled through the speakers, and a moment later Guinevere appeared through the open terrace doors.

My heart arrested at the sight of her.

Her long, thick hair was a big, soft corona of curls around her face and down her back, beneath such a sheer veil it seemed woven from the cloud of her breath in the cold. I could still see through to those luminous dark eyes, large and fringed in heavy lashes, filled with love so tangible it was as if her gaze had fingers to reach through my chest, to hold my heart and force it to restart painfully.

She looked ethereal, Proserpina in her white froth of a gown, only lace webbing over her arms and the points of her fingers, a sluice of unblemished silk over her upturned breasts and the slight curves of her hips. Innocence personified but for the slash of crushed-berry red painted on her full mouth, a tantalizing hint of the huntress she could be if the need arose.

John walked her down the aisle, but no one existed for me but her.

La mia stella cadente.

La mia cerbiatta e la mia cacciatrice.

My Vera.

When John placed her hand in mine, I felt as if the earth moved, tectonic plates sliding irrevocably into place.

"Hi," she said with that sweet, shy smile that had first enchanted me so many months ago.

"*Ciao bella,*" I echoed, giving in to the urge to tug her indecently close, pressing our bodies together, hips to thighs. "I missed you."

Her features softened behind the thin veil, mouth a generous moue. We had been apart for one night, but we both suffered from nightmares without the other in our bed.

"I missed you before I even knew your name," she confessed.

Love filled my chest so full I found it difficult to draw breath.

"You once told me *segui la tua stella,*" she murmured, as if there was no audience to our union, "to follow my destiny. I started on the path to my fate, to my soul mate, the day I set foot in Italy, and I would not change a single hardship I have ever endured, because I know it led me to you. I know we earned this happily ever after."

"'*E quindi uscimmo a riveder le stelle,*'" I said, dipping to kiss her through the veil. The effort marked the sheer white with the blood red of her lipstick. "'And so we emerged once more to see the stars.'"

The final line of Dante's *Inferno* was inscribed on the inside of the thick gold band she slipped onto my finger minutes later, when we had finished exchanging our vows.

"What kind of happily ever after does a King Below warrant?" I quipped when Carmine, acting as our officiant, declared us husband and wife.

Guinevere's grin was wild and wicked and free when she rose to the toes of her heels to bring her mouth close to mine and whisper, "A dark ever after with his huntress by his side."

PLAYLIST

"Ready or Not"—Mischa "Book" Chillak (featuring Esthero)
"Nothing's Gonna Hurt You Baby"—Cigarettes After Sex
"Closer"—Isabel LaRosa
"The World We Knew (Over and Over)"—Frank Sinatra
"A Different Age"—Current Joys
"Phantoms and Friends"—Old Man Canyon
"In the Devil's Territory"—Sufjan Stevens
"Tell It to My Heart"—MEDUZA (featuring Hozier)
"To Be Alone with You"—Sufjan Stevens
"I Wanted to Leave"—SYML
"No Love for a Sinner"—Shaya Zamora
"Who Are You, Really?"—Mikky Ekko
"Second Chances"—Gregory Alan Isakov
"Fine Line"—Harry Styles
"Lights Are On"—Tom Rosenthal
"Happiness is a butterfly"—Lana Del Rey
"Città vuota"—Mina
"Mystery of Love"—Sufjan Stevens
"Piazza Grande"—Lucio Dalla
"Lovesong"—Adele

"The World (Is Going Up in Flames)"—Charles Bradley (featuring Menahan Street Band)
"Dark Red"—Steve Lacy
"In My Blood"—Tommee Profitt (featuring Fleurie)
"Say Yes to Heaven"—Lana Del Rey

ACKNOWLEDGMENTS

Writing the end of Guinevere and Raffaele's story is bittersweet because this is truly one of my favorite worlds and love stories I have ever written. The combination of all my favorite things—age gap, Italy, action and adventure, personal growth, literary and historical references, sex in public spaces—made this duet a pure delight to indulge in. I hope you love this series even half as much as I do.

I have to thank Montlake Publishing for giving me the absolute dream opportunity to write for them.

Lauren Plude, for welcoming me into the Montlake family and making my experience so incredible. Thank you for believing in my words.

Sasha, you are the best editor I have ever had the pleasure to work with, and I am so eager to reunite someday soon on another project. Thank you for lending your expertise to make this duet the best possible story it could be.

To the rest of the team at Montlake, thank you for polishing this manuscript into something clean and beautiful for the world to enjoy. I appreciate it so much.

Georgana Grinstead, for being the best agent and publicist in the world but also one of my most treasured friends. Thank you for all the ways you love and support me. I can't believe how lucky I am to know you.

My assistant, Jess, who amplifies and organizes everything I do. There is not a single day I take working with someone as bright and lovely as you for granted.

To Pang, my other assistant, and the loveliest woman. I am very lucky to have you on my team.

Valentine, my other beloved Grinstead, for being my girl and confidante. Your sense of humor and our sisterhood bring me joy every day.

Sarah, for being my creative sounding board and ride-or-die friend. Talking to you is one of the highlights of my every day.

Becca, my bestie, thank you for being there for me through everything personal and professional. Being with you is like drinking a warm cup of tea on a rainy day while reading under a blanket.

Veronica Capo, my Italian consultant and wonderful reader, thank you for lending your expertise to this story. You have made it authentic and beautiful with your advice.

My Darlings, who are my safe space on the internet and a place I can go every time I need a smile or a reminder that people care about the stories I tell. Thank you for being so positive and supportive all the time. I'm so in debt to you all for making my dreams come true.

My ARC and content creator teams, thank you for being the most supportive and kind readers ever! You make a world of difference in my career, and it means so much to me.

Brittany, I love you, and that's the beginning and end of it. I love going through the wild, crazy bookish world with you and knowing I can always count on you for life advice.

Kandi, for inspiring me every day with your creativity, work ethic, bright spirit, and beauty. Thank you for being such a wonderful friend.

To the women who have supported me for years and celebrate my every success—Fiona, Lauren, Madison, Armie, Bridget, Lisa. Knowing and loving you has been a highlight of my life.

To the men who have seen me and supported me since I was a girl—Al, Devo, Kevin, Sammy, Spencer, Colin—I wouldn't be me without you, and how beautiful is that?

To my French family, who took me into their home and their hearts when I moved to France for the first time at eighteen years old, much the same way Guinevere moved to Italy. I will always be grateful fate saw fit to throw us together, because I would not be me without you. And special thanks to Charlotte, who inspired Guinevere's chronic illness and who talked me through the ins and outs.

To my sister, Grace, who is my best cheerleader and has been since I was eight years old and told her I wanted to be an author one day. You were one of only two people who believed in me then, and it means the world to me.

To my dad, the other person who believed in my dreams and who would be so proud of how far I've come. I miss you every day, and I wish I could hug you just one more time.

To my mum, who shares some characteristics with the Stones only in that her love and fear for me sometimes conflict with what I need to make me happy. Thank you for loving me even when I have made choices that have deviated from your norm.

And last but never least, my husband. I will never tire of saying that, "my husband," or waking up beside you in the morning or holding your hand when we walk down the street. Even the little things still hold so much awe and wonder for me. "I get to love you," I think almost every day. "How cool is that?!" In fact, I know it is the coolest thing I will ever do.

ABOUT THE AUTHOR

Photo © 2024 Paige Owen

Giana Darling is a *USA Today*, *Wall Street Journal*, and Amazon Top 40 bestselling Canadian romance writer who specializes in the forbidden and angsty side of love. She currently lives on an island in beautiful British Columbia, where she spends time riding on the back of her husband's bike, baking pies, and reading while snuggled up with her golden retriever, Romeo.

To get the latest info on her books, upcoming events, bonus content, and more, visit Giana's website at https://gianadarling.com, where you can also sign up for her newsletter. Connect with the author on social media via Instagram (@GianaDarlingAuthor), X (@GianaDarling), or YouTube (@gianadarlingauthor). You can also find her on Facebook (check out her readers group, Giana's Darlings), TikTok, Goodreads, and BookBub.